THE COMPLETE CASES
OF COLONEL KASPIR, VOLUME 1

THE COMPLETE CASES OF

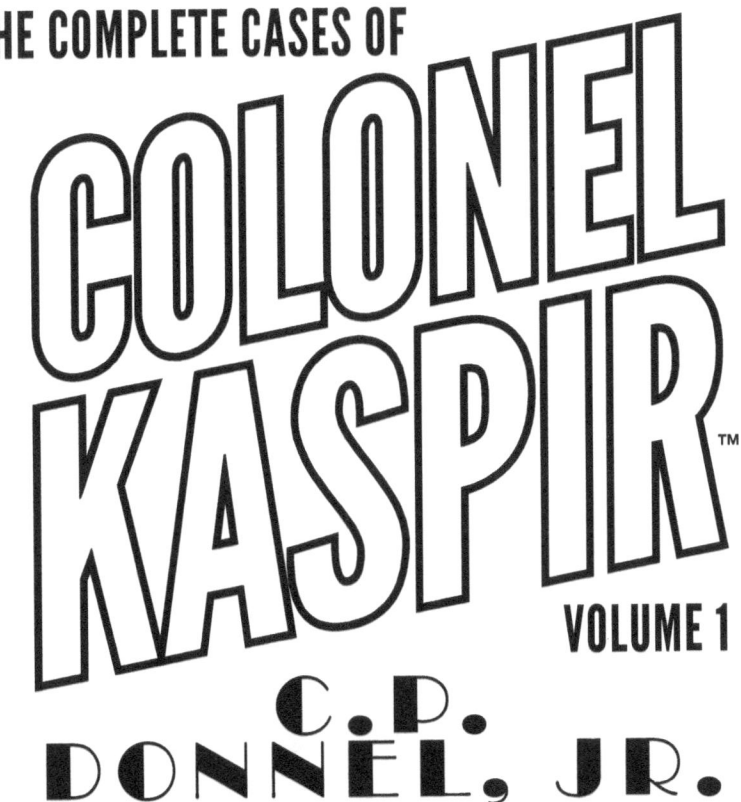

COLONEL KASPIR™

VOLUME 1

C.P. DONNEL, JR.

INTRODUCTION BY
JOHN WOOLEY

ILLUSTRATIONS BY
JOHN FLEMING GOULD

POPULAR PUBLICATIONS • 2024

TABLE OF CONTENTS

C.P. DONNEL, JR.: THE ONE WHO WALKED AWAY

HERE'S THE way Cornelius Philip Donnel, Jr., summed himself up for the readers of the November 1943 *Argosy* magazine (which featured his novel-length adventure story "Invasion, Limited"):

> A native of Bala, Pennsylvania, which is a suburb of Philadelphia, I've made my home in Norfolk, Virginia, since 1913. Attended Blair Academy at Blairstown, N.J.,and Yale, wrangling an A.B. from the latter in 1929.
>
> Followed nine years newspaper work on the *Norfolk Virginian-Pilot*; jobs ranged from subbing as woman's page editor to police reporting and day city editor. I turned to fiction in the false hope that it would be less strenuous.
>
> My hostages to fortune are a wife who likes my stories; Connie, age 10, who likes the Oz books; and Donnie, seven, who wants a scout knife.

Knocking out pulp fiction may indeed not have been less strenuous than the newspaper racket, but by the time Donnel's mini-autobiography appeared, he had firmly established himself as a prolific and reliable craftsman, working almost entirely for the top-rung Popular Publications. What's more, he'd already created two series characters for the company, both debuting in 1941. First came Doc Rennie, a big-city "psychological detective" who helps a rural sheriff solve small-town crimes. The Doc first hit the stands in the January 1941 issue of the groundbreaking detective pulp *Black Mask,* via a story called *"The Man Who Knew Fear";* it appears to be the first piece of magazine fiction that Donnel ever sold. (Popular Publications had bought *Black Mask* from Pro-Distributors, its previous publisher, about six months earlier.)

Donnel's second series began not long afterwards, in *Black Mask's* sister magazine, *Dime Detective.* And while it started in an issue cover-dated months before Pearl Harbor, it was unquestionably a wartime series, featuring the corpulent Colonel Stephen Kaspir, chief of Section Five, a little-known counterintelligence operation of the U.S. government. The first eight of those fascinating tales are collected here.

We'll get back to the Colonel and his supporting cast shortly. But first, let's take a closer look at their creator.

LIKE A lot of his fellow pulp scribes, Donnel came out of the newspaper business. Learning how to knock out stories, albeit nonfiction, on tight deadlines was a plus for those writers who jumped from newsrooms to pulps and needed to produce their fiction at a high rate of speed in order to make a living. There was also the advantage of what newsman-turned-author Gene Fowler allegedly said about reporters having "a front-row seat on the circus of humanity," getting exposed to all sorts of personality types that could ultimately enrich fictional efforts.

Donnel got a third benefit out of his newspaper career. As an unbylined February 11, 1944 piece in his former newspaper, the *Norfolk Virginian-Pilot* noted, "[O]ften his stories have been of the detective mystery type in which his knowledge of police work is apparent. For several years he was police reporter on this newspaper and worked constantly with sensational crime cases."

C.P. Donnel, Jr.

During that stretch, on at least one occasion, he violated that old journalistic taboo—albeit unintentionally—about how a reporter should never be part of the story. It happened in 1934, while Donnel was still working the crime beat for the *Virginian-Pilot*. That was a morning paper, and it fell to its afternoon counterpart—which had recently been bought by the *Virginian-Pilot*—to tell the tale.

"Alleged Burglar Nabbed by Sleuth and Reporter," blared the headline in the January 22 *Norfolk Ledger-Dispatch*. The article told how a 29-year-old Black man named Richard Scott, aka Thomas Williams, had been "arrested by Detective J.G. Wright on the second floor of a house in the 1000 block of Wood [S]treet early this afternoon."

In an account that may have included an inside joke on Donnel, the unnamed reporter wrote:

> Detective Wright and Phil Donnel, Virginian-Pilot police reporter, who should have been asleep after being up most of the night, jumped in a squad car and sped to Wood [S]treet after headquarters received a telephone message that a burglar was in the house at 1010.
>
> Donnel covered the outside of the dwelling while Wright entered the place. The detective flushed the Negro on the second floor. The latter, a bundle of blankets and sheets under his arm, started toward a window, but seeing Donnel waiting for him with open arms, changed his mind and surrendered to Detective Wright.

According to research from John Locke, Donnel had assumed the *Virginian-Pilot* crime beat after stints at other jobs with the paper, something Donnel himself mentions in his *Argosy* bio. "First byline (Phil Donnel) found on Dec. 6, 1929," writes Locke. "He was the Market Reporter (produce prices) through the end of 1932. After a while he filtered in additional reporting on radio programming and sporting events. After 1932, no more Phil Donnel articles. He did byline one article as C.P. Donnel, Jr., in 1936, on Virginia history. I suspect he was promoted to police reporter in 1933."

(In those days, bylines were not exactly handed out like Christmas candy, and Donnel appears to have toiled anonymously during his entire time on the crime beat.)

Not long after his 1929 graduation from Yale, Donnel had married a woman from New London, Connecticut named Grace Kingsbury Arms, the daughter of a rear admiral in the Navy. By 1940, Locke believes, she, *sans* her husband, had moved to Groton, a town just across the Thames River from New London. During World War II, Groton was known as the Submarine Capital of the World, thanks to the electric-boat division of General Dynamics, which was assembling submarines for the Navy at a breakneck pace. An obituary for Ms. Donnel, in the July 11, 1969 edition of the *New London Star,* noted that she had worked as "a draftsman at General Dynamics-Electric Boat for about 14 years until 1954"; given both her and her father's profession, it seems likely that she left Norfolk to contribute to the war effort—even before it had officially started. It's not known whether she took their two children, who would've been about seven and four years old, with her. What we do know is that Donnel quit the *Virginian-Pilot* in 1941—the year he began selling to the pulps—and, despite what he says in his *Argosy* bio about still living in Norfolk, joined his wife in Groton in August of that year. By that time, he'd placed at least a half-dozen stories in pulp magazines, with many more on the way.

ALTHOUGH HE filled out his draft card (race: white; eyes: blue; hair: brown; complexion: light brown) on October 16, 1940, when he was 34, Donnel apparently never served. Throughout the World War II years, he continued to write—mostly for the pulps, but occasionally hitting the slicks, a goal of just about everyone in his circumstances. When he did, it was sometimes enough to warrant a local-boy-makes-good story in his former paper. For instance, the January 30, 1943 edition of the *Virginian-Pilot* included a piece celebrating Donnel's appearance in *Collier's Magazine* with a story titled "Strangers on the Place." The article noted that he was not only the paper's police reporter "for a number of years," but "also was identified with the Little Theatre."

And one from the newspaper's February 11, 1944, number, previously mentioned, carried the headline "Donnel Story in Satevepost," noting that "C. P. Donnel, Jr., former member of the news staff of the Norfolk Virginian-Pilot, has 'hit the big time again' with his fiction, this time in the current issue of the Saturday Evening Post. It is a breezy short story, 'You've Got to Live with People,' his first appearance in this magazine."

Still, for the rest of his career, pulps made up the overwhelming portion of Donnel's published work. And then, as the rough-wood mags began plunging to their deaths like lemmings off a cliff, something happened to C.P. Donnel, Jr. While many of his fellow fictioneers sought opportunities in other media, including movies, television shows, detective-story digest magazines, and paperback books, just about all Donnel got published in the early '50s was a handful of poems for the slicks, mostly *The Saturday Evening Post*. (His final pulp story seems to have been "I Call Everybody Darling," published in the November 1951 *Popular Detective*.) Writing poetry, then and now, did not provide anything like a decent living, and Donnel's motivation for switching to verse may never be known. If nothing else, though, his efforts were good enough to regularly hit one of the major mainstream magazines of the time.

Then, apparently, he gave up and walked away from the whole business.

DONNEL'S OBITUARY in the December 19, 1977 issue of *The Day*, out of New London, which carried a Mystic dateline, told its readers that the 71-year-old Donnel had died the previous Saturday (December 17) "at the Mary Elizabeth Convalescent Hospital [in Mystic] after a long illness." (Donations to the Heart Fund were being solicited in his memory, which would indicate his cause of death.) The obit noted that his wife had passed in 1969, and that they had both lived in Mystic; Donnel for the past 15 years.

And then, this bit of information: "Mr. Donnel was a freelance writer, retiring about 20 years ago." No indication was given that he'd gone into another line of work or established any other kind of income source. He had just "retired" in the 1950s from his vocation, which was writing, and stayed retired until his late 1970s death.

Indeed, there's no evidence that any new material appeared from Donnel after the early '50s. Perhaps he did something pseudonymously, but there's nothing in his past to indicate he ever wrote under any name but his own. However, if you were reading crime fiction in the late '50s through the '90s, or even watching Czechoslovakian or West German television, it's possible you ran onto a specific piece of his work.

The story titled "Recipe for Murder" first showed up in the *American Legion Magazine* from January 1947 (sold for Donnel by famed pulp-writer agent August Lenniger). A brief tale set on the French Rivera, it concerns a police inspector's questioning of a handsome woman who he believes has killed her previous two husbands. The twist ending is ingenious and unusual, and apparently gave the story its significant legs.

"Recipe for Murder" was reprinted in the June 1950 issue of *Ellery Queen's Mystery Magazine,* showed up again in the January issue of *Verdict Crime Detection Magazine* seven years later, was included in the Alfred Hitchcock anthology *13 More Stories They Wouldn't Let Me Do on TV* (1959), and was given the audiobook treatment in volume six of Otto Penzler's *The Greatest Mysteries of All Time* (1997), read by British actor Christopher Cazenove. It was also dramatized on TV in the two countries mentioned earlier—Czechoslovakia in 1969 and West Germany in 1973.

So, for all his hundreds of thousands—probably millions—of words knocked out for the pulps, the only tale of C.P. Donnel's to see print after the Pulp Era seems to have been a brief story with a non-pulpwood origin.

That is, until now.

RIGHT OFF the bat, it's tempting to theorize that Col. Stephen Kaspir, the cherry-chocolate-loving big man with the cupid's-bow mouth, was inspired by British actor Sydney Greenstreet—especially Greenstreet's portrayal of the suavely villainous Gutman in the third movie iteration of *The Maltese Falcon* (based on the Dashiell Hammett novel that first saw life in the pages of *Black Mask*). After all, Gutman's first name is Kasper.

There's only one thing wrong with that theory. The first Colonel Kaspir story came out in the August 1941 issue of *Dime Detective*, which means it actually hit the stands at least a month earlier than its cover date. And *The Maltese Falcon*—which was Greenstreet's first movie appearance— didn't hit movie houses until October of that year. Donnel seems to have been a reasonably cultured man, so it's possible he'd seen Greenstreet in one of the many stage appearances he made before finally debuting in films. Or maybe he took the physical attributes of Kaspir from Hammett's description of the character in the novel.

A more likely inspiration, though, is Nero Wolfe, author Rex Stout's portly and eccentric detective, whose novels (beginning with 1934's *Fer-de-Lance*) had become quite popular, spawning a couple of '30s movies. They all carried on the long detective-story tradition of a secondary character—in this case Archie Goodwin, Wolfe's right-hand man—telling the stories, an approach Donnel used as well in the Kaspir tales.

In addition to narrator Mike Kettle, the ex-newspaperman turned Army captain, the Kaspir yarns feature an array of intriguing supporting characters, starting with Kaspir's lovely receptionist Maude and extending through the likes of the African-American Joe, who guards the old brownstone ex-boardinghouse that's now Section Five headquarters, and Lieutenant Charlie Wu, of Chinese heritage. Both are introduced as racial stereotypes of the time, and both quickly show themselves to be something else entirely. (A cautionary note: Most of these stories came out during World War II, so there are names used for ethnic groups that are now considered offensive.)

As is the case with Joe and Wu, many of these stories are built around people being something other than what they seem, about appearances vs. reality. They're good stories, solidly constructed and well-told, and, if nothing else, their resurrection in book form gives contemporary readers something of Donnel's to savor beyond his much-anthologized twist-ending short story that, somehow, took on an existence of its own, outliving its creator's writing life by decades.

— John Wooley
Foyil, Oklahoma
18 September 2024

(Big thanks to the invaluable FictionMags Index (philsp. com), the unflaggingly helpful publisher Matt Moring, and John Locke, the rajah of researchers.)

FRAULEIN JUDAS

RHYS-ECCLES AND I FELT
PRETTY RELIEVED THAT THE
WAR INDUSTRIES REPORT WAS
FINISHED AND READY FOR
WASHINGTON. WE HARDLY
EXPECTED ANY TROUBLE
FROM GESTAPO AGENTS HERE
IN THE VIRGINIA MOUNTAINS.
AND THAT'S WHERE WE WERE
WRONG. IT ALL STARTED WITH
THAT KID HAVING A TUMMY
ACHE ON THE PICNIC....

CAMP GREENWOOD is for people who like to rough it in log cabins with French windows and tiled baths. It occupies a lush clearing halfway up Apple Orchard Mountain in the soft, purple Blue Ridge range northwest of Lynchburg, and the fried chicken served in its pine-paneled dining-hall is not a dish, but an experience, like love at first sight.

Over a platter of this unrivaled chicken, Martin Rice scowled at me. Not a personal scowl. Simply an expression of his attitude toward the human race, of which I happened to be the nearest unit.

I countered with a smile. Rice and I had every reason to be gay. The Rhys-Eccles Report, offspring of Martin Rice's peculiar brain and my own crudely efficient typing—born paragraph by paragraph over three days and nights of paralyzing mental labor—reposed in my inside pocket and crackled reassuringly as I speared another chicken breast.

Tomorrow—Monday—we would leave Camp Greenwood for Washington. There I would deliver Martin Rice and the Rhys-Eccles Report into the hands of Colonel Stephen Kaspir, chief of Section Five, who would start them on their way to Great Britain. In Britain the Rhys-Eccles Report would undoubtedly start something.

My smile broadened as the chicken breast parted obediently under the affectionate stroke of my knife. Martin Rice was alive, the Rhys-Eccles Report was completed, and Colonel Kaspir was a false prophet. He had predicted trouble. It had failed to materialize. No shots from ambush, not even a hellish attempt to sabotage my typewriter ribbon.

I would prick him with that one tomorrow. "No," I would say sweetly, "not even an attempt to sabotage my typewriter ribbon." And he would squirm.

Kaspir had hinted, through chocolate-stained teeth, of possible action by one Maria Hencken, who, I had gathered, was a sort of Gestapo superwoman. Description of Maria Hencken? "None available," Kaspir had muttered, twiddling pudgy fingers and wagging his fat head dramatically.

Maria Hencken indeed! My lip curled as I surveyed the dining-hall for perhaps the fiftieth time in three days.

TAKE PROFESSOR Davis and his little girl, for instance, who had been on our train and ridden up in the station wagon with Rice and me Friday afternoon. A hawk-nosed man in his late thirties, Davis was a widower, and his fortified black eyes softened only when he addressed his daughter. His eyes were soft now as he cut up a piece of chicken for the child, and his mid-Western voice was a caressing murmur as he said something to her across their table. The child, a pallid little thing of ten or eleven, small for her age and shy almost to mutism, watched her father with large, luminous eyes. Her right arm, recently fractured in some playground mishap, was in a sling, and the triangle of black silk that narrowed to her chin intensified her pallor.

Miss Ogilvie had found
Effie lying unconscious at
the foot of the stairs.

Then there were the Misses Alicia and Alethea Ogilvie, gaunt, gray-haired twins nearing sixty, addicted to
long khaki skirts, mannish coats, and floppy straw hats.
They came up from Norfolk each year at this time (it was

May) to paint the laurel blossoms which lay like snow over the spur hills about the camp. Of forbidding aspect in the mornings, the Misses Ogilvie, I had noted, mellowed amazingly by dinner time. Annie, the rawboned mountain woman who cleaned the rooms, ascribed this mellowness to bottles of gin which, she informed me resentfully, the Misses Ogilvie kept locked in their trunks.

And, finally, there were the Hinkles, John and Martha, as thoroughly anesthetized by love as any bride and groom I have ever seen. Their assault on the chicken was punctuated by long, ineffable looks. John Hinkle, big, blond, serious, was a telephone company official from somewhere in Delaware. Martha was dark, sleepy-eyed, exotic. Her figure, as outlined by a sweater suit, was something a man might die for, and Hinkle was obviously ready to make the supreme sacrifice at a moment's notice.

And that was all our company, aside from the servants and Oliver Sparklet, the owner, manager, desk-clerk, social secretary of Camp Greenwood, pink of cheek and oppressive with innkeeper's charm.

MY EYES returned to Martin Rice, now scowling at his plate. A tiny gamecock of a man, white hair rising from his narrow skull like an angry crest. A face ever ridden by the memory of that night in London when a stray bomb, whistling down through the clouds like a satanic judgment, had taken his wife, his daughter, and his left arm.

A shadow at my shoulder, a whiff of eau-de-cologne introduced Oliver Sparklet. He treated Rice and me to a heavenly smile. Rice grunted in pure, unadulterated ill-humor. I raised an eyebrow.

"You'll join the picnic, of course," Sparklet beamed.

"Not interested." This from Rice in clipped accents of disapproval.

I said, "Picnic?"

"We go each Sunday afternoon to Lichened Rock," explained Sparklet alluringly. "I cook the steaks myself."

"Who's going?" I made it offhand.

"Everyone." Sparklet included the whole dining-hall in a womanish wave of his plump hands.

"You go," snapped Rice at me. "I have work—"

"In that case," I cut in, disappointed, "I'd better—"

"I said you were to go, Potts." It was a command. I flushed. But I was—for Camp Greenwood's benefit—Rice's secretary, so what could I say? I nodded to Sparklet. He passed on to the Ogilvies, who accepted with old-maidenish squeals of delight.

Rice stuck out his single, blue-veined hand. "Give me the report." He had sense enough to keep his voice down.

I shook my head. His eyes flamed.

"Give me that report." His voice rose. I glanced quickly around the dining-hall. No one was watching. I whipped out the master copy as surreptitiously as possible, thrust it at him under the table. He got up, stuffing the dozen typewritten sheets into his coat pocket. I jumped up and followed him outside, boiling.

On the flagstoned veranda he faced me, peppering me with short, hot words before I could tell him what I thought of his idiotic action in the dining-room. He made it very clear that he looked upon Kaspir and me as imbeciles—that our fears concerning the Gestapo were childish—that he, Mortimer Rhys-Eccles, resented this three-day seclusion under the name of Martin Rice, and that his opinion of our Government Intelligence and Counter-Espionage services was—

I interrupted angrily, reminding him that future British policy would be vitally affected by the report—that any Axis agent would give his ears for a five-minute perusal of it. "Furthermore," I threw at him, "that report may eventually affect my country as well as yours. I can't permit you to take chances."

He subsided to a tone of quiet contempt. With exaggerated deference he told me that he simply intended to sit in his room and review it in detail—that my presence would only distract him—that if there were any last-minute changes we could make them together that night.

I agreed to join the picnic on two conditions. The first: that everyone else in camp went. The second: that he would promise to lock both the hall door of our two-room suite and the French window giving on our private porch.

He exploded into an exasperated affirmative and stalked off to the big guest cabin.

I rejoined the others in the lounge of the main lodge, and at three thirty we all went down to the guest cabin for blankets and wraps. Rhys-Eccles had been as good as his word. The door was locked. He unlocked it peevishly, returned to his big chair and lost himself immediately in the report. On my way out I closed the door and rattled the knob suggestively until I heard him stamp across the floor and turn the key.

WE STRAGGLED lazily up to Lichened Rock, only half a mile from camp. From the rock the forest dropped away beneath us to Wheat's Valley, and the valley stretched like a toy panorama into the warm afternoon haze.

We loafed in the ripe sunlight. Little Effie Davis climbed around the rock, followed by her father's anxious eyes. The Ogilvies sketched. The Hinkles disappeared hand-in-hand up a leafy side trail, returning while Sparklet and I were laying a fire under a grill set into a cleft of the rock. In the dying rays of the sun we ate our excellent meal.

Two incidents marred the party.

Little Effie Davis complained, in her semi-audible whisper, of a tummy pain. Miss Alethea Ogilvie solicitously insisted upon accompanying the child back to camp, ordering Professor Davis to stay and enjoy himself. Overwhelmed, Professor Davis gave in.

The other incident came about three-quarters of an hour later, just as a golden moon-rim showed in Gunstock Gorge. Heavy feet crashed along the trail. Someone was running, gasping. The raw-boned Annie burst into the circle of firelight, an apparition of disheveled hair and wild eyes. Her first dozen words sent Davis and me streaking back to camp, plunging recklessly ahead by the wavering beam of a flashlight I had snatched from Sparklet.

Annie's words sent us first to Davis' suite on the second floor of the guest cabin. Miss Alethea Ogilvie hovered distractedly over the bed. On the bed lay little Effie Davis, cheeks like skimmed milk, a great purple bruise down one side of her small face.

Davis bent over the child. Miss Ogilvie, almost incoherent from terror and gin, blurted out her tale.

She had brought Effie back, laid her on the bed. The child, already better, had sipped water, declined medicine, quickly dozed off. Miss Ogilvie had gone to her own room, next to the Davis suite, and sat there with the door open, in case Effie should awake and call out. Downstairs she could hear "Mr. Rice" moving about.

Some fifteen minutes later Effie had appeared at Miss Ogilvies door, a handkerchief tied peasant-fashion around her head, a doll in her good arm. She said she was all right and was going downstairs and play on the front veranda. Miss Ogilvie heard her go down the steps. Almost immediately there was a cry, a rustling noise, another cry, then the sound of running feet. Rushing down, Miss Ogilvie had found Effie lying unconscious near the foot of the stairs, the handkerchief torn from her head and exposing the great bruise. Her assailant was nowhere to be seen, nor could Miss Ogilvie tell which way he ran out.

Miss Ogilvie had run down the hall to our suite to seek help from "Mr. Rice." The door was open. "Mr. Rice" was in the big chair, apparently asleep. She had shaken him by the shoulder several times, until she realized....

Then she had screamed until Annie ran down from the main lodge. Together they got Effie, now mumbling something about a "big man" who had struck her, upstairs again, and Annie had run for Lichened Rock.

I left Miss Ogilvie, dived downstairs to our suite. Rhys-Eccles was quite dead, his scrawny throat rasped reddish-brown by whatever had strangled him. Three minutes of frantic searching convinced me that the Rhys-Eccles Report was gone. Not that I didn't have a carbon copy in the money-belt around my waist, but what good, now?

I left Rhys-Eccles to his calm contemplation of the ceiling and tore for the main lodge and its telephone. It took me five dancing, cursing minutes to get through to Kaspir in Washington. He mumbled something about a military plane and said he'd be at the Lynchburg airport in less than three hours. I ran to the servants' quarters and snatched Joe, the Negro handyman-chauffeur, away from his supper with the rotund black cook, ordering him to get out the station wagon at once. Fortunately he knew the airport. As I hurried back to the guest cabin the station wagon whizzed past me and its tail light sank away down the mountain-side like a falling star.

Circling Rhys-Eccles' still figure in a second and more thorough search of our rooms, I found nothing of importance. In his steamer trunk, insolently undisturbed, were the three hundred-odd typewritten reports which his fine machine of a mind had condensed, in three days and nights, into the Rhys-Eccles Report, for which His Majesty's Government was waiting impatiently.

I dropped helplessly into a chair and lit a cigarette. It seemed impossible that I had known Rhys-Eccles—and Colonel Kaspir, too—for only four days. It seemed more like years.

MY WEST coast assignment had ended in a blaze of glory the previous Tuesday when Weber had walked into my arms in the lobby of a San Francisco movie theater, a stroke of dumb luck. That afternoon I was ordered back to Washington. I boarded the plane determined to ask for a transfer to Propaganda the minute I hit the capital. I'd done enough in Frisco to convince me that Counter-Espionage was not my racket.

Captain Ed Bell, my immediate superior, met the plane at the Washington airport Thursday morning. He stuck out his hand. "Nice going, Kettle. Thought you told me you'd never make an Intelligence man?"

"Pure dumb luck." I said it wearily, knowing he wouldn't believe me.

"Horsefeathers!" He clapped me on the shoulder. He looked around. The other passengers were almost to the gate.

"Kaspir wants you," he said, half under his breath. "I've got your orders here." He shook his head as I extended my hand. "Verbal orders."

"Who's Kaspir?" I'd never heard the name before. "What does he want me for?"

"I don't know." Bell was embarrassed. "As near as I can find out, it's a new department, hush-hush as hell—kind of a bastard by Treasury out of State. Some sort of liaison tie-up with the British. Overlaps into C.E. work now and then. I know one thing though."

"Go on," I said grimly.

"Kaspir's the white-haired boy around Washington just now," said Bell, with inter-departmental jealousy. "What he asks for, he gets. Took Williams and McCreary off us last week."

"What are they doing now?" I was startled. They were top men in our line.

Bell blushed. "I don't know." He looked around again. "At least, I'm not supposed to."

He bent even closer to me. "I did think I saw Williams this morning," he said darkly. "Driving a cab. What do you think of that?"

"How're my chances of getting into Propaganda?" I said hastily.

Bell stiffened officially. "Here are your orders, Kettle."

When he finished his spiel I just looked at him. His mouth twitched. "No kidding," he said, and walked off.

So I took a cab downtown and caught a bus. When I reached a certain corner I got off and ambled along a row of

old, tall, brownstone houses until I found the number Bell
had given me. A colored houseboy in a white coat answered
my ring. It seemed to be a boarding house. But as the boy
led me up to the second floor I noticed a bulge on his right
hip. At the foot of the dark wood stairway leading to the
third floor he stopped, jerked his thumb upward.

"Last door down, boss." His accent was that of an uned-
ucated Virginia Negro, but—

"New York University," I said on impulse.

His puzzled look made me feel like a fool. Then he
smiled and shook his head. The puzzled look had been
an act.

"Columbia Law School," he said, smiling, and turned
away.

Still following Bell's instructions, I mounted to the third
floor, entered the door at the end without knocking, to find
myself in a crudely equipped office that obviously had once
been a bedroom. There was an inner door. It was shut. I was
reaching for its knob when a man's voice, high, neighing,
gusty with passion, cut through its flimsy panels.

"Where did you put 'em?" demanded this neighing voice.
I stopped dead.

A woman's voice, low, angry, answered: "Where you
won't find 'em. And you know why."

Brief silence, during which I could visualize the antag-
onists glaring at one another.

The man's voice went up a quarteroctave. "I order you
to tell me—"

"Fiddlesticks!" High heels clicked across the inner room.
I jumped back and to one side. The door flew open and a
tall woman flounced out. A second glance showed her to
be a superb blonde, beautifully turned out, probably thirty.
Under her plentiful but skillfully-applied make-up her face

was scarlet with anger. To my amazement she flung herself down at a typewriter desk and began to pound the keys of an old Underwood. I coughed introductively. She looked around quickly.

"Who're you?" she demanded pettishly.

This was too much. "I'm beginning to wonder," I barked.

"Then you must be Mike Kettle," she retorted. "What're you waiting for? He's in there." She shrugged a shapely shoulder toward the half-open door. Whereupon she ignored me and the Underwood began to chatter like a mad thing.

THE DOORWAY filled slowly with a man. From a small, precise mouth set in a great moon face the same neighing voice, now controlled and courteous as a politician's, said: "Welcome to Section Five, Lieutenant."

Momentarily speechless, I bowed.

"Come in." The figure turned on its heel, showing a back broad as a barn door.

I paused irresolutely in the doorway, hand on the knob. A swivel chair squealed in agony as the owner of the neighing voice dropped into it.

"Don't bother to close the door," said Colonel Kaspir, with some bitterness. "She'll only listen at the keyhole."

The typewriter had stopped. Behind me the blond woman snorted contemptuously.

Kaspir waved a fat hand toward a straight wooden chair, and, as I sat down, lost himself in thought, eyes closed. I seized the opportunity to take stock of my new boss.

Weight about two-eighty, but the fat hands and round face make him look tubbier than he really is, I decided. Suit of good tweeds, expensive shirt, grotesque tie. But untidy. Looks as if he'd been held down and clothes put on him by force.

"Nursemaid job," said Kaspir suddenly, eyes opening full on mine. "You can typewrite, can't you?"

"I was an editorial writer on the *Sun*," I replied with dignity. Then a forlorn hope. "That is why Propaganda is really my—"

"Lot o' reports," said Kaspir. "Took 'em months. Their men, our men, working together." This meant nothing. I noticed his teeth were stained, as though with tobacco juice.

"This feller Rhys-Eccles'll do it, though," continued Kaspir, nodding solemnly in admiration of Rhys-Eccles. "All brain, no brawn." He smacked his lips. "Put 'em all together. That's where you come in."

His voice trailed off. I realized incredulously that he believed he had told me everything, that my instructions were now complete, and that the interview was over.

"Oh!" Kaspir's face lighted up, his middle finger snapped against his pulpy palm like a small firecracker. He had remembered something. "Hencken."

"Hencken?" I don't know why I bothered to ask. I suspected that the answer would mean nothing, and it did.

"Yep, Hencken." Kaspir was impatient now. He jiggled in the swivel chair, which cursed him. "People over there"— he waved in the direction of the rising sun—"give a good deal for Rhys-Eccles' results, o' course. We've heard some woman named Hencken is due to try for 'em—you'll have to watch out—"

His train of thought was obviously miles past me, but I leaped figuratively for the caboose. "May I have a description of this Hencken woman?"

He leaned forward, highly pleased at my grasp on the matter in hand. "None available," he said, staging a pantomime with fingers and head to emphasize the utter unavailability of a description of the woman Hencken. "Just have to do the best...."

"Where do I—" I began desperately. If whitecoated attendants had rushed in and thrown Kaspir into a strait-jacket at that moment it would not have raised a single pulsebeat of surprise in me.

Kaspir rose, all six and a half feet of him. "Rhys-Eccles demands quiet—no distractions. Camp Greenwood. Got tickets here." He rummaged in his pants pockets. "He'll be Martin Rice, author. You'll be Potts, his secretary"— still digging deep—"Get it? Your name's Kettle. You'll use Potts. Easy to remember?" A laugh rumbled up from his ample belly. Both hands came up clutching wads of what looked like waste paper, and a roll of greenbacks tumbled to the floor. Kaspir frowned down at it. "Maude!" he bawled.

NEITHER OF us had seen the blond woman poised statuesquely in the doorway. Now she stepped forward with a purposeful swing of her rangy hips. She retrieved the money, slapped it down on the desk. From Kaspir's hands she snatched the crumpled papers. She sorted them swiftly, efficiently, and handed me two railroad tickets. She faced Kaspir. "May I put in my dime's worth now?" she inquired, plucked eyebrows arched.

"Why, of course!" Kaspir was genuinely hurt at the implication that he was a petty tyrant.

Maude turned fine brown eyes on me.

"A joint British and American commission has just completed a survey of our war industries," she said. "Potential production, potential aid-to-Britain—that sort of thing. Dull but extremely important."

I sighed with relief as the room's atmosphere became tinged with sanity.

"It adds up to three hundred-odd separate reports," went on Maude. "They need a digest of this material in London at once. Rhys-Eccles is a political economist and a bit of a mental freak. They brought him along just for the job. He's to go off to some quiet place with these reports. They say that in three days he'll be able to come up with a four or five-thousand word summation which will give the British government a basis for immediate formulation of policy.

"Section Five has been assigned to look after Rhys-Eccles. We're sending him up to Camp Greenwood in the Blue Ridge. You'll go along to do his typing, give him whatever assistance you can, and see that he lives to finish the job."

Kaspir was pacing up and down inspecting his fingernails. "I told him all that," he put in, bored.

"Keep him alive?" I said.

"Just this," said Maude. "The Gestapo people most certainly know of the commission's work. We have reason to believe they're keeping an eye on Rhys-Eccles. We even have information that an agent named Maria Hencken has been assigned to obtain his summary. About Maria Hencken we know nothing."

"Nothing," neighed Kaspir from the window, with gloomy pleasure.

"Rhys-Eccles is at the Tuart Hotel under the name of Martin Rice. You'll be George Potts, his secretary. Pick him up tonight at eight. Your train leaves at eight thirty. Take a portable typewriter, of course. You'll find Rhys-Eccles difficult. Put up with him as best you can. And if anything should happen—"

"Call me," said Kaspir over his shoulder. I scribbled down the private number Maude gave me.

"Now run along and be a good boy," ordered this surprising woman, bestowing a motherly kiss on my forehead as she pushed me gently toward the door. The kiss sent a tingle down to my heels. Outside, in the hall, I paused to stuff the tickets into my wallet.

"Now," I heard Kaspir say menacingly, "where did you put 'em?"

Maude's voice was full of shrewish satisfaction. "I threw 'em every one out of the window."

Kaspir's shrill moan rattled the door. "The whole box?" he screamed.

"If you think, with your figure," said Maude acidly, "that you're going to sit in that office and stuff down those nauseating chocolate cherries all day...."

I hurried away to preserve what remained of my reason. The Negro house-boy-Columbia law graduate let me out. His intelligent mouth broadened at my dazed expression, but his "Good-day, suh," was strictly in character.

THAT WAS how I met Colonel Stephen Kaspir, the strange head of Section Five. Now I sat beside Rhys-Eccles' cooling corpse. Voices in the night told of the return of the rest of the picnic party. I went out to take charge of things until Kaspir arrived.

I relayed Miss Ogilvie's account of the attack on Effie Davis and the finding of Rhys-Eccles' body to Colonel Kaspir as soon as we had laid him on the bed in Rhys-Eccles' room. It was two A.M. and he had just arrived, wobbling into the guest cabin supported by Maude, resplendent in mink over a dazzling dinner gown, and Joe, the chauffeur. Kaspir was in full evening dress, very rumpled, and there were spots on his shirtfront.

Maude said crisply to Joe: "Bicarbonate of soda. Plenty of it."

She turned to me. "Plane-sick all the way from Washington. When he got out at Lynchburg he got ground-sick. In the station wagon he was car-sick."

She wheeled on Kaspir, who lay with his eyes shut, his broad face the color of a mud beach at low tide. "Have a chocolate cherry?" she cooed cruelly, throwing off the mink wrap and filling the room with the glitter of sequins. "Well, what happened, Kettle?"

So I told everything. Kaspir struggled up on an elbow. His eyes were on the sheeted figure in the big chair, but I could feel him listening. When I got through he rolled himself to the edge of the bed.

Maude smoothed the sequins over her hips. "Well," she said to Kaspir, "what about it, Steve? Do we form a posse and beat the woods for the masked intruder?"

Kaspir pursed his lips contemptuously. When he spoke, it was to me, an unintelligible mumbling accompanied by a village-idiot waving of the hands.

"In English," said Maude resignedly, "that means 'where is everybody now?'"

"Professor Davis and Effie are in the room overhead, of course," I replied. "The others are all in their rooms. The Ogilvies are next to the Davises. The Hinkles—that's the bride and groom—are in the suite next to this one. The servants are in their own quarters. Sparklet, the owner, has rooms at the main lodge. I told him to stay there."

Kaspir spoke clearly now. "What else did you do?"

"Not a thing, except call you," I returned defensively. "Murder's not in my line. My specialty is propaganda."

Kaspir chuckled delightedly. "We'll make something of Kettle yet." He was on his feet now, a monolith of black broadcloth and smudged linen. The weakness seemed to have passed.

"I hope so," I said sourly. "Something in Propaganda preferred."

"Balderdash," said Kaspir goodnaturedly. "You haven't seen a lady bare-back rider in camp, have you?"

"Not a spangle of one." What could you do but humor the big maniac? "Unless its Mrs. Hinkle. Why?"

"Hinkle?" said Kaspir. "First name?"

"Martha."

"Hmmm!" He addressed the silent Maude. "Heard today that the Hencken female used to be a circus performer—"

His bulk became suddenly animated, so unexpectedly that Maude and I both jumped. He minced over to the big chair and twitched the sheet from Rhys-Eccles with a magician's flourish. Bending with a grunt, he peered into the dead man's face. Then he drew a forefinger down the stiff left cheek, like a man sampling wet paint, and stared myopically at the fingertip, clucking softly to himself. I glanced sardonically at Maude. To my surprise, her expression was no longer scornful. She was watching Kaspir intently.

Kaspir flung the sheet carelessly over Rhys-Eccles' peaked face and turned to the paneled wall beside the chair, his back to us. The next instant he walked with short steps over to the French windows and flung them open, sticking his head into the night, still clucking. He withdrew his head after a minute and slammed the French window. A pane of glass fell in gleaming shards at his feet.

"Clumsy, eh?" He was beaming. He looked at the big chair. "Poor little guy. Not much to live for now, except his job. Done that."

He addressed me directly. "Keep Maude amused. Gotta see some people." And he left the room, apparently under the impression that because he was tiptoeing he was making no noise. The door banged behind him like a studio sound effect.

Maude looked pityingly at me. "You're bearing up better than most," she said. "He gave one man Cheyne-Stokes breathing." She passed me slowly in an aura of gardenia perfume and once more brushed my forehead with her lips. Again I tingled. She sat down on Rhys-Eccles' bed, crossing her admirable legs. "Listen," she said.

So we listened, and my muddled brain conceived the notion that Rhys-Eccles was listening, too. I had a feeling that if I removed that sheet I would find a mocking smile on his thin lips.

Colonel Kaspir was very busy. We needed no television set to follow his progress through the guest cabin.

He clumped up the steps and went to the Davises' suite, directly overhead, first. His chat with Professor Davis was mild and brief. Next we heard him knocking at the Ogilvies' door, and for a few minutes high, harsh, undistinguishable words caromed about the whole cabin. The door slammed.

Then the stairway shook again and he pounded on the Hinkles' door down the hall from us. He involved himself in a neighing altercation with John Hinkle that gradually simmered into whispers.

Next he poked his head in our door and Maude, after a long look at the grimace on his face, got up.

"Come on," he neighed gaily. "We're all going up to Effie's room."

I'LL NEVER forget that brief quarter-hour in "Effie's room," which was really her father's.

In the first place, it was strangely like a courtroom, with the child herself, propped up in bed, chalk-white except for the bruised area on her face, as the judge. A little red wrapper around her shoulders hid most of the long-sleeved, old-fashioned nightgown she wore. The white edge of the plaster cast around her right wrist framed the wrist like a cuff inside the black silk sling.

Kaspir sat mountainously on the bed beside her, fingering a heavy oak walking stick belonging to Professor Davis. As the company straggled in, the Ogilvies heavy-eyed but apparently sober, the Hinkles oddly apprehensive, I noticed that Professor Davis shifted, too casually, to a position beside John Hinkle, and that Hinkle was breathing hard.

Kaspir drew a bead on John Hinkle with the walking stick.

"Left the picnic awhile, didn't you?" he asked unpleasantly. His blue eyes glinted. "Effie," he said very gently, his other hand touching the child's thin shoulder, "Mr. Hinkle was the man you saw leaving Mr. Rice's room—the man who knocked you down—wasn't he?"

Effie's eyes were riveted on Hinkle. We could barely hear her "Yes."

Hinkle's laugh was a feeble effort.

"I want," said Kaspir with flute-like clarity, "that report."

But Hinkle was gone, tearing himself from Professor Davis' frantic grasp, upending an Ogilvie sister as he dived for the hall. Davis was after him like a fighting hound. Kaspir, clutching the oak stick, materialized beside me and shot after them, screaming "Close the door!" I ran after Kaspir, jerking the door shut.

Davis and Hinkle were struggling on the floor at the head of the stairs as Kaspir and I reached them, a tangle of thrashing fists and feet. Kaspir took what I instantly saw to be very bad aim with the walking stick. Before I could catch his arm it hissed downward. A dull sound of wood on scalp and bone.

"Ah!" said Kaspir, straightening himself and looking down at the unconscious figure of Professor Davis. He stretched out a long arm, helped Hinkle up. "Stay with him," he said to Hinkle, indicating the prone Davis. "Also," he added, turning away, "thanks."

We re-entered the bedroom. I was quite resigned now. Somebody was crazy. I only hoped it was Kaspir, not me.

Kaspir lumbered over to the bed. "Your father's quite safe, Effie." His ironical tone was like a slap at the child's face. An Ogilvie sister stepped forward angrily. Maude held her back.

"Let me see that arm of yours, Effie," demanded Kaspir, stretching out his left hand. His right still gripped the stick.

Then I went sick inside.

For Kaspir snatched the plaster cast-enclosed arm from its black silk sling and was battering the plaster to pieces with the handle of the walking stick—

I can't remember the rest in detail, but I do remember something flashing in Effie's free hand and Kaspir screaming, "Little devil!" and his great hand snaking out and closing around her little throat.

Then there was turmoil among the spectators as Kaspir and the child flopped across the bed in an absurd, squirming battle that was awkward but deadly.

It ended with Kaspir flinging Effie heavily against the headboard. The impact dazed her. We crowded around the bed as Kaspir rolled off and got to his feet. I heard Maude gasp. The Ogilvie sisters clung to each other, whimpering.

The struggle had ripped away the upper portion of Effie's nightgown. A single glance explained many things to me: why Effie always wore long-sleeved dresses and little cape-like coats, why she spoke in a whisper, why woolen stockings always encased her spindly legs.

For Effie Davis was a woman. Her torso, bare, made that very plain. And her thin arms were weirdly muscular.

A midget, if you like, but a woman.

Kaspir paid no attention to her, even when she stirred, sat up, and cursed him shamelessly in a shrill, evil voice.

He was plucking bits of plaster from the Rhys-Eccles Report, newly freed from the plaster cast that had encircled Effie's "broken" arm. He said quietly: "I suppose that thing out in the hall is your husband, eh, Maria?"

Effie's reply, describing her relationship to Davis, was unprintable.

"HANDKERCHIEF BUSINESS, you see o' course," mumbled Kaspir thickly through a ham sandwich. He gulped two mouthfuls of scalding coffee. "Powder on the old boy's cheek. That gin-swizzling female don't use it. Clean plaster on cast, too. And porch. Got that?"

Maude's sequins rattled venomously as she tossed pad and pencil to the bed, lit a cigarette, and fixed Kaspir with a grim, uncompromising eye. "Tell it straight and I'll take it down," was her ruthless ultimatum.

The relaxed hulk of Kaspir filled the big chair lately vacated by Mortimer Rhys-Eccles, who had been removed and deposited on the bed in my room. The Hinkles were present by invitation. Upstairs the Ogilvies slumbered alcoholically. Behind the main lodge, we knew Annie and Joe sat with shotguns before the strong door of the vegetable dugout, serving as a detention cell for Maria Effie Davis Hencken and her "father."

Kaspir looked diffidently at Maude.

"Oh, all right," he said mildly. He put the sandwich down, leaned forward. Maude reached for the pad, poised the pencil above it in her slender crimson-nailed fingers.

"Little she-Judas strangled Rhys-Eccles, o' course," began Kaspir. "See a lot o' midgets doing bareback stuff—acrobatics—in circuses around Germany, Poland, Hungary.

"Old Miss Gin-Swizzler lays Fraulein Judas on bed after coming back from picnic. Miss Gin-Swizzler goes to own room. Little she-Judas eases outa bed, slips off plaster cast, slides down porch support to Rhys-Eccles' porch—" He nodded toward the French windows. "Taps on window," he said.

"Who'd Rhys-Eccles open French window for but child? Lost his own in London. Likes children. They probably knew that—reason they used little Judas-devil. He opens window, lets her in, sits down in chair. She, affectionate, goes coyly around back of chair, slips arm around his neck. About time Rhys-Eccles begins to wonder where plaster cast on arm is, little she-Judas tightens arm around his neck—braces herself against back of chair.

"You saw that arm. Like wire rope."

Maude's pencil flew across her pad. The Hinkles were hunched forward in their chairs.

"Garroted, Rhys-Eccles was, by that little arm. But he fought. Banged Fraulein Judas' head against wall. But he caved in. She took report, shinnied back up to own room, unlocking hall door of this room before she left.

"Face badly bruised, though. Must be explained somehow. Ties handkerchief around head to hide bruise, replaces cast on arm, goes to old Miss Gin, tells her she's going out to play. Goes downstairs. Stamps feet, cries out, tears handkerchief off, lies down, swears she's been struck down by mysterious man. Bruise visible now. Ha! Simple!

"Rest's easy. Davis and little she-Judas get rid of old cast, make new one around Rhys-Eccles Report.

"Powder was give-away. Fraulein Judas had to powder up to look pale and frail. Left some on Rhys-Eccles' cheek when she"—here Kaspir was human enough to shudder—"cuddled her cheek against his. Also some on wall when face banged against it. And how could child with broken arm tie handkerchief around head, unless she used 'broken' arm?"

"But why that scene with Mr. Hinkle here?" I protested.

"Davis armed," growled Kaspir. "Wary, too. So told him Hinkle was man—get ready to help. Very pleased to, Davis was. Wonder what Davis' real name is. Maybe Washington knows."

He yawned cavernously. The Hinkles got up, silent.

"Siddown," ordered Kaspir hospitably. They sat. "Chat with Maude and friend Kettle-Potts here." He glanced at his watch. "We leave at daylight, and that's only an hour."

He yawned again. "Little nap," he murmured apologetically and ambled into the next room.

"There's only one bed in there," I called hastily, cringing at the thought of what reposed on that bed.

Kaspir turned benignly in the doorway. "Won't disturb him," he said, drawing the door to behind him.

Through the closed door we heard the bed creak. "Move over, old boy," said Colonel Kaspir. Then all was serene.

THE BODY TRAVELS EAST

WHEN THE BEHEMOTH BOSS OF SECTION 5 SHIPPED THE AIRPLANE-FORTRESS TO ENGLAND ON A DEFENSELESS LITTLE FREIGHTER WE ALL THOUGHT THAT THIS TIME HE REALLY WAS STICKING HIS FAT OFFICIAL NECK OUT— BUT COL. KASPIR PROVED HE COULD OUTSMART A NAZI AS EASILY AS HE WOLFED HIS CHERRY CHOCOLATES.

J OE, THE Negro houseboy who holds a law degree from Columbia, and whose white serving jacket conceals a .45 automatic, let me in and silently ushered me upward through the dim old dwelling.

In the outer office of the musty attic suite, Maude, her superb blond head tilted back to keep the cigarette smoke from her fine eyes, punched away with scarlet-nailed fore-fingers at the ancient Underwood which represents the office equipment of Section Five, strangest of the many strange government bureaus existing in Washington today. A magnificent opal flamed and danced on Maude's busy right hand, and reflected ruefully that my month's salary would not have paid for the imported silver-gray sweater suit she was wearing.

She rose, and my pulse broke into its usual double-shuffle. A still of Maude in that sweater suit would never get past the Hays office.

"At long last, Mike." She spoke without taking the dark jade cigarette holder from her lips. Her violet eyes, on a level with my own, were inexcusably provocative. A slender thumb made the hitchhiker's gesture toward Col. Stephen Kaspir's lair. "He's waiting."

"What is it this time?" I growl at Maude for reasons which I fear are not secret to her.

We saw the submarine
breaking water.

"God only knows." Her tone lacked its customary
sardonic edge. "Something big's on the fire. He's been
stewing for two weeks now—like a chunk of tough beef."

She waved down my exclamation at the mere idea of anything worrying the self-rising Kaspir. "He even talks of going on a diet."

This floored me. Colonel Kaspir's waking hours are largely devoted to a series of high-protein meals strung together on an endless chain of chocolate cherries. Maude winked, tiptoed to the inner door and flung it open without knocking.

"Aha!" she cried. Over her shoulder I saw Kaspir's bulk galvanized into sudden and guilty movement. I knew what it was: he was trying to hide a bag of his beloved cherries. The flurry over, he faced Maude blandly, his moon face with its absurd Cupid's-bow mouth a caricature of innocence.

"Wipe your mouth," ordered Maude resignedly. "Mike Kettle's here."

Kaspir dabbed quickly with a handkerchief at clean lips, then realized he had been tricked. He transfixed the languid Maude with a martyred glare.

"It's ten to ten," volunteered Maude, glancing at her nails.

This got results. Colonel Kaspir bounded to his feet—six feet six of billowing white linen. He snatched a wad of papers and stuffed them into a coat pocket. His rotund figure—he weighs close to three hundred—is amazingly lithe in action. He rummaged in a desk drawer and came up with a rolled Panama, which he unfurled and clapped on his head.

Maude cocked a critical eye at the result. "Why don't you," she inquired acidly, "have holes cut for your ears?"

He muttered something under his breath and stalked from the room. In a second he was back.

"Whatinell's the matter with you?" He was addressing us both, and petulantly. "Come on."

Maude shut her eyes. "What for?"

"Take notes, o'course. Minutes o'meetin'—that sorta thing."

Maude opened her eyes. "You know perfectly damn well," she announced distinctly, "that I can't take short-hand."

"Who said shorthand?" demanded Colonel Kaspir, fidgeting in the doorway. "Scribble on a pad, that's all. Look like you're doin' something. Impress 'em. Very important session."

"And what do I do?" I asked mildly.

"Look wise," instructed Kaspir, turning to go. "Look like an expert at something. Show 'em I got a smart staff."

AND HE was gone. Maude plucked a floppy creation from an old hat-tree as we sped through the outer office after him, and succeeded in patting it over her perfect permanent as she clattered ahead of me down the dark oak stairway, swearing under her breath. Thirty seconds later we were crammed warmly into a taxi which Joe, the house-boy, apparently had produced from his hip pocket. Kaspir bellowed unintelligibly at the driver, who miraculously understood, and we shot away down the steaming street.

Maude, jammed between us, wriggled forward to preserve the floppy hat. Kaspir patted his foot, hummed off-key, and looked out of the window.

"I suppose," threw out Maude, in a faraway voice, "it would be too much to ask where we're going, or why."

"We're goin' to a beanfeast at Benny's." For the first time since my assignment to Section Five I detected an effort behind my chief's flippancy. "Big mad on," he explained. "Everybody scowlin'."

"Oh, talk sense."

"Fact," declared Kaspir airily, smacking his lips and peering a little too casually from the window. "Hoke and the Gen. are out for my hide. Don't like the way I'm runnin' this show. They got Benny all worried." He resumed his foot-patting and humming, convinced that he had explained everything in lucid detail. The chorus of his half-swallowed song emerged: "They're gonna hang Steve Kaspir to a sour apple tree."

I gave it up and began to chew on the first morsel he tossed us. "Beanfeast at Benny's." Only one prominent figure in Washington is known as Benny—and as that only to initiated angels who fly high in the political stratosphere. He's the Secretary for Defense—a post in these days almost tantamount to supreme authority—and his full nickname is "Bellowing Benny." Since we could hardly be going to a beanfeast—whatever that meant—at Bellowing Benny's marine-guarded office, I abandoned the problem to time, which resolves all mysteries. Maude leaned back a little and her wrist brushed my knee, which tingled. This gave me something to think about until the cab turned up a driveway and stopped before the servants' entrance of a fat mansion on F Street.

The marine sergeant waiting inside the kitchen door seemed to be expecting Kaspir, and led us through a maze of pantries, down a broad hall, and into a large library. The curtains were drawn, and several reading lamps furnished the light.

Five men were seated around the broad mahogany table, which was cleared for action. As Colonel Kaspir had predicted, they were a grim lot. Least grim of the five was a chunky man with a prize-fighter's jaw, bright black eyes, and a Hitler forelock. This was Bellowing Benny.

The five stood perfunctorily for Maude, sat down simultaneously with her as Bellowing Benny waved us into chairs. Kaspir remained standing a moment, a tower of white linen, his survey of the board faintly hostile and frankly wary. He jerked his head toward Maude and me. "Gentlemen, my assistant, Lieutenant Kettle, my secretary, Miss Umph...."

A thin-lipped fellow with high collar and gold-rimmed spectacles opened his mouth. Colonel Kaspir drowned him out with a full-bodied and patently artificial cough.

"Meet Mr. Oliver Wendell Hoke," he said, pointing rudely at the thin-lipped man, who barely inclined a narrow skull topped with thinning, slicked-down blond hair. I recognized the name as that of a well-known manufacturer of military aircraft.

"Mr. Prettyman," continued Kaspir shifting his forefinger to an immensely tall skeleton of a man, a hook-nosed individual with a black patch over his right eye. "Major Duff-Dawson"—a plump man with a red face and gray mustache nodded pleasantly, eyes on Maude. "General Tancred"—the owner of the reputed second-best brain in our Military Intelligence setup shrank ill-naturedly into his rumpled alpaca coat, and his saucer-like ears looked sullen. "And the Secretary for Defense," concluded Kaspir, decent respect in his voice at last.

BELLOWING BENNY smiled briefly, glanced at his watch as he stood up. He spoke directly to Colonel Kaspir.

"Two weeks ago," he snapped, "I requested you to arrange to get the last of the Hoke Gibraltar's to England."

Kaspir nodded over the flame of a match he was holding to a crumpled cigarette.

Tancred, the G-2 brass hat, grumbled, "I've always maintained that this decentralization of Intelligence activities is—" An irritable twitch of Bellowing Benny's expressive mouth shut him up, and he pulled sulkily at a lobeless ear.

"Mr. Hoke," continued Bellowing Benny, "refuses to complete tests on the last and latest Gibraltar type unless he approves your plan for transferring it to England. He has heard a rumor...."

Kaspir inspected his thumbnail, and I tingled again. That meant he was intensely interested.

"... that you intend to ship it from Norfolk," went on Bellowing Benny's staccato voice. Short pause, with everyone tightening up. "On a small freighter."

"Sure," said Colonel Kaspir.

Consternation! Gabble of voices! Tancred boomed: "Most idiotic damned thing I—"

But it was Oliver Wendell Hoke who bounced to his feet, pale eyes hot behind the thin lenses of his spectacles. He managed to control his voice.

"I suppose you are aware," he addressed Kaspir, "that the Hoke Gibraltar represents England's first chance for a truly effective defense of her cities against enemy bombers."

"Sure," repeated Kaspir brightly. "Quite a plane, I bet."

"Did you know"—Hoke's solicitous tone carried the maximum insult—"that only four Gibraltar's have been built—and that three of these are now on the bottom of the ocean?"

"Sure," agreed Kaspir genially. "Shipped from Canada. U-boats picked right ship out of convoy three times runnin'. Bad leak somewhere." His baby blue eyes flickered to Tancred. "Intelligence cooperated with Canada in arrangin' sailings, didn't it?"

It was Tancred who sprang to his feet this time, furious. "Are you insinuating—"

I noted that Bellowing Benny was watching Kaspir intently.

"Insinuatin' nothin'," said Kaspir softly. "But they're gone, ain't they?"

Hoke took over, fingertips on the gleaming mahogany. "It takes eighteen months—*and* a million and a quarter— to build a Gibraltar. They *must* be tested under war conditions before we freeze the design and produce in quantity. This last one *must* get across. And you intend to ship it on a freighter—entirely unescorted—from Norfolk?"

"Surest thing you know." Kaspir's eyes, hardening, met Hoke's angry gaze head-on.

Hoke flung out a blue-veined hand. "I appeal to you, Mr. Secretary"—emotion thickened his words—"this criminal gamble—"

"Sure it's a gamble," snapped Kaspir. "What ain't?"

Bellowing Benny, noted for a trigger mind, for once looked doubtful. "Really, Steve," he began. "A small freighter—"

"Good, clean boat," asserted Kaspir fatuously. "Fast little hooker—sixteen knots."

I couldn't blame Tancred for his disgusted, "Good Godalmighty!"

The skeleton-like Prettyman spoke for the first time. His words were delivered with a faintly British inflection. I recalled his name as that of Hoke's chief executive in Hoke Aircraft, Inc.

"Suggest a compromise, gentlemen," Prettyman put a claw-like hand to the black eye-patch, adjusted it the merest trifle. "The British cruiser *Himalaya*'s at the Norfolk Navy Yard, isn't she? In for repairs? Then ship the Gibraltar on Colonel Kaspir's freighter, but wait until the *Himalaya*'s ready to convoy her over. Surely a week or two—"

KASPIR LOOKED meaningly at the gray-mustached Duff-Dawson. Duff-Dawson's face was somber.

"I'm afraid Mr. Prettyman is not aware," he said slowly, in the ripe accents of Oxford, "that the *Himalaya* met forty Stukas near Malta."

"You mean…?" Prettyman's single eye lighted with quick apprehension. Obviously the man's background was British.

"It will be six months before the *Himalaya* is ready to sail," answered Duff-Dawson simply, adding, after a pregnant pause, "if at all. She's been in a week. They've not got all the bodies out of her forward compartments yet."

Once more Hoke's slender hand sought Bellowing Benny's attention. "This absurd freighter idea! I positively refuse to—"

I thought I intercepted a momentary exchange of glances between Duff-Dawson and Colonel Kaspir. Tancred was up again, insisting upon being heard.

"I back Mr. Hoke's stand most vigorously. Colonel Kaspir must not… Did you know," he barked suddenly at Kaspir, "that we had a report yesterday that Willie Spruhe is in the United States?"

"Willie Spruhe?" This from Bellowing Benny.

"Yes, sir. One of the—no, I'll say the best of German Intelligence men. If he's here he's certainly smelled out this Gibraltar business."

"Little Bill ain't so smart," tossed in Kaspir bumptiously. Even Bellowing Benny's hackles rose at his tone.

"You know him, I suppose?" Tancred's tone was murderous.

"Never seen him. Heard of him. Big feller, tall as me and fatter. Works with a queer bird called Major Hansa. Pulled some tricks in Budapest that were hot stuff in '36. Dead now, I hear."

"You're crazy!" exploded Tancred.

"Maybe," admitted Kaspir. His moon face suddenly acquired certain hard angles I had never seen in it before. At my side, Maude's breathing quickened and she stopped doodling on her pad. My stomach went hollow with apprehension. Colonel Kaspir was about to declare himself.

"Listen, Benny—"

I gasped. Maude's head came up. Bellowing Benny was still watching Kaspir intently. He showed no resentment at the familiar form of address.

"Why'd you organize Section Five?" Kaspir's small mouth made the words crystal clear, and somehow he kept the question from sounding disrespectful.

Bellowing Benny did not hesitate. "To deal with emergencies outside the normal scope of Intelligence work."

"Why'd you pick me to run it?"

The Secretary for Defense hesitated this time.

"Go on." Kaspir smiled tightly. "I ain't modest."

"Because," replied Bellowing Benny in a lecture-room tone, "the Pr—because we knew that an eccentric approach will sometimes solve an abnormal problem."

"This Gibraltar business," pursued Kaspir. "It's an emergency—an abnormal problem, ain't it?"

"It most certainly is."

Kaspir treated the secretary to one long look.

"Then gimme a free hand," he demanded, leaning back in his chair, big paws folded across his chest. The room was very still.

"It's yours," announced Bellowing Benny, at length. "But if—"

"I getcha. Shot at sunrise—that sorta thing." Kaspir rose. The mantle of authority was almost visible on his bulging shoulders.

HOKE TOSSED a gold pencil he'd been fiddling with onto the table, where it clattered viciously.

"The plane's at the hidden field near Langley, ready to test?" Kaspir fired at Hoke.

"Yes, but—"

"But nothin'. You'll test this afternoon, dismantle at once, load 'er tonight. That freighter—what's-er-name, Dawson?"

"The *Lochgair*," supplied Duff-Dawson.

"I got barges ready on the James near the test field," said Kaspir. "We'll load the plane on them, bring 'em right downstream and up the Elizabeth River to the *Lochgair*. She's at the Army Base piers. She'll clear the Capes by daylight tomorrow."

Hoke spluttered and Kaspir bent forward threateningly.

"If you don't wanta do it," he said, "I'll commandeer the whole works and have it done m'self."

"I'll do it," muttered Hoke. He no longer went through the formality of veneering his personal animosity toward Kaspir.

"Good. You got your private flying boat at Anacostia, ain't you?"

Hoke nodded sourly.

"We'll fly down with you this afternoon," said Kaspir flatly. Bellowing Benny stood up and the rest of us followed suit. Maude flipped shut her notebook and I felt her trembling.

Tancred could contain himself no longer. Broad mouth bitter, he stalked up to the towering Kaspir. "If this moron's gamble of yours goes bad," he ground out, "I personally will see to it that you—"

Colonel Kaspir interrupted with something that sounded to my flustered ears like, "Ibble-dibble-dibble."

"What's that?" roared the purpling general.

From his great height, Kaspir regarded the general gravely. "Ibble-dibble-dibble," he repeated blandly.

General Tancred drew an ominous breath. "Your rank, sir, is that of colonel. There are certain formalities—"

He flounced away angrily as Kaspir clapped him on an outraged shoulder. "Keep your shirt on, old boy. Kentucky colonel only. Strictly civilian in this show."

Well! I'd served in Section Five for seven months and never known that. I was still recovering from the shock as we crowded into another overheated taxi. Maude's color was returning, but she was far from her old, ironical, biting self. She asked, very seriously: "Steve, why don't they fly the Gibraltar across?"

"Top speed's only sixty-five per," answered Kaspir absently, taking up his foot-patting.

This nonsensical retort reduced us both to a fuming silence. Kaspir stopped the cab at a glittering candy store. "See you both at Anacostia at four. Gotta have my staff along, y'know." He grimaced, waved a huge hand, and lumbered across the hot sidewalk.

I said something I'd been trying to say for seven months: "Maude, will you have lunch with me?"

"Why, Mike, I'd love to!"

But our lunch was not the gay affair I'd planned. Kaspir and Hoke and the Gibraltar and Willie Spruhe (known to Colonel Kaspir as "Little Bill") sat as skeletons at the feast.

Maude put it succinctly, capping a silence between courses.

"Thinks he's so damn smart," she complained childishly. Then, "Mike, I'm scared."

I'd never seen her really human before. I went soft and couldn't say a word.

TWO SURPRISES marked the flight to Norfolk for me. The first came at five thousand feet over the Potomac when Oliver Wendell Hoke's private flying boat, which on the water at Anacostia had appeared as plump and slow as a well-fed mare, overhauled and left behind the Washington-Norfolk afternoon plane, which does its hundred and fifty-nine miles in around fifty minutes.

The second surprise came a little later.

The trip down was not a gay one. Hoke ignored the lot of us. He sat poring over papers with Prettyman and radiating hostility to the world at large.

Hoke's steward, Davidson by name, a gorilla-built, middle-aged man with a flat, seamed face, resented Kaspir's bringing Joe, the houseboy from Section Five, along. Joe was relegated to a rear seat, where he dozed.

I was sulky because Kaspir had preempted the seat beside Maude.

Finally Prettyman, whose social sense apparently got the better of his feelings toward us, left Hoke and came to chat with me. I liked the man. He'd obviously knocked around the world more than a little. He talked in a way that interested me strongly—me, who had been drafted from an editorial desk on the *Baltimore Sun*, presumably to do propaganda work, and who had been out of my depth ever since. This was due, first, to an inexplicable transfer to G-2; second, to an equally inexplicable transfer to Colonel Stephen Kaspir's Section Five—that weird, anomalous bureau with headquarters in the attic of a brownstone ex-boarding house in southwest Washington.

Prettyman rambled on. He had flown ore-carrying planes in a venture beyond Burma, he told me, and after a jungle crash had cost him an eye, had landed a job as executive on one of the government-backed freight lines in South America. It was here that Hoke had discovered him and lured him north. Prettyman was up-to-date on military plane design now, and his analysis of the vulnerable points of a Messerschmitt was fascinating. But when I baited him about the Hoke Gibraltar, he shut up. "Wait'll you see her," was all he'd say. It was plain that he worshipped Hoke and the Gibraltar.

"There's Chesapeake Bay," he said at length, and went forward to talk to Dave Urban, Hoke's personal pilot, who in another hour was to take the Gibraltar on her final hop. Prettyman was back in a moment, said something to Hoke, then resumed his seat beside me. "Goin' to have a look at the *Himalaya*," he said. "We're ahead of schedule."

We swung in low over the brown Elizabeth River and ignored the city of Norfolk on our left for the sprawling, steaming activity of the great Norfolk Navy Yard, grinding away at a thousand jobs beside the narrow, deeply-channeled Southern Branch. We recognized a lean cruiser in drydock as H.M.S. *Himalaya*. Giant patches of canvas over portions of her deck and sides hid the gaping Stuka wounds, and even from the air we could spot the heavy force of guards that kept all visitors at a distance.

We wheeled north toward the James and the field where the Gibraltar awaited us. Prettyman fell silent, then, apparently to help relieve the tension that was taking hold of the cabin, called Davidson and ordered soft drinks. Hoke had abandoned his papers and was drumming absently on the table before him. Even Maude was subdued, staring out of the heavy glass window. Only Kaspir was airy, stuffing down chocolate cherries from a bag in his pocket in open defiance of Maude.

Davidson served the drinks, then carried a glass of ginger ale forward to Urban. I watched him disappear into the pilot's cabin. The man's physical strength, as evidenced in his shoulders and dangling arms, was almost frightening.

Thirty seconds later Davidson came hurrying from the pilot's compartment and his pasty gray face brought me at once to my feet. He stumbled down the aisle to where Prettyman and I were sitting, spilling ginger ale right and left from the glass he still held.

The flying boat lurched sharply, and Hoke glanced about him in quick alarm.

PRETTYMAN GRABBED Davidson's white sleeve.

"Mr. Urban!" gasped Davidson. Obviously he was badly frightened. "Heart—fell over—"

The flying boat yawed sickeningly. Prettyman was away to the pilot's compartment in a flash, beating Hoke to the door by a pace, while Kaspir and I brought up the rear. Behind me Maude half-stifled a highly feminine squeal.

Hoke appeared, hauling the sagging form of Urban into the main cabin. Through the forward door I could see Prettyman folding his angular length into the pilot's chair.

Immediately the low wing tip arced up and we resumed level flight.

The righting of the plane enabled Hoke to hoist Urban up into a seat, fending off, with a pointed elbow, Kaspir's attempt to help. Hoke's bloodless fingers found Urban's pulse. A second or two later he thumbed back the pilot's eyelids. Slowly he got to his feet.

Kaspir seized the opportunity to flop to his knees and go through substantially the same routine as Hoke. A shoulder pressed mine and the scent of honeysuckle told me that Maude had joined us. Hoke did not look around. He addressed the back of Kaspir's big, round head, and the venom ran deep in his voice.

"I suppose," he said, "that you will deny now, Colonel, that the Nazis are fully aware of your plans."

Kaspir looked up, eyes questioning.

"Urban was poisoned," said Hoke flatly. "Someone has tried to kill us all." If Hoke valued his own life, no quiver in his tone betrayed the fact. "It must have been done at the airport," he mused. "Timed to take effect on the way down."

Kaspir laughed, a brassy, neighing laugh that filed our nerves like fingernails scratching a blackboard.

"Relax," he told Hoke. "You're seein' bogie-men."

Hoke stiffened furiously.

"Th' poor feller's heart just quit on him," announced Kaspir. He stared at Hoke's white cheeks. "Yours'll do the same if you don't calm down."

Hoke's thin lips were framing a blistering comment on this incredibly ill-timed levity when we all pitched forward a step or two. Maude's nails nearly punctured my right biceps, but in a second we realized that Prettyman was bringing us in to a fast landing beside a small pier on the left bank of the broad James River.

But even I had noticed a condition at the base of Urban's nails, and the ghastly tinge of the lips, which told me that Kaspir's diagnosis of the pilot's death was no more than wishful thinking. And it was not until we were ashore, and gathered before a jerry-built hangar at one end of a lengthy and secluded emergency field, that the sight of the Hoke Gibraltar going aloft (Prettyman substituting at the controls for Dave Urban, deceased) dissolved the hard lump of apprehension in my chest.

For the Hoke Gibraltar broached a wellspring of optimism in me that ran dry only at the conclusion of the flight—when Colonel Kaspir began to behave in a manner that clearly indicated incipient insanity.

Of the Hoke Gibraltar I can say only this: only the fact that she flew (if you could call that awkward passage through the air flying) entitled her to recognition as an airplane.

Two broad planks laid across the ends of a coffin would give you an idea of her general lines. Two motors nestled under each of these wings. I say "wings" because, since they were of equal length, it was hard to know which one to call the tail.

As this monstrosity lumbered down the field and thunderously hoisted her dark gray bulk into the air, I realized that Kaspir's statement of her maximum speed had not been a bad joke, but the unvarnished truth.

Then it dawned on me! The Gibraltar was designed for sluggishness! For when Prettyman had her a thousand feet up, flaps drooped suddenly from her wings and she became, to watchers from the ground, almost stationary in the late afternoon haze.

Did I tell you she was knobby as a toad? No twenty feet of her body surface but had its gunblister or gunport, and the good half of these apertures carried heavy stuff—far heavier than I had dreamed could be put upon a plane. The rest of the gunports exhibited machine-guns of bulbous design in batteries of three.

The picture of the whole took shape in my mind: dozens of these air-borne forts crawling back and forth through the sky over the cities of England, their very slowness rendering their fire amazingly accurate. I imagined a Heinkel squadron passing between two of these behemoths—or, say, through a box formation of four of them operating at different levels—and visualized grimly what would be left of the attackers after a bath in the Gibraltars' shell-streams. And fighting planes? Why, one Gibraltar could stand its ground in the clouds and rip squadron after squadron of fighters to shreds.

And so I could understand the fierce pride emanating from Oliver Wendell Hoke's ascetic face as he watched the Gibraltar settle heavily to the dusty field and put out four fat wheels to soak up the landing shock. And why Maude, shoulders back and firm chin up, winked her glistening eyes.

THE GROUND trembled as Prettyman taxied the Gibraltar over to the hangar. Colonel Kaspir, who had watched the test with a poker face that must have maddened Hoke, said to him: "Did'ja do what I said?"

The hangar swallowed up the Gibraltar as Hoke nodded. We walked over to it. A guard admitted us through a side door.

Maude and I gasped simultaneously, and even Kaspir's eyes widened. The Gibraltar had preceded us into the hangar by less than two minutes, but already she was coming apart. The place swarmed with mechanics. More than two hundred, I should say, had been cooling their heels in that lofty frame structure while the Gibraltar bellowed her way through the final test.

Now they were upon her. Even as I watched, one whole gun-blister disintegrated into a collection of metal panels and sections of bullet-proof glass.

At the far end of the hangar, stacked to the ceiling, were the crates—big crates and little crates, hundreds of them. Already twenty or thirty huskies were trundling these up to the Gibraltar on squat tractors. The gun-blister I had watched dissolve disappeared like a magician's egg into one of the smaller crates, and, as a tractor drew the full crate aside, the dozen-odd men of the mechanics' crew were at work on another part of the plane.

Prettyman, pilot's role aside, was now supervisor of dismantling. His grotesquely long legs carried him swiftly about the rapidly-changing Gibraltar. His black eye-patch would hover briefly over a group of workmen. He would say something and illustrate his remark with a wave of his antenna-like hands. Then the work would go on a little faster, a shade more efficiently.

Hoke led Kaspir and Maude and me to a pine-board office. He hesitated only long enough to see us seated. When he spoke, I knew that the sight of the Gibraltar had humbled him.

"Colonel Kaspir," he began, and there was no hint of animosity in his tone, "for the last time I beg of you to reconsider your plan."

Kaspir, teetering back in a creaking wooden chair, said, "Huh?"

"I made no issue of it at the time," said Hoke, "but I feel that you know as well as I do that Urban was poisoned. This plan of yours is known."

Maude pressed her hands together until the knuckles whitened, for Hoke's voice was shaking, and you could feel, deep in you, the awful price his pride was paying for this plea.

"Well?" said Kaspir rancorously. He was going to make Hoke pay full price. Maude's violet eyes blazed at him.

"I beg of you," said Hoke simply, "to re-arrange matters so that this last Gibraltar—the best of the four—can go out adequately guarded, with at least a fair chance of reaching England."

Kaspir creaked forward until his elbows were akimbo on a low drafting table. A cigarette in his pursed lips began to bob up and down as he answered.

"Nothin' doin'," he said. Hoke's thin frame sagged. "You tried convoys outa Canada. Where'd it getcha?"

"But a freighter—a small freighter—unarmed? And this man—the spy—Spruhe, and his organization?"

We all felt Kaspir's ultimatum coming. "I got everything ready. We load tonight. And the *Lochgair* runs for it."

Kaspir's moon face darkened to an ugly red and his long, thick arm snaked out. A pudgy forefinger poked Hoke's bony shoulder, none too gently.

"Listen, feller." Hoke drew breath. "You saw those marines outside? Then get this. You try any funny stuff—callin' Washington or slowin' up the work"—he jerked his head toward the clamor beyond the thin door—"and I'll have you—yes, and Prettyman too—in the brig at Langley Field in twenty minutes. Maybe fifteen. That's all."

Maude jumped to her feet, all her pity for Hoke, all her fury at Kaspir starkly revealed in her attitude and, when she could speak, in her voice. With a tongue like a scalpel she carved Kaspir's hide and laid bare his vanity and what she aptly described as his "bull-headedness." These she held up to our scorn.

Colonel Kaspir's round blue eyes were speculative as he listened. When she finished he turned to me. "Your turn, Kettle. You got an oration on your chest, too?"

I shook my head. "I think," I said, "that Maude has covered the ground."

He was hurt, not play-acting, but genuinely hurt. "Kinda thought you two 'ud string along," he said. For a moment I softened, but the thought of his treatment of Hoke set me like plaster.

What happened next made me wonder seriously if the strain of the Gibraltar incident had not affected Kaspir's mind. I'd long suspected he was a man who could not stand opposition. He stalked from the room, and when he returned, Prettyman was with him—and a marine lieutenant.

"I'm takin' over at this point," he announced calmly. It was deep dusk outside now, and the single naked bulb in the office only emphasized the bareness of the place. "They're beginnin' to cart your baby down to the barges," he went on, addressing Hoke. "Now listen—" This was to all of us—"You don't like my party. Well, you can just take Hoke's plane and get the hell over to the Chamberlin at Old Point Comfort and stay there. Take a coupla rooms and sit up for me. None o' you's goin' anywhere, get me? No phone calls."

He cocked an eyebrow at the marine lieutenant. "They're all yours, son. Take 'em."

OF ALL the petty jack-in-office stuff I ever saw, this took the grand prize! Even Maude was speechless. I had long ago decided one thing. Section Five and Colonel Kaspir were not for me. I was going to get into Propaganda, where I belonged, if I had to tear Washington apart to do it.

Silently we made our way from the clamorous hangar—the whole crew engaged on the big job now, that of crating the Gibraltar's immense body—and shuffled down through the dark and dust to the pier where Hoke's flying boat waited. Prettyman and Hoke walked together, talking in low tones. Hoke's voice was angry, Prettyman's replies growing more and more disgusted as he listened to Hoke's tale of what had taken place in the hangar office.

Thirty minutes later the marine lieutenant, who had roused my ire by his attentiveness to Maude, was herding us into a small suite high in the lofty hotel. Apologetically he collected the keys from the three doors after locking them on the inside. We paced the floors and peered from the windows into the moonless night. Far down the bay, flashes and reverberations told of night anti-aircraft practice at Cape Henry.

Twice the marine lieutenant unlocked one door. The first time was to admit a waiter bearing many sandwiches and much coffee. The second time—about two A.M.—was to admit Colonel Stephen Kaspir. I was happy to see he looked drawn and worried. Hoke and Prettyman stared at him.

"She's loaded," he said wearily. He shook his head, and for the first time I spotted self-doubt in his mind. "Body-crate wouldn't fit the damn little hold," he said. "Hadda lash it on deck."

Hoke and Prettyman paled. That crate, on the afterdeck of a small freighter, would be an advertisement plainer than a neon sign!

Kaspir drew a chair to a window and gazed into the night, the smoke from his succession of cigarettes drifting back into the room. The marine lieutenant and Maude started a game of Russian bank. Prettyman stretched his elongated body on a bed and bored holes in the ceiling with his one eye. Hoke sat enveloped in black thoughts. In the far room Joe and Davidson slept, Davidson noisily.

At three A.M. Kaspir's shoulders straightened. "There she goes." He said it half to himself, but the room came alive in a second as we crowded to the widows.

From a high room in the Chamberlin you can almost spit into the channel that races between the boat-landing and Fort Wool—the tiny island that squats in the junction of Hampton Roads and Chesapeake Bay.

There, heading east, almost directly beneath us, was a small, furtive freighter. The dark shape of the tremendous crate on her after deck identified her as the *Lochgair*. She slid past Fort Wool, and as she stuck her nose into the bay, her half-dozen lights winked out.

Funny thing. As the *Lochgair* became one with the black bay water, I had a feeling I would see her again. This feeling persisted like a headache through the restless remainder of the night, and was still strong upon me when we boarded Hoke's flying boat off Fortress Monroe. We left the water smoothly and Prettyman pointed our blunt nose in the general direction of Washington. In those comfortable seats we settled down to our thoughts.

I WAS dozing off when Colonel Kaspir, beside me, leaned suddenly across me and looked out of the window. Idly I followed his gaze. My heart skipped a beat.

There should have been green fields and the gray-green Potomac down there. But there was nothing but open water. For some reason, Prettyman had eased the plane gently around and was heading to sea.

Colonel Kaspir rose very quietly and started up the aisle toward where Davidson stood with his back to the door of the pilot's compartment.

The cabin of Hoke's flying boat is sound-insulated, so we could hear Davidson quite plainly. He said: "Stop right there, Colonel."

I was wondering why Kaspir obeyed so promptly when, past his elbow, I saw the two heavy automatics in Davidson's stubby hands.

"Sit down!" barked Davidson. He included Hoke in this order, for the little man, who had been sharing his seat with Maude, had shot up like a jack-in-the-box.

"Sit down!" repeated Davidson harshly when Hoke was about five feet from him. Kaspir's hand caught Hoke's arm and for a second this Mutt-and-Jeff combination faced the white-coated steward. Davidson brought the gun muzzles up an inch or two.

"Better do what he says," advised Kaspir, pushing Hoke back into the seat beside Maude. "Now, my man," he began pompously, "just what is all this rigamarole?"

Now, this wasn't Kaspir's style at all, and the fact penetrated the dizzy whirl of speculation and apprehension in my brain.

For answer, Davidson drew up a foot and banged three times with his heel against the door behind him. Prettyman appeared almost immediately, stooping low to pass through the small doorway. With a single motion of his head, Davidson turned the situation over to Prettyman. He shoved the guns into Prettyman's lean hands and vanished into the pilot's compartment. At once the increasing vibration of the big boat told us that Davidson had opened up her engines to full throttle.

"Prettyman!" The amazement in Hoke's voice made one thing quite plain. This was no desperate venture to save the Gibraltar from the possible consequences of Kaspir's plan. This was something entirely different.

"Sorry, Oliver." Prettyman's tone was pure irony, and the black patch was momentarily like the evil winking of an eye. Kaspir dropped into a seat almost at Prettyman's feet. "Keep your hands on the table," ordered Prettyman. One gun barrel wavered in Kaspir's direction.

"Here, boy, move up," called Prettyman, stretching his long neck. Quickly up the aisle came Joe, his intelligent eyes glazed, his whole face a mask of terror. At Prettyman's direction he took a seat across from me. Somehow this terror didn't strike me as Joe's style.

"We'll have no trouble," announced Prettyman. His eye blazed suddenly at Maude. "What are *you* doing?" he snapped.

"Powdering my nose," snapped Maude.

"Take your hands off that bag." Maude's white hands drew back slowly. Prettyman, with a single five-foot stride, stepped forward and hooked Maude's white linen hand-bag with the little finger of one gun-hand. He hefted it. His expressive mouth broadened. "And what," he inquired archly, "were you about to do with that, me proud beauty?" He dropped the bag on the floor for emphasis, and it struck with a peculiarly heavy thud.

Maude's hands patted her permanent. "Shoot you," she answered, tucking in a stray lock. "Right through your good eye."

Prettyman chuckled. His hand went up and raised the black patch. The eye under that patch was a perfectly good one, and it blinked in the light.

"What was it?" he inquired of Kaspir, who had slumped into extreme dejection. "What was it you said yesterday at the Secretary's house: 'Little Bill ain't so smart'?"

Kaspir shot bolt upright. "Why, Willie," he exclaimed, genuinely admiring, "you cute thing. So you're Little Bill." His blue eyes ranged Prettyman's emaciated figure. "Well, I'll be damned," he said. "I'd always heard you were a fatty. How'dja lose it?" This time it was the envy that was genuine. I believe I mentioned that Kaspir weighs close to three hundred.

"Fever." Prettyman grinned. "South America. Waiting for someone like Oliver here to recognize my talents and make a place for me in American aviation. Shed a hundred and ninety pounds, Kaspir, and you'll have the best disguise that ever was—like me. You see it's—"

But we never heard the rest of this, for the door behind Prettyman resounded to heavy knocks from the pilot's compartment. Prettyman's light manner fell away on the instant. Eyes still on our group, he opened the door a crack and hurled something over his shoulder in German. We could just catch, out of Davidson's reply, the word *Lochgair.*

IT WAS a different man who spoke to us through Prettyman's mouth. "Get over there." This was to Kaspir and me. He herded us into the seats opposite Maude and Hoke. Joe moved up to the seat lately vacated by Kaspir.

"Now," said Prettyman—or Willie Spruhe, if you like, "listen." He glanced at his watch and nodded to himself. "You will all remain in those seats. If anyone moves I shall kill him—or her. You may look"—he could not control the tension that was setting his lean body a-quiver—"out of the window."

The flying boat slanted slightly as Davidson sent her into a long, slow curve. We were throttled down again. We peered down. Of the five of us, Colonel Kaspir was the only one who did not cry out. Two thousand feet below, a toy boat rode through sun-dappled waters. Across her after-deck was lashed a crate like an immense coffin. She was a tiny and very gallant object on that broad expanse of sea, but that was not what had made us cry out. The *Lochgair* was not alone. From our elevation we could see what could not be seen from her bridge.

Two long, dark shapes, perhaps half a mile apart, lay under the water like sinister gate-posts. The *Lochgair* was heading directly between them.

Davidson kept the flying boat in a giant circle with the freighter for its center. Maude's hands, on the table, were white-knuckled fists, and I found myself gritting my teeth until my jaws ached.

Beside me, Kaspir turned and spoke to Prettyman over his shoulder. "Gonna take 'er or sink 'er?" It was as though he had said, "Will you have Scotch or bourbon?"

"Sink her, of course." The stupidity of the question irritated Prettyman. "I have duplicates of the essential plans, of course. Which is more," he added meaningly, "than Oliver has."

A strangled sound drew my eyes to Hoke for the first time in many minutes. What little blood he had, seemed to have been siphoned out of him. Everything that had made him such a forceful, vital little figure was gone. One of Maude's hands flew to his shoulder in a spontaneous gesture of pity and sympathy.

"I am sorry, Oliver"—Prettyman's voice lost a shade of its mockery—"but I was forced to destroy the originals before we left Washington."

"Then," said Colonel Kaspir, briskly and cheerfully, "we shall have to use the ones you've brought along, Little Bill." He added, "It was you tippin' your gang about the Canadian convoys?"

Prettyman nodded. "I had to go up there, of course, to help load. And of course we managed to have a man or two on the ships."

Maude gasped, "Look, Steve!"

The submarines were breaking water—an insolent, open move that set my blood boiling. Only sure information regarding the *Lochgair's* defenseless state could warrant a maneuver like that. I shoved against Kaspir, even as Maude half-climbed over Hoke, to get a better look at something I had decided I did not want to see.

A blob of white issued slowly from the deck-gun of the sub nearest us. Davidson was bringing the flying boat lower now, for I could see the *Lochgair's* white wake fading into green and gold as her engines stopped.

And now there were men running frantically along her decks, eddying and charging about the lifeboats which flanked the great crate on the afterdeck, holding the Gibraltar's body.

Prettyman stepped closer to us, gazed down critically. "Panic!" he said scornfully. "They have nothing to fear. Our U-boats will take them all aboard—even as they will take us aboard. This will be one of the great mysteries of the sea and air."

"All gonna be very uncomfortable," said Colonel Kaspir.

There was a brittle tinkle in Kaspir's tone which I thought I alone had detected. Instinctively I looked at Prettyman. His ears had caught it, too. "Listen, Kaspir," he began warningly.

"Little Bill," said Kaspir solemnly, "this is gonna be kind of tough on you."

We all gaped at him.

"Lookit," he advised.

IF I'M a trifle incoherent about what happened next, forgive me. Merely thinking about it can still set my pulses pounding.

Two of the frantic groups on the *Lochgair's* decks suddenly left their work at the lifeboats to run to the sides of the great crate. Five seconds later the crate sides were down and shunted aside.

"Old stuff," grunted Colonel Kaspir to Prettyman, without turning. "Old stuff, Little Bill," he repeated, "but pretty goddam effective."

Then the crews of the two guns on the *Lochgair,* free now of the concealing crate, went to work with a vengeance. They were North Sea-trained and salty, those boys, and this in-fighting was right up their alley. The third shell from the spitting starboard gun rocked the smaller sub and spilled overboard the men who were bringing its tiny deck-gun to bear. Two more shots, planted with the lethal accuracy of a fine boxer's one-two punch, and the smaller sub was merely a blunt bow reeling drunkenly heavenwards in a boiling circle of oily foam.

But the larger sub was making a fight of it. Her commander brought her swiftly around so that, before the *Lochgair's* port gun-crew could bracket her effectively, she presented an infinitely smaller target. A ventilator beside the *Lochgair's* gun-crew disappeared as the sub's deckgun opened fire.

Prettyman, almost at my shoulder now, yelped something in German. Then there were two ghastly explosions in the cabin, seemingly right in my ear. Maude screamed. For a second I was sure a chance shot from the fight below had found us. Then a weight fell upon me and the next instant I was on my feet and struggling blindly and awkwardly with Prettyman—until I realized that Prettyman was not fighting back and that my fingers were digging into a limp and lifeless body.

Something white across the aisle moved. "Nice goin', Joe," grunted Kaspir, who had wheeled with the rest of us.

Joe's white teeth flashed briefly as he slid his own automatic back inside his white serving jacket. "A pleasure, Colonel," was all he said. Then I knew that Prettyman's attention must have been deflected by the shock of the events below.

Prettyman was very dead as he lay in the aisle where I had dropped him. The two big bullet holes in his forehead were not half an inch apart.

Kaspir nodded toward the pilot's compartment. "Step in there, Joe," he said, "and tickle Major Hansa's ear with that bean-shooter o' yours. Tell him to keep circling."

He looked down at Prettyman. "I wish he coulda seen this," he said regretfully, as we turned to the window. "Oh, my God!" he cried.

And Oliver Wendell Hoke echoed it hysterically and lashed out at Kaspir with both thin hands. His fists smacked sharply against Kaspir's full face. Kaspir caught the flailing hands, held them. Hoke struggled. He was cursing now, and tears and sobs were mixed with the flow of invective. Then I thought to look down, and knew why.

The sub was heeled over now. She was finished.

But the *Lochgair* was finished, too. One final, desperate torpedo had taken her amidships, for the black hole in her side was fully visible and she was settling fast. The gun crews and lifeboat gangs were getting her boats into the water smartly, though.

But Hoke's ravings struck home to me with re-doubled force. The subs were gone—yes. But the Hoke Gibraltar was now joining her three sisters on the bottom of the ocean. Kaspir had won the last round, all right. But he had lost the fight on points.

Kaspir's placid face, as he gripped Hoke's weakening hands, somehow infuriated me.

"Let's go for'ard," he grunted. I got out of his way. He hauled Hoke across Maude and hustled him up into the pilot's compartment. The flat-faced Major Hansa—lately Davidson, steward—was still at the controls, and Joe's automatic was very close to his head.

HANSA LOOKED around with grim enjoyment at the three of us huddled in the cramped space. "You've got me, Colonel." His dark eyes glinted. "But would you not rather have had the Gibraltar?"

"Head back for Norfolk," said Kaspir. "Gonna hang you in a few weeks."

"Hang me, Colonel?" Major Hansa altered the controls slightly.

"For poisonin' that what's his name—that Urban fellow—Hoke's pilot. Slippin' him that quick stuff in the ginger ale," replied Kaspir. "I suppose you hadda get him outa the way so's Prettyman could fly us out here."

"Ah, yes, of course." Major Hansa was bringing the flying boat around, straightening her into level flight. "But are you not going to stop here and assist those men in the boats?"

Kaspir glanced at the rectangular watch on his beefy wrist. "There'll be somebody along in a few minutes to pick 'em up." Again that brittle note in his voice.

Hansa's eyes narrowed. "You will have much fun," he suggested, "trying to recover the remains of the Gibraltar from eighty fathoms of water." The man was trying to reassure himself of something. I discovered with a shock that he was on the verge of breaking.

Kaspir was supporting the dazed Hoke with an affectionate arm.

"Drop down to about three hundred," he instructed Hansa. Hansa shoved the wheel forward and the flying boat's nose dipped.

Kaspir was peering ahead at the gleaming ocean and his wide blue eyes were dancing as the opal had danced on Maude's hand. He inhaled suddenly. "Lookit!" he said.

So we looked, Hansa craning his neck with the rest.

At first it was nothing but a dark gray bow and some smoke. But our speed was bringing it toward us as though we were reeling it in on a drum.

Colonel Kaspir leaned closer to our pilot. "You ain't supposin', Major," he said very softly, almost in Hansa's ear, "that I really shipped the Gibraltar out on that little of freighter, are you?"

Hansa's eyes must have been better than mine, just as his comprehension was, for before I could grasp the full significance of the approaching vessel, the gorilla-like major had leaped from the pilot's seat and was flying at Kaspir's crouching bulk in vain, unprofitable fury. Very vain and very unprofitable indeed, for Joe swung the blue-steel barrel of his automatic heavily against the back of the major's head. The major became a limp tangle of long arms and bandy legs. Joe opened the door to the cabin and removed his second victim.

Colonel Kaspir's small mouth stretched dangerously into a grin as he shoved Hoke gently into the pilot's chair. Hoke's hands and feet went automatically to the controls. He still stared at the oncoming ship, and he made no attempt to hide the tears.

The vessel below would pass under us in another minute. I ran back to the cabin, threw my arm around Maude's warm shoulders, and drew her to a window. Joe, the house-boy, joined us.

We looked down at the gray efficiency of His Majes-ty's Ship *Himalaya,* and I knew then why Kaspir and Duff-Dawson, of the Embassy, had seemed to be sharing a secret that morning at Bellowing Benny's.

The canvas patches were gone from the Himalaya's decks now, and there were no Stuka scars visible—because there had never been any.

Across H.M.S. *Himalaya's* afterdeck, beyond her guns, was lashed a huge, wooden, coffin-like crate, exactly like the dummy crate that had disfigured the *Lochgair's* after-deck. But this one, I knew now, held the body of Gibral-tar, just as the cruiser's hold held the remainder of Hoke's remarkable plane.

So the *Himalaya,* bearer of the Gibraltar, slipped away under us, heading east across the shining ocean—hull down for England. As you may have heard, she arrived safely.

A moon face rose over my left shoulder.

"Pretty, ain't she?" said Colonel Kaspir.

PRESSURE ISLAND

WE NEVER COULD KEEP UP
WITH THE ANIMATED-DYNAMO
CHIEF OF THE DEFENSE
BUREAU'S SECTION 5. BUT
THE WAY OUR BEHEMOTH BOSS
UNVEILED THE "SUICIDE" OF
ONE OF HIS BRIGHT YOUNG
MEN AT THE SUBMARINE BASE
AS MURDER, AND TRAPPED
THE NAVY'S SINISTER
SABOTEUR LEFT US GASPING.

PERMIT ME to say right here that the incident of the gentlemanly Japanese had no connection whatever with the Pressure Island affair—so far as we have learned.

Type recently reported that "Col. Stephen Kaspir, hulking, moon-faced chief of the Washington defense bureau known as Section Five, keeps milkman's hours"—whereupon Maude commented bitterly, "It's a lie. He keeps all hours." She was right. All hours of the twenty-four are alike to Kaspir, who stokes his great frame with endless pounds of chocolate cherries and sneers at folk who require sleep.

This night was a case in point. We'd been nightclubbing. This would suggest three hours of boredom at a ringside table, four or five drinks, then home to bicarbonate of soda and bad dreams.

Not so with Kaspir. We "did" four nightclubs, and Kaspir, an animated mountain of black broadcloth and starched linen, was offensively the life and soul of the party at each. He swilled champagne with half of official Washington. He bellowed quips across indignant tables to acquaintances in far corners. Worst of all, he dragooned Maude and me into countless conga lines, where his behind looked for all the world like a dancing elephant's rump when the band plays "Yankee Doodle" in slow time. And finally, at the

"Try this," the Colonel
said affectionately.

Troika, he danced Maude into an inoffensive Japanese
waltzing gracefully with his Russian wife and became so
abusive that the management asked us to leave.

On the sidewalk Maude, her cameo upsweep unruffled
by the evening's acrobatics, stared at gray streaks in the east
and murmured gratefully, "Home, by God!" A cab appeared
and she turned, queenly in her silver lame, to me. "Kiss me
good-night, Mike. I don't want to see either of you guys for
a week." Her mocking lips made me feel weak....

"Whaddaya mean—home?" demanded Kaspir. He was
completely sober, although he had wallowed in champagne. He pushed us into the cab. "We ain't through yet,"

he said, wriggling himself between us. He gave the driver a southwest Washington address and Maude moaned, "Oh, hell." She put her blond head on my shoulder and snored ostentatiously.

Kaspir hiccoughed, blasphemed the champagne, halted the cab at an all-night drugstore, and squirmed out. He came back ripping the gaudy wrapping from one of those two-pound boxes of chocolate cherries that are forever on sale. Popping a couple into his cupid's-bow mouth, he tendered the box to me. For answer, I shuddered. He stuffed in two more and champed juicily, regarding me from the corner of his eye.

I knew exactly what he wanted. He wanted me to demand why he had staged this absurd binge when we were dead beat from the Panama business; why we were returning to the old brownstone ex-boarding house that is Section Five's G.H.Q. I forced my weary mind to review the evening. "The Jap?" I asked, at a venture.

"He ain't a Jap." He said it so peevishly that I knew I'd guessed right. "He's unique."

Bait. I refused to ask why. He'd tell me anyhow.

"He's a Chink," said Kaspir, smirking at my surprise. "Only Chink I ever saw who can pass for a Jap."

"Friend of ours?" I inquired.

"Too soon to tell. Skittish. I been wooin' him a bit."

THE CAB squealed to a stop. I suffered a pang when Maude removed her lovely head from my shoulder.

Joe, the Negro houseboy, was buttoning his white linen jacket as he opened the door. I glimpsed the handle of the shoulder-holstered automatic that Maude swears he sleeps in.

"The Navy Department's after you, Colonel," he announced as the familiar mustiness of the old place enveloped us. Joe saves his drawl for visitors.

Kaspir swore, leapt up the stairs. He stopped halfway. "Joe—"

Joe was lifting the chinchilla cape from Maude's white shoulders.

"I'm expectin' a yeller man," called Kaspir from the dim stairway. "Gentlemanly feller. Show him right up. And Joe—"

"Yes, Colonel."

"Frisk him first," said Kaspir, and bounded upwards. Maude sprang after him in a flurry of long, shapely legs and chattering jewelry. I caught up with her on the third floor and we hurried along the creaking boards to her office, the anteroom to Kaspir's. Kaspir was already neighing irritably into the phone, "I want Admiral Dickerman." Pause. "Good God, man, is he gonna sleep all day?"

I touched Maude's bare shoulder and showed my wrist watch. It was five A.M. We went in. Kaspir was glaring at the telephone receiver.

"These Navy fellers," he began, as we entered. Then, "Oh, *there* you are. Whereinell you been, Sam?" Long pause, during which the unintelligible crackling of words in the transmitter made the only sound in the room.

"Nope," said Kaspir at length, very positively. "You guys lay off. I'll 'tend to it. I gotta free hand at Anacostia, I suppose?"

He broke the connection, dialed again. "Get me Captain Ardsley." Another fretful wait. "Ed? Steve Kaspir. You gotta coffee-grinder handy that don't go like this?" His big hand made a series of dips, like a child imitating a roller-coaster. Captain Ardsley apparently understood. "Then gas 'er up, will you? We'll be there in less'n an hour. Thanks." He heaved himself up, lumbered to the closet where he keeps a skeleton wardrobe.

A cigarette Maude was tamping on a gold case slipped through her fingers. "Who is it this time?" she addressed Kaspir's back, in a curiously strained voice.

Kaspir stripped collar and tie from his fleshy neck with an exasperated yank. "You never met Williams, did you?" He said this to me. I said no. Maude was very pale.

"You never will," said Kaspir, fumbling at his vest. "Now beat it, you two. See you at Anacostia in forty minutes."

Knowing Maude, I expected a wrangle. None came. In the cab I got a clue to her forbearance. "Steve thought a lot of Williams," she said. I wondered jealously how much Maude had thought of him.

"We got him fresh from Yale Law when Steve organized Section Five," she added. "Steve knew his father."

My jealousy relaxed. Maude's near thirty. Williams must have been far too young…. We pulled up in front of the Willard Hotel.

"Steve's out for blood," said Maude. "See you at 'costia."

Rolling on through the yellowing day to my own hotel, I pondered the fate which had driven me from a snug editorial desk on the *Sun* to whirl me through Army Intelligence into Section Five; which had welded my existence to that of Maude and Colonel Kaspir; which had me gravely concerned over something—I knew not what—that had happened to a young man named Williams, whom I would never meet.

AT ANACOSTIA the propellers of the big Navy patrol plane ticked over restlessly. Maude and Kaspir were already aboard, Maude smart in mink jacket and scarlet wool, Kaspir untidy in tweeds, his face apprehensively green.

Our pilot gunned his motors. The air-sickly Kaspir retched. Only our heartless persistence on that flight tore any information at all from him. Over the Delaware River he gasped that we were heading for New London. Over Sandy Hook, between groans, he related that Williams, acting on a vague tip picked up in Washington, had been "wet-nursin' Jack Tucker on that funny island." Over New Haven he implored us to go to hell, but as we glided in to a landing at the New London Submarine Base he revealed that Williams had apparently committed suicide.

A wonderfully courteous Navy lieutenant put us aboard a waiting PT boat and we thundered down the Thames at a modest fifty m.p.h. I enjoyed that ride. The echoing rush under the bridges and past the sprawling Electric Boat Company plant where, in plain view of all the river, eleven black cigar shapes a-crawl with workmen were becoming submarines.

To starboard rose the Pequot Light. We whipped around it as around a pylon. Ocean Beach slid past. Our goal was now obvious—a small, green island, dotted with three white buildings. It grew larger. The roar of our three motors softened to an angry muttering as we approached a small pier. Kaspir shook an ungrateful fist heavenward at the Navy patrol plane, now droning back to Anacostia. In another minute we had the firm planking of the pier under our feet and the PT was a dwindling white wake.

Colonel Kaspir addressed the world at large. "Wherein-ell *is* everybody?" His color was returning.

A red head appeared at a corner of the pier shed and said cordially, "Be with you in a second, bud." It vanished, reappearing a second later followed by a body. It was a gob, very young, very green, but wearing a highly official automatic.

"You lookin' for Doc Tucker?" inquired Redhead, eyes on Maude. "He's over at the basin. They're takin' Alice down this morning."

Kaspir swelled. "Ain't there guards here?"

"Sure," said Redhead. "Me. The other boys are out patrollin'." He pointed to sea. We saw a gray launch. "We don't let no pleasure boats come within a quarter-mile," he explained.

"Take me to Tucker," ordered Kaspir.

"Sure." Redhead led us off the pier, up a grassy path.

"What about this feller Williams?" barked Kaspir, perspiring up the slope.

Our guide put a grimy forefinger to his forehead, cocked his thumb, snapped it. "That's all I know," he said simply. "We heard today that some high muck-amuck from Washington was comin' up to— Say, you ain't...?"

"Lead on," said Kaspir grimly.

It was downhill now. To our left the three white stucco dwellings made a triangle on a green slope. At the foot of our path, on a small cliff at the water's edge, a crane had been erected. It was attended by four figures in dungarees. The breeze brought us the grinding machinery. Something was being raised from the water.

"That's Alice coming up," said our guide cryptically.

So intent were the workers at the crane that not a head turned at the slight bustle of our arrival. Redhead led us to the cliff edge. The crane was drawing a dripping steel cable from green water.

"Aha!" exclaimed Redhead. A shining shape broke water. "That's Alice. Well, folks, I gotta leave you."

"Alice" ascended, streaming. She was a shiny metal ball, perhaps nine feet in diameter, her bottom pocked with many valves. In her top, near the cable ring, was a hatch the size of a porthole.

The crane arm swung inshore, lowered Alice gently to a crude wooden base not a dozen feet from where we stood. The dungaree-clad workers ran to her. One climbed on her shoulder and applied a wrench to the hatch bolts. The hatch swung out, an arm pushing from inside. The worker seized the arm and pulled. There appeared a head, as big as Kaspir's and bald as a billiard ball. Then narrow shoulders and a round belly. The hatch was a tight fit. The head cursed without heat. Beside me, Kaspir snickered. "Jack Tucker ain't built for this sorta thing."

IT DAWNED on my tired mind who Jack Tucker was. Dr. Johnson Tucker, of course—the physicist, the bathysphere man, the treasure-hunter extraordinary who'd raped the wreck of the *Grenadier* off Los Cocos Key to the tune of a million and a half in gold. So this fat little fellow floundering down Alice's swelling side was the Dr. Tucker who'd had five wives and who was reputed to know more about submarine construction....

Tucker's shiny pate became one of a cluster of five heads bent over a wooden table littered with plans. We three, consumed with curiosity, edged nearer. Tucker was jabbing a thumb at one plan and saying something in a soft voice. A blond youngster with enormous hands seized a pencil and noted some change.

Tucker returned to the dripping Alice and, standing on tiptoes, made some adjustment in what appeared to be a master valve. "Three millimeters," he called. Again the blond youth changed the plan.

Kaspir fidgeted, grumbling under his breath. Maude lit a cigarette.

Tucker drew himself up Alice's shoulder to the hatch, struggled through, disappeared. The blond giant climbed after him, screwed shut the hatch. Then he returned to the crane. The dark-haired workman who accompanied him walked with a peculiar swing of the hips.

Maude noticed it, too. "It's a woman, Mike."

The other two came over to the cliff edge, pulling out watches.

"Stopwatches," grunted Kaspir. I had never known him to remain unobtrusive so long before.

The crane motor whirred. Alice rose, turning slowly on her cable. The crane arm swung over the water. Alice descended, settled "waist-deep" in sunny ripples. The cable went limp. She was floating.

The silent pair with the watches had their eyes on Alice now. The dungaree-clad woman was squinting at a gauge by the cable drum.

Water boiled suddenly at Alice's waist. The men near us clicked their stopwatches.

Alice sank. Since she was obviously designed to sink, why did we gasp then, and hold our breath? Because she sank so swiftly that it was as though she had been transformed in a second from a hollow sphere to a solid thing. Already she was a distorted, indistinct shape far under the surface. Then we could no longer see her. The cable stopped, shuddering.

One of our neighbors said in a shaky oddly accented voice, "What do you make it, Gideon?" For answer the other man called, "What was it, Rosa?"

The woman in dungarees spoke without taking her eyes from the gauge. "Ten—no, eleven fathoms."

"What did you make the time?"

"Twelve seconds exactly," answered the woman. "Bring him up, Davy."

Eleven fathoms—sixty-six feet—in twelve seconds!

Alice returned to her base. Dr. Tucker was again extracted, his khaki shorts and sleeveless shirt drenched with sweat.

"Eleven in twelve!" boomed the blond youth triumphantly.

"That'll do," said Tucker tensely. Then, surprisingly, he walked straight to us, hand outstretched to Kaspir. "Hello, Steve." His voice was almost a lisp. "Haven't seen you since Miami. Here about Williams, I suppose?"

With a shock I realized that I had all but forgotten the purpose of our trip.

"Moody lad," murmured Tucker, his liquid brown eyes wavering briefly toward Maude. "He seemed afflicted with some sinister theory that I am in danger. He prowled at night. Annoying. I must say, Steve, that you people in Intelligence—"

"I *ain't* in Intelligence," interrupted Kaspir, rudely and vehemently, reddening at Tucker's tone.

"—are a rather useless crew of romantics," concluded Tucker calmly. His assistants were ranged behind him now, listening.

KASPIR GOT a grip on himself. "Just what happened?" he asked. His tone, in the face of Tucker's bland insult, was quite friendly.

"Blew his brains out," said Tucker critically. "Oh, definitely unbalanced. Really, Steve, supposing I were in danger...."

I felt Maude stiffen. I was raging mad. Kaspir turned to us, smiling. "Don't mind Jack. He always was an insultin' little buzzard, weren't you, Jack?"

Tucker's answering smile was almost pathological. "I've been under a strain," he apologized. He waved a dimpled hand at Alice, now drying in eccentrically shaped patches.

Kaspir said, unimpressed, "Just what is this toy you're playin' with, Jack?"

Dr. Tucker's transformation from brassy calm to naked anger was almost frightening. Lips trembling, he hotly informed Kaspir that his work was too important for explanation to morons. Then, without abating his heat, he explained it, in a volley of furious technicalities.

The outburst confirmed my own inferences from Alice. Tucker had developed not only a variation of the Kingston valve, but also a system for placing Kingstons along a sub's ballast tanks which would double—nearly triple—the crash-diving rate. By doubling the number of Kingstons (through which a sub takes water when diving) and increasing the number of vents (through which the air is expelled)....

Kaspir yawned. "Your old pig-boat'll fold up like a Chinese lantern if you bore 'er fulla holes."

Tucker's emotional storm blew itself out with uncanny suddenness. He laughed.

"Cross-bracing the ballasts, Steve, that's the answer."

"Suppose you *do* dive 'em quick," persisted Kaspir. "What's the diff?"

"My dear Steve,"—Tucker spoke as though to a third-grader—"submarines in war zones now cruise double-banked—partly submerged—to facilitate diving when enemy planes appear. Subs with Tucker-Kingstons will cruise on the surface, thereby increasing their speed and useful range nearly twenty-per cent. Equipping a hundred subs with Tucker-Kingstons will be the equivalent of adding twenty new ships—in a short time and at very little cost."

Kaspir said grudgingly: "There's just a chance you know what you're talkin' about. Well, that's your business. Young Williams"—he swept Tucker's assistants with a cold eye—"is ours. Suppose you start makin' known your folks here...."

"Certainly," purred Dr. Tucker.

So we met Dr. Tucker's co-workers.

The woman—now seen as a voluptuous type, full-breasted and warm-eyed—was Dr. Rosa Bain, a physicist. "Also my fiancée," said Dr. Tucker.

The blond giant was Davoll Morgan, a mechanical engineer. ("One of Troop's M.I.T. geniuses," added Tucker, and the giant blushed.)

"Dr. Gideon Landsberg," he continued. The small, precisely handsome Jew bowed. ("Who has done wonders, despite frequent glandular disturbances in the presence of Dr. Bain," said Tucker, and Landsberg's black eyes glowed briefly.)

Tucker concluded: "My first assistant—our ray of sunshine—Dr. Etienne Jean McCarty. Dr. McCarty, as you might guess from his name, is the happy outcome of an international romance."

McCarty's grin broadened in his puckish face; his frank eyes were friendly. Then the smile faded. "You forgot one thing, Jack."

"Really?"

"Really." McCarty addressed Kaspir. "I'm the man who does not believe that your Mr. Williams committed suicide."

"Why?" Kaspir spoke sharply.

"Wrong type," answered McCarty emphatically. "I can assure you—you see, he roomed at my cottage—that he was an unusually well-balanced young man. Now if it had been you, Jack, with your sadistic mind and sexual neuroses...."

"Yes...?" Tucker's syrupy tone sent a tingle up the back of my neck.

"I should have regarded it as a perfectly natural act," said McCarty, grinning again.

"Of course," agreed Tucker. He turned to us. "You must forgive us," he begged. "We have been under considerable pressure—both water and mental." He chuckled. "That is why we have renamed this place 'Pressure Island.'"

"Let's get to Williams," said Kaspir shortly.

WE STRAGGLED up the path, past the largest of the three stucco dwellings. "My place," said Dr. Tucker. "Also our common dining hall." ("Very common indeed," muttered Dr. Landsberg.) Maude clung to my arm. I have seen her weather scenes of physical violence without turning a blond hair, but Dr. Jack Tucker's ageless face, his eel-like temperament, his bland smile at impossible moments, were corrosive to the nerves. Not, apparently, to Colonel Kaspir's however. He and Tucker walked together, deep in what appeared to be amiable conversation.

McCarty's cottage lay perhaps a hundred and fifty yards below Tucker's place. As we approached, McCarty pushed ahead, taking out a key. We all crowded into the tiny living-room. The flat odor of blood and death was present.

McCarty nodded toward a door. Kaspir flung it open, and for a second his bulky figure filled the doorway. Then he strode in, Maude and I at his heels. Without ceremony, he jerked a sheet from the lumpy shape on the bed and I got my first look at young Williams, late operative of Section Five.

Williams was on his back, dressed except for his coat. The blue eyes stared vacantly at the white plaster ceiling. The regular features and scholar's forehead were placid and unmarred, but the upper part of the head….

Powder burns showed that the gun muzzle had been jammed against the temple. The heavy automatic was still in his hand, his forefinger curled around the trigger.

I looked from Maude's pale face to Kaspir's. Around his eyes was the same greensickness I had noticed in the plane. I remembered Maude saying that Kaspir had known Williams' father.

Quickly, carelessly, Kaspir replaced the sheet, turned away. Maude twitched it straight. We followed him back to the living-room.

"Exactly what happened?" inquired Kaspir gently of McCarty and Tucker, who were standing together. I prepared my mind for a long, circumstantial account. Actually it lasted less than a minute.

Last night, McCarty said, just at seven, he had rapped on Williams' door and told him to come along to supper. Williams had called back that he would be along in a minute. So he, McCarty, had climbed the path to Tucker's house.

McCarty looked at Tucker. Tucker took up the narrative.

"I was standing out front, enjoying the sunset. Dr. McCarty arrived, saying Williams would be along in a minute. Dr. Bain, Davy, and Dr. Landsberg arrived from the other cottage. We heard the shot and ran down at once to McCarty's cottage. Williams was on the bed as he is now. The gunpowder smell was still in the air."

"And then…?" said Kaspir.

"Why, we went in to supper," said Dr. Tucker artlessly. "After supper I notified the Navy Department, which I assume notified you. And now, Steve, if you will excuse Dr. McCarty and me—"

"Where you goin'?"

"To Groton." Tucker's easy volubility returned. "At the Electric Boat Company the submarine *Trout* is on the ways. The cross-bracing of the ballasts has been done and the extra air vents cut. It is merely a matter of installing the Tucker-Kingstons. We shall be diving her by tomorrow noon."

"Diving!"

Tucker smiled. "Some seventy of the best submarine mechanics in the country are ready to start in the installations."

"You comin' back tonight?"

"Oh, yes. We'll return to Groton tomorrow, but then it will simply be a matter of adjusting the valves before the actual submersion tests—which I shall direct." The smile had become almost a benediction.

"Take the body along," said Kaspir.

"Of course." There was a general shuffling of feet.

"One more thing," said Kaspir, loudly and suddenly. Everyone turned.

"IF IT'LL ease your minds," said Kaspir, "Williams was a suicide. No sign o' murder."

"I was quite satisfied that that was the case," said Dr. Tucker. "Come along, Etienne." They departed. So did Dr. Bain, accompanied by Landsberg and Morgan.

Maude dropped wearily to a sofa, her sea-green eyes on Kaspir. "About the suicide," she said shakily, "that was a damned lie."

"Yep," said Kaspir. "Yep."

Which was all we got out of him that day. The enlisted men came for Williams' body. As soon as we heard the motor of the launch carrying it and Tucker and McCarty to Groton, Kaspir began a search of the cottage that lasted the entire morning and afternoon, irritably refusing assistance, flatly ignoring our questions. He even declined an invitation from Landsberg to lunch at Tucker's house.

After lunch Maude and I, bored, took a walk around the island. We looked in on Kaspir three times. First we found him rooting like a terrier in a trash pile behind the furnace, which occupied a room adjoining what had once been a kitchen and was now used, judging from the bottles, chiefly as a bar. The second visit discovered him rapt before the bathroom cabinet, apparently entranced with the usual miscellany of shaving tackle and patent medicines. The third time, he was asleep. We woke him from his nap and he lumbered silently up the hill to Tucker's house.

To my surprise, the supper was actually gay. The work was well along at Groton. McCarty was talkative, and Tucker, shaved and shining, played the genial host. Only Kaspir was glum, and he cheered up noticeably when McCarty invited us all down to the cottage for the evening, mentioning that he had been hoarding a half-case of "good fizz" for just such an occasion. All accepted but Tucker, who declined gracefully, pleading work to do.

It was taken for granted that we three would stay on Pressure Island that night, Kaspir having expressed a wish to remain over and inspect the *Trout*. Maude was to share Dr. Rosa Bain's room and Landsberg insisted upon yielding his room to Kaspir and bunking with Morgan. That left Williams' room for me. I didn't fancy the prospect, but was ashamed to say so.

We tramped down through bright moonlight to the cottage. The evening opened with Scotch-and-sodas. Things picked up at once. McCarty tended bar, darting back and forth between living-room and kitchen. Dr. Rosa Bain, eye-arresting in sweater and skirt, wrestled Kaspir in a rumba that shook the walls. Landsberg switched off the radio and proved a handy man at the piano, and the blond Davy Morgan uncovered a good tenor voice. It was after one when McCarty popped what he almost tearfully described as "the las' bo'll," and we drank a sobering toast to young Williams.

As McCarty and I saw the rest off, I noticed Landsberg and Dr. Bain walking very close together. It occurred to me that Tucker might have good grounds for disliking Landsberg.

McCarty filled his lungs with the sharp night air. "God, I'm glad it's over!" He threw back his head. "Good job, well done. Now for a rest. Florida." His odd accent, English compounded with French and a brogue, was attractive.

"Worried about the tests?" I asked.

"Hell no." He became serious. "Like him or not, it's a privilege to work with Tucker. That valve system…" This was the undiluted admiration of an expert for a better man's mind.

"I still don't understand it," I said.

"Easy as ABC." He yawned. "It's all in the sequence, the rhythm with which the valves open. On the face of it, you'd swear that with so many valves and vents your boat'd wallow and turn turtle, but adjust the four master Tucker-Kingstons according to his formula and—bingo! you're down ten fathoms before a bomber pilot could blink twice."

HE YAWNED again. "Jack's up rather late," he said absently, looking up at Tucker's lighted window. He glanced at his wrist watch. "Extremely late. Midnight's his usual hour. He's up at five every morning." A twang of excitement crept into his tone. "Listen, Kettle—"

"You think we'd better go up?" I asked.

"I'd feel easier," said McCarty apologetically. "Young Williams… Frankly, Kettle, I can't say much for your super-sleuth. There's some simple explanation for that Williams business, but it ain't suicide."

I reflected that McCarty would probably feel even less well disposed toward Kaspir if he had overheard Kaspir's final words to me, transmitted under cover of a song. "Keep your bright eyes on our buddy, McCarty," he'd whispered. "Nope, I ain't expectin' anything. Just watch him."

"Let's go," I said.

To our left, lights were winking out in the Bain-Landsberg-Morgan cottage, but ahead, Tucker's light burned with ominous steadiness.

"Easy," warned McCarty as we reached Tucker's porch. "If he's awake he'll raise holy hell. Remember what he said about young Williams prowling around."

We eased into a vestibule dark as the pit. "There's a switch somewhere," whispered McCarty. I heard his hand fumbling along the wall. "Damn!" he whispered. "Say, what the—"

A sudden and furious struggle. Who was the third person in that vestibule? "Grab him, Kettle, he's—" A thudding blow hammered McCarty's cry into a groan. I lunged forward toward the sound, hands outstretched.

Then the world exploded into colored lights and I was dropping… dropping… dropping….

I swam back to consciousness on a wave of pain. My head throbbed in unbelievable agony. I rolled over. Something knobby ground along my ribs. I managed to get to my feet. The darkness was stifling. Where was I? Then I remembered. I felt for my cigarette lighter, twirled its wheel with a clumsy thumb. The feeble flame was eerie. More light was the first need. I saw the switch McCarty had been seeking. Going to it, I stumbled over something. I fell against the switch, flipped it on.

At my feet lay McCarty, the red smear on his forehead broadening into a crimson blot on his cheek and collar. Then I thought of Tucker.

I threw open the inner door and ran—or rather, staggered—across the living-room to Tucker's door. It was unlocked.

Tucker, in pajamas, lay on his back on the floor. The hole between his eyes looked bigger than it actually was, because of its brownish-purple border. Someone must have held the gun very close to his head. I saw no gun.

My thoughts rocketed back to that business in the vestibule, to Kaspir's warning. Could McCarty have faked that—slugged me, shot Tucker, then tapped himself and lain down under the switch? I knelt by Tucker's body. No. Tucker had been dead a couple of hours at least.

I tiptoed back to the lighted vestibule. McCarty's pinched, slightly comical face was ghastly pale. His heavy breathing hinted of concussion. Then I saw what had hurt my ribs when I had first come to: a blackjack, red with McCarty's blood and mine.

And suddenly a sick horror of Pressure Island and all its works turned me panic-stricken and drove me out into the night. Holding a hand to my burning scalp wound, I pitched and tottered down through the dewy grass to rouse the other cottage by banging on the door and bawling for Kaspir.

I remember Kaspir's face, grim as fate, as he hauled me inside. And Maude's, "Oh, Mike!" and the touch of her cool hand, trembling. And Dr. Bain's eyes staring, not at me, but at Dr. Landsberg.

PRESSURE ISLAND dropped astern, its stucco buildings violently white in the morning sun. No sign of life was visible, and for a good reason. In Tucker's house, I knew, sat Dr. Landsberg, Dr. Bain, and the powerful Davy Morgan, silent and very conscious of the body in the next room. And with them sat the red-headed sailor and another, both armed.

I thought of Kaspir's parting speech to this trio. "I'm comin' back here in a little while and have words—a lotta words—with you three." Then, to Redhead, "Watch 'em, son."

Kaspir had tried to persuade the bandaged, white-faced McCarty to postpone testing the *Trout* until he had fully recovered. I recalled with a thrill McCarty's furious, "I'll be damned if I do. What do you think we've been killing ourselves on this island for, day after day? Speed, you fat fool. D'you think I'm going to slow up Jack Tucker's work for a rap on the head? Get me my clothes."

And now the four of us were off for Groton in the Navy launch, which, since there was no reason now to patrol Pressure Island, McCarty had commandeered. McCarty had enlivened our departure by fainting on the pier. Revived, he had sulphurously insisted, over our protests, upon carrying on.

The Thames opened up before us as we rounded Pequot Light. The sailor at the tiller set his course cross-river for the lofty water towers, one black, one silver, of the Electric Boat Company. McCarty conned a blueprint. Kaspir, his face a mask of melancholy, stared at our bilge and did not look up until the din of the E.B. ways was loud in his ears.

Our launch circled in to a pier, docking directly behind a submarine, which McCarty told us was the *Trout*. To all appearances it was identical to two subs we had passed in the river. Then I recalled that the Tucker-Kingstons were under water, on the ballasts down near the keel.

A group of naval officers and civilians beside the *Trout* looked curiously at McCarty's bandaged head as we approached. McCarty addressed a four-striper. "Everything set, Captain Virney?"

"Just finished. All valves in perfect order. Nothing now but the adjustment." The captain's tone was almost deferential. Then the inevitable, "Where's Dr. Tucker?"

"Sick," snapped McCarty. "I'll make the adjustments. Won't take ten minutes."

"Delaney's taking her down for you," said the captain. A fresh-faced young lieutenant came forward, escorted McCarty up the pier. They disappeared inside the *Trout*. Several civilians, presumably Electric Boat officials, followed. The rest talked shop… "negative buoyancy at twelve fathoms"… "kept boppin' her nose on bottom, and by God, they'd hit a fresh-water spring"… "now these German subs are built like washtubs"… "Yeah, but…."

Captain Virney met Kaspir's eye, then strolled off toward the *Trout*. Kaspir said: "You look kinda feeble, Kettle."

"But I feel just dandy," I said sarcastically. The rattle of the rivet-guns behind us was hell for my throbbing skull and a senseless tension was tying my stomach into knots. Ten aching minutes dragged by... twenty....

Maude exclaimed, "Look!"

A stir of men at the *Trout's* conning tower. We ran up the pier, Kaspir pounding ahead.

They were carrying someone up the little gangplank to the pier now. We arrived in time to hear Delaney saying to Virney, "Completed the adjustments, sir, checked 'em—then collapsed."

Kaspir pushed through the crowd. Through the path he opened I could see McCarty, on his feet, supported by two gobs. I struggled through after Kaspir, Maude in my wake.

KASPIR ADDRESSED Captain Virney pompously. "This man can't make a dive today. It's concussion. I was a fool to let him come here at all."

McCarty's eyes blazed in his milk-white face. "Keep this meddling idiot away from me," he flared. "Let's go back, Delaney."

Kaspir gripped McCarty's thin shoulder. "Listen, McCarty—"

McCarty tore himself free, staggered, almost fell.

Captain Virney barked, "Who are you?"

Kaspir didn't answer. He said to McCarty, "Did you finish the job?"

"Certainly," answered McCarty weakly. "But I want to observe. Don't you understand? All that work..." It was Kaspir who caught him as he toppled.

"One dive," mumbled McCarty. He was pleading now. A lump the size of a hen's egg rose in my throat. "All that work," he repeated. "This'll be play."

"Suppose you let Delaney do the diving," suggested Virney reasonably. "His observations will be adequate,

I'm sure. Then, when you're better, you and Dr. Tucker will be able to—"

Delaney said eagerly, "Sure, Mac. I'll get the dope on the first dive, and then tomorrow or the next day—"

McCarty yielded. "You'll be sure to take her slow the first time, Delaney. They'll be stiff, you know."

"Sure, Mac." Delaney smiled his thanks and hurried aboard.

We got McCarty to a small office at the pier-side and made him comfortable on a bench, a folded peajacket under his head. Maude said, in a choked voice, "We'll get you to a hospital right away."

"No hurry," said Kaspir callously from the window. "Look, Kettle—there she goes!"

McCarty struggled up and peered out at the *Trout* sliding away from the pier. Despite the rivet-guns near by, the office seemed quiet, and I could hear McCarty's quick breathing. The *Trout* passed from sight down the sun-dappled river and McCarty sat down suddenly on the bench.

"I got somethin' here that'll set you right in no time," said Kaspir. "Better'n aspirin, any day."

His thick arm shot out. With no apparent effort he lifted McCarty clear of the bench.

"Try this," said Colonel Kaspir affectionately, and knocked McCarty spinning with a brutal blow. I went sick inside. Kaspir had gone stark crazy.

Kaspir yanked McCarty up, threw him to the bench. To my astonishment, McCarty was conscious.

"Didn't think you'd have the guts to go down-river with those boys," said Kaspir genially. "No hara-kiri for you, eh Mac?"

McCarty shifted a little on the bench. At Kaspir's words a half-smile flickered around the thread of blood at each corner of his mouth. Kaspir nicked open his silver case and chose a cigarette with exaggerated care. Something in his eyes froze the smile on McCarty's battered mouth.

"I was sucker enough to think you'd hold off on Tucker until today, Mac," he said. "But say, you didn't really think I was gonna let Delaney dive that sub after you'd cooked the valve system—now did you? Delaney's under strict orders not to touch his divin' gadgets."

The danger signals were so plain in McCarty's eyes that Maude screamed even before he leapt from the bench. His attack was singularly futile. Kaspir dropped the cigarette case and caught the swinging wrist.

"From Williams, with love," he said softly, and drove a ham-like fist into McCarty's face. "Get Virney, Kettle. Tell him we want a plane. We're takin' this gallows-bird back to Washington."

OVER NEW Haven Kaspir said irritably, "O' course I knew young Williams was murdered." The plane dipped. Brief interlude while Kaspir fought down the onslaught of nausea.

"Young Williams," he said finally, "heard in Washington that somebody was out to scotch Tucker's show, so I sent him up to nose around. McCarty must ha' got nervous. So that afternoon, prob'ly while Williams was nappin' or just restin', McCarty sneaked his gun, wrapped it in somethin', and blew Williams' brains out. Then he planted the gun in Williams' hand and went up to supper."

"But the shot?" I argued. "Tucker said McCarty was talking to him when they heard…."

Kaspir's head wobbled impatiently. "Hoariest trick known to man or beast." We could feel McCarty listening now. "Mac rigged himself a firecracker with a long fuse. He shoots Williams, tosses the cloth he muffled the shot (and prob'ly concealed the gun) with, into the furnace, lights the firecracker fuse and strolls up the hill. He's talkin' to Tucker. Blam! A shot! When they find Williams it don't occur to anybody—except me, later—to question its bein' a shot. Later Mac cleans up the firecracker fragments."

Over the Delaware River: "O' course Mac was layin' for Tucker. From his livin'-room he could watch Tucker, up the hill, movin' about in his room, so the idea of a long shot naturally occurred to him. So he got him with a rifle... Where'd you get the silencer, Mac?"

"Try and find out."

"I guess you'd been meanin' to shoot him some night and take your chances o' being caught. When we blew in, you got a brighter idea. You staged that drinkin' fiesta, knowin' Tucker didn't drink and had work to do. And after supper, Mac, you planted that cardboard box with the alarm clock in it, set for eleven, outside Tucker's window in some bushes. And you made damn sure to be in the kitchen fixin' drinks at eleven so's you could step into the furnace room and stick that .22 o' yours out the window. And when the alarm went off, and Tucker opened his window to see what the hell that muffled ringin' was—

"He must ha' made a beautiful target there, Mac, with the light behind him. And us raisin' so much Cain we couldn't ha' heard the shot even if you *hadn't* used a silencer. Then, after we'd left—"

So it *was* McCarty who'd staged that little act and put the slug on me, after pretending he'd been downed himself. "But why—" I began.

KASPIR PRODUCED a little brown bottle from his pocket.

"So's he could step in," he answered, "and put some powder burns on Tucker's wound. That was his alibi—eh, Mac? The condition o' Tucker's body would prove he'd been shot while the party was ragin', and we all knew Mac hadn't left the party. So the powder burns would 'prove' that Tucker had been shot with the gun muzzle right against his head."

He tapped the bottle. "Potassium permanganate crystals. Give you as pretty powder burns as ever you saw. McCarty dabbed some on the bullet hole while you were snoozin' in the vestibule, Kettle. They burn in a minute or so. Then he put the bottle on the shelf in Tucker's bathroom and went back and sapped himself with the blackjack just hard enough to draw blood. Then he lay down, waitin' for you to come to and find him.

"If you'd been able to ditch that alarm clock, Mac, you'd ha' made things tougher. But when I found that—and saw the bottle on Tucker's shelf just like the one I'd seen on yours that afternoon—and then thought to dig in your coal pile and find that classy little .22 complete with silencer— that's when I began to get the full beauty o' your mind.

"That, Mac, was when I phoned the sub base and told Virney on no account to let that sub dive. I was afraid, Mac, that you'd get aboard and dive the whole works, yourself included, to the bottom. But no, you fixed those valves so's she'd turn turtle and fill through the vents, and then you fainted again. Very artistic.

"O' course," concluded Kaspir, eyes shut and body rigid against the vibration of the plane, "the whole idea was to do the Navy outa the Tucker-Kingstons. With Tucker dead and a boatload o' fine fellows gone to glory on the first trial, it was a safe bet the Navy'd be scared off Tucker's proposition for a coupla years at least, but—"

Kaspir's eyes opened and his voice was hard. "Listen, Mac. The Navy'll work out that adjustment O.K. And in three months we're gonna have a fleet o' pigboats that'll knock spots off anything your crowd's got. I don't know who your crowd is, Mac—yet. But the F.B.I. boys'll find out before we hang you. And they ain't gonna be tender while they're findin' out. Them days," hummed Colonel Kaspir, "is gone forever."

Joe, the houseboy, was on the pier at Anacostia. "Colonel," he said, as we stepped ashore, "that Sino-Japanese gentleman you were expecting the night before last, appeared on the doorstep just after you left."

"Good. Wha'd he say?"

"Nothing, Colonel. Someone had cut his throat."

"Jumpin' saints!" yelled Colonel Kaspir. "We gotta get to the Coast right away. Kettle, you beat it over to the airport and get the tickets, and Maude, you—"

Joe held out a fat envelope. "The tickets are here, Colonel. Your plane leaves in forty minutes."

"Then what're we waitin' for?" demanded Colonel Kaspir.

FOOTPRINTS ON THE CEILING

THE RUMOR WAS ONE OF THE UGLIEST EVER CIRCULATED IN WASHINGTON—CONCERNING, AS IT DID, ONE "MR. SMITH" BEHIND WHOSE FOREHEAD MESHED THE GIGANTIC GEARS OF OUR WAR EFFORT—AND IT HAD TO BE SCOTCHED BEFORE IT DAMAGED PUBLIC MORALE. SO THEY CALLED IN COLONEL KASPIR OF SECTION FIVE, WHO CAME FORWARD WITH THE STRANGEST STRATEGY OF HIS CAREER.

CHAPTER ONE
THE RUMOR

THERE ARE people in Washington today who term the incident of Madame D'Herelles the most wantonly brutal, the most shockingly vengeful piece of Fifth Column work yet perpetrated in the United States. And there are some who, remembering her kindnesses, still make a dolorous pilgrimage once a fortnight or once a month to see her. Among these pilgrims is Colonel Stephen Kaspir, chief of Section Five, who has no reputation whatever as a sentimentalist.

Unless you are among those who enjoyed the lavish hospitality of Madame D'Herelles, her name is probably blankly unfamiliar to you. Nothing was ever published about the manner of her passing from the Washington scene.

For that matter, nothing has ever been published, in the American press, about The Rumor.

It was a big rumor, and by far the ugliest of this year notable for ugly rumors—too ugly, in fact, to be juicy. Confirmed gossips did not nibble at it twice, for it left a dry, bitter aftertaste, like the aftertaste of malarial fever.

Most rumors are social coin in Washington, assets exchangeable for cocktails, dinners, and even, in extreme cases, the favors of ladies. But this one, as swivel-tongued individuals quickly discovered, was most emphatically a

A knife had ended Alanson's
tour of duty with Section Five.

liability, good only for a tongue-lashing or a punch in the
nose. One ill-advised embassy hireling who mouthed it
aloud at a Press Club smoker immediately lost two front
teeth, and was later interrogated, with chilling insistence,

by two young men from the F.B.I. From his bruised lips they learned what they already knew: nothing.

The Rumor was about Mr. Smith, which is not his name. You know "Mr. Smith" as a radio voice which makes periodic reports to the nation on our war effort—a radio voice

which has, in a few short months, become the third, if not the second, most important radio voice in the world. The capitals of the world tune in to hear "Mr. Smith"—even as they do when the President, himself, is on the air.

But did you know that behind "Mr. Smith's" forehead mesh the gigantic working gears of our war effort? Did you know that it is his brain which is functioning as the timer for such potent cylinders of our war engine as the White House, the W.P.B., and the Army and Navy Departments? That it is his brain which now has these cylinders beating in the smooth and terrible rhythm which is driving us ahead with irresistible speed and power? Perhaps you did. But there were men in Berlin and Tokyo and Rome who knew it before you did. And thereby hangs my tale.

THE RUMOR arrived at Section Five under awesomely official auspices, its bearer being none other than the G-2 brass hat, Major General Altemus Tancred himself.

Tancred's reluctant respect for Kaspir was equaled only by his unconcealed dislike for every facet of Kaspir's many-sided personality. In return, Kaspir treated Tancred with a gruesome lack of tact which sustained their relationship on a high level of hostility.

That Tancred should have condescended to visit the old brownstone ex-boarding house in southwest Washington, which has been the headquarters of Section Five since early in '40, was in itself a testimonial to the status of "Mr. Smith."

We—Kaspir, Maude, and I—had arrived in Washington that morning by airliner from Chicago, where Kaspir had dealt sharply with a gentleman named Winkle who had been corresponding indiscreetly with a Mr. Togijara.

At the Chicago airport some enemy of mankind had informed Kaspir of a new remedy for airsickness. It consisted of repeating aloud, at the approach of nausea, some soothing poem.

An hour out of Chicago, Maude and I and every one of our dozen-odd fellow passengers knew "Trees" (the Kaspir version of the Joyce Kilmer original) by heart. Two hours out (the air was bumpy) I felt as though each word had been engraved permanently on my brain with a rivet gun.

Incredibly enough, however, this thing worked. And Kaspir, who usually spends his airborne hours commuting wanly between his seat and the lavatory, now became offensively hearty and actually began stuffing himself with chocolate cherries. And I, who had been looking forward to an uninterrupted session with Maude, suddenly found the aroma of cherry syrup so overpowering that I was forced to hustle my squeamish stomach aft no less than four times.

Maude, regal in mink-trimmed black broadcloth, poised her classic head at an aloof angle and refused to notice Kaspir, until he proffered a chocolate cherry. Whereupon she struck it from his hand and applied her quivering nose to a vial of smelling salts. Whereupon Kaspir transferred his attentions to others in the plane. We glided in over Washington just in time to prevent his being lynched by a drumhead court martial composed of all on board.

At the airport café Maude and I, hollow-eyed, irritable, sipped black coffee while Kaspir stowed away a gigantic breakfast. We taxied at once to headquarters, pausing only at a drugstore to allow Kaspir to purchase a gaudy box of chocolate cherries and a five-pound sack of English walnuts.

In the musty front hall of headquarters, Joe, the Negro houseboy, told us we could expect General Tancred any minute.

"What's eatin' Tancred?" demanded Kaspir, trying to conceal his surprise.

"He didn't say." Joe's bland eyes flickered just a trifle and Kaspir, who for all his bumbling manner never misses anything, snorted.

"But you gotta good idea?" he insisted.

"I have," said Joe. "It could be only one thing."

"Well," began Kaspir impatiently, "whatinell's keepin'....?"

The doorbell interrupted him, and Joe left us to do his duty. Joe holds a law degree from Columbia, and his white serving jacket conceals a .45 automatic, but his "Come right in, gentleman," was delivered with a pure Virginia Negro accent.

"Oh, don't give me that minstrel routine, Joe," we heard Tancred say irritably. He came in, a small, paunchy man with a shrewd little face flanked by round, almost lobeless ears.

Of the two men with him, I knew one, a stocky individual with the unobtrusive manners of an undertaker. This was Dave Primrose, late of the White House Secret Service detail, more recently attached to the person of "Mr. Smith."

Our third visitor I had never seen before. He was as tall as Kaspir (who is six feet six) but in place of Kaspir's barrel-like bulk he ran to broad shoulders and slim hips. He had a square, pleasant face topped with close-cropped red hair, and his blue eyes were friendly.

"Kaspir," began Tancred, "I want you to meet—"

"Let's go up," broke in Kaspir rudely, and lumbered up the stairs, his rotund form mountainous in the baggy tweeds he affects. The rest of us stood aside for Maude and fell in behind her. Behind me I heard Primrose inquire of Tancred, "Is he always like that?" and Tancred's spiteful, "No, usually worse."

KASPIR WAS dumping walnuts into a wooden bowl when we reached his office on the third floor rear, Maude cocked an apprehensive eyebrow at me—wondering, I knew, what line Kaspir would take with Tancred this time. In a minute we found out. Today Kaspir was being athletic. He picked up a fair-sized wooden armchair with one hand and held it out carelessly to Tancred. "Here," he directed, "have a seat by the desk." The gambit was painfully obvious. Tancred would have to use both hands, and puff and strain....

"Allow me, General." It was the tall, redhaired man interposing. His long, freckled paw slid past Tancred and seized the chair back. "Thanks." He nodded to Kaspir and relieved him of the chair. Using only one hand, he placed the chair by the desk with no visible effort.

Kaspir frowned, plucked a walnut from the bowl and folded his great hand about it. There was a splintering sound as the shell yielded to the pressure.

"Nuts?" Kaspir held the bowl out to Tancred, who shook his head. There was no nutcracker in the bowl. Maude also refused, glaring. Primrose said: "No thanks."

The tall man, however, took one. I thought I saw a glint in his eye, an almost imperceptible twitch of his wide mouth. He held the heavy-shelled nut between a long thumb and forefinger and contracted his hand. There was a crisp sound as the shell split evenly along its seam. The meat dropped intact into his palm. Kaspir turned a sullen pink. He has tried to do this, and can't.

Tancred watched the byplay impatiently. "If you're through showing off," he snapped at Kaspir, "perhaps we can get to business." He introduced Primrose and the redhaired man, who was a Doctor Somebody.

"My—er—secretary, gentlemen." Kaspir pointed to Maude, who crossed her long legs and smiled. His thick thumb indicated me. "Lieutenant Kettle, one of my— you call 'em operatives, don't you, Tancred, just like in the storybooks?"

Tancred exploded. "Oh, for God's sake, sit down, Kaspir!"

Kaspir obeyed meekly and promptly, a pleased light in his eyes, his great moon face smug. He had got Tancred's goat. Now we could get to business.

"I suppose you've heard the rumor," Tancred opened. "By the way, you've got a radio here, haven't you?" He glanced at the redhaired doctor. "We wouldn't want to miss—"

"There's a table model in the outer office," I told him.

"Nine thousand eight hundred and sixty-four rumors," said Kaspir provocatively. "Which one you nursin' now, Tancred?"

The Secret Service man answered slowly and frigidly: "The one about my new boss cracking up."

A tingle crept up the short hairs of my neck, and I heard Maude's gasp. Kaspir's baby-like eyes widened a trifle, and he pursed his cupid's-bow mouth. We all knew who Primrose meant. He meant "Mr. Smith!"

KASPIR RELAXED ever so slightly. "Nine thousand, eight hundred and sixty-four times," he said bumptiously. "Good lord, man,"—this to General Tancred, who bristled like a porcupine—"ain't you too old to be gettin' butterflies in your tummy over—"

He broke off abruptly, and in the dead silence his eyes, narrowing, jumped from Tancred's face to Primrose's, then to that of the tall doctor. When he spoke again, leaning forward, with his palms against the desk edge, the last trace of his skeptical manner was gone.

"How much o' that rumor is true?" he asked harshly.

Tancred stared at his blue-veined hands. "More than I care to think about," he answered soberly. He glanced at his wrist watch. "Say," he exclaimed, "bring that radio in here, will you? He'll be on in three minutes."

As I went to fetch the radio, I recalled that this was the day of "Mr. Smith's" initial "Report to the Nation," the first of the three scheduled, the first on the new phase of the war effort.

Returning, I heard Tancred saying to Kaspir, apparently in reply to a question, "… and terribly depressed. All the vitality seems to have gone out of him."

"Does he realize it?" demanded Kaspir fiercely. Tancred shot a glance at the red-haired doctor.

The doctor nodded. "Definitely." His lean hand rasped across his square chin. "I might add," he said, with no hint of professional nonchalance in his tone, "that he is making a very gallant and remarkable effort to overcome it, as you might expect. But, in view of the already tremendous strain upon him, this additional effort is almost too much."

"Shhh!" This from Tancred, fiddling with the radio.

Five seconds later we were listening to the voice of "Mr. Smith." Before that speech was five minutes under way, I found my fists clenched and my whole body tense and straining, just as you thrust yourself forward at a race, as though by so doing you could help your man along.

I glanced around the room. Tancred, biting his lip, was watching Kaspir's face. Maude was leaning forward, elbows on knees, chin in her cupped hands, her fine violet eyes dull. The cigarette between Primrose's lips had gone out, and he was glaring at the radio as though somehow it was responsible for what we were hearing. The redhaired doctor, sprawled out in his chair, stared at the ceiling, his blue eyes as deep and inscrutable as the rest of his freckled face.

Kaspir was making a great show of being unimpressed, but his pallor betrayed him as surely as did the occasional nervous flaring of his nostrils.

The speech went on. Here and there we caught a flash, like the glimpse of a country lane from a fast train, of fire and warmth and confidence. But for the most part, even the most optimistically phrased passages were deadened, and rendered tortuous, by the effort in "Mr. Smith's" voice. And (worse!) here and there the voice became that of a man who is losing faith in himself and his cause— although after each such lapse the speaker, as though realizing it, would rally his forces and produce a minute of blood-warming, spine-tingling confidence.

But the finale! Written as a stirring appeal to the nation for fresh courage and renewed faith, it sounded as uninspiring and mechanical as the "click" which came when Tancred stretched out a pale hand and switched off the radio.

"You understand now?" said Tancred, in hollow triumph, to Kaspir. The question was wholly unnecessary.

KASPIR IGNORED him and turned to the redhaired doctor. "What's your angle on this, Doc? Seems like it's your nut to crack, not ours. Tonic, complete rest for two weeks, change diet—that sorta thing."

The redhaired doctor smiled thinly. "I thought so myself, at first." He left it at that.

Kaspir swelled, reddened. The sight of Tancred's glum face seemed to infuriate him.

"Godalmighty, Tancred!" he burst out suddenly. "Can't a guy get a touch o'liver without you fellers seein'boogey-pictures of the end o'the world?" He shifted his guns to Primrose. "Dammit, Dave, I should think your crowd'ud have more sense than to get steamed up over... How long's he felt this way? Not more'n a month. I saw him a month ago, and he was—"

"About three weeks," supplied Primrose, taking offense at Kaspir's tone. "But that—"

Tancred took over, pulling one lobeless ear in a characteristic gesture. "For your information, Kaspir—since we've come to you—all indications have been of mild depression caused by overwork and overstrain. Loss of appetite, irritability—the regular signs. That is why Admiral Bensinger consulted my friend here." He indicated the redhaired doctor. "The doctor agreed—with reservations."

"The reservations," added the doctor, "increased in number when I found that the patient did not respond in any degree to the customary treatment. In fact, he—"

"The depression has grown steadily worse," said Tancred flatly. "He is fully aware of it—and of its implications. He has been getting all the rest possible under the circumstances, although—"

"I suppose," interrupted Kaspir, "it never occurred to one o'your great minds to come right out and announce that he don't feel so good, and that he'll have to pull a stretch in bed. People'll swallow anything, you know, even the truth."

"It did occur to us, Kaspir." Tancred's sallow cheeks flushed. "We're not all complete idiots, you know."

"Then—"

"Read this," directed Tancred expressionlessly. He drew a folded paper from the side pocket of his rumpled coat and slid it across the desk. Kaspir ran a hasty eye over it, beckoned to Maude and me. Reading over his shoulder I felt Maude, beside me, shivering as though with cold.

Frankly, I was unimpressed. It was nothing but a mimeographed propaganda sheet, in Portuguese, setting forth in lurid detail what we had just been discussing. Apparently aimed directly at the South American capitals, it was brief but trenchant.

"The man behind the new American war effort has himself lost heart," it concluded. "He has given up the struggle. Desperate efforts are being made in Washington to conceal this fact. Do not be misled by them. Insist that your diplomats see him and talk with him themselves. We do not ask you to believe us. Let your representatives speak with him, then believe their own ears and eyes." It wound up with the usual guff about the invincibility of the Axis powers. I'd seen dozens of pieces like it, of course. But none taking this particular line and singling out an individual.

Kaspir flung the thing back to Tancred. "We've all read tons o' this toilet tissue," he sneered. "Somebody's capitalizin' on a rumor. So what?"

"Just this," answered Tancred quietly, and for some reason I knew he was about to demolish Kaspir's attitude. "We confiscated a batch of these things the other day, all done up in envelopes and addressed to South American embassies and offices. Dave Primrose turned them over to the F.B.I. And the F.B.I. discovered a surprising thing, Kaspir."

"All right," challenged Kaspir. "Surprise me."

"You remember that gang we caught in Montford two months ago?" asked Tancred.

"You mean the America-Now-and-Forever-Heil-Hitler lads?"

"Yes. Big batch of subversive literature on the premises."

"Go on," directed Kaspir, with mock weariness.

"We destroyed their mimeograph machine on the spot."

"So what?"

"This"—Tancred tapped the propaganda sheet—"was mimeographed on that machine."

KASPIR'S REACTION was all Tancred could have desired. He shot up from his chair, which toppled over with a crash. His jaw was loose, his eyes astonished. "What?" he bellowed.

"Fact," said Tancred, still sourly. "Some smart youngster in the F.B.I. happened to compare this with the samples we confiscated in Montford. No doubt about it. Done on the same machine."

"Then—"

"This letter was set up and mimeographed at least eight weeks ago," said Tancred shortly. He sucked a rubbery underlip, tugged again at his ear.

Kaspir said apologetically to the redhaired doctor: "I begin to see your point, Doc."

"Exactly." There was no rancor in the doctor's voice. "When a hostile agency is able to predict a man's ailment five or six weeks before he or those nearest him are aware of it, it begins to look as though—"

"Don't tell me," begged Kaspir. "I heard enough. What's your best guess then, Doc?"

"I have none—now," replied the doctor. "My first—er—guess was a poisonous drug. That was Bensinger's theory, too, but…" His voice trailed off.

Primrose was shaking his head. "Can't be. We've eliminated that possibility." He stood up and rammed his hands into his pants pockets. "Kaspir," he said, "we've checked and analyzed every bit of food 'Mr. Smith' has taken for over two weeks. We've checked the water supply, investigated grocers, analyzed samples from pots and pans."

"Cigarettes?" said Kaspir.

"Good God, yes!" Primrose's laugh was brittle. "Even the air in his bedroom and office. Watched all employees. Cut down the visitors' list until we're afraid to cut it any further. Nothing helps."

Kaspir, lying back in his swivel chair, inspected the pink roses on the ceiling paper.

Maude said: "Shaving cream, toothpaste, medications?"

Primrose smiled bitterly. "Elementary, lady. Do you know what one of my jobs is now? Each morning, Torby—he's the fellow who straightens up 'Mr. Smith's' office—eight years at the White House, by the way—each morning Torby and I take twenty minutes over that vacuum water bottle 'Mr. Smith' keeps on his desk, the one he uses during the day. While Torby's rinsing it out with boiling water, I'm getting out the special jug of analyzed mineral water from which we fill it. I pour the mineral water into the vacuum bottle myself. Torby—with me following—takes it straight to the boss's desk. When the boss leaves the office in the afternoon, Torby—with me watching—puts the vacuum bottle in the safe. Next morning, same routine. I tell you this simply to give you a rough idea of the pains we're taking. Besides…" He looked to Tancred.

"If they can get slow poison to him," said Tancred, "why not quick poison instead? Why not plain assassination?"

Kaspir rocked forward, put his elbows on the desk. "Hypnotism," he suggested, with a faint ring of triumph.

"You do these gentlemen an injustice, Colonel." It was the redhaired doctor again. "That happens to be my specialty."

Kaspir looked his surprise.

"I'm a psychiatrist," said the doctor. "We all have to know something about hypnotism. It so happens that I've gone ahead with it experimentally. You can take my word for it"—I took it immediately, for the man's manner was utterly compelling and convincing—"that it's not hypnotism."

Kaspir drew a long breath. "Then why," he asked, a little wildly, including our three visitors in the question, "did you fellers come to me?"

Tancred was up now, his black eyes snapping ill-naturedly. "Because," he answered, "we've applied all available sane and reasonable minds to this matter, with no luck. So we thought we'd give you a shot at it. Besides, you've got a lot of funny friends around the country. If you get anything, let Primrose or me know at once."

"Why?" inquired Kaspir innocently, drumming on the desk top.

General Tancred did not deign to reply. He stalked out, his pinched face purple, and Primrose stalked after him. The red-haired doctor, a wraith of a smile about his mouth, shook hands with Kaspir and me and bowed to Maude before he let his long legs carry him after his colleagues.

Kaspir looked at the hand the doctor had shaken. It was white in patches, but the blood was returning slowly.

"Smart guy," he said pettishly, and I knew he had tried his crusher grip on the doctor.

"I thought he was darn nice," said Maude belligerently. "Well, Steve, where do we go from here?"

"I kinda thought of droppin' in on Baritone Mamie this afternoon," murmured Kaspir vaguely. "Tackle some o' those pet Poles o' hers. They hear a lotta stuff." He spoke without conviction. "Besides," he added, brightening, "maybe she's got some o' that Veuve Cliquot left… Give 'er a ring, will you, Maude, and ask her will she put us up for the weekend?"

Maude tossed me a helpless look and sat down to the telephone. "I wish that nice, redhaired doctor were going to be there," she said, with calculated malice.

"That walnut stunt he did," said Kaspir, stung. "Showy." He plucked a nut from the bowl, clamped it between thumb and forefinger. His face flushed as his hand strained. The nut split evenly, even as the doctor's had.

"Not a bad feller at all," he said, delighted. " 'Ja catch his name, Maude?"

"Rennie," answered Maude. "Dr. Walter Rennie."

CHAPTER TWO
BARITONE MAMIE

JUST BEFORE we left for Madame D'Herelles' place at Chevy Chase that afternoon, Tancred, telephoned. Kaspir was at the barber's, so I took the message. Tancred let me have it all unsweetened.

The public reaction to the "Report to the Nation" had been very bad. The State Department had already had discreet but significant questions from the British embassy. Worse, representatives of half a dozen South American countries, obviously under pressure from their capitals, had been politely insistent upon an interview with "Mr. Smith"—"as soon as possible." And there was a new rumor abroad: that today's "Report to the Nation" had been a faked recording.

"Tell Kaspir," concluded Tancred's wheezy voice grimly, "that we've gone overboard on this end."

"Overboard?" I asked.

"Yes, overboard. Invited the whole shooting match to attend the next broadcast and see the man for themselves."

"But that's only a week from today!" I gasped.

"Exactly, Lieutenant. So tell your man to stir his stumps."

"HI, MAMIE."

"Stefen! My dear Stefen!" Madame D'Herelles' plump, powdered arms pulled Kaspir's head down. There was a squashy kissing sound. She released him, to pounce on Maude, "My darrrling! You are lofelier than ever! Iss she not, Stefen? Do you still adore her, Lieutenant?"

Fortunately Madame D'Herelles does not insist on answers. She swept us along the broad hall. Kaspir daubing at a blotch of lipstick, Maude with an unexpectedly shy glance at my red face.

Kaspir gazed after the waddling form of our hostess. Even black velvet could not conceal the fact that Madame D'Herelles is inches close to being as broad as she is long. "Pardon me, boys," he said, half under his breath, "is this the Chattanooga choo-choo?"

Luckily this outrageous remark was lost to Madame D'Herelles in the flood of her own remarks. The burden of her lament, as nearly as I could gather, was a lengthy explanation of why, with seven servants in the house, she had had to answer the door herself. She paused at the bottom of a broad stairway. "Osca'!" she bawled hoarsely. "Osca'!" She bent an ear toward the upper part of the old Georgian mansion.

"Maybe he's coming," she said. She patted the thick tire of badly dyed blond hair which encircled her round head like a washed-out halo. "He iss not feeling so good today. One of hiss bad days. He iss thinking of Warsaw," she explained. I will not attempt to reproduce fully her French-cum-Litvak accent.

A lean, elderly man with hollow eyes, so thin that his big hands and feet looked doubly outsize, appeared at the top of the stairway, started down with a heavy, lifeless tread.

Kaspir said, quick and low: "Wanta talk to you soon's possible, Mamie."

"Library," said Madame D'Herelles, barely moving her lips. "About twenty minutes." Then aloud to the descending skeleton, who, I saw now, wore an approximation of a footman's uniform: "The luggage is on the porch, Osca'. You feel all right to carry it?"

The man nodded, marched past us without a word. His footfalls thudded like those of a man twice his weight. Madame D'Herelles watched him with sympathetic eyes. "I tell him he does not haff to work," she complained. "But he says, 'I work or go crazy.' So I let him work." She shook her head. "He lost much in Warsaw. He iss sorry hiss life was not included." She patted Maude's arm, cocked an arch eyebrow at Kaspir. "I go now to help Anna—that iss my maid—help the cook make canapes, but I will be in the library in twenty minutes. Osca' will show you your rooms, Stefen. I put you and the handsome"—a lush glance at me—"lieutenant together. You don't mind, eh?"

We said certainly not, and she rolled off. The silent Osca' returned with the bags and led us upward. In the spacious chamber assigned to Kaspir and me, by the bureau, shone a champagne bucket on a stand.

"That's Mamie for you," said Kaspir affectionately, yanking the bottle from the ice and going to work on the cork.

"Here's to the Madame," I suggested, when he handed me my glass.

"Let's drink one to Osca' instead," said Kaspir. "Long may he work."

This didn't sound like Kaspir, somehow, but I let it pass without comment and drank. Kaspir was definitely twitchy today. Tancred's late message had upset him, although he would not admit it.

I drank hurriedly, for I wanted a second glass and Kaspir's conscience does not apply to wine. He poured it grudgingly, then tilted the bottle for his own third. I was raising my glass when a sudden contraction of my stomach muscles, a leap of the pulse, made me whirl toward the door. The wine slopped on my bare wrist and I shivered.

OSCA' WAS there. Despite those large feet, I had not heard him enter the room. He was staring at us. The man's forehead was magnificent—the forehead of a scholar—but under it the features were skeletal. His eyes were large and luminous. Oddly enough, his attention seemed directed more at me than at Kaspir. I had an uncomfortable feeling that I had seen Osca' somewhere before.

Kaspir spoke without turning (so he *had* heard Osca' come in!): "Turn on the heat, will you, Osca'?"

The pictures danced on the walls as Osca' tramped across the room. He fiddled with the radiator, rose and looked at Kaspir.

"Think we'll have any luck this trip, Mike?" said Kaspir conversationally, addressing me but looking at Osca'.

Before I could answer, Osca' nodded slowly, like a toy mandarin.

"That'll be all, Osca'," said Kaspir shortly.

Osca' marched out. As he passed Kaspir I was amazed to see a human twinkle in his hitherto-dead eyes. To Kaspir he breathed, "How's he doing?" with a minute inclination of the head that most certainly meant me. Kaspir smiled and nodded, as though to say, "Oh, pretty well."

At the door Osca' stopped and held up both hands with the fingers spread apart, then two fingers of one hand. I thought at first of the "V" for victory sign, then realized that the signal meant twelve. Twelve what? Twelve o'clock?

But the gesture had conveyed more than that to me. Kaspir, watching, saw the dawn of comprehension in my eyes. I knew now who Osca' was. Kaspir shook his head to cut off the exclamation I was about to make, and strolled to the window and raised it. I joined him.

"That's Alanson," I said, incredulous.

"Yep." He twisted the champagne glass slowly between his fingers. "Taking a sabbatical. He seems to remember you."

Alanson had been assistant professor of Romance languages at Harvard during my undergraduate days, and I had been his earnest, if not very competent, student. He was a moody bird with the gift of tongues. He was popularly supposed to speak eleven languages, and actually, I learned later, spoke fourteen.

"Borrowed him off Tibby Bigelow late in '40," murmured Kaspir. "We cued him back into this country on a shipload from Lisbon. He gravitated here to Mamie's about four months ago. First class gent. Only man we've got who can understand most of what's said in this house."

"You can't mean that you suspect Madame D'Herelles of—"

"Good God, no!" Kaspir sounded genuinely shocked at the idea. "But think what a happy huntin' ground this joint is for the other crowd."

I hadn't thought of it in that light. But of course, in the heterogeneous collection of foreign derelicts and pensioners who passed through Madame D'Herelles' charitable hands, there must be a certain percentage of bad eggs. It made me hot to think of it.

However much people laughed at Madame D'Herelles, her cubic figure, the pathetic artificiality of her tarnished gold hair, her hoarse voice and ill-kept nails, and the creaking machinery of her sprawling household, there was no one in Washington to accuse her of hardness of heart or tightness of purse-strings.

She was the widow of a Toulon Frenchman, one of the industrial giants of the late 20s. Around 1935 he had met and married Mamie Jablonsky, who was then a concert singer known only to the smaller concert halls of middle Europe.

In 1940, when the supposedly great men of France were turning into despicable figures of clay and straw, D'Herelles was one of the few who threw all his available money and influence into the final war effort. When France fell, his shrift was short.

How Mamie D'Herelles escaped his fate, only she knew. She arrived in the United States to find herself, to her surprise, still a wealthy woman, for D'Herelles' interests in this country had been large. She had purchased this estate on the edge of Chevy Chase and thrown it open to the vast and shifting class of folk whom Hitler had turned into wanderers on the face of the earth. Czechs, Poles, and Free French formed the majority of her beneficiaries, and they ranged from ex-cabdrivers to authentic Middle European princes and princesses with royal eyes and no baggage.

Nor was Mamie D'Herelles' charity confined to room and board and cash handouts. She functioned as a sort of unofficial adjunct to our overworked Immigration Bureau, fought the State Department for passports for her charges, and, once they were in this country, never lost sight of them. And on two occasions, I recalled now, her sharp little eyes had perceived the wolf behind the sheep's clothing and she had notified Kaspir. And we had added to the growing collection of Gestapo small fry behind our bars.

Kaspir's uncharitable nickname of "Baritone Mamie" for our hostess was the result of one of her less success-ful bursts of energy, in which she had tried to help launch a young Polish pianist by appearing as guest soloist at his debut. In the middle of her first number Madame D'Herelles realized that her voice had dropped an octave or two since the fall of France. She had stopped at once and announced to the astounded audience, "I am making a damn fool of myself," and waddled off the platform, not without a certain dignity.

Standing there at the window, I had to chuckle at the recollection of this episode. Kaspir read my mind. He said: "I told Mamie she oughta get a good plumber to go over her pipes." He glanced at the thin gold watch on his beefy wrist.

" 'Bout time," he said. "Let's gather in Maude and go down."

IN MADAME D'Herelles' lofty-ceilinged, untidy library Kaspir opened the ball with a frankness that floored me.

"Mamie," he said. "Pennsylvania Avenue's gettin' hot these days." He blew his cheeks into a ruddy balloon and went "pop!"

Meaningless as this sounds, Madame D'Herelles understood him perfectly. She pursed her own rouged lips. "I heard some'sing," she admitted cautiously.

"Who ain't?" Kaspir's fingers drummed on the brocaded arm of his chair. "I was hopin' you *knew* somethin'. I'm tellin' you straight, Mamie, we're up a tree."

"Do you not think, Stefen," said Madame D'Herelles gently, "that if I knew some'sing I would come quick and tell you?"

"Sure." Kaspir, abashed, shifted his ground. "Who's eatin' here now?" he inquired, still drumming.

Madame D'Herelles smiled. "I seldom know, these days. Six—maybe eight—maybe ten, beside yourselfs."

"Charlie Doll still here?" Kaspir is not pretty when he tries to look arch.

"But certainly!" Madame D'Herelles actually preened herself. "What would I do without him? He iss my secretary, my major-domo, my—he is indispensable, Stefen." The black eyes flashed. "You don' think, Stefen…?"

I remembered "Charlie Doll," which was as close as Kaspir ever came to the name. He was Major Kyrlo Dolle, late of the Polish army—an intense, silent young man obviously suffering from shellshock or some other war neurosis. He was about half Mamie D'Herelles' age.

"Good God, no!" Kaspir's vehemence was reassuring. "But he gets around a lot, and I just thought—"

"This *affaire* of Pennsylvania Avenue," said Madame D'Herelles, her guttural voice softening, "iss it really so bad, Stefen? Iss this new man really depressed—decouragé? I tol' you I heard reports, but one hears so many…."

"Yep." Kaspir plunged his hand into a bowl on the table, came up with a walnut. He sat turning it between thumb and forefinger.

I saw a strained, impatient expression cross Maude's face. I knew what she felt. I wasn't at all sure of the wisdom of this line Kaspir was taking with Madame D'Herelles. The Madame was all right, of course, but there were undoubtedly others in this house not fully accounted for. And Kaspir had not lowered his voice.

A discreet knock at the library door. Madame D'Herelles interrogated Kaspir with her bushy, graying eyebrows. He nodded vaguely.

"*Entrez*, Kyrlo," she called. A new note in her voice brought me a look from Maude. There were rumors abroad about Madame D'Herelles and young Dolle—the usual thing—but until this moment I had scorned them. Now I wondered.

ENTER MAJOR Kyrlo Dolle, darkly handsome, but with something of Osca's dead look behind the eyes. Even the sight of Maude, whose blond perfection usually sends Slavs into spasms of heel-clicking, hand-kissing, and tender glances, failed to elicit from him anything but the most perfunctory of polite greetings.

Madame D'Herelles indicated Kaspir with her eyes. "*L'affaire* Pennsylvania Avenue," she said simply. "He wants our help."

The merest flicker of interest lighted Dolle's eyes momentarily. "A report," he said (his English accent was superior to that of Madame D'Herelles), "which I preferred not to believe."

"You can start believin' it any time you like, Charlie," said Kaspir dourly. "You'll be safe enough."

"Then I am most sorry." Dolle took a cigarette from an ormolu box beside Madame D'Herelles, tamped it thoughtfully. It was as though he had expended all the interest he was capable of expending on a single topic. He told Madame D'Herelles, in French, that their house guests were beginning to come downstairs, and that the cocktails....

"Seen this one, Mamie?" Kaspir had been occupied with getting the walnut into position. Dolle looked distinctly annoyed at the interruption.

"Lookit!" said Kaspir. The muscles of his hand and wrist quivered. We were rewarded by a crunching sound, immediately followed by the spectacle of Kaspir bounding into the air like a performing bear.

"Damn!" shouted Kaspir, wringing his hand. "Damn!" He ceased dancing and gesticulating long enough to pluck from his thumb a sharp sliver of shell. He poked the wounded thumb into his mouth and mumbled through it. Then he drew it out and inspected it. A large bead of blood was welling up.

Maude smiled seraphically, and I was enjoying it, too. But our pleasure at Kaspir's mishap was destroyed by a singular occurrence.

Madame D'Herelles' throat squeezed out an odd, choking noise. We turned just in time to see her fat, animated face go slack. The whole flabby mass of her relaxed in a faint.

Instantly Major Dolle became a thing of fire and fury. "You fool!" he screamed at Kaspir, his dark face contorted. The tone was so vicious that I jumped up. But Major Dolle's attention now belonged wholly to Madame D'Herelles. He rushed to a side table for brandy, and brushed Maude aside as he knelt by Madame's chair and put the glass to her lips.

Madame D'Herelles recovered speedily, but I could see that she was badly shaken. The pallor brought out liver-colored circles under her eyes, and her trembling mouth suggested her real age.

When he saw Madame coming around, Dolle bethought himself of his violence to Kaspir. His apology was fulsome. Madame, it seemed, was unable to stand the sight of blood. He had fears for her heart. His own nerves, too—the war, you know. Colonel Kaspir would forgive him?

"Sure, sure," said Kaspir, to stem the flow of words. He had a handkerchief around his thumb now. He was watching Madame D'Herelles—not, I noticed, with proper solicitude, but speculatively. Kaspir is regrettably callous to all human suffering except his own.

Madame D'Herelles was also apologetic. It was awkward of her to frighten us that way, but ever since France, the mere sight of a drop of blood....

Under other conditions I might have suspected Madame D'Herelles of theatrical shenanigans aimed at the sympathy of Major Dolle. But her collapse had had all the earmarks of the genuine article.

When Madame was able to walk, we went out to meet the other guests. They were a strange assortment, most of them newly arrived from the breadlines and terrors of Europe.

The table talk that night was rare and wonderful. I thought longingly of the old days on the *Baltimore Sun*, before world events had yanked me from an editorial sanctum and pitchforked me into Section Five, that oddest of odd counter-espionage bureaus. What I could have done with a typewriter and even the least of those stories told at the table of Madame D'Herelles! But tales of incredible horror and incredible courage are a dime a dozen these days.

Despite the stories and the excellent food and wines (with Alanson, late of Harvard, being deft with dishes and decanters) there was a weight upon my spirits that not even the champagne could lighten. I could see the same thing in Maude's face, even as she laughed at the sallies of a giant Czech with a spade beard.

I thought of the radio speech, of Tancred's worried face and grim message on the phone. We had so much to do, so little time, and not a handle whereby to grasp this thing.

I glanced down the table at Kaspir. His bull shoulders were hunched yearningly toward a pretty little mademoiselle, a distant cousin of a distant cousin of the late M. D'Herelles. Suddenly I was disgusted with my own-incompetence, and Kaspir's fumbling, and with the world as a whole. And this feeling rode me like an old man of the sea throughout what should have been a gay and amusing evening.

It was well past eleven, and most of the party had already retired, when Kaspir's mouth spread in a trumpet-like yawn that he made no effort to hide. Behind Madame D'Herelles, who was leaning on Major Dolle's ever-ready arm, we ascended the broad stairway step by slow step.

CHAPTER THREE
FOOTFALLS AT
MIDNIGHT

ONCE INSIDE our room, Kaspir made no move to undress, and shook his head when I started to peel off my coat. "Make a noise like you're goin' to bed," he whispered, and refused to elaborate.

So we went solemnly through an absurd routine that made me feel like a low-grade idiot. We dropped shoes on the floor. We conversed as two men sharing a room might reasonably converse while preparing for bed. Kaspir was maddeningly thorough, even to contriving proper sound effects on the bathroom fixtures. At length, after much creaking of bedsprings (a listener outside might have thought Kaspir was doing flip-flops on his bed), we switched off the lights and lay there in the silent darkness, Kaspir's cigarette alternately burning bright orange and dying to a dull red between puffs.

Once I thought I heard angry voices on the servants' floor overhead, but the altercation, if it was an altercation, subsided quickly. I was just dozing off when I heard the familiar heavy footfall of Osca', apparently descending the back stairs. Our room was in the rear of the house.

The sound galvanized Kaspir into life. "What's he makin' all that damn racket for?" he whispered, furious.

Osca' (for there was no doubt in my mind as to who it was) was approaching our door now. Kaspir was on the edge of his bed. He deliberately ground his cigarette into the rug with his heel.

Heavy as the footsteps were, they were somehow muffled. They did not stop at our door, as Kaspir had evidently expected. They went on up the hall in the direction of Madame D'Herelles' suite.

Kaspir sighed, apparently with relief. "Guess Mamie must've rung for him," he whispered. "He'd have had to answer." But he didn't sound as if he believed it.

We both crept to the door. The footsteps continued for perhaps a dozen halting paces, then stopped. The silence and darkness twisted my nerves taut. I wanted to yell to relieve the tension.

Kaspir opened the door, turning the knob as you might unscrew the detonator of a shell. There was a soft noise up the hall, as though someone had dropped a pillow.

But Kaspir was staring down at the polished oak floor directly in front of him. In the half-light I saw footprints, messy footprints—muddy footprints.

Muddy footprints hell! Bloody footprints!

Kaspir left me. For all his bulk, he can move quietly as a cat. When I could make my trembling knees function, I set out after him, treading close to the wall to avoid the horrid, foot-shaped blotches. It looked as though a bare-footed man carrying a badly leaking can of red paint had passed that way.

Under a shaded wall lamp opposite Madame D'Herelles' door I found Kaspir. He was kneeling beside something. Even before additional light sprang from the small pocket flash in his hand, I knew what I would see, and my throat tightened.

A knife had ended Alanson's tour of duty with Section Five. I sickened as Kaspir, cradling the dome-like head in one big hand, exposed the wound to the beam of light from the other. It was ghastly plain why Alanson had not cried out. A single sweep of a sharp blade had severed the windpipe, then curled back and upward to nick the jugular vein.

I felt a sudden pang of shame. Here was a man near sixty who, mortally wounded, had been able to march his dying body down a flight of stairs and along a long hall, for some grim purpose of his own. And here was I, young and unmarked, on the verge of collapse. I stiffened, and the slow tide of anger put new strength into my buckling knees.

Kaspir thrust his tiny metal flashlight into my hand. The wavering beam passed over the wall above Alanson's body. Before I could check it, a grunt of astonishment escaped me. Kaspir grimaced like a gargoyle for silence. I pointed.

Someone had dipped a finger in Alanson's blood and left a sign. It was crudely drawn, but then the swastika is a crude sign.

Kaspir seized my wrist, directed the flashlight beam once more at Alanson's head. His fingers went to the gaping mouth. My stomach heaved. For a split second I thought he was trying to pull out one of Alanson's teeth. But when his hand came away, I saw it held what seemed to be a folded slip of paper, damp with saliva but not bloody.

Behind us, the flat voice of Major Dolle said: "Who has killed Osca'?"

KASPIR WAS up in a single bound, and a single stride took him to the major. Dolle's left hand flew to his hip. But Kaspir was not attacking. He was merely insisting upon silence. He gripped Dolle's arm, said something in his ear. I saw Dolle nod, start back obediently for his room, which was at the far end of the hall, beyond ours. Kaspir motioned to me. We trod softly after Dolle.

To reach Dolle's room we had to pass the intersection of an "L" of the old house. From the shadows here stepped Maude. Dolle stopped, staring at her.

Maude began, "I heard—" Like Dolle, she was in a dressing gown over pajamas.

Kaspir whispered urgently: "Get your duds on and come to Dolle's room." He pointed to the door. Maude turned away without a word.

In Dolle's room Kaspir raised his voice above a whisper for the first time. "You know who got Osca', I suppose." It was not a question, but a statement.

"I can give an excellent guess," said Dolle evenly, reaching for a silver cigarette case on the bureau. For all his calm, however, there was a hard, excited light behind his eyes.

"You gotta gun?" demanded Kaspir.

Dolle put the cigarette case down, opened a bureau drawer and produced a long-barreled automatic of some foreign make.

"You wouldn't object to cuttin' yourself a slice of the Gestapo, would you, Charlie?" said Kaspir gently, as one offering a juicy bone to a dog. "They're still in the house, y'know."

Dolle's hand, closing on the automatic, began to tremble.

"Get out the back way, quick's you can," ordered Kaspir. "Maude'll be along in a minute. You can take the back, Maude'll cover the front." His hand went up against Dolle's protest. "She's a better shot than you are, Major. Do as I say, now. Kettle and I will do the inside work. If they come your way, let 'em have it. But I don't think they'll get that far."

He opened the door with a peremptory sweep of his arm. Dolle hesitated, stepped out. Maude joined us, in slacks and topcoat, her eyes questioning. Kaspir handed her his own pet, a flat, light .32 automatic. He pushed her after

Dolle, who was starting for the back stairs. "The major'll explain," he whispered. "Go with him."

"Come on," whispered Kaspir to me.

I caught his sleeve. "Let me get my gun," I said. If Kaspir's theory about the murderers of Alanson were true, it would never do to embark on the hunt unarmed.

"Gun, hell!" grunted Kaspir disgustedly. "Come on." And with that he started back for Alanson's body. I followed, highly uneasy.

I have seen Kaspir do callous and even brutal things during my association with him, but his actions of the next few minutes topped them all. Had we been attacked, I doubt if I could have raised a hand in our defense, for I was weak and sick.

First, he twitched the shade from the small hall light near Alanson's body, and in the naked glare of its bulb the body, and its trail of footprints, became things of added horror.

Next, without a word to me, he opened Madame D'Herelles' door and entered her room, closing the door behind him. Through it I, shivering in the night air, heard his voice, rough and insistent—then Madame's, sleepily hoarse.

The door opened and Madame appeared, in peignoir over nightgown. Kaspir loomed behind her. "Look," he said, and pointed over her shoulder.

It was several seconds before Madame's eyes, blinking in the sharp light, saw what he meant.

I AM no weakling, and Kaspir's physical strength is immense, but I do not exaggerate when I say that for two or three minutes Madame D'Herelles, middle-aged and apoplectic, came very close to being a match for the two of us. No fainting this time. Neither did she cry out. But she slavered and struck at us as we held her back from her bedroom window, and twice she broke away and nearly hurled herself through the glass. It was sheer blind panic at the sight of the blood, verging on insanity.

Finally we, or rather, Kaspir, succeeded in flinging her on the immense Louis XIV bed from which he had roused her, and she became calmer.

At this point Kaspir, seated physician-like on the edge of the bed, with a precautionary hand on Madame's bulbous shoulder, began to talk. It was the most amazing balderdash. I didn't hear all of it, for between breaths he sent me into the bathroom to hunt up a sedative.

He was still talking when I returned, after an exhausting session with Madame's thousand odd face creams and lotions, with some small blue pills that looked like sodium amytal. He was reeling off Polish and French names and asking Madame about them. For a man who couldn't pronounce "Kyrlo Dolle," he showed an astonishing familiarity with many tongue-twisting titles and places. As nearly as I could tell, he was inquiring about many of the people whom Madame had aided in this country, and about their origins. He seemed to be probing about in her subconscious mind, trying to strike some profitable vein. Not exactly the method I would have chosen to soothe a woman whose nerves were shot to pieces.

But Madame only stared numbly at him, her eyes large under the crazy disorder of her hair.

I thrust the capsules under his nose, but he pushed them away. Madame's eyes were glazing with sleep, the drugged sleep that follows a devastating emotional blow-up. Right in the middle of one of Kaspir's long-winded passages her jaw dropped, and from her flattish nose issued an unmistakable snore.

Kaspir jumped up, disgust written large on his face. I was past wondering at Kaspir's actions or reactions. I was a stooge in a nightmare now. If Kaspir had ordered me to dive headlong from the window, I think I would have done it unquestioningly, in the belief that I would wake up later.

"Give her a couple hours," muttered Kaspir, frowning down at Madame. He hooked his thumbs in his vest pockets and teetered on his heels. He was dejected, and if I read his eyes correctly, puzzled.

"I don't suppose it means anything to you," I said, with lofty sarcasm, "but there's a Heinie with a knife loose in this house somewhere."

"Oh, him," said Kaspir carelessly. "I'll fix him later."

For some reason this fool remark touched my temper. "Maude's outside," I flared, "and Dolle. Suppose—"

"Say!" Kaspir's face lighted up. From a vest pocket he drew the folded slip of paper he had discovered in Alanson's mouth. He unfolded it and hurried over to a table lamp. "Lookit," he said, studying it under the light, his brows drawn together.

Curiosity downed my impatience momentarily. I joined him. Behind us, Madame D'Herelles snored on.

"Whaddaya make of it, Mike?"

It was a prescription. Printed at the top was the name of a well-known Washington eye, ear, nose and throat man. But the words and symbols written below, in purple ink, meant nothing to me.

"Listen, Mike!" Kaspir's finger bit into my arm, which went numb to the nails. "Get downstairs on the phone and call Tancred."

"Tancred?"

"Dammit, pay attention." This so loudly that Madame stirred in her sleep. He fell silent until her snores became rhythmic again. "Yes, Tancred. Find out where that Rennie's stoppin'." He pushed the prescription into my hand. "Read him this junk over the phone, best you can. If it's what I think it is—" He was almost shaking with excitement now. "While you're doin' that, I'll have a look around Alanson's room."

This unexpected but welcome eruption of enthusiasm, coming when it did, fired me. We left the room together. Kaspir's first move was to replace the shade on the bulb over Alanson, and I was grateful as the stark outline of the body, with its gory swastika above, softened in the dim light.

"Come up as soon as you finish," whispered Kaspir and lumbered off toward the back stairs.

I made my way down the broad sweep of the front stairway, clutching the prescription, and back to the library.

Tancred must have been up, for he answered his phone on the first ring. "Kaspir got something?" he asked eagerly, when I had identified myself. From his tone it was obvious that his end of the investigation had not progressed. I told him we didn't know yet, and his "Oh" was hollow and hopeless.

"Rennie?" he said, in reply to my next question. "He's here. I'll put him on."

MY CONVERSATION with Rennie was brief. He interpreted the prescription for me without hesitation. I went up through the house to the servants' floor, stopping at our room to pick up my own automatic. I located

Alanson's room without difficulty, for the door was open and the light on.

"Wha'd he say?" demanded Kaspir softly, kneeling by a wastebasket with both hands full of trash. By the bed, a brownish puddle showed where Alanson had been when the knife was applied.

I closed the door quietly and told him.

"What?" He goggled, for all the world like an angry frog.

"It's a prescription for cough syrup," I repeated patiently. "Rennie says it's one of the old standbys."

Kaspir was on his feet in an instant. He snatched the paper. "I'm gonna talk to that Rennie," he grated. "Listen. Stay in this hall out here. If one o' these flunkies starts roamin' around, conk him and lay him in here." With that he was gone, before I could argue the point.

There was nothing to do but obey. I took my shoes and patrolled that stygian hall for two mortal hours. Several times I trod on dry, hard ridges—Alanson's trail, now coagulated.

Dull? Not exactly. Once, about thirty minutes after Kaspir had left, I heard a quick footfall (not Kaspir's) in our hall below. I sneaked halfway down the stairs, but by then there was silence. Soon afterward I could have sworn I heard a flurry of movement in one of the rooms below, but again the silence fell so quickly that I could not be sure.

It was about fifteen minutes after that that I heard—no mistake, this time—the thing that sent my hackles up in pure, undiluted fear. I slipped down to the foot of the stairs.

In one of the rooms (I could not tell which one) someone was walking with heavy, hesitating footsteps. Not loud, but heavy. Heavy, hesitating footsteps, exactly like....

But Alanson was dead!

I am ashamed to admit that I did not investigate. I followed my initial, panicky impulse, which was to spring back up the stairs. I paused halfway up, panting, my hands and brow clammy.

No more footsteps. All quiet now. I waited, straining my ears until I was almost dizzy. Two minutes passed. Five. I sat down, weak-kneed, only to leap up, clutching my gun desperately, as a dark figure materialized at the foot of the stairs. I shrank against the wall and raised my automatic for a crushing blow.

"Quit playin'," muttered the dark figure peevishly, a second before my arm descended. "C'mon."

"Wait a second." I seized Kaspir's shoulder. "Did you hear someone walking?"

"Walkin'? Where?"

"You'll think I'm crazy," I whispered, "but it sounded the way Alanson sounded when he passed our door tonight. It was somewhere near Madame D'Herelles' room."

"That's where we're goin'," muttered Kaspir, still peevish, as though I should have known. "We'll have a look-see."

I gave up and followed him into Madame's room. She was about as we had left her, sleeping the sleep of utter exhaustion.

There were half a dozen floor and table lamps in that room, and Kaspir switched them all on. The blaze of illumination hurt my eyes, and I narrowed them against the glare. Kaspir sat down beside Madame D'Herelles and jiggled her shoulder. "Mamie!" he called. "Wake up!" In his hand was the prescription for cough syrup.

Madame stirred and tried to turn over on her side to get away from his voice.

"Wake up, Mamie!" Kaspir slapped her fat cheek lightly. A strangled protest rose in my throat. After what Madame had been through—

"Shut up," growled Kaspir. He took her jaw, wobbled her head. "Wake up, Mamie! Wake up!"

Madame D'Herelles blinked, threw a fat arm across her eyes to shut out the light.

Kaspir pulled the arm away. "Wake up!"

She rubbed her eyes. "Wake up!" urged Kaspir, holding the prescription open, a little way from her face. "What's this, Mamie?" He shook her again. "What's this?"

She was awakening now. I could see her pupils contracting in the strong light as the room came into focus for her. She started to mumble something. Suddenly her eyes fixed themselves in a stare that sent a chill into my stomach.

She was staring at the ceiling, and in that moment I saw the dawning light of reason fading from her eyes, to be replaced by a very different expression.

I tilted my head back to follow the direction of her gaze. Even as I gasped, my thoughts flew back to the heavy footsteps I had heard from the stairway. I knew now what they had been.

Across Madame D'Herelles' white plaster ceiling, from the door of the bathroom past the door by which we had entered…! I looked again, to make sure. Unless I was crazy (which was a definite possibility now) someone had walked across the ceiling of Madame's room—someone with large, bloody feet!

Kaspir saw the new expression settling upon Madame D'Herelles' face. He shook her frantically, stuck the prescription blank almost against her nose. "Who is this for, Mamie? Who is this for?"

A momentary gleam in her eye. She spoke, quite clearly, a name.

Then she returned to her contemplation of the ceiling. Kaspir repeated the name she had spoken, but she was silent now, and smiling.

That was the new expression: the bright, vacant smile of an idiot!

"We're gettin' outa here," said Kaspir, and pulled me from the room.

CHAPTER FOUR
WORSE THAN POISON

OBSERVE ME now: Lieutenant Mike Kettle, of Section Five. It is about four A.M. Madame D'Herelles is still lying on her back in bed. She is smiling up at me.

I am on a stepladder. In my hand is a paintbrush. Before me, on the ladder apron, is a bucket of white paint which Kaspir somehow procured from the chauffeur at the garage. The household still sleeps as I ply my brush over the footprints. Madame smiles as though in approbation.

Kaspir and Maude are in the library, telephoning. My job is a tedious, back-aching affair. I don't know why I am doing it, save that Kaspir told me to.

"What have you done to her?" A darkhaired, swarthy girl, with hot eyes and a certain sultry beauty, is in the doorway. In her hand, bearing steadily on me, is an automatic. She glances from Madame D'Herelles to me, back to Madame D'Herelles, who still smiles.

"What have you done to her?" There is a definite menace in her tone. Ordinarily this apparition, the open threat of the gun, would frighten me a little. But this night has placed me temporarily beyond shocks or surprises or fear. I ease one hand inside my coat and grasp the butt of my own gun. Shoot or be shot. Woman or man.

The girl's hot eyes see my move. In a detached sort of way I note that her hand is tightening around the trigger. She is about to bring me down.

Something flashes against the girl's dark head from behind, making a sharp, uncompromising sound against her skull. My gun is out now, but she is crumpling, face forward.

"That must be the damn maid," says Colonel Kaspir, sticking his great round face around the door. It was the barrel of his gun that had struck her down. "Hurry up, Mike," he says irritably. "Maude's bringin' a car around front. We're goin' to town."

I paint on, hurrying. "Where's Dolle?" I inquire.

"The hell with him. We're in a hurry," says Kaspir.

MAUDE DROVE US to town. I gathered from her driving, and from one or two of her curt remarks to Kaspir, that she was in a black rage at having been left outside on guard while Kaspir and I were busy inside the house.

I dozed on that trip, too weary to ask questions. I wondered vaguely whether Kaspir would leave Dolle guarding the rear until daylight.

Tancred and Rennie and Primrose were on the side-walk in front of Tancred's hotel, their faces pale in the dawn. They crowded into the car and we shot away. Tancred attempted to learn from Kaspir where we were going, but Kaspir was in one of his airy, noncommittal moods, so Tancred soon lapsed into an angry silence.

We sped over dew-damp streets into southwest Washington, Kaspir humming under his breath and patting his foot. Tancred took this attitude as a personal insult, but I knew Kaspir was worried.

I thought at first that we were bound for our headquarters, but half a dozen blocks away, Maude slowed the car to allow Kaspir to see the house numbers. "Here," said Kaspir finally, and she put on the brake.

"Come on, Mike," said Kaspir, climbing out.

Tancred said sulkily: "Hadn't we all better——"

"Nope," said Kaspir. "You wait right here."

It was a lofty brownstone house made over into walk-up apartments. Kaspir thumped upstairs to the second floor, stopped to look at a card beside a door.

"Andrew Torby," it read.

Torby! That was the name Madame D'Herelles had uttered just before she began to smile.

Kaspir laid his splay thumb against the bell-button and held it there until the door was opened by a large man with blue jowls. He wore striped pajamas.

"What do you want?" His beefy face was suspicious.

He stopped there, because Kaspir had him by the throat.

Torby's right hand moved swiftly, but Kaspir's left caught it. Kaspir drove his knee forward and upward into Torby's groin.

We had to help Torby down the narrow hall to the tiny living-room, and support him while he was sick into a waste basket. He moaned as, the spasm of retching over, we let him down on a couch. Kaspir sat down beside him. Kaspir was white around the mouth.

"I ain't gonna waste any time on you, Torby," said Kaspir. He held out the cough syrup prescription. "Where do you take this to be filled?"

Torby shook his head. You could see by his eyes that he knew what Kaspir meant. You could also see that he had no intention whatever of answering.

Kaspir wasted no time in further questioning. Torby's shake of the head had reduced the situation to a very simple proposition.

Kaspir's hand shot out and gripped Torby's throat once more. Torby's hands clawed at Kaspir's wrist, but his strength had left him.

"You're outa luck, boy," remarked Kaspir conversationally. "Because I'm just so damn anxious to find out about this little piece o' paper that I can't wait."

The pressure was still on. Torby's face was purple now, and he was making noises in his throat. His eyes were bulging.

Kaspir let him go. He fell back, massaging the red streaks left by Kaspir's fingers. He mumbled something.

"What?" asked Kaspir, a hand cupped to his ear. "I missed that."

Torby tried again. This time we got it. "I demand to be arrested," he croaked.

"The old refrain," said Kaspir genially. He was deathly pale now. His face, beside Torby's, was like a peeled potato beside a beet. "Where do you take this little slip o' paper to be filled?" he asked again, and his hand took a fresh grip on Torby's throat. I had to turn away. The sound was bad enough without having to watch Torby's face go purple again.

I heard no word, but Torby must have made some sign of capitulation.

"Go down and get the others, Mike," said Kaspir. So I went down and ushered them up. As we trooped down the narrow hall we heard Kaspir saying: "You're an ingenious feller, Torby. But I don't think Primrose'll like you any more. This bein' a democracy, you're liable to lose your job. You got one o' the things here?"

Torby nodded.

"Get it," ordered Kaspir. "Go with him, Mike."

I followed Torby's faltering steps into a two-by-four bedroom. From behind a picture he hauled a flat metal box. We returned to the living-room, and the others crowded around as I opened the box.

It held two lozenges, translucent and almost transparent, each perhaps an inch in diameter.

"Now, where'd you get these?" demanded Kaspir. His amiability vanished as a mulish look appeared in Torby's eyes. He held up his right hand before Torby's sullen face. "I ain't a bit averse to performin' in front o' spectators," he said, and advanced a step, his china-blue eyes stormy. "Matter o' fact, I think—"

Andrew Torby, late attendant at "Mr. Smith's" office, answered hastily and huskily. "At ——'s Pharmacy."

I recognized the name as that of a small neighborhood drugstore not three blocks from our headquarters."

"Who from? Always the same man, I suppose."

Torby nodded again to save his throat. "The night man," he said.

"How do you use 'em? I gotta pretty good idea," said Kaspir, "but I think these gentlemen 'ud find it more convincin' if they heard it from your own ruby lips."

TORBY GLANCED uneasily at Primrose, whose hard eyes were boring into him now.

"At first," he muttered, staring at the floor, "I used to warm one and stick it to the inside of the water carafe every day."

"The carafe!" exploded Primrose. "You mean the vacuum bottle on the boss's desk—the one he drinks out of every day?"

"Yeah. And after you made me start sterilizin' the carafe with hot water every morning, it was easier." A malicious edge sharpened Torby's husky voice. "Once the bottle was hot inside, all I had to do was slip one of these in with my thumb—while you were getting the drinking water ready, Mr. Primrose."

"They dissolve slowly in the water, I suppose?" cut in the redhaired doctor smoothly, as Primrose flushed.

"Yeah, I suppose so."

" 'Suppose' "—warned Kaspir.

"I don't know nothing about them except what I was told to do," cried Torby hoarsely. "All I know is my orders. Every week I'd get one of those prescriptions in the mail. It had a different prescription on it every time. I'd take it to the night man at ——'s Pharmacy and he'd slip me a box with a half-dozen of these in it." He pointed to the lozenge in my hand. "Whatever code was on those prescriptions, I didn't know nothing about it."

"Major Dolle mail you the prescriptions?" demanded Kaspir. Silence. "Did he?"

"Yeah."

The redhaired doctor took the lozenge from me, broke it, put it to his tongue, then smelled it.

"Probably one of the barbiturate group," he said. "Done up with some solution to make it stick fast to a slick surface like the inside of a carafe." He touched his tongue with it again. "A very clever bit of compounding, Colonel Kaspir. Tasteless in water, odorless, dissolves slowly and evenly, I dare say. Virtually invisible in the carafe."

"Poison?" asked Primrose.

"No," answered the doctor. "A little worse." His face was grave. "A drug that, little by little, day after day, works with a slow, cumulative effect. Induces nervousness and, after a week or two, a pronounced depression, very hard to fight against and impossible to conceal." He handed me the broken lozenge and I replaced it in the box. "Yes," said Doctor Rennie, "that was undoubtedly it."

"The—er—cure, Doctor Rennie?" asked General Tancred. "Will it—er—how long will it take?" He had the forthcoming "Report to the Nation" on his mind.

Rennie smiled. "Quick and easy, General. Three days should be more than enough, now that we know what the trouble is."

"Ha!" exclaimed General Tancred. His pinched face seemed to fill out before our eyes—"like a prune in water," as Kaspir described it later.

"You found this prescription at Madame D'Herelles' house?" asked the general of Kaspir. "How, and where? And who put you on to Torby?"

"A little bird," said Kaspir sweetly. "And don't look at me in that hungry way, General. He ain't gonna sing no more—for nobody. And by the way," he added innocently, "when we left Mamie's this morning there was some kinda scrimmage goin' on among the servants. Somebody might ha' got hurt. I'd suggest you take some men out there and clean up the mess before it gets into the papers."

BY SPECIAL invitation, Tancred, Primrose, and the redhaired doctor were guests at a small affair in Kaspir's office on the day of the second "Report to the Nation." They arrived just as Kaspir switched on the radio in his office.

You remember that second address, I'm sure. Clear, vital, ringing—the speech of a man made strong by infinite faith and courage. It had a profound effect on the South American delegation who sat opposite "Mr. Smith" as he spoke into the microphone—a profounder one, I should guess, upon certain officials in Berlin responsible for flooding South America and Allied capitals with pamphlets similar to the letter Tancred had confiscated.

When it was over and we dipped our noses into some Scotch, Tancred leaned back in his chair. "That was a fine mess we found at Madame D'Herelles' place last week," he murmured, eyeing Kaspir.

"Really?" Kaspir was all attention. "Just what did you find, General?"

"In the hall"—Tancred ticked the items off on his fingers—"a footman with his throat cut and a bloody swastika over him. In Mamie D'Herelles' dressing-room was that feller Dolle, dead as a doornail with a knife between his ribs—"

"Major Dolle!" cried Maude and I together.

"In the bedroom was Mamie D'Herelles herself," went on Tancred smoothly, eyes still on Kaspir. "She was picking at the covers and smiling, her mind all gone.

"But the strangest thing of all," concluded Tancred, "was on Mamie D'Herelles' ceiling. Someone had walked across that ceiling—someone with bloody feet. You saw nothing of those footprints, I suppose, Kaspir?"

"The day I see bloody footprints on a ceilin'," retorted Kaspir, "I'm gonna send for our friend here."

"At your service any time, Colonel," said Rennie, and Tancred rose to leave.

WHEN HIMMLER'S show was plantin' agents in France in '35," began Kaspir, when he and Maude and I were alone, "they scored one ten-strike. They planted Mamie Jablonsky right in D'Herelles' bed. D'Herelles was in on things—a big shot. You can figure how valuable Mamie was to her side. When they shot D'Herelles, Mamie 'escaped' to this country and set up in business helpin' the victims of that 'feelthy Adolf.'" He mimicked Madame D'Herelles' guttural voice.

"She really helped 'em, too," went on Kaspir. "Lady Bountiful. It made 'em trust Mamie. So much"—his face darkened—"that they confided in her a lot of stuff about who helped 'em on the other side, before they made the United States. Then Mamie would make up a little list and send it over to her pals in Berlin—

"Alanson—that was Osca', Maude—got a bee in his bonnet over Mamie and came to me. We got him in at Mamie's. He managed to intercept a couple o' those lists. And Alanson and I, we nursed Mamie along.

"Until this 'Smith' business busted—" said Kaspir. He broke off short and snorted. "Tancred and Primrose wonderin' why poison wasn't used...."

"Well, why wasn't it?" asked Maude.

Kaspir snorted again. "S'pose they'd poisoned 'Smith.' What permanent good 'ud that do 'em—except make the whole world a little madder and a little more determined to—"

"I see your point," said Maude.

"But if he was to begin to look bad, to look discouraged and depressed, *then* they'd have something that 'ud make itself felt in every capital from Buenos Aires to Moscow.

"So when Tancred tackled me after the first broadcast, I figured on tryin' Mamie first, she bein' our nearest, best, and biggest bet. I'd been wonderin' about Charlie Doll, too.

"You see, Alanson was on to something. He conveyed that in the room that afternoon—remember, Mike? My guess is that he found one o' those prescriptions in Charlie Doll's room and was gonna bring it to me at midnight.

"But Charlie Doll missed the prescription—that's a legitimate inference—and had ideas about who had it—ideas that, unfortunately for Alanson, were correct. So Charlie went to Alanson's room and tackled him on this topic that night after we went upstairs. Alanson must ha' slipped the thing into his mouth when Charlie attacked him. Charlie knifed Alanson, and left him for dead.

"An' Alanson, bein' a gutty gent, got up and walked downstairs. He was aimin' for our door, Mike, but he was too far gone to spot it."

"That much I believe," I said. "But explain the swastika. We were out in that hall in a minute. Dolle couldn't have—"

Kaspir looked long-suffering. "Did it occur to you, Mike, that Alanson might have scrawled that swastika in one last effort to let us know who'd got him?"

I SAW the end o' paper stickin' outa Alanson's mouth," went on Kaspir confidently, "and Doll saw me take it. And the minute I jumped Doll in the hall I knew he was the one who'd done Alanson in. Remember him reachin' for his hip, Mike?"

"But Alanson wasn't shot," I objected.

"Ever see a picture of an S.S. man in uniform?" inquired Kaspir acidly. "Knife worn on left hip.

"So I sent Charlie Doll out on guard," continued Kaspir, up now and pacing the floor. "That showed I trusted him.

"When the prescription turned out to be cough syrup, I put you on guard, Mike, and called Rennie myself. I told him about Mamie's blood-phobia. He told me another shock might make her talk.

"So I went back to Mamie's room and was standin' there in the boudoir, chewin' my nails and tryin' to dope out a

Number Nine jolt for the old girl, when in pussyfoots Charlie Doll.

"Charlie shoves a knife against my ribs and invites me, very polite, to hand over that paper I'd found on Alanson.

"So I removed"—Kaspir's eyes twinkled—"said knife from Charlie Doll's hand, toute suite. Bein' flustered at the time, I must ha' returned his knife to him point first." Kaspir smiled.

"You killed Dolle?" Maude gasped.

"Yup. An' then I saw how Charlie might help me with Mamie.

"So I took off my shoes and socks and dabbled my little pink tootsies in the puddle Charlie was so obligin'ly furnishin'. Ever squish around in blood, Maude? Just like cylinder oil. Then I proceeded to put the prints o' my dainty dogs along the ceilin' where they'd greet Mamie's eyes as soon as she came to."

Maude swore aloud. I said: "We give up. How did you walk on the ceiling?"

For answer, Kaspir seized two small wooden office chairs by their backs and swung his huge body aloft into a handstand, one hand gripping the back of each chair. Our office ceiling is high, but his feet reached it easily. Then, using the chairs as a man might use a pair of crutches upside down, he walked across the room, raising a chair and moving it forward with each step on the ceiling.

Kaspir swung himself down, red and panting. Maude and I stared at the ceiling, at the dusty prints left by his shoe soles on the flowered ceiling paper.

"See?" inquired Colonel Kaspir, refreshing himself with a chocolate cherry.

THE UNDERTAKER HAS COLD HANDS

THE COLD AND HAUGHTY STARE OF THE COPPER COBRA IN THE PAWNSHOP WINDOW HAUNTED ME IN MY SLEEP— WHERE I SAW IT SWIM INTO THE PANAMA CANAL AND BLOCK IT. BUT IT WASN'T TILL COL. KASPIR, OUR ERRATIC CHIEF OF SECTION 5, GOT TO WORK ON THE ESPIONAGE MURDERS THAT THE COBRA'S VENOM WAS DRAINED OUT OF THE BIG DITCH TO MAKE IT SAFE FOR OUR VITAL SHIPPING.

THE COBRA stared haughtily. I glared back. The creature's self-esteem was galling. The pretentious flare of the hood, the arrogant little red eyes abraded my nerves.

A man in top hat and tails paused at my shoulder. "Some day," he announced tipsily, "I'll buy that brute and chuck him in the river."

The cobra's eyes turned malevolent. "Yah," said my top-hatted friend defiantly and twiddled scornful fingers at his nose before he passed on. I recognized him as Ackermann, the sportive undertaker whose place was in the next block.

I shrugged my sandwich-boards to a less painful position. Three consecutive sixteen-hour days as A human billboard must have left me light-headed. I remember wondering what the up-curling devil of a snake had to be arrogant about. He was nothing but hammered copper with bits of ruby glass for eyes, and his abode was a pawnshop window beneath three gilt balls and a sign: *Aunt Jane's, Inc., Loans and Jewelry*. He rose no more than eight inches from his imitation ebony base, and dangling from his jaw like a badge of shame was a price tag, blank side to the public.

Far off, a thoughtful clock began to pound the hour. The ninth stroke hung lonely in the summer air. I shuffled along the nearly-deserted street toward the distant neons of Joey's Hot Dog Palace, which employed me.

My raw feet sent up distress signals, and I conned them along with the promise of a hot bath. So lost was I in this vision that I failed to allow for the weaving progress of the man lumbering toward me.

He was a big man, mellow drunk. He blundered against a sharp corner of my sandwich-boards in a way that jarred us both to the heels. It was almost as though he had sought the collision.

A great hand seized my shoulder and shook me as a woman flaps a dustcloth. The sandwich-boards flogged my shins. I smelled garlic and sour wine.

"Listen, you—" I began furiously, then bit my tongue as the result of an especially violent shake. Whereupon I struck at him.

A sandwich-board is a defensive structure. Cramped like a turtle in its shell, I barely grazed the craggy chin. Immediately the hand loosed my shoulder and curled into a large, dirty fist which sledgehammered me to the warm concrete of the sidewalk.

The fist became a vise at my throat. Another hand went through my pockets, about as gently as a steam shovel. But deep in my addled mind I rejoiced. This was merely thuggery.

The horny hands withdrew. The departing footsteps were quick and furtive—the footsteps of a sober man.

I STRUGGLED up and made my numb way to the alley door of Joey's Hot Dog Palace. Joey, a fat Litvak, regarded my battered face incuriously once he had satisfied himself that his sandwich-boards were undamaged. To keep in character I forced down a greasy dog and blistered my mouth with his unspeakable coffee before I left.

My day's wage just paid for the taxi to the brownstone ex-boarding house in southwest Washington which has served as Section Five's headquarters since early '40. Joe, the Negro houseboy, opened the fly-specked door. His dark, intelligent face spread in a grin as he noted my villainous cap, my stubbled face, and my general air of down-and-outness.

"How is yo', Massa Lieutenant Kettle, suh?" He received my cap with exaggerated servility. "You-all had a ha'hd day at de office, suh?"

"Anybody home?" I asked.

Joe abandoned his minstrel routine. "The

His hands slipped off the iron railing, and he slid headfirst from our sight.

colonel's anxious to see you," he said. "General Tancred's with him. The Canal business. Who socked you?"

"Who knows?" I murmured. "Watch out for visitors."

Joe patted the bulge under his left armpit reassuringly. I plodded up the stairs toward the sound of voices.

Kaspir's full moon of a face shone briefly as I entered his office. "Whatcha got?" he inquired, too casually. I shook my head.

Kaspir snorted, lolling back in his outsize swivel chair, mountainous in white linen, his beloved battered Panama crammed down over his large ears. A deflated paper bag on the desk informed me that he was full of chocolate cherries. His lounging pose told another story. He was worried.

Major General Altemus Tancred said, "Ah!" and tugged at a lobeless ear. His narrow, shrewd face was pale with the pallor Army Intelligence men take on these days when the topic is the Panama Canal. "If only we had something to go on," he muttered.

Kaspir snorted again, this time with deliberate intent. Tancred bristled. "Personally," he said, "I think you have a bee in your bonnet."

"No room for a bee in that bonnet, General," said Maude critically. She was standing, her slender body provocative in white sweater and skirt, her bare legs golden-brown. Her violet eyes strayed from my face to Kaspir's Panama. "That hat," she added, "is full of head—fathead."

This outrageous comment created the diversion she sought. Kaspir, stung, sat up. General Tancred, whose military mind abhors insubordination in any form, knitted his brows. But the tension was eased.

Kaspir pursed his cupid's-bow lips. "Michaelson in Panama says this Dan Perkins is a wrong gee. He admits he don't know why. But Michaelson's no fool."

General Tancred fished in his black alpaca jacket and pitched a packet of letters onto the desk. Kaspir's baby-blue eyes gleamed, but Tancred blew out the spark. "Nothing in 'em," he snapped. "Best code men we've got have been going over 'em. Drawn a complete blank. Dan Perkins writes his mother what you'd expect an affectionate son to write. The mere fact that he's a Canal Zone engineer and that his mother runs a shady pawnshop in Washington hardly indicates a hellish (the adjective was heavily sarcastic) plot to interfere with the use of the Canal."

"Why don't you say 'blow up the Canal'?" demanded Kaspir unfeelingly. Tancred winced. "You know damn well that's what's in your mind." Kaspir shook a lone remaining chocolate cherry from the paper bag and champed it juicily, eyes on Tancred's reddening face. "By the by," he added, in the nick of time to avert an explosion, " 'ja check on Old Lady Perkins?"

"Fully." The general clutched at his temper. "Seldom leaves her shop. Meets no enemy agents or persons remotely under suspicion. Uses her phone only to order groceries. We've checked on every person who's entered her shop. But there's no use"—his angry black eyes bored into Kaspir—"offering you our list. You have your own."

KASPIR ACTUALLY had the grace to blush. My hand went instinctively to my inside pocket. Tancred spotted my move and grunted angrily. Maude hummed a little tune.

"Sure I put Mike Kettle in that block," blustered Kaspir. "Thought he might spot somethin' your fellers missed." He rubbed his chin. "Meant to tell you," he lied feebly. "Forgot."

I could have killed him. To set me to pounding the pavement before Aunt Jane's, Inc. (which was Mrs. Jane Perkins's firm name) in those absurd sandwich-boards, while Tancred's highly competent operatives snickered at my disguise, was too much. My body ached afresh as I thought of those weary hours wasted.

Tancred observed with satisfaction the effect of his little bombshell. He rose. "From now on," he said to Kaspir, "play your own hunches." The official rasp in his tone was unpleasant. He drove his point home. "Intelligence has problems of its own. The next time you play on my curiosity, to save your own organization a bit of effort, I shall make an issue of it."

Kaspir was silent. Tancred is only human. "I'd suggest you and this Michaelson get your heads together over a ouija board," was his Parthian arrow as he put on his hat. "If you should achieve anything, I beg you not to let me know."

"I may do that, General." As repartee this was pathetic, and the general ignored it. But Maude caught the tinkling undertone and arched a silky brow at me.

General Tancred nodded curtly in our general direction and pointedly failed to acknowledge Kaspir's florid farewells. As his heavy footsteps faded down the hall Maude wheeled on Kaspir, eyes crackling.

"Fat-head," said Kaspir thoughtfully, before she could speak.

"You know blinkin' well why I said that," she fumed. "He was about to bite you. Now what about that crack about Michaelson and the ouija board?"

"Michaelson?" mused Kaspir absently. "Oh, *Michaelson!*" These histrionics were maliciously calculated to irritate her. "Tancred's developin' a psychic streak in his

THE UNDERTAKER HAS COLD HANDS 157

old age," he went on. "That was an inshot about the ouija board."

I expected Maude to flare up. Instead, her eyes widened fearfully. "Steve, you don't mean...?"

Kaspir's teeth came together with a click. "Michaelson was killed by a hit-and-run car outside a bar in Panama City last night. Coincidence, huh?"

Maude fumbled with the catch of the gold cigarette case which cost me a month's pay on her last birthday. I struck a match, telling myself that it was weariness which made my hand waver.

Kaspir flirted a thick thumb at the giant wall map of the Canal Zone behind his desk. "You see," he murmured, "we're movin' a good hunk o' the Atlantic battle fleet through the Canal into Hirohito's puddle early next month. I heard that first from Michaelson. Michaelson heard it from a gent who had no business knowin' it. That gent was Dan Perkins. Get it?"

I got it, although I didn't want it. My stomach was hollow and chilly. Mechanically I held the match to Maude's cigarette.

Maude spoke through a trickle of blue smoke. "Just what have we got, Steve?"

"We got Michaelson's hunch," replied Kaspir darkly. "And nothin' else. Unless you count me. Tell you what: let's all drop in on Don Bill the Gaucho and mooch us a drink. Elena's gonna help me polish my rumba," he added fatuously.

"I'm going home to bed," I said, disgusted.

"Also,"—Kaspir resettled the Panama at what he considers a devil-may-care angle—"Don Bill's been hintin' he's turned up some dope on a gang in Colon that Tancred's had his rheumy eye on...."

"Give me time to shave and change," I said hastily.

Kaspir cocked a glance at my bruised face. "Better douse that glim o' yours with some raw beef," he advised. "Who trod on it?"

I outlined my encounter with the garlic-breathing gorilla.

"Why didn'cha kick his teeth in?" demanded Kaspir unreasonably.

"I was afraid I'd hurt him," I replied gently. "Besides, if there's anything I just adore, it's to have a hairy giant slug me down and go through my pockets and—"

"O.K., O.K." Kaspir detests all long-winded sarcasm but his own. "You gonna stand there gabbin' all night?"

DONA ELENA Velez welcomed us to her apartment with a heavenly smile, saying, "So you did find time after all, Steve." She included Maude and me in the quiet warmth of her pleasure.

A spate of laughter from the living-room, followed by a floor-shaking bump.

"That is Bill," said Dona Elena to me, "showing off before Uncle Henry." Her fine eyes swung back to Kaspir and asked a question. Kaspir nodded.

"Go ahead, Elena," he said.

She hesitated. "Will you speak to Bill?" she whispered.

"About what?" Kaspir was being willfully dense.

"You know he's meddling in your kind of work, Steve. You know how foolhardy he is." She caught her breath. "Men are watching this apartment," she breathed.

"Elena!" This from the living-room. "Bring them in."

"Do what I can," promised Kaspir unconvincingly. We moved down the hall. An immense-shouldered, darkly handsome young man in slacks and crew shirt materialized in the living-room doorway.

"Come in and watch," cried Don Bill the Gaucho. "I have a new one." I heard his wife sigh resignedly.

Don Guillermo Velez spotted Maude. He gazed soulfully into her eyes. "Is this 'the face that launched a thousand ships'?"

"G'wan wid yer blarney," ordered Maude, not displeased.

Don Bill's brown, muscular hand closed on mine. "Lieutenant Kettle, this is a pleasure." He made me feel my appearance was the one bright spot in his evening.

We straggled comfortably into a living-room friendly with chintzes and American antiques. Awaiting us was a short, grayhaired man, whose sleepy eyes and merry mouth lent distinction to his round face. He was Don Enrico Tuila, Dona Elena's "Uncle Henry." I had heard of him as an able physician with a large practice among South Americans in Washington.

"You have entered a circus," Dr. Tuila warned us. His English was less perfect than that of the Velezes. "Bill is bursting with agility. His vitamins overwhelm him."

"I feel good," said Don Bill. He drew breath. "Barto!" he bellowed. "Barto!"

From somewhere in the big apartment rose an answering bellow.

"Three rum superbes!" shouted Don Bill. "Step on it!" Then, in an undertone to Kaspir, without changing his expression, "I've got something." He held a gold lighter to Kaspir's cigarette.

"Canal?" said Kaspir indifferently. I tingled.

"Yes." Don Bill snapped off the lighter. "Later." He raised his voice to include everyone. "You are just in time," he announced, "to witness the greatest feat"—he flung open a French window to reveal an ornamental iron balcony; some thirty feet below slumbered a small garden—"of all time, in which I defy death, vertigo, and gravity, and in which—"

"Bill," interrupted the Dona Elena, smiling, "these people are thirsty."

Don Bill smote his forehead. "That Barto! Slow as death and not nearly so sure." He hurried out, calling, "Back in a minute. Prepare your nerves."

I GLANCED around the room. The Velezes had taken up America and its ways with a vengeance. A chair beside me was a genuine Tracy Windsor. That three-tiered piecrust table would have been cheap at five hundred. Not that money mattered to our host and hostess. Don Bill the Gaucho was reputed to own vast ancestral acres on the west coast of South America, which had been in the family since the days of the Spanish hidalgos—the Velez name was a power in Spain even today.

They seldom journeyed home. Don Bill, with a passion for sports and the easy informality of North America, found Washington much to his liking and had wangled himself some minor post in his country's embassy as an excuse for remaining. Like so many other foreigners, they had become more North American than ourselves, dressing and comporting themselves as though their heritage was that of New England rather than some gigantic plantation overlooking the Pacific.

I had met them once or twice at parties—they were tremendous favorites with the younger set—but this was the first time I had visited their home.

Dona Elena drifted up. I suspected that Don Bill's delight in risking his neck was more of a strain than she cared to admit. "You, too, will try to persuade Bill, Lieu-tenant?" she begged. "I tell him that counter-espionage is for professionals like Steve and yourself. I say, wait until our country is at war, then fight if you hate the Germans so much." She bit a red lip. "But he is a child," she sighed. "He feels he must be dashing—romantic." Her hand on my arm awakened my pulse. "You'll try?"

Before I could pledge myself to her cause, Don Bill bounced back into the room with three tall frosted glasses. "That Barto!" He shrugged helplessly. "Fumbling the limes, spilling the rum." He dealt out the glasses.

"Now!" he proclaimed. "This one Barto taught me. Did you know he was once a circus acrobat?"

He strode to the balcony, returned seven measured paces to the living-room. Back to the balcony, he spread his tapering legs. His muscles tensed, his eyes narrowed. I sought Dona Elena's face. Her lips were trembling. Dr. Tuila smiled.

"Hola!" Don Bill the Gaucho whipped backward, muscles functioning like tempered steel. Two back flips, smooth and perfect, carried him to the French door. The third shot him corkscrew-wise onto the balcony. My heart skipped a beat. He was going over— No! Those powerful hands met the iron railing.

"Hola!" Don Bill was in a handstand on the railing, feet aloft, toes together. Automatically I set my hands to applaud. The stunt would have taxed a professional; as an amateur's parlor trick it was superb.

I never applauded. Suddenly the figure on the railing, outlined against the glowing summer night, went slack. There was a strangled sound in some throat in the room. I froze. Kaspir sprang for the balcony like a bulky tiger, arms outstretched.

Don Bill went "Uh!" very faintly, and I saw those brown hands slipping. Quietly he slid headfirst from our sight. There was a sickening thud in the garden.

Kaspir peered down, whirled. "Quick!" This to Dr. Tuila. I found myself clattering downstairs behind them. Behind me clicked the high heels of Maude and Dona Elena. We ran out through the lobby and around to the garden. Kaspir kicked open a small iron gate.

Don Bill the Gaucho was on his back, head and shoulders on a flagstone walk, body and legs on the soft turf. The moon touched his wide forehead and straight nose with peaceful highlights.

"Knocked cold," muttered Kaspir, bending over the kneeling Dr. Tuila. This optimistic opinion failed entirely to account for the flat hush which had settled upon us. The angle of Don Bill's neck, something in the position of his limbs....

Dr. Tuila's swift fingers took the pulse, slid under the neck.

Kaspir grunted, "Mike, better call an ambulance."

Dr. Tuila rose and touched Kaspir's arm. The gesture was enough. He didn't even bother to shake his head.

Maude cried, "Mike!" I turned in time to catch Dona Elena as she crumpled.

Dr. Tuila looked sadly at the limp figure in my arms. "Better so," he said gently. "Please carry her upstairs." He took off his checked sports coat and spread it over Don Bill's face. Then he led the way back to the apartment.

I LAID Dona Elena on a bed. Dr. Tuila said, "Call Barto, please. I wish some brandy for her."

I could not bring myself to raise my voice. I went to look for Barto, who, I surmised, was the servant. When I returned with the brandy Dr. Tuila was saying to Kaspir, "Yes, the neck. Broken. An easy death, thank heaven." He took the little glass from me. A minute later Dona Elena coughed and stirred. Her eyes opened to transfix Dr. Tuila with a dreadful question. His voice was very gentle as he told her that Don Bill had died instantaneously and without pain. He turned to me. "Where is Barto? He is their friend."

My throat tightened. Kaspir stared at my white face. I stammered, "I'll get him," and beckoned to Kaspir. Maude followed us through a pantry into a spacious kitchen.

On the waxed floor, in the path of the soft breeze blowing in through the open door, lay a giant of a man, his great belly curving upward. The breeze ruffled his thick black hair. From the left breast of his white duck serving jacket jutted the wooden handle of a kitchen knife. There was almost no blood.

Maude's sharp nails bit into my arm. Kaspir stood over the dead hulk. "So friend Barto had company," he said. He stepped to the open door, glanced out, shook his head. "Quick and dirty," he said. The silence hummed like distant bees.

"Why'd Don Bill's hands slip?" demanded Kaspir suddenly and fiercely. He rammed his hands deep into his pockets. "Let's look upstairs."

We hastened past the bedroom where wept Dona Elena, and mounted to the apartment directly overhead. Kaspir held his thumb against the bell. Ten seconds later he said, "Nuts!" and drove his heavy shoulder against the door. A second lunge did it. Wood splintered.

When we left that place we had learned exactly nothing. The apartment was unoccupied, in order, with no sign of a break-in. We learned later that the Methodist bishop who lived there was on a tour of his diocese.

"Let's go down," said Kaspir shortly, his moon face stormy.

Dr. Tuila was in the hall.

"Gotta talk to Elena," said Kaspir.

Dr. Tuila's sleepy eyes flickered. "She has had a sedative," he protested.

Kaspir brushed him aside and entered the bedroom. Maude was on a chair beside the bed. On the bed Dona Elena's swimming eyes turned to Kaspir as he loomed above her.

"Did Bill tell you anything about that business he was working on?" he asked.

Dona Elena's handsome head turned slowly on the pillow in a movement of negation.

"Didn't think so," said Kaspir brusquely. Then as brusquely, to Dr. Tuila, who had followed us in, "Come outside."

Tuila reddened at the tone. In the hall Kaspir tapped him on the chest. "I'm gonna have to search you, Doctor," he said. "Nope—I ain't got time to argue. That Barto guy's lyin' in the kitchen with a knife in his pump."

TUILA'S JAW dropped. Some of the color drained from his cheeks and he shrugged with the air of a man beyond protest or astonishment.

Kaspir searched him thoroughly, then returned the various oddments he had culled from the pockets.

"Pray, what did you expect to find?" inquired Dr. Tuila icily, re-distributing his belongings about his person.

"I'll be damned if I know," said Kaspir, squinting at him. "Sorry." But he didn't sound as if he meant it.

"Would you show me Barto, please," suggested Dr. Tuila mildly. Kaspir stalked toward the kitchen, Tuila following with short, even steps.

"There will have to be an inquest," he said thoughtfully, as we stood once more over the late Barto.

"Inquest hell," snapped Kaspir ill-naturedly. He draped a handkerchief over the knife handle and pulled. The soughing sound curdled my stomach.

"I beg your pardon," objected Dr. Tuila formally and firmly. "Don Guillermo's death I can certify as accidental, but this—"

"This is private stuff," said Kaspir flatly. "You know me; you know what my job is. I'll have no policemen's big feet tramplin' through this case. And it ain't gettin' in the papers, either."

Dr. Tuila's mouth was obstinate. "Without some authority—"

"I got authority enough right here," said Kaspir. He hauled out a dog-eared leather wallet and from it twitched a gold badge that I had never seen him show before. This he shoved under Dr. Tuila's nose.

Dr. Tuila's gaze lingered on the engraved legend before he looked up. "What do you propose?" he asked, in a different tone.

"Call an undertaker," ordered Kaspir. With Tuila acquiescent, he became less overbearing. "Put 'em both on ice. Tell the undertaker to keep his trap shut till he hears from me."

We left Tuila at a telephone in the pantry and returned to the living-room. Kaspir dropped limply into a deep armchair and looked at me. My head throbbed painfully.

"I'm tired," said Kaspir simply.

The shock almost floored me. The person who has never witnessed Kaspir's childish, consuming pride in his own resiliency, or his equally childish contempt for mortals whose flesh is weaker than his own, can have no idea of the significance of such an admission.

He saw my amazement. "Tired up here, o' course," he qualified irritably, tapping his forehead. "Michaelson gone—Don Bill gone." He drank deeply from one of the frosted glasses, without apparent effect. "Nothin' to work on," he continued. "And all hell at stake."

I felt suddenly ashamed of my preoccupation with my own headache and fatigue. Kaspir's bumptiousness, his posturing vanity, his irritating mannerisms are so obtrusive that I too frequently forget they are no more than protective coloration for a keen mind and a very real and deep sense of obligation and responsibility. I looked at his restless eyes, his drawn mouth, and guessed at some portion of the load he was carrying. I searched my mind for some phrase of decent sympathy.

He read my thoughts, and colored. "If you think I'm gonna let my hair down and cry," he snarled, with some hint of his old manner, "you're mistaken. Now listen, Mike—"

The approach of Dr. Tuila silenced him.

"I have called Ackermann," said the little doctor in a subdued tone. "A first-class undertaker. He will be here soon."

"Then we'll be movin' on," said Kaspir, heaving himself to his feet. His animosity toward Tuila was gone. "Turn 'em over to Ackermann and tell him I'll see him in the morning. If Elena remembers anything, lemme know. Would'ja like to have Maude stick around?"

Tuila nodded gratefully.

"Then tell her Mike and I are shovin' off," said Kaspir. He retrieved his Panama from a hall settee and clapped it on his head.

I STOOD rooted in the hall. "Come on," he urged. I didn't budge. In the dark reaches of my mind a thought had gleamed and vanished like a will-o'-the-wisp, and I was hunting desperately for it. Ackermann? The copper cobra? No. But I was getting warm.

"What's eatin' you?" Kaspir nagged. I hurried back to the kitchen, Kaspir padding behind. I heard myself say, "It must be on the right leg, because I was on the inside." Then to Kaspir, "Roll up his right trouser-leg, will you?"

Kaspir, baffled, knelt by Barto. "Hocus-pocus-diddly-docus," he said. "Shapely little gam." The hairy calf he exposed might have been a section of tree-trunk. "Say, who kicked Superman in the shin?" The bruise was yellow and purple, and the size of a small ashtray.

"Me."

"You?"

"My sandwich-board did," I explained. "That's the garlicky citizen who slugged me and went through my pockets."

Kaspir stood up. For a full minute there was silence. "Very interestin'," he said finally, trying to sound offhand.

"What do we do now?"

"Go home to sleep," he said. " 'Perchance to dream.' "

Which was all I got out of him that night. Nor was he more communicative in the morning when we visited the undertaking parlors of Mr. Henry Ackermann in the block below Aunt Jane's, Inc.

The furnishings of Mr. Ackermann's reception-room bespoke a carriage trade. A somber youth in a dark suit took Kaspir's name and glided out. Soon afterward Acker-mann glided in.

By day, Mr. Ackermann was a very different person from the dandified gentleman of the night before. Now his costume partook of the hush of his establishment, and the amber eyes behind the gold pince-nez were bland as milk. His handshake was a solemn rite, and his hand was so cold that I wondered shudderingly what he had been doing when we came in.

To my surprise, Kaspir showed the gold badge again. "I wanta see the two bodies from the apartment on Blake Street."

"Of course." Ackermann inclined his balding head with professional courtesy. "This way." He ushered us down a carpeted hall.

Kaspir was inexplicably chatty. "Very tragic case," he remarked. "Widow's a beautiful woman; young, too."

Ackermann assented politely. He opened a door at the end of the hall and stood aside. A short flight of steps led down to an extensive basement chamber of white tile. Kaspir clumped down without hesitation, but I had to pause a moment as the chill, heavy atmosphere, with its suggestion of formaldehyde and other potent preservatives, seized me by the throat.

"Which would you like to see first?" Ackermann's words echoed hollowly off the tiles. He approached a sort of giant chest of drawers built into the far wall and fingered one of the shining handles.

"Don't matter," said Kaspir. "Long as they're both here." He tittered. "Mere formality, y'understand?" The person-ality he was projecting was nauseating.

Ackermann pulled gently. The drawer slid out with only the faintest gurgle of ballbearings.

THERE WAS no doubt as to whose clay reposed under that starched sheet. The great arch of the belly was ample identification. But Kaspir must needs pull the sheet down to the waist.

Repairs had been made on Barto. The knife wound was barely visible under the matted hair of the chest, so fine were the stitches.

"Nice," said Kaspir approvingly. Ackermann bowed and smiled. He replaced the sheet expertly, and with one manicured forefinger pushed the drawer. It shut with a click. "Latest type," said Ackermann to Kaspir, as one connoisseur of mortuary equipment to another. "Special refrigeration. And now for the younger man."

Another drawer; same business. I caught my breath as Ackermann displayed the fine features and magnificent shoulders of Don Bill the Gaucho.

I hoped that Kaspir would omit the fuller examination. He did, turning away the instant he had satisfied himself that the marbly face, frozen into a handsome peace, was really that of Don Bill. The click of the drawer had a ghastly finality about it.

"Has any decision been reached on the—ah—destination of the bodies?" asked Ackermann, when we were back in the reception-room. "You see, it makes a difference to me."

Kaspir frowned. "Don't get you."

"Dr. Tuila—charming gentleman, by the way—has indicated the widow's desire that her husband's body be transported back to his native country in South America for final interment; also that of the servant."

"Still don't get you," said Kaspir apologetically.

Ackermann's smile was patient. "A body must be specially prepared for a long journey to a warmer climate." This was not intended as humor. "To put it crudely, Colonel, human remains deteriorate quickly."

Kaspir flushed. "Stupid of me. Of course. Naturally, certain formalities must be observed before the bodies can leave the country by boat. Papers to be signed—that sorta thing. I'll see to it myself. Tell Dr. Tuila so, will you?"

Ackermann dry-washed his slender white hands. The atmosphere of harmony was almost oppressive.

"Capable feller, Tuila," bleated Kaspir. "Has he been in Washington long? I don't seem to recall—"

"Five or six years, I believe," said Ackermann. "Formerly had a large practice in—let me see—"

Kaspir snapped his fingers. "California, wasn't it?"

"Quite right. California it was."

"Well, good day."

"Good day to you, sir."

We hailed a cab. As we passed Aunt Jane's I noted that the cobra was still in the window.

OF THE next three days the less said the better. Kaspir ignored his work and slaved for Dona Elena until Maude and I suspected the worst. He interviewed shipping officials. He saw old acquaintances in the State Department. He pulled strings. On the afternoon of the third day, which was Thursday, Maude and I accompanied him to the Velez apartment and heard him inform Dona Elena that arrangements had been completed to ship the bodies on a freighter leaving Baltimore on Saturday.

Dona Elena managed a pale smile and retired to her bedroom. Dr. Tuila and Kaspir settled the details over a rum punch. The bodies would have to be put into coffins in the presence of government men—since the ship would pass through the Canal—and Kaspir said he would be happy to look after this part. Quarters had been arranged for Dona Elena on the freighter. Dr. Tuila would accompany Dona Elena and the coffins to Baltimore the next day and remain with her until the boat sailed.

On the way back to headquarters Kaspir sloughed his geniality like a snakeskin.

By the way of bait, I said: "Maude and I were thinking of a twirl at the Troika tonight."

"Do your twirlin' on your own time," said Kaspir nastily.

"Have I got any?" I inquired equally nastily, thinking of those endless hours with the sandwich-boards.

"Nope," said Kaspir. That disposed of that.

Maude said: "Of course, if there's something you want us to do...."

"There is." This very grimly. "Just stick around."

So we stuck. It was gruesome. Kaspir, feet on his desk, dozed and fidgeted. Maude and I made feeble pretense of working a crossword puzzle, but our energy petered out and Maude withdrew to the outer office to slumber on a brokenlegged sofa. At eight Kaspir awoke and sent Joe for a box of chocolate cherries, six ham sandwiches, and a half-gallon of coffee.

We ate our way through this clammy collation without enthusiasm. Kaspir then inveigled Maude into a game of cribbage, and I sought to hypnotize myself to sleep by concentrating on the map of the Canal over Kaspir's desk.

I must have slipped into a semi-nightmare. I distinctly recall watching the copper cobra, complete with red glass eyes, wriggle up the wall and onto the map. It swam into the Panama Canal and stuck there. I urged it to move on, pointing out reasonably that it was blocking the Canal, and that it was not wearing its price tag.

The creature hissed. This infuriated me. "You know you're no good without your price tag," I told it.

"What's no good without a price tag?" boomed a voice from nowhere.

I strained at the shackles of sleep, determined to prove my point. "The cobra, of course," I cried. "The price tag belongs on its jaw."

Then lights shone in my eyes and I awoke, heart pounding, hands and face bathed in sweat. Maude and Kaspir were standing over me. I squinted past them at the wall map. The cobra was still there, still covering the Canal.

"Wake up, Mike," said Maude. "You've had a nightmare." But Kaspir asked, in a queer voice, "What's that about a cobra?"

I stretched and knuckled my eyes. Needles of sleep pricked my legs. I laughed weakly. "The cobra from Aunt Jane's window," I said. "It just fitted the Panama Canal—tail in Panama City and head in Colon." The prickly sensation was moving up my spine now. "It just fitted," I repeated.

Kaspir said, "Shut up," and stared at the map. Then, very slowly, as though the slightest haste might disorder his thoughts, he opened a desk drawer and produced an automatic pistol with a stubby silencer fitted to its nose. This he handed over. "Get down to the hot dog joint and get into those sandwich-boards," he told me. "Flash your badge if the guy argues. Then be outside Aunt Jane's in twenty minutes." He grimaced impatiently as I glanced down at my suit. "No time to get into your old duds. Get movin'."

EXACTLY TWENTY minutes later I was outside Aunt Jane's, Inc., sandwich-boards and all. I would have been there sooner but that, remembering my experience with Barto, I lacerated Joey the Litvak's finest feelings by carving the "O" out of "Hot" on the front board in case I had to use the gun. And Kaspir had not handed me that gun as an idle jest.

Headlights shone on the cobra as a taxi pulled in to the curb. The price tag was no longer on the jaws. It had been moved down to a curve nearer the base. The price was visible now: $8.25.

Maude got out of the cab and waited until it had pulled around the corner before she came over to me. "Steve wants the snake," she said. "He says to—"

"Wait." I pulled her away from the window as a dark figure in top hat and tails approached. What Ackermann the undertaker thought about a modishly dressed young woman chatting with a sandwich-man I could not guess. He stopped at the window and lit a cigarette, keeping the match alight, I thought, an unnecessarily long while.

When he strolled on, Maude slipped off a high-heeled shoe and limped over to the window. I wandered to the corner and sauntered back, whistling. I saw her arm draw back.

The crash of plate glass was like an exploding bomb in that quiet street. The first blow was not enough. She swung again. I hastened up with some vague idea of using the butt of my pistol. Then I saw the top-hatted figure sprinting toward us in the shadows.

I intercepted Ackermann not a yard from Maude, who was gamely reaching in for the cobra. When he found me blocking him, one white-cuffed wrist went to a hip pocket.

I fired through the hole where the "O" had been, blessing my foresight. In the heat of the moment I aimed at his heart. I am a poor shot. Ackermann screamed hoarsely and his gun clanked on the sidewalk.

Maude said, "Bring him along," and started off with her loot. The cobra's head leered at me over her shoulder. I shoved Ackermann after her, and he stumbled along moaning over his shattered hand.

Colonel Kaspir, waiting in the doorway of Ackermann's place, hustled the three of us inside. In the reception-room the somber youth trembled in his dark suit, his face the color of skimmed milk. When he saw Ackermann he tried to speak, but couldn't.

Kaspir seized the youth's arm. "You know what you're to do?" The boy nodded, terrified, and ran from the room. Kaspir wheeled on Ackermann. "Keep quiet, man!" But Ackermann continued to moan and held up his injured hand as a dog holds up a hurt paw. Kaspir hit him with merciful efficiency on the point of the chin and carried the limp body to an inner office.

"Only got a few minutes," he said when he returned. "Stow those boards away, Mike. Maude, put that conceited-lookin' cockatrice you're totin' on the desk." He himself stepped over to the mantel and examined a pair of fat blackout candles.

Outside, taxi brakes squealed. "Siddown," hissed Kaspir. Maude and I tumbled into chairs. Kaspir lounged against the mantel.

We heard the front door bang open, then a woman's voice, hysterical, calling for Ackermann.

"Come in," shouted Kaspir.

She burst into the reception-room, blinking at the lights. Terror had wiped most of the beauty from Dona Elena's face. She glanced wildly around the room. "Where's Mr. Ackermann? He called me—said something was wrong—"

"Something is." Kaspir nodded solemnly. "That was me called you. Siddown."

I shoved a chair forward just in time. It was not until she was seated, I think, that Dona Elena recognized us.

Kaspir stamped his foot twice and every light in the building went out.

THE SUDDEN darkness choked me. Maude gasped, "Mike!" Something scraped and flared in Kaspir's hand. He held the match to the blackout candles. They flickered up into a steady flame.

Dona Elena leaned forward, a hand at her throat.

"Bodies deteriorate quickly when the refrigeratin' device goes off, so Ackermann tells me," remarked Kaspir from the mantel. By some chance combination of light and shadow his beefy face appeared as though suspended in mid-air. "It's off now, Elena."

"You must turn it on," said Dona Elena Velez thickly. She gripped the arms of her chair. "You don't know—"

"Don't I?" asked Kaspir softly.

She flinched as though he had hit her in the face. "What do you want?" she pleaded, in that same thick voice.

"Straight answers," replied Kaspir quickly. "What's that cobra for?" She glanced in the direction of his pointing finger. I saw her stiffen, saw her frightened eyes harden and her lips become a straight line.

"It oughta be gettin' kind o' stuffy in those drawers down in Ackermann's morgue," said Kaspir calmly. "I wouldn't care to wake up in one o' those cubbyholes."

Maude's voice was brittle. "For God's sake answer him, Elena!"

"The cobra's the Canal," said Dona Elena suddenly. "You knew that. Now will you turn on the current?"

Kaspir held up a huge hand. "What's the price tag for?"

"To show the position of the new locks. For the love of heaven, Steve!"

"What do the figures on the tag mean?"

"The code name of the man we were to contact on the ship." The words were coming with a rush now.

"Did Dan Perkins send the dope on the new lock to his ma?" She nodded. "Then why'd Mrs. Perkins use the cobra? Why didn't she just call Don Bill or Tuila?"

"Because she knew she was being watched. The cobra was for emergencies like that. Oh, Steve, please!"

"Tuila doped out this refrigeratin' gag, I suppose?" Again she nodded desperately. "But how'd you figure on getting air to your hubby on the boat?"

"The coffin, you fool. Ackermann fixed that. A panel inside, hidden. When you slide it back there are air-holes."

"One last thing." Kaspir was hurrying his words now. Dona Elena was cracking up. In another minute she would be useless to us. "How were the explosives to go on board. I think I can guess, but—"

She nodded for the last time. "Barto," she said, and I thought I saw Kaspir shiver a little.

"Before you scream and faint," he told her, "lemme tell you that the refrigeratin' plant in Ackermann's morgue ain't on the regular building circuit—just in case of emergencies like this." Incredulous relief flooded Dona Elena's face. Kaspir thrust out his under lip. "You don't think I'd let my old pal Don Bill the Gaucho spoil on my hands, do you? Listen, sister, when he's defrosted, it's gonna be under proper conditions, because I'm gonna hang him for killin' Barto."

He thumped twice with his heel on the floor and the lights came on. The frightened assistant was obeying his cues.

"REASON WE never had a line on any o' this gang before," said Kaspir, "is that they been savin' them for this Canal fiesta. Didn't let 'em mess with petty stuff. Kept their noses clean for the big day. If Michaelson hadn't got that hunch on Perkins down in Panama...."

We were still in the reception-room. Kaspir said we were waiting for "the bomb squad," whatever he meant by that.

"This was their super-dooper extra-special ace in the hole," he continued. "No crude stuff like plantin' bombs in packin' cases for the inspectors to find. This idea had brains and guts behind it, and good timin', and it called for two coffins and two corpses.

"One coffin was to contain a corpse *and* explosives. The other was to contain a corpse that could rise and touch off the explosives in the first coffin—at the proper time—which was when the ship was nestlin' in those new locks in the Canal.

"You see the problem. They don't let corpses go on ships these days without at least a cursory inspection of 'em—particularly when the ship's goin' through the Canal. The problem was to turn Don Bill into a corpse that would pass inspection, yet not ruin him permanently.

"Don Bill faked that garden business, o'course. He took that plunge deliberately. While we ran downstairs, he arranges his neck to look broken. Doc Tuila goes hocus-pocus over him and pronounces him dead. He throws his coat over him, and Dona Elena diverts our attention by faintin' artistically.

"But at first I couldn't fit Barto in. Because Barto was dead. That I knew. It looked like Don Bill had stabbed Barto when he stepped out to help with the drinks that night. But why?

"Tuila and Ackermann had laid their plans to turn Don Bill into what you might call the workin' corpse. In Los Angeles in '35 a doc named Willard quick-froze monkeys, huntin' a cure for T.B. He found he could freeze a monkey stiff as death for three-four days and thaw him out good as new, or better. He swore it'd work on humans, but the D.A. wouldn't let him try it. And Tuila was in Los Angeles in '35, and I don't doubt he picked up some o' Willard's technique.

"Tuila and Ackermann fixed up one o' those morgue drawers downstairs with special freezin' coils. That's where they put Don Bill that night he 'died.' And the next day—remember, Mike?—we could ha' sworn he was dead.

"You get it now. Dan Perkins writes his mother (an arranged code that Tancred's boys couldn't break down) and gives her the location of the new lock. Old Lady Perkins arranges the price tag on the cobra. Ackermann drops by, strikes a match, and picks up the information, which he was to turn over to Dona Elena tomorrow morning.

"The coffins are ready. Government men'll witness Barto's and Don Bill's bodies bein' put in 'em. They'll seal 'em. Once aboard the lugger and everything's jake. There a stooge in the crew who'll slip Don Bill grub and spring him at the proper time, which is when the boat is in the new locks. Bill fixes the fuse on Barto's coffin, then he and Elena and the stooge'll scram for the stern and take their chance when the bow o' the boat blows up and takes the new locks with it. *And,* the Atlantic fleet, which was to have passed through that way a little later, will have to take the long way around through wolf packs o' subs, and get where it's goin' about a month late."

"BUT WHY did Barto slug me?" I demanded.

"They suspected you, Mike, seein' you in front o' Aunt Jane's every day. They couldn't take chances. Lucky you didn't have a badge on you that night, or Barto might have—"

"You keep talking about blowing up Barto's coffin," objected Maude indignantly. "How could they have it full of explosives right under the nose of the government men?"

"It wasn't the coffin that was loaded," said Kaspir.

"But you said—"

"Some boys from the F.B.I. bomb squad are droppin' by here in a few minutes," said Kaspir. "You can watch 'em if you want. They'll take a sharp knife and run it real easy—real, real easy—along that big belly o' Barto's, and I'll give you seven to one they find Ackermann and Tuila have got him stuffed like a turkey with TNT half-pints, or one o' them new explosives."

Colonel Kaspir yawned cavernously. "It was a real pretty set-up they had," he said. "Just think, Maude, it would ha' worked, but for one thing."

"What?"

"Me."

HAND, EARS, AND TONGUE

CHARLIE WU SNAPPED THE CORD THAT BOUND THE LITTLE BROWN BOX, OPENED IT AND LIFTED OUT A STRIP OF PAPER NEATLY PRINTED WITH JAPANESE CHARACTERS. "THE HAND GIVEN IN FALSE FRIENDSHIP," WU TRANSLATED SOFTLY; "THE EARS THAT HEARD AND RETAINED; THE TONGUE THAT BETRAYED...."

CHAPTER ONE
CHARLIE WU OF HARVARD

IF CERTAIN of Colonel Kaspir's actions during the course of this story outrage your sense of what is fitting in a highly-placed Government servant, I can plead only that Colonel Kaspir is Colonel Kaspir, and that war is war.

Maude answered the phone that summer morning in Kaspir's office, high in the brownstone ex-boarding house in southwest Washington which has served as the headquarters of Section Five since the early days of 1940. She turned to Kaspir: "New York calling."

The chief of Section Five, dozing uneasily in his swivel chair after a night of calls to the West Coast, made grumbling noises in his throat.

Maude's long, red-nailed fingers worried Kaspir's beefy shoulder a second.

"Unless somebody is kidding me," she said, "it's a Lieutenant Wu calling."

Kaspir sat up and stared at her through a fog of sleep. "Gimme that phone. That's Charlie Wu." His great hand closed around the phone and he went "Huh?" Then he settled back with the receiver at his ear and seemed to be taking a nap. Then he made an unintelligible sound and hung up. He struggled to his feet, yawned a mighty yawn, and reeled to the wall closet, fumbling therein for his coat and hat. "Why ain't you callin' the plane?" he asked irritably.

Maude raised her eyebrows at me. "What plane?" she said resignedly. "When, to where, and how many reservations?"

Kaspir turned. "New York plane," he said patiently, as though he had explained this a dozen times already. "Charlie Wu's waitin' for us."

Maude compressed her lips and began to dial the airport. "Are Mike and I going?" she inquired.

"O' course." Kaspir wrestled into his white linen coat and pulled his beloved Panama down almost over his ears. "Wha'd you think you two were gonna do—sit here and play post-office?"

He yawned again and lumbered out while Maude was reserving three places on the next plane for New York. I followed him down the dim old stairway. Before we reached the ground floor, Maude was treading on my heels, swearing under her breath as she tried to adjust a picture hat over the blond perfection of her hair.

Joe, the Negro houseboy, whose intuition is a wonderful thing, was waiting in the downstairs hall.

"Goin' New York," mumbled Kaspir, rubbing his eyes. "Be back some time. Murray Lane Hotel. S'long."

Joe's grin flashed at Maude and me like a green light. He swung the front door open just in time to prevent Kaspir from walking right through the glass.

The taxi was there, all right, like a coach-and-four conjured up by a fairy godmother. Kaspir, with the usual selfish wriggle of his broad hips, appropriated an even half of the available seating space. I could not complain, for it brought Maude and me very close, and the fragrance of her

We stared in horror at the objects
laid out on the drain board.

honeysuckle perfume and the soft pressure of her shoulder
and hip made me forget my weariness.

"Who's Charlie Wu?" snapped Maude, as Kaspir's lids
were closing over his wide, baby-blue eyes.

"Head of our New York office," muttered Kaspir as
though exasperated at her not knowing. "I pinched him
off the Alien Squad. Valentine's sore as hell."

I felt Maude stiffen. "I didn't know we had a 'New
York office.' I don't know this Charlie Wu, and his name
isn't on our payroll." Her tone was sharp. Maude, among
other duties, is charged with the thankless task of keeping

Section Five's records, and only a thick streak of purely feminine stubbornness has kept her from chucking the whole effort a hundred times.

"I put him in last week," murmured Kaspir, reddening. "Meant to tell you. Slipped my mind."

MAUDE HAD to laugh. The situation was so typical of Kaspir's methods that it stood forth as a shining and practically flawless example of the office efficiency of Section Five. Yet Kaspir has a religious belief that he runs his peculiar department with a machine-like precision which other Washington agencies—including Army Intelligence and the F.B.I.—would do well to copy.

Kaspir accordingly resented that laugh. He roused himself and half opened his eyes. "Can't think of everything," he protested shrewishly. "Forgot you and Mike gotta have blueprints before you can wipe your noses."

Maude's blistering glare shut him up. He closed his eyes again and affected sleep. He broke his silence only twice on the plane. The first time he held a mammoth bag of chocolate cherries over his shoulder and under our noses and croaked: "Have some goo?" It was then shortly after eight A.M. The second time, just as we were gliding down a long incline of summer air into LaGuardia Field, he said: "Shouldn't wonder if this call o' Charlie's don't have something to do with that bit o' glass."

I rummaged in my mind for an explanation of this cryptic remark. Then I recalled a week-old conversation dealing with "Pool's 7," which is the Army's unofficial designation of the optical formula for the new bombsight lens.

Beside me, Maude sat up a little straighter. "Pool's 7" was hot stuff. With it, as Kaspir had said the week before, a bombardier could "drop a marble down a drain from 30,000 feet"—and he meant it almost literally.

The last of my weariness vanished. Counter-espionage, especially as practiced under Colonel Kaspir in Section Five, can be the most wearing of all professions. But it has its moments, and the mere mention of "Pool's 7" made this one of them. Kaspir hates plane travel; it turns him green. Yet his instantaneous response to the mysterious call from the equally mysterious Charlie Wu was clear proof that this jaunt, for all of Kaspir's elaborately casual manner, was no pleasure hop.

My own interest in meeting Charlie Wu increased, and when Kaspir pointed him out as he strode across the sunbaked airport to meet us I was not disappointed.

Maude hummed in my ear: "Did you ever see a safe walking? Well, I do." Her imagery was perfect. That was what Charlie Wu reminded me of, a safe. He was slightly under five and a half feet, and his cubical figure, neatly draped in dark blue gabardine, looked as solid and uncomprehending as a bank vault. A gray snapbrim shaded his almond eyes, and the lower part of his face was as round and childlike as Kaspir's. One thing spoiled the balance of his appearance: his arms belonged by rights to a man of Kaspir's towering build. When he raised his hat I noted with more than a mild shock that Charlie Wu had no ears.

Charlie Wu's broad hand met Kaspir's big paw and I thought I saw Kaspir wince a trifle.

"Allee samee velly nice day, Cholly," said Kaspir amiably. Maude and I had brought up against his broad back and the four of us stood like a river rock in the eddying stream of passengers. Behind us, on the field, motors spat and roared unceasingly.

"Allee samee big piece fine day," agreed Lieutenant Wu gravely. His friendly eyes included Maude and me in the quiet warmth of his welcome, and I thought I saw a faint gleam behind them. "You plenty fat, boss man."

Kaspir coughed, and I knew he was drawing in his tummy. He stood aside and waved his hand toward Maude and me. "Missie Maude Number One girl, Section Five," he said by way of introduction. "Captain Mike Kettle, Number One boy."

Lieutenant Wu bowed. Maude and I bowed.

"Taxi wait," said Lieutenant Wu, and led the way.

THE CAB spun away from the airport and Lieutenant Wu doffed his hat and laid it in his lap. He looked at Kaspir.

"Somebody's fingers itchin' for that bit o' glass?" inquired Kaspir, glancing out of the window.

"Too soon to tell," said Lieutenant Wu. "Perhaps. But I rather think it's something else." His accent was now reminiscent of Harvard Square and a chord of memory vibrated in my mind.

"You played end in '31," I said.

Lieutenant Wu smiled. "I left college junior year," he said. "You were the shining light of old Barrett's English Three about then."

He caught me staring at his lack of ears; so did Kaspir. I flushed. Wu's smile broadened.

"Charlie interfered with some Jap sailors smugglin' silk on the docks a couple years back," said Kaspir unfeelingly. "They pruned his head for him."

"It's amazing how well you can get along without them," said Lieutenant Wu to Maude.

"What's this clambake you promised me?" inquired Kaspir.

"I ran into Stuyvesant Cooper at the Harvard Club last night," said Lieutenant Wu. "His Jap houseboy has something on his mind. I asked him to bring the boy over to my place this morning. I thought you might be interested." He glanced at the yellow gold watch on his thick wrist. I had a feeling that he was holding back his climax. So did Kaspir.

"Spill it, spill it," he commanded irritably, squirming and nearly unseating Maude as the cab turned into Lexington Avenue.

Lieutenant Wu considered. "The boy claims to have proof"—you could feel him picking his words—"that the Den-Kaigi has an active branch in New York."

Kaspir sat up straight rapping his head against the ceiling.

"Also," continued Lieutenant Wu delicately, as though fingering a Ming vase, "the boy tells Cooper that the Den-Kaigi is working with the German crowd here."

"I'll be damned if I believe that!" exploded Kaspir. "That's against the Den-Kaigi's house rules."

Maude tapped a cigarette on her dull gold case and a lighter appeared like magic in Charlie Wu's hand.

"And now," said Maude, a shade bitterly, through the smoke, "for the sixty-four dollar question. What's the Den-Kaigi?"

Lieutenant Wu was framing a courteous reply when Kaspir cut in impatiently: "One o' those Jap secret societies—all high-rig-a-ma-jig and ceremony. You gotta have nine thousand ancestors to make the inner circle, but they ain't above usin' hoi polloi for their knife work."

A scream from the taxi's brakes killed the question that was hovering in my throat. We had stopped at a small, false-front apartment house in the late Sixties, East. Charlie Wu led us up one flight and into a small service apartment furnished in Swedish modern, like a hotel. He twitched the cord of a Venetian blind and peered from the front window.

"They're on time," he said. We heard a cab door slam. "That's Stuy's way."

Colonel Kaspir abandoned his nonchalance and began to pace the floor. Maude touched my arm lightly. Her violet eyes had turned diamond-bright, as they do when she is excited.

Lieutenant Wu moved stolidly to the hall door and ushered in a very tall man with a lean, brown face, and a short individual whose cheeks were pasty yellow. Stuyvesant Cooper's narrow shoulders are bowed under a great family name and a greater family fortune. He possesses the grand manner and is the greatest yachtsman in the world, but even Lieutenant Wu's courtesy could not conceal the fact that we were anxious to get the formalities over with and hear what the little yellow man had to say.

Stuyvesant Cooper introduced the yellow man as Komagichi Yesuda, his "servant and friend." He was about to elaborate on this introduction when I think he sensed the urgency in our attitudes. He said, "Please tell them what you told me, Gichi," and sat back in his chair.

CHAPTER TWO
THE BUTTERFLY

"**MY BROTHER** and I were brought to the United States when I was five and he was eight," said Komagichi Yesuda. He spoke with—if there is such a thing—a New York accent. His lips were thin, and there was none of the buck-teeth-and-thick-glasses look of the cartoon Jap about him. "Our parents were employed by Mr. Cooper's father. I have served Mr. Cooper since the death of his parents and mine. The United States is my country."

"Where's your brother now?" put in Colonel Kaspir.

"Here—in New York. He has a small bakery—the Oriental—on Tenth Avenue," said Yesuda. He waited politely for further questions, but Kaspir waved him on.

"Have you ever been back to Japan?" asked Lieutenant Wu, as Yesuda's lips parted to resume his story.

"My brother and I visited relatives in Japan in 1932," replied Yesuda. "We stayed only four months. We did not care for it much."

"Please go on," said Wu, leaning back, his liquid eyes as still and even as a millpond.

"Several days ago—Monday, to be exact—I received a phone call from a man I did not know. He said that his name was Shintaro Kato, and that he was a Japanese-born

American," continued Yesuda's soft voice. "He said that a group of New York Japanese were banding together to aid the American war effort, and invited me to the meeting.

"I was interested. I suggested that he call my brother Kanju. He did. Kanju was interested, too. We attended the meeting together. It was held in some clubrooms on lower Third Avenue."

Komagichi Yesuda put his fingertips together and bowed his head a moment. When he continued, there was just the suggestion of a tremor in his voice.

"The meeting," he said, "was not as represented. Only four men were present besides Kanju and I. They informed us, without beating around the bush, that they represented the Den-Kaigi, and intimated that it is well-established in New York."

I saw Wu's eyes waver ever so slightly in Kaspir's direction. Kaspir stared at his fingernails and began to pat the floor with a large foot.

"To make a long story short, gentlemen," said Yesuda, and there was no mistaking the fear in him now, "my brother and I joined the Den-Kaigi. Not as full members, of course; full membership is a very select affair. We were taken in as 'kumi'—that is, affiliate members who work under orders." Yesuda's almost translucent hands were trembling. "We were not invited to join," he murmured. "We were simply informed that we were members working under strict orders. We were instructed to return Thursday night—tonight—and receive certain assignments. There is no doubt that espionage of some sort, or even sabotage, will be involved."

For a few seconds there was silence.

"No use asking why you didn't refuse to join," said Wu.

Komagichi Yesuda smiled palely. "Then you know something of the Den-Kaigi. Kanju and I heard about it first from our parents. We heard of it also in Tokyo in 1932. There was something very deadly, sir,"—this to Kaspir—"in the calm assumption of Shintaro Kato that Kanju and I would obey orders."

KASPIR NODDED solemnly. His customary bumptiousness seemed to have received a knockout blow. "What about the Gestapo?" he said.

"There is apparently a definite working agreement between the Den-Kaigi and the Gestapo branch in New York," said Yesuda earnestly. "Once my brother and I were members, Shintaro Kato and the others talked quite freely over some wine we all shared. For example, no secret was made of the fact that tonight German submarines will shell Virginia Beach, on the Virginia coast, and a new shipbuilding plant below Wilmington, North Carolina—while a Japanese submarine off Los Angeles will stage the first bombing of an American city."

Maude made a quick sound of unbelief. A prickly sensation mounted my spine rung by rung and lost itself in the short hairs at the base of my skull. But Kaspir only nodded without amazement, and Lieutenant Wu, hands folded across his hard belly, crossed his legs.

"Plane from a sub, I suppose?" said Kaspir conversationally, and Yesuda nodded.

Kaspir looked impatiently at the surprise on my face and Maude's. "The speech—the speech!" he snapped. Then I got it. The President was to speak that night. The Japs had pulled the same trick before—a token shelling to steal headlines. Only this time they would sacrifice a small plane from one of their giant subs in the interests of bigger type.

"That is all the exact information that was given in my presence," concluded Komagichi Yesuda. "I might mention that there is a short-wave radio set concealed in a standard RGA-Acme set in the clubrooms. Also, just at the very end, there was talk about some mutual assistance deal that the Den-Kaigi and the Gestapo have made here...."

"Ha!" exclaimed Kaspir. He was on his feet now, and his bulk seemed to fill a corner of the room.

"It seems," said Yesuda, "as though the Den-Kaigi recently assisted the Gestapo materially in some enterprise. In return, the Gestapo has undertaken to deliver something—I do not know what—to the Den-Kaigi. But that apparently will not take place for a day or so. Shintaro Kato talked as though the Gestapo's gift to the Den-Kaigi will be of immense value."

Komagichi Yesuda looked hesitantly from Cooper to Lieutenant Wu, and I saw that his mask had completely fallen away. There was raw fear in his small brown eyes, and his mouth had begun to twitch like a hysterical woman's.

"If I might have a small glass of something," he whispered, as though afraid to raise his voice. His lips had gone greenish-white.

Lieutenant Wu moved very swiftly for such a solid figure. It seemed as though the request had barely reached his ears—or rather, the place where his ears had been—when he was back in the room with a water glass half full of brandy for the little yellow man. Yesuda tossed it off gratefully and his eyes watered.

Kaspir was standing over him. "I don't like to ask a guy to do something that 'ud give me the heebie-jeebies to do myself," he said slowly. "But you're in a cleft stick, Yesuda."

I saw Yesuda, by force of will, make his eyes meet Kaspir's.

"I think I understand, sir," he said. "I shall have to attend the meeting tonight. But in the future—"

"We'll get in touch with you through Mr. Cooper," said Kaspir quickly. "I might's well give it to you straight. If I'd known what you were gonna tell us, I wouldn't have let you come here today. But that's done now, and we can't help it. In the future you'll take no more chances than you have to." Some of his unwonted seriousness left Kaspir's manner. He held out his hand. "You're a rare, delicate plant right now, Yesuda. We wanta keep you blooming for selfish reasons. You go to that meeting tonight and pass on the dope to Mr. Cooper. Cooper, you meet us at—say—Pierre's, around noon, and dish out the dirt over some grub."

KOMAGICHI YESUDA stood up, squaring his thin shoulders. His small hand disappeared inside Kaspir's in a brief handshake. In that moment, as his sleeve slid back an inch or two, we all saw the butterfly tattooed on his wrist just above the hand. He saw our eyes on the mark and pushed the sleeve farther back.

"My father put that there," he said, smiling. "He learned the art in Japan, when he was a boy. My brother has one too, and—"

He glanced at his employer. Stuyvesant Cooper laughed as he shoved back his own cuff and sleeve. His butterfly was identical to that of Yesuda. The colors, the shadings, were exquisite.

"Takakimi—that was Gichi's father—put one on me, too," said Cooper. "Much against his better judgment and after much begging on my part. My mother raised particular cain when she saw it, but I think the artistry of the thing won her over."

"My father was a real artist," said Yesuda proudly. He looked Lieutenant Wu in the eye and the corners of his mouth spread with a humor that was purely American. "Just a trifle above the Chinese art, wouldn't you say, Lieutenant?"

"Perhaps," admitted Wu. He took down the address of the Den-Kaigi clubrooms, then opened the door for Cooper and his valet-friend. "See you at Pierre's tomorrow, Stuy," he said, as they left. The door closed softly and Wu turned thoughtfully to Kaspir.

"Looks as though we've struck oil," he said. "Although I hate to trust any Jap."

"Where's your phone, Charlie?" said Kaspir. "We'll put a double-check on that story of Yesuda's that'll X-ray it right to the core."

"How?" This from Maude, skeptically.

"Get Tancred to arrange a reception committee for those babies tonight," he explained with a patience that was more galling to Maude than any caustic comeback. "If they show up on schedule we'll know we've got something. If they don't, I'm gonna take a personal interest in Mr. Yesuda's private life that'll surprise even him."

He stalked out to the phone, which was in the hall, and immediately embroiled himself in a heated controversy with the long-distance operator because she could not get Major General Altemus Tancred, of Army Intelligence, on the line in something under twenty seconds. There was an extended interlude of argument and rude sarcasm. Then Kaspir bumbled back full of his triumph over Tancred's natural skepticism about Yesuda's story. Tancred had promised to arrange for the receptions on both coasts.

That night at our hotel, when we were sitting by the phone waiting for a report from Tancred's office regarding the outcome of the submarine affair, Kaspir was more fidgety than usual. I think he was on the verge of admitting that he had been completely taken in by Yesuda's yarn. But the telephone saved him, and for the next half-hour his face was the face of a man who has discovered a Titian in a pawnshop.

You read about it, I'm sure. Our little yellow friend had been accurate to the last gasp. While the President's speech was still going on, two PT boats and a pair of Navy dive-bombers located and boxed that giant Jap sub off Los Angeles. Her plane never got out of its deck-hangar. And on the East Coast, dancers at Virginia Beach ran down on the sand and cheered as night bombers clipped a U-boat a scant two miles offshore. The one on the Carolina coast lobbed a couple of three-inchers ashore before they found her, then crash-dived and got away. But there was oil on the beach the next day, and other evidence that she was crippled.

Kaspir and Maude and I turned in and slept the sleep of the righteous dead. Next morning, we gulped our food, then fidgeted for two solid hours while the hands of the clock crawled toward their noon rendezvous.

Lieutenant Wu was waiting outside Pierre's, and even from a distance we could see the worry on his normally placid face.

"What's eatin' you?" inquired Kaspir brusquely.

Charlie Wu glanced up and down the busy, sunlit street before he answered. "I got the wind up about half an hour ago," he said uneasily. "I called Stuy Cooper's place. No answer."

Kaspir chuckled. "Mrs. Cooper's prob'ly out havin' her hair curled," he suggested. "Yesuda's buyin' bacon and beans for the evenin' meal and Cooper's down at his broker's gnawin' his knuckles over Amapola Copper."

"I hope you're right," said Charlie Wu.

FORTY-FIVE MINUTES later it became painfully apparent that Kaspir was wrong—badly wrong. He admitted it himself in his own eccentric way—by bundling us suddenly into a cab and bellowing at the driver to drive like hell to Cooper's address in the middle Seventies. He continued to bellow at the driver, with such effect that when we debarked before a sumptuous apartment house I was forced to lend Maude an arm for support. By the time I had finished paying the angry driver and piloting Maude to the second floor, Kaspir and Lieutenant Wu had already tired of pressing the Cooper bell and were preparing to put their shoulders against the door.

It was a solid door. But Kaspir is a deceptively solid man, and Charlie Wu is constructed of some sort of animated granite. The third time they hit it, the lock parted company from the wood with a shriek and we found ourselves in a hall almost oppressive with quiet luxury.

It was several minutes before we located the Coopers. They came to light as four staring eyes in a bedroom clothes closet. Their bonds of sheeting were miracles of efficient craftsmanship, and their gags of powder puffs and sheeting no less admirable.

Mrs. Cooper, a stately brunette, was regal until her knees gave way and she was borne off by Maude and put to bed. I'm afraid my own nerves had been slightly jangled by the past twenty-four hours, for I had to battle an absurd impulse to giggle as we delivered New York's most impressive male socialite from mummylike wrappings and watched him gargle away the particles of his wife's dusting powder which had collected in his throat from the powder puff which had occupied his aristocratic mouth for nearly twelve long hours.

I recovered my gravity quickly enough when Cooper told his tale. It was chilling in its brevity and implications.

Cooper's first question was about Yesuda. Kaspir and Wu shook their heads in unison. Yesuda was not in the apartment. Of that they had made sure.

It seemed that Cooper and his wife had gone to the theater, returning shortly after midnight. Cooper had gone to Yesuda's room hoping to hear about the Den-Kaigi meeting, but Yesuda was asleep, so Cooper decided that morning would be time enough.

Not long after Cooper and his wife had retired he had been awakened by a light in his eyes. Beside the light he saw a gun. He turned his head to look at his wife's bed. Two dark figures were already busy there. Cooper tried to rise, but at least two men forced him back and began to bind him. A minute later he was tumbled into the clothes closet. Beside him, to his immense relief, he felt his wife.

Stuyvesant Cooper stood up, massaging his cramped limbs. Kaspir's face was red and stormy.

"The little yeller feller was tellin' the truth," said Kaspir softly. "He must ha' gone to the meetin'. Then, after he left, the high muck-a-mucks sat up for the returns on the short wave. When they heard what happened, they added two and two and got Komagichi. So they came for him."

Lieutenant Wu, who had stepped out of the room, returned, enveloped in gloom. "I've checked with the police," he said. He shook his head.

"Did'ja check the flower show?" demanded Kaspir sourly. "He might be under a potted plant. Listen, Charlie, you get hold of some o' your old pals from the Alien

Squad, and we'll step down to that Den-Kaigi hang-out and take a look."

"They're meeting us two blocks from there in ten minutes," said Charlie Wu.

THE RAID on the Den-Kaigi clubrooms—four plainly furnished rooms over a nondescript saloon on lower Third Avenue, was depressingly nonproductive. There was nobody home, and no indication that anyone would ever return. Kaspir meditatively drove his heel through the expensive short-wave set concealed in a big cabinet-model RGA-Acme while Charlie Wu and three silent, thick-set efficient members of the Alien Squad went through the place with a fine-tooth comb.

The one real find told everything. Behind the conference room was a smaller chamber whose furniture included a long table of heavy wood. There was quite a bit of blood on this table, and some had dripped to the floor. In the wood were several indentations, evidently from the blade of some cutting tool.

"I wonder," said Kaspir thoughtfully, staring at the table, "just what that blade passed through before it hit wood."

Maude, pale as skimmed milk, set her shoulders and left the room with what dignity she could muster. A pang almost like a sickness settled in my chest as I thought of the mild and mannerly Komagichi Yesuda being led into this room by his fellow-members of the Den-Kaigi. I wondered what had become of the brother Kanju.

Kaspir and Wu were wondering the same thing. Not a dozen words were spoken as we left the Alien Squad in charge and joined Maude on the sidewalk. Wu hailed a cab. I asked Maude if she wanted to go back to the hotel, but she shook her head grimly.

Ten minutes later we pulled up in front of a retiring little establishment across whose fly-specked window marched peeling gold letters: *Oriental Bakery*.

Kaspir said: "Better see what the neighbors think of Kanju first." He asked Wu to wait in the cab with Maude. We became investigators for a credit union and made the rounds of the block checking on Kanju Yesuda's rating for the new list we were supposedly compiling.

SEVERAL STORE owners informed us flatly that Kanju Yesuda was a spy and should have been taken up by the F.B.I. long before—but under some bullying by Kaspir they admitted that their evidence of Kanju's treason was confined solely to the color of his skin and the name of his race. In that whole block we obtained only one interview that yielded anything like a thoughtful and honest estimate of Kanju Yesuda.

This came from an undertaker named Williams, a ruddy-faced man with an Irish cast of countenance. In the dead air of his reception-parlor, amid coffins that yawned with cheap pink satin mouths, Williams told Kaspir in no uncertain terms that Kanju Yesuda was an unjustly maligned Jap. Williams had evidently had words with some of the neighboring tradesmen on the subject.

"I've known the little guy a dozen years, off and on," he orated belligerently. "He wouldn't fool me a minute if he wasn't right. But these harpies around here can't seem to get the idea that this is a democracy. They want him lynched on general principles. I told one Hunky yesterday: 'Yesuda's been in this country longer'n you have. He don't go around squawkin' that you're a spy just because you don't talk English as good as he can.' The guy got sore. I told him: 'All right, put up your dukes.'" Williams gazed affectionately at his beefy red fist. "But he wouldn't. He went off and begun to whisper to Ike Cohen. They'll be puttin' me down for a spy next. Then I'll hafta break somebody's jaw."

He thrust his professional card on us as we departed.

A neat colored girl was in charge of the bakery. She eyed us curiously, but without alarm. Kanju Yesuda, it seemed, was out making some early-afternoon deliveries. Kaspir left Lieutenant Wu's phone number and a request for Yesuda to call it as soon as he returned.

"How come Kanju Yesuda is still breathin' freedom's air?" inquired Kaspir as our cab headed uptown. "You'd think they'd ha' cold-beefed Kanju on general principles."

Charlie Wu contributed the not-too-helpful guess that there'd probably be some simple explanation of Kanju Yesuda's survival.

In this he was very much mistaken. Kanju Yesuda's escape was anything but a simple affair as we heard it from his own lips not an hour later. We did not hear it, however, until after the incident of the small brown box.

CHAPTER THREE
PLEASE FIND
ENCLOSED —

THE SMALL brown box lay invitingly on the floor before Charlie Wu's door.

Wu picked it up. It was perhaps eight-by-six-by-four inches. On the brown paper wrapping was printed, in bold letters with purple ink: *Lieut. Charles Wu. Personal.*

Charlie Wu hefted it absently. Then he shook it, a move which struck all of us as foolhardy in the extreme. Even Kaspir stepped back. Charlie Wu smiled thinly.

"I was on the bomb squad a year," he said. "I can smell 'em. This is no bomb."

So much to the good. Wu led us back into his compact, shining pantry-kitchen and set out a heartening array of bottles of glasses. He handed me a rubber ice tray. Kaspir turned a bottle of brandy in his hands and smiled.

Charlie Wu hooked a finger in the heavy brown cord which bound the box and snapped it. He undid the paper slowly. Maude had a tinkling glass in her hand now, and Kaspir was slopping brandy into an especially large tumbler that he had pinched for himself. "Show us your Christmas present," he urged, as Charlie lifted the lid.

To my amazement, Charlie Wu did what seemed, at the moment, a very rude thing. He whirled so that his body was interposed between Maude's curious eyes and the box.

But Maude had seen something, and the crash of her glass on the floor splashed my ankle with icy liquid.

"Will you please go," said Lieutenant Wu to Maude.

Maude said thickly, "I think I will," and the swinging pantry door flapped sullenly at her exit.

Charlie Wu laid the contents of the box out on the drain board, one by one. There were five items. The first was a strip of paper down which ran a dozen-odd neatly printed Japanese characters.

In the hall the telephone had begun to ring, but to my dizzy, dulled ears it sounded a mile away. Charlie Wu was studying the strip of paper.

"For God's sake, Charlie," said Kaspir, "what's it say? You know some Japanese."

"A free translation might be: 'The hand given in false friendship; the ears that heard and retained; the tongue that betrayed,'" said Charlie Wu gently.

I stared at the objects on the drain board. It was not until Kaspir picked up the largest one and held it first to his eyes, then to his nose, that I groped blindly for the door and pushed through to the hall.

Maude put down the telephone and looked at me with sick eyes.

I discovered that I still had a glass of light brown liquid in my hand. I drank half, and the cold stream opened my throat.

"They were Komagichi Yesuda's, all right," I said. "Hand, ears, and"—I just made it—"tongue."

We stared at one another, and slow anger began to stiffen my melting knees and watery wrists. There was no doubt about the hand being Yesuda's. Whoever had lopped it off had left enough of the wrist to show the whole delicately tinted butterfly.

"Who was that on the phone?" I asked.

Maude said weakly: "The Oriental Bakery. A man with a soft voice told me that he has very good bread for sale."

In the silence that followed we could hear Charlie Wu, in the pantry, saying, "… probably with a short sword—except the tongue, of course." And Kaspir's answering grumble.

It was evident that Charlie Wu was all too well known to the Den-Kaigi, so Kaspir and I left him behind on our second visit to the Oriental Bakery. It was risky enough for us to go there—risky for Kanju, I mean—but we had already established our characters as credit investigators and Kaspir figured it might be safe. And the sooner we talked to Kanju, the better.

On the way we dropped Maude at the hotel. She said she thought she would lie down for a little while.

KANJU YESUDA was a slightly older, somewhat smaller edition of his late brother. He wore spectacles, and there was something very like death in his sallow face.

Before we could speak, Kanju laid two loaves of fresh bread on the counter and reached for wrapping paper. Kaspir produced a black notebook and fiddled with a pencil.

"I suppose you know what happened to your brother," remarked Kaspir in a low tone.

Kanju Yesuda tore a piece of wrapping paper from a roll behind the counter and slid it expertly under the loaves. "Yes," he said.

"Are you willing to help us?" said Kaspir, scribbling meaningless figures in the notebook.

"Yes," said Kanju Yesuda, with utter finality. Mechanically his hands were constructing a neat package of the bread and paper. His eyes met Kaspir's squarely.

"Were you at the meeting—the first meeting—last night?" pursued Kaspir.

"Yes." Yesuda took a turn around the package with white string from a ball on a peg. I moved restlessly. Kaspir flipped over a leaf of the notebook.

"Did you learn anything new?"

Kanju Yesuda drew breath, his first sign of tension. "Yes." He pulled two more loaves from the stack beside him. "Two of the new bombsight lenses have been stolen by the Germans. One will be turned over to the Den-Kaigi tonight." He shook his head at the question in Kaspir's eyes. "I do not know where. I did not hear."

"How did you know about your brother?" asked Kaspir.

Kanju Yesuda's jaw-line hardened. "Because I was there," he said. "It was I who cut off his hand."

I started. Kaspir flung me a hard look before his glance swung again to Yesuda. Kanju had completed the second package. He took two more loaves from the stack.

"They came for me early this morning," said Yesuda. He was talking quickly now, and I knew why. The longer we remained in that bakery, the longer the odds against Yesuda's life. "They took me to the rooms on Third Avenue. My brother was already there. He looked at me, and because he is—was—my brother, I knew what he meant. He was as good as dead. He wanted me to save myself.

"They told me he had betrayed them. I denounced him in the name of our ancestors and in the name of the Emperor. Then the man called Shintaro Kato handed me the short, heavy knife of execution.

"My brother laid his right arm on the table. I cursed him and brought down the knife—a clean, quick stroke."

"A single blow?" murmured Kaspir.

"Better that than awkward blows by another."

"And then…?"

"The others finished the Rite of Betrayal upon Komagichi. I was saved. I had proved myself. They did not require me to do any more. I was glad of that. I do not think I could have."

Kanju Yesuda adjusted his spectacles with a quivering hand. Kaspir shut his notebook and dabbed at his brow with a handkerchief.

"Will you please go quickly now?" said Yesuda.

"I'm at the Murray Lane Hotel," said Kaspir. "You'll call me if you get anything new?"

"Of course." Yesuda's voice was sharp-edged with impatience. "What do you think I am living for now?" he breathed. "Good-bye."

KASPIR CALLED General Tancred in Washington immediately upon our return to the hotel. Maude wandered in, pale but composed, just as he got Tancred on the line.

Kaspir's relations with Tancred have never been marked by excess geniality, and the present instance was no exception. The fault, I should say, lay with Kaspir. In extenuation I offer the fact that Kaspir had been through a good deal that day, and his flippancy was the flippancy of a man on the raw edge of despair.

"You know those little bits o' glass we were talkin' about last week. General?" Kaspir cocked his feet on the bed. General Tancred apparently replied that he knew all about the bits o' glass.

Kaspir leered at Maude and me. "There's a couple missin'," he said. He held the receiver from his ear until Tancred quieted down and inquired how in blazes he knew.

"Feller told me," said Kaspir sweetly. "Very reliable feller. Be dead soon, I'm afraid." A long pause. Then, more seriously: "No, I'm not kiddin'. You better make a quick check on the deliveries. Lemme know as soon as you find out anything."

"Steve, cut the fooling," said Maude, when he had hung up. "Are any of the lenses really missing?"

Kaspir nodded soberly. "Kanju Yesuda says so. And I got a feelin' he knows. Tancred says there've only been two batches of eight each turned out so far, and they've been sent to advanced bomber fields for testing."

"Where are they made?" This from me.

"Right here in little old New York: Brase Optical Company, Ninety-ninth just off Broadway." He glanced at Maude. "Kanju says the German gang is turnin' one over to the Den-Kaigi tonight in return for favors received."

"What are you going to do?" Maude's voice was little more than a whisper.

"What can I do?" he burst out. "Yesuda don't know where the ceremony's takin' place. Nothin' to do but wait'll we hear from Tancred. It's just possible Yesuda don't know what he's talkin' about."

It was an hour almost to the minute before Tancred called. Again his end of the conversation was lost to me, but there was no mistaking the fact that he was modifying his tone to Kaspir considerably. Kaspir himself had little to say, a thing unusual in itself. He listened closely, said, "I'll let you know," and hung up. All trace of levity was gone from his face and tone.

"There *is* one missin'," he said. "In the batch that went to Anson Field, Tancred says. They hadn't even been unpacked. When Tancred called he held the phone till they unpacked 'em. They found one was phoney as a ten-cent diamond—probably an early test grinding that should have been destroyed. But it wasn't. Somebody saved it, and packed it, and kept a gen-u-wine one for himself." He glanced at his watch.

"Three twelve," he said. "We'd better hurry."

As we piled into the cab I felt as though my whole life had been spent being jammed into hard corners of cabs by Kaspir's bulk.

THERE WAS nothing in the exterior of the Brase Optical Company, a small firm on the second floor of a middle-aged building, to hint of the guards and activity within. One of the guards, virtually salaaming before Kaspir's gold badge, sped off on winged feet to locate Mr. Brase, who was somewhere in the grinding room.

The short wait was not unpleasant. Behind the reception desk sat one of the handsomest women I have ever seen: red hair, creamy skin, royal eyes, a passionate mouth. According to the small brass plate on her desk, her name was Miss Katherine Doorn, and I decided then and there that if Maude were ever to give me a decisive "No" I would look up Miss Doorn without delay. Miss Doorn and Maude eyed each other with the deadly, instinctive dislike of two handsome women meeting for the first time.

The guard came back all too soon and ushered us down a hall and into Mr. Brase's private office.

Mr. Brase was a small, nervous type in gray serge, the kind of man Kaspir terrifies. This case was no exception. By way of introduction he flashed his badge.

"Listen," he said belligerently, and Mr. Brase quailed, "who O.K.'d those two batches of Pool's 7's that went outa here last week?"

"I did," quavered Mr. Brase.

"Then who packed 'em for shipping?"

"James Worker, my plant superintendent—under my supervision."

"It's Worker who has charge of destroyin' the test grinds, I suppose?"

Mr. Brase swallowed hard. "Yes. Why?"

"Where's Worker now?"

"Home—he's been ill with flu for the past several days." Some blood seeped back into Mr. Brase's cheeks. "May I ask…?" he began.

"You got his address?"

"Miss Doorn has it. May I ask you why…?"

Kaspir stood up. So did Mr. Brase, flushing.

"One o' those Pool's 7's in the Anson Field Shipment turned out phoney—an old test grind," said Kaspir. "Think it over, chum."

"Oh my God!" said Mr. Brase weakly, and sat down.

Five seconds later Kaspir was demanding James Worker's address from the creamy Miss Doorn. She bridled at his tone and her fine eyes lit with a battle light. In the nick of time Mr. Brase, staggering down the hall after us, called: "Let him have it, Kathie. Quickly!"

Miss Doorn turned reluctantly to a small filing cabinet and took her time finding what we wanted. As we sailed out with it, it was Maude who called a sardonic "Thank you." Miss Doorn did not reply.

"I'll buy you a bottle of fizz if he's home," said Kaspir gloomily in the cab.

Maude did not get her fizz. The talkative landlady at Worker's boarding house informed Kaspir at great length that Mr. Worker had left the house around noon, saying something about going back to work. No, she did not know any other place he might be found. He was a quiet man, and his diversion was symphony music. No, she did not know any of his friends. No one ever called on him at the boarding house.

On the pathetically feeble hope that Mr. Worker might actually have returned to the optical company, we stopped there on our way downtown. It was quitting time. Maude and I waited in the cab while Kaspir elbowed his way upstream against the departing flow of workers.

"There's your friend," said Maude, a brittle tinkle in her voice. I feigned ignorance. "She seems to have a boy friend," said Maude. "Two, in fact."

That turned my head, just in time to catch a devastating glimpse of long, shapely legs as Miss Doorn inserted her gorgeous body into an expensive-looking convertible sedan behind our cab. The sedan pulled out. As it was passing us, Miss Doorn turned to speak to the man on the back seat. In that instant I got a flash of the driver's face—a mere flash, but sufficient.

The next thing I knew, I was in Mr. Brase's office and Brase and Kaspir were staring at my white face.

"The Doorn woman!" I gasped. "That undertaker—Williams—the one who spoke up for Kanju Yesuda—he was waiting for her." I started out. "Come on."

"Wait." Kaspir was fumbling at his notebook, swearing purple oaths. "Gimme that phone." He nearly spun the dial from its spindle.

"That you, Charlie? Listen, there's an undertakin' joint on Tenth Avenue just a few doors from the Oriental Bakery—

yeah, Yesuda's place. Get over there right away. Watch the place. For the luvva Pete don't let anybody spot you. We'll join you soon's we can make it." He slammed the receiver into place and bellowed, "Come on!"

But an idea was rapping at my mind. I said to the flabbergasted Brase: "Does this man James Worker have gray hair and a prominent nose? Does he ever wear a tan Palm Beach suit?"

Brase nodded numbly.

I said to Kaspir: "He was in the back seat."

As we ran out we heard Mr. Brase's despairing, "Oh my God!"

CHAPTER FOUR
CORPSES MADE TO ORDER

LIEUTENANT CHARLIE Wu said: "Two men and a woman went in. One of the men's still in that room that looks on the street. He acts like a look-out. Fellow with gray hair."

We were in an odorous confectionery diagonally across Tenth Avenue from the sign that read: *W. Williams, Mortician.*

Kaspir said, in a controlled tone: "Friend Kanju's lockin' up kind of early, ain't he?"

We stretched our necks. Several doors beyond the undertaking place I saw the unmistakable figure of Kanju Yesuda locking the front door of the Oriental Bakery.

"He's gonna pay a social call," said Kaspir flatly.

When Kanju Yesuda turned in at the undertaking place, my heart began to pound in great, slow beats.

"Maude, drift over and get the lay of the land," said Kaspir.

It seemed hours before she returned, switching her hips into the confectionery for all the world like a chippie on the make.

"Worker's the only one in the front parlor, Steve," she said. "The others must be in some back room."

Kaspir swore. "Worker's the look-out, all right. And if we rush the front, he'll—"

Charlie Wu said quietly: "There's a shade on that window, Steve. When I pull it down, that means come on over." And with that he was gone. He crossed the street, stepped out briskly. When he reached Williams's door, he stepped inside without breaking his stride. Less than a minute later the shade came down.

"You stay here," said Kaspir to Maude, and pointed at her shoes.

"These damn high heels!" wailed Maude.

WE STOOD in that musty reception-parlor and listened. At Charlie Wu's feet lay James Worker, very still, the marks of Charlie Wu's fingers purpleblack on his throat.

"Before we go back there," breathed Kaspir, "get this: nobody makes a move until I tip 'em the sign."

From somewhere in the rear came a muffled laugh—a loud laugh that suggested Williams's red face and hearty manner. Charlie Wu, silent as a ghost, drifted down the hall leading into the rear. Kaspir and I, at his heels, were palsied with the fear of stumbling. An odor of formaldehyde grew stronger; also the sound of voices. I heard the Doorn woman say something. Then Williams laughed again, and there was that in his laugh which suggested that all was not well with the conference.

The laugh served our purpose, however. It placed the conference very definitely behind the last door on the left, a door with an upper half of frosted white glass. Charlie Wu ducked under the light sifting through the glass and took up his stand on the far side of the door. I leaned against the frame, being careful not to get any part of me silhouetted against the glass, and Kaspir, at my shoulder, breathed into my ear.

"You Japs are cold-blooded fish," Williams was saying, and you could hear the forcing of the jovial note. "Here we've got the world by the tail and you don't even want to celebrate. Come on, Yesuda—bust this bottle with Kathie and me."

"I wish to see the lens," came Kanju Yesuda's even voice. It was neither friendly nor unfriendly.

"I tell you the lens is right in this room. Good lord, man, I don't carry it around in my pocket. Say, have you seen the new short-wave set Worker rigged up? Here, Kathie, gimme that bottle."

A cork popped. There was a gurgling noise.

"Here's yours, Yesuda—it's the best you can buy these days. Here, Kathie...."

Then Kathie Doorn's voice: "Your health, Mr. Yesuda." Silence.

Kanju Yesuda said, "Why don't you drink, Miss Doorn?"

A short, sharp sound of a glass being set down on a hard surface.

"Do you think I am so stupid as not to know there is poison in that wine?" inquired Kanju Yesuda.

Williams's chuckle was a ghastly effort. "What makes you think we'd try to poison you, Yesuda?"

I could almost see the curl of Yesuda's thin lips. "Because you have been ordered not to let my country have that lens. You stole only one, and that is intended for Germany."

Williams abandoned all pretense. His voice came from deep in his throat. "You little yellow snake, I'll break your back."

The shot and Kathie Doorn's scream came simultaneously. Under our feet the floor vibrated slightly with the thud of Williams's body.

"Where is the lens, Miss Doorn?" asked Kanju Yesuda.

"I don't know where it is. And if I did know, I wouldn't... Don't—oh, don't!"

"I cannot have you in my way while I am searching," said Yesuda, and our hallway echoed with the second shot.

CHARLIE WU was in a half crouch, eyes on Kaspir. I looked around. Kaspir shook his head.

Judging from the sounds, Kanju Yesuda's search was a very thorough operation. Twice we heard him move one of the bodies in the course of his hunt. Then a pause, and I knew that Yesuda was standing in the middle of the room, thinking, gazing around. Then a sound, and another. Yesuda was using the telephone.

"O.K.," said Colonel Kaspir quietly.

I hit the door a half-second ahead of Charlie Wu—hit it with all the tension that had been accumulating in me while we waited and listened. Glass and wood gave way with a crash that was momentarily deafening.

Kanju Yesuda's back was toward me. He had a telephone receiver at his ear, and his free hand went automatically to the coffin beside him at the hubbub of my entrance. Even as I saw the gun in the coffin I reached his shoulders and rode him to the floor. He wriggled clear like an eel, but Kaspir and Charlie Wu had their hands on him by then.

I saw for the first time that we were in the embalming-room of Williams's establishment, as tiled and gleaming as the operating-room of a small hospital. The equipment was perfect, even to the corpses. Yesuda had lifted Kathie Doorn's body onto the operating table, and beyond the coffin lay Williams on his back.

From the broken bottles on the floor rose an overpowering stench of some formaldehyde compound. I was about to comment on the short-wave set reposing comfortably in the open coffin when the sound of footsteps in the hall froze us for a moment.

Maude wrinkled her nostrils as her blond head came in at the door. I saw her eyes widen at the sight of Kanju Yesuda with Charlie Wu's arm crooked about his neck, widen further as they took in the bodies of Kathie Doorn and Williams.

"Now that you're here," said Kaspir ungraciously, "you can give us a hand in lookin' for that lens. I got an idea it's in this room, just like Williams told our sharp-shootin' buddy here."

"What does it look like?" Maude's handkerchief was at her nose.

"Mushroom-shaped, grunted Kaspir. "Thick, round, with a bulge at one end. Although how you expect to find it by curtsyin' aroun' holdin' your nose...."

"You mean like this?" said Maude. She leaned over, and with squeamish fingers plucked a chunky bit of clear glass from the sticky mess of formaldehyde and bottle shards on the floor.

Kaspir's nerve is immense. He took it without batting an eye, rubbed it clean with his handkerchief, and held it up to the light. "Yeah," he said, "that's it."

BY THE by," said Kaspir to Yesuda, "how's your brother Gichi gettin' on? I trust he's sittin' up and takin' notice."

Maude exclaimed, "Steve!" in a choked voice. I had a vision of Charlie Wu taking those grisly items from the brown box.

Kanju Yesuda said calmly "He's doing very well, thank you, Colonel."

Kaspir's mouth twitched at the horror in Maude's face. "Save it," he said. "Dear little Gichi ain't dead. He just can't move the fingers of his right hand, that's all—because the hand ain't there."

Kaspir read the question marks in Maude's face, in mine, in Charlie Wu's.

"Don't you get it?" he exclaimed. We said no, we didn't get it.

"The Pool's 7 was just a secondary consideration to our yellow friends," said Kaspir. "They got vision. They were playin' for big stuff. Their aim was to get one o' their guys so deep into the confidence of our Government agencies that we'd trust him right down the line. And he'd keep buildin' up our faith in him with tips, and they'd be straight tips.

"You see the scale they were playin' on? They threw that big sub o' theirs away last night—and the two Jerries—all for what? To build up our confidence in what Komagichi and Kanju told us.

"To make this Den-Kaigi yarn stand up, Komagichi is to become a 'martyr' to his devotion to the dear old U.S.A.

"The pair of Yesuda boys and prob'ly Williams and Worker staged that kidnapin' at the Coopers' apartment last night. Then they came back to this stiff-parlor and Komagichi goes under ether in this operatin'-room, and when he comes to, he's shy a hand. By the way, Kanju, who did the cuttin' and sawin'?"

Yesuda pointed to the body of Williams. "He was a doctor in Germany once."

"So the hand, complete with tattoo mark, is sent around to Charlie Wu's, along with a tongue and an odd pair o' ears that Williams had been keepin' on ice for the big moment.... Whose tongue and ears were they, Yesuda?"

"A cousin of mine died the day before yesterday," said Yesuda grimly. "We had been waiting for it. He had been ill a long while. He was proud to think that even in death he could serve."

"You get it now?" demanded Kaspir triumphantly. "We've got Komagichi established as a martyred American. We've got Komagichi's brother carryin' on in his place, very bitter against the Den-Kaigi. Kanju here would have fed us more tips—straight tips—until he had us believin' everything he said. And they'd throw away half a dozen more subs, or maybe a squadron or two of planes, backin' up Kanju's tips to us—because they'd be gamblin' for the big shot later on. Because one o' these days Kanju here would have fed us a tip that would ha' led maybe half our Pacific fleet into a death trap."

I got it then.

"I SAID the bombsight lens was secondary," said Kaspir. "It was. But it was important. The minute the Yesuda boys found out Williams and his crowd expected to get hold of one, they got itchin' palms. So they worked up a deal with Williams's crowd. And that's where the whole business began breakin' down—just like everything else Japan and Germany try to pull off together is gonna break down.

"How can they work together when Germany's whole premise is that she's gonna run the world after the war. This bla-bla-bla about Germany sharin' world domination with

Japan is just that, and nobody knows it better than Kanju and his pals."

"If I might ask a question—" said Kanju Yesuda.

"Shoot."

"May I ask how you spotted the hand and ears and tongue for a hoax?"

"I didn't, right away. But you told me you'd used a knife to lop off Gichi's hand, and when I remembered seein' the marks of a surgical saw on the wrist bone, it naturally made me wonder. Now lemme ask you one."

"Please go ahead."

"Didn't you know that when a man's telling the truth he don't sweat under the arms? Well, when you were handin' me that spiel in the bakery today, you pretty near sweat yourself to death."

"Oh," said Kanju Yesuda thoughtfully.

THE DOG WITH THE GOLDEN EYES

HOWIE SUGG WAS A GOOD KID, AND HE HAD THE MAKINGS OF A GREAT REPORTER—TILL HE STUMBLED ONTO SOMETHING A BIT TOO HOT FOR HIM TO HANDLE. PERHAPS HE MIGHT HAVE SURVIVED IF HE HADN'T KNOWN HIS SCRIPTURE SO WELL, FOR HE FOLLOWED TO THE LAST THE PROVERB THAT WAS THE KEY TO THE WHOLE CASE: THE WICKED FLEE WHEN NO MAN PURSUETH; BUT THE RIGHTEOUS ARE BOLD AS A LION.

FIRST I rang. Then I knocked. No one answered. There was certainly nothing sinister about the house. On the contrary, it fairly reeked of a suburban peace. Yet as I walked away down the flagstoned path I experienced a very definite disinclination to turn my back on the place.

In fact, only a minor triumph of will power saved me from hastening my departure like a small boy scuttling from a dark room.

I reminded myself that I had had a long day; that I was weary to the point of collapse; that my nephew's death was less than forty-eight hours old.

At the gate I looked back. The fierce moonlight of a warm Virginia September night silvered the white frame walls and turned the green shutters jet black. The scene belonged by rights to a drowsy Vermont village, even to the backdrop of sound thrown up by a million crickets.

It was hard to believe that there was a confectionery store a long block away; that two blocks beyond the confectionery, across a children's playground, ran a bus line which would take me in five short minutes into the heart of that teeming, fabulous city which the war has made out of the quiet seaport city of Norfolk.

In a flash I knew what had happened to Howie—and
then I heard footsteps behind my back.

I marshaled these comforting facts in my mind as I waited for the unaccountable trembling of my knees to stop. It did not stop, but it lessened sufficiently to allow me to set out for the corner. I must have gone all of twenty yards before I discovered that I was being followed.

To say that I was surprised is a gross understatement. The realization came with one of those paralyzing nervous jolts that strike a man hot and cold simultaneously, and leave the brain and pulses in confusion.

It must have been the crickets which had kept me from hearing the faint clicking of toenails on the sidewalk behind me.

My companion, seeing me rooted, sat down and regarded me with patient eyes.

I flushed. It was just a dog. Not a hostile dog, either. But on the other hand, not friendly. He just sat there, waiting.

I like dogs. Besides, I was ashamed of my panic. I stooped down, snapped my fingers, urged weakly: "Come here, boy."

He did not budge. Nor did he take his eyes off me. They were large eyes—he was a large, shapeless sort of brute—and they shone golden in the moonlight like a Persian cat's.

I shuffled toward him. He rose and moved beyond reach of my outstretched hand. He did not bristle, nor did he show fright. He merely made it plain that I was not going to touch him.

I straightened up and walked on. The click of his nails on the sidewalk began at once.

I stopped again. We went through an absurd little maneuver. I ran at him. He wheeled away, glancing back.

I set out with quick steps for the confectionery. He turned immediately and trotted after me, matching his pace to mine. He had made something else quite plain. He intended to follow me until... until what?

At this point I noted for the first time that his shaggy coat was black. A black dog!

It was here that I began to go to pieces.

MY INITIAL impulse was to stand my ground and bawl for the police. Deep inside me I knew that this was a wise impulse and should be obeyed. But the fear of making a fool of myself overrode my fear of the black dog and all that his presence implied.

I do not remember entering the confectionery, but my agitation must have been written large on my face, for the proprietor stared.

Two young men who had been chatting with the proprietor threw some money on the counter. I jumped at the ring of silver. They said: "Good-night, Sam."

They went out. The proprietor trudged back behind the counter to where I sat on a stool. He was a big man in a greasy apron, and he needed a shave.

"Beer," I quavered.

He glanced at the wall clock over the pinball machine (the Virginia licensing laws are strict). Eight minutes to twelve. He raised a lid. "What brand?"

"Any brand," I snapped, watching his hairy hands moving among the ice and bottles.

I downed that first bottle sloppily. I did not even bother to wipe my dripping chin, although normally I should have had my handkerchief out in a second. Silent, unsmiling, he opened another bottle, although I had not asked for it.

I heard myself saying huskily: "Do you know who in this neighborhood owns a big black dog?"

He affected to consider, throwing back his head, passing a hand over his stubbly chin.

I caught my breath. It was overdone, this indecision. I could see the wary glow behind his eyes. He shook his head. "No," he said.

Now it would have been the most natural thing in the world for him to follow that with "Why?" but he did not. The subject of the black dog was left quivering in the air.

I looked toward the front of the ill-lit store. Across the window straggled a meaningless assortment of gilt letters. Instinctively I reversed them in my mind. They read: *Vogelsang's Confectionery.*

There was no sign of the black dog out there, but I knew he was waiting. I tilted the second bottle to my lips. It was good beer, and cold. I looked around me. A telephone booth.

"If you have any sense at all," I told myself, "you'll phone the police and tell them to come get you. After all…."

But what could I tell the police when they arrived: that I was afraid of a black dog?

I envisioned a large, calm sergeant, notebook in hand, asking if the dog had attacked me. I squirmed as I heard myself answering: "No, but he's following me."

Staring at the beer bottle, I struggled to phrase my explanation. "You remember that newspaper reporter, Howard Sugg, who was killed the night before last?" I would say. "He was my nephew. I am investigating his death. Just before he died he mumbled something about a black dog—and pigeons."

In my mind's eye I could see the sergeant's eyebrows going up. I could hear him objecting: "Yes, but Sugg was killed near Ocean View—a good ten miles from here."

I could persist, of course, with: "How about Detective Will Adams of your own force, the man who made the report on Sugg?"

At this point my imaginary sergeant said briskly and suspiciously: "Who are you?"

And I would have to identify myself as Captain Michael Kettle, U.S. Army Intelligence, operating on special assignment with—

But when you belong to Section Five you don't broadcast it, even to the police.

What, then, would I achieve by calling the police? Nothing, beyond giving some Norfolk policeman the well-warranted impression that I was either drunk or a skulking moron afraid of a black dog.

I gave it up. I told myself, as the last icy trickle of beer burned past my Adam's apple, that it was high time I behaved more like Army Intelligence and less like a neurotic woman. I would cross those fields, catch a bus to my hotel, and call Colonel Stephen Kaspir, my chief in Section Five, and lay the matter before him.

I planked down two dimes on the counter and left the store without a word. I felt, rather than heard, the black dog padding behind me as I took the hard dirt path across the first of the two fields. I stiffened my shoulders against the returning fear that crawled like a slow beetle up my spine.

I made the playground. The swings and slides were spidery black in the white moonlight.

I was not a dozen feet from where the path wound round the corner of a caretaker's toolshed when I knew that the black dog was no longer with me.

Of all the events of the past quarter hour, this was somehow the most terrifying. I had seen enough of the black dog's actions to satisfy myself that he was no idle wanderer of the night. He was doing a job for which he had been trained. Presumably that job was now done. Which meant...?

The explanation occurred to me just as I reached the corner of the toolshed, a second before the dark figures stepped out behind me. In a flash I knew what had happened to Howie Sugg. And what would happen to me. In that instant I drew breath.

I got rid of that breath in a wordless shout as I heard the steps—human steps this time—not a yard from my back.

Of the next five seconds or so I can recall three things. First, I remember the sharply outlined shadows of their arms on the moon-white ground as those arms rose and fell, and the heavy, painless blows numbed me.

Second, I can revisualize the glimpse I caught, as I went down twisting, of the black dog dwindling on the path as he returned to his post.

And I can remember thinking, as the gritty ground met my cheek: "Well, I doubt if we could have proved anything anyhow."

I HAD hesitated about showing the letter to Kaspir at all. We were squarely in the middle of the business of the Spanish envoy when it arrived, and it infuriates Kaspir to be distracted by "trifles"—which means any matter in which he is not personally interested.

It was hot that day. Kaspir's office, on the top floor of that old brownstone ex-boarding house in southwest Washington, which has housed Section Five since early in 1940, was a double-insulated oven.

In that oven Kaspir and Maude and I baked like potatoes in their jackets. We were dressed in our social best, and we had a quarter hour to kill before leaving for the cocktail party which the Spanish envoy was expected to attend.

Colonel Kaspir's flannels were too tight, his stiff collar was abrading his thick neck, and his full moon of a face was apoplectic red. He was waspish and peevish and irritating.

Maude, a dream in white moire topped by a picture hat like a broad halo, was not as saintly as she looked. She and Kaspir were snapping at one another in senseless exchanges of pure temper.

I said nothing. Tom Larssen's letter was in my pocket and its contents lay heavy on my mind. I wanted to show it to Kaspir, but I was afraid he might say something flippant or callous. If he did that, I would explode.

"You and your indigestion, Steve," Maude was saying acidly. "You stuff yourself with those nauseating chocolate cherries all day and then wonder why…" She tapped a small foot impatiently.

A mulish look took possession of Kaspir's hot face. Very deliberately he opened a side drawer of his desk. He fetched up a melting mass of chocolate, inserted it into his Cupid's-bow mouth, and licked his fingers smackingly.

The tempo of Maude's foot became faster, and she averted her eyes. The click of her dull gold case as she took out a cigarette was somehow the last straw. I took Tom Larssen's letter from its envelope and pitched it onto the desk in front of Colonel Kaspir.

Something in the action, something in my face, stopped the tapping of Maude's foot. Kaspir chewed less noisily as he picked up the single typewritten sheet.

"Who's this Tom Larssen?" he grunted, after a single glance.

"We were cubs on the *Baltimore Sun* together," I said. "He's managing editor of the *Virginian-Dispatch* in Norfolk now. When Howie quit college last winter I got him a job under Tom."

Maude said, in a very different tone from the one she had been using with Kaspir: "You mean your sister's boy—Howie Sugg—that bright-eyed youngster who came to see you last year—the one who was trying to get in the Army?"

I nodded grimly.

"Has something happened to him?" Her violet eyes were questioning and the pitch of her voice had risen.

I nodded again.

"Oh, Mike!" Her hand was on my arm now, and her eyes were sorry. She flared at Kaspir: "And you and I were sitting here gassing while Mike...."

Kaspir, eyes still fixed on the letter, blurted something which sounded suspiciously like "Oh, nuts!" He hooked a splay finger in his collar and tugged. The collar parted with a tearing sound. "Ah!" he said, relieved, and read on.

Maude jumped up, trod on her cigarette, and went and stood behind Kaspir to read over his shoulder. So did I, although I knew Tom Larssen's letter by heart.

Dear Mike,

Howie Sugg was killed late tonight in an automobile crash. I persuaded the police not to wire your sister. Thought you'd rather break it to her yourself.

The police found his car folded up against a telephone pole on the Ocean View road. He was inside. Skull fractured. I got to the emergency-room at St. Paul's Hospital just as they were giving him a spinal puncture. He rallied for a second or two, said something about a "black dog," and muttered a word that sounded like "pigeons." Then he died.

There was a slight fog on when the accident occurred; I say "accident" because that's what we've called it. But I wasn't satisfied that that's what it was. Neither was Will Adams, the detective who investigated, although he didn't mention it to anyone but me.

Mike, the boy had had something on his mind for weeks. He hung around the waterfront a lot in his spare time. Do you suppose he could have turned up something important? You know what a red-hot spot Norfolk is these days.

I understand you're doing some sort of hush-hush work in Washington now. Could you get down here for a day or two? It would ease my mind.

Believe me, this is not an easy letter to write. And when you notify your sister, please add my condolences and those of the whole staff.

Howie was a good boy. And he had the makings of a first-class—no, I'll say a great—reporter.

YES, I knew Howie. My sister's been on the West Coast ever since her husband vanished in the South Pacific early this year. There was no holding Howie when his father was reported missing. He quit the University that day and spent a full two months trying to get into the war. But he was frail, and his eyes were bad. He wouldn't go back to college, so as a stop-gap I got him the job with Tom.

A vague, dull anger began to sharpen as I stood there behind Kaspir. Poor Howie! A sailor would have said that Howie was over-engined for his beam. He had too much heart, too much energy, too much courage for that body of his.

I was about to say something when Kaspir picked up the phone. He spun the dial thoughtfully, growled: "Gimme Admiral Blank." Then, without preamble: "Listen, Oscar, what's the graph on the Fifth Naval District these days?"

I pricked up my ears. Norfolk is the heart of the Fifth District.

Admiral Oscar Blank apparently understood this cryptic question, for Kaspir listened at some length, his big face darkening. Finally he said: "Got nothin', huh?" and hung up. He stared right through Maude, his small blue eyes vacant.

I said: "Don't you think I'd better…?"

"Yep." He heaved his bulk from the swivel chair. "Yep, you better had."

"What was that balderdash on the phone?" demanded Maude caustically. "Code?"

Kaspir ignored this. He addressed me. "Blank says it's a new mess off the Virginia Capes, these past few months. U-boats huntin' in packs again. Four outa five boats leavin' Norfolk attacked within a hundred miles. Naval Intelligence is wild—workin' night and day. They swear the U-boats are operatin' on definite and accurate dope." He hesitated. "They got some fellows under observation down there," he said, "but they ain't made a false move. Not one."

"Who are they?" I said. "If I'm going down there I'd better know."

Kaspir considered this question for a full fifteen seconds. He shook his head slowly. "I ain't gonna tell you," he said.

It was Maude who said "Why?" Icicles hung from the word.

To my amazement, Kaspir answered mildly: "Because Mike ain't strictly a professional. The Navy lads are. They're good."

This was just true enough to stifle my anger momentarily. I went into Army Intelligence from an editorial desk on the *Baltimore Sun*. Kaspir borrowed me when he first formed Section Five. It is true that we do counter-espionage work, but not of the ordinary kind.

"I still don't understand." Maude's tone was a little less frigid.

"Mike's got a certain gift for blunderin' into things," said Kaspir. I flushed. This was also true.

"Now..." He became what is, for him, business-like. "Get down there right away, see? Talk to this detective feller. See 'f you can get a slant on what really happened to the kid. And if you run into anything hot"—here his voice became urgent—"for the luvva high holy heaven don't try to be a lone eagle. Call me. Got that? Call me."

I got it. It was tactless, and I didn't like it much, but I got it. I stood up, put the letter in my pocket, and stalked out without a word.

It did not occur to me until an hour and a half later, when I was on my way to the airport, that behind Kaspir's assault on my vanity might lie a very genuine concern for my personal safety. I felt ashamed.

THE TAXI decanted me in front of the finest newspaper plant in the South. The old, familiar atmosphere of tapping typewriters, odorous ink, warm paper, and hurrying feet enveloped me as I entered the high-arched lobby. A neat Negro elevator girl who took me to the second floor said that Mr. Larssen had just come in. It was six o'clock of a grand September evening.

There was a real thrill in walking into the newsroom of the *Virginian-Dispatch* and seeing Tom's blond head and square, calm face behind the city desk. It had been nearly three years since I had laid eyes on him. He smiled his slow smile and nodded me into a chair at one corner of the desk, then went on talking to a jolly-looking, gray-haired man of vaguely clerical appearance.

I heard the gray-haired man saying, with real feeling, "… and I cannot tell you, Mr. Larssen, how distressed my sisters and I are about young Sugg. In all my dealings with the press, I have never encountered a more sincere, a more courteous young man. I trust—"

Tom stood up. The gray-haired man was momentarily puzzled.

"This is Howie Sugg's uncle, Captain Kettle," said Tom, and I rose, too. "I think he would like to hear what you are saying, Mr. Knott. Mike, this is Mr. Knott, who heads one of our finest local war enterprises."

Mr. Knott's large, soft hand met mine more than halfway. He repeated, in substance, what he had just been saying to Tom. His voice had a touch of pulpit oratory in it, but his gray eyes were utterly sincere.

He concluded: "Selfishly speaking, I don't know what we shall do without him, my sisters and I. He was most sympathetic and helpful at all times about publicity."

I thanked him in my sister's name. He turned to Lars-sen. "That notice of our last meeting—the one I gave young Sugg—if you would be so kind as to run it tomorrow…?"

"Proverb and all, Mr. Knott," said Tom kindly. "We'll run it tomorrow in the regular column of church notes."

Mr. Knott bade us a grave farewell. I said to Tom: "Welfare worker?"

He nodded. "Pretty good type, too. Single-minded enthusiast. Had some sort of brokerage business until the war. When the ships began to sink and the survivors were brought in here in droves, he quit everything else and started a place down on the East Side called 'Little Home Ashore.' Sort of recreation hall for merchant seamen. He helps re-outfit the stranded ones, too, and begs money around town to keep the things going. His sisters help him. Nice old girls."

I said perfunctorily that Mr. Knott sounded like a fine person. I glanced around the room, which was a swirl of action, this being the hour when a morning paper really gets into its working stride.

"That desk in the far corner was Howie's," he said, pointing.

"About Howie—" I began.

Tom took my arm, piloted me into a small side office and switched on the light. He took one of my cigarettes and smoked it thoughtfully for a minute or two. I was not impatient. I knew he was going through the old reporter's routine of sorting his facts and deciding on his lead paragraph.

"I told you in my letter," said Tom, "that Howie had something on his mind. You could see it in his eyes."

I had to smile. I knew those eyes of Howie's well, bright and intense, young and eager behind the thick lenses he had worn since he was twelve.

"But he didn't say anything," went on Tom. He seemed to be having trouble getting started.

That was Howie, all right—hugging his secrets close to his breast until the moment arrived for some startling disclosure. I think he did it to foster a sense of mystery and superiority within himself.

"I figured it might be some little feature yarn he'd dug up and would tell me about in his own good time," continued Tom. "He was always noting around off his beat. He hated that church-and-civic club routine."

WE BOTH smiled, a little sadly. It's hard lines, when you are itching to set the world on fire, to have to confine yourself to the grind stuff. But necessary.

"Night before last," said Tom, gazing at the ceiling, "he came in about eleven. I didn't ask where he'd been. He was so evasive and offhand that I could see he was strung up pretty tight underneath it all. So I figured a little routine would help him back to earth, and asked him to type out some notices that people had brought in for us to run in our church note column.

"I watched him. He'd type a few lines, then stare at his typewriter; type a little more, stare some more. And then, without word to me or anybody else, he jumped up, grabbed his hat, and was out of the office in nothing flat."

I sensed that Tom was coming to the hard part.

"The next time I saw him," he said, and I tingled, "was in the emergency room at St. Paul's. Adams, the detective, had been driving in from Ocean View when he came upon Howie lying in the wreck of that little coupé he had. Adams brought him in to the hospital and called me.

"The doctors were working on him when I got there. Adams and I went over to the table. They'd just drawn off some fluid from the spine to relieve the pressure on the brain—he had a bad skull fracture. Just as they did it, he opened his eyes."

My hands were clenched now, and clammy. Tom Larssen was a little pale around the mouth.

"Adams and I saw his mouth working," said Tom huskily. "The doctor said: 'You'd better listen while you can.' We knew what that meant, and we leaned over.

"He just said it once: 'Black dog.' We both heard the words. Then he mumbled something that sounded like 'pigeons' or 'pickings'—we couldn't be sure which. Then he was quiet, and a minute or so later the doctor looked at one of the nurses and she pulled a sheet over his face."

I was anxious to get away from this scene. I said quickly: "But you wrote that his car had hit a telephone pole. His eyes were bad, and you have the dim out here, don't you? Surely that could have been an accident. What gave Adams the idea...?"

"We stayed for the examination," said Tom. "They found three separate fractures, all near the base of the skull. Now a man whose car runs head-on into a telephone pole...."

"I see," I mused.

"Of course, as the doctor suggested, he might have turned around, or been thrown around in the seat just before the car hit the pole. Possible. But Adams was leery. He said he was going to look into it further. A good man, Adams; quiet, but very thorough."

There was an undertone in Tom's voice that I could not quite account for.

"Then the first thing for me to do," I said, "is to see Adams and—"

Tom Larssen's blue eyes widened. He stood up.

I said: "What the hell?"

He was only gone a second. He came back with a newspaper and thrust it at me. "I thought you'd seen this."

"What?"

"Here." Tom's long forefinger pointed to a single-column cut on the front page just below the fold. The caption was: *CRASH VICTIM.*

The picture was that of a long-faced, pleasant-looking man with dark hair, straight dark eyebrows, and a good square mouth. Below it a one-column headline read:

DETECTIVE DIES AS CAR
PLUNGES INTO CULVERT
W.H. Adams, Popular Officer
Second Dimout Traffic Victim in 2 Days

I looked up, speechless.

"Coincidence?" said Tom dryly.

For the moment I couldn't answer. This thing simply kicked the props right out from under me. Numbly, mechanically, I read on. Adams had been found dead in the wreck of his police cruiser in a culvert in a suburb called Berkley.

"Berkley near Ocean View?" I asked.

Tom shook his head. "Opposite direction."

I stood up to ease the tension that was beginning to cramp me. I needed something to satisfy the craving for physical action which I knew would endure until my mind got something to chew on. I took a final look at the story on Adams' death and noted that it had occurred almost twenty-four hours to the minute after Howie's.

"Where's the Hillwell-Bowen Funeral Home?" I said. That's where both bodies were being held.

Tom took his hat from a wall peg and opened the door to the newsroom. He yelled: "Harry, take the city desk a while. I'm going out." He turned to me. "My car's in the alley," he said.

TOM LARSSEN and I looked upon the unmarked face of Detective Will Adams. It was composed and peaceful.

"Did he look like that when you got him?" said Tom. "The face, I mean."

Bowen, the undertaker, a soft-spoken, youngish man with an easy manner, said: "No. His face was contorted. I imagine that at the last minute, when he realized he was going into the culvert…" He left it at that.

A vast depression was settling over me. Below, in the morgue, lay my nephew Howie Sugg. A few seconds with Howie had been enough. Howie's pinched face had not lost, even in death, that quality of youth and eagerness, and as I had stood there gazing down at him something had become taut in my throat.

I felt shackled and helpless. Tom and I had been through the undertaker's envelopes containing the articles collected from Howie's pockets and those of Adams. Whatever it was that those two had guessed or learned, they had committed no portion of it to paper.

That this was a case for Kaspir I was now positive. Yet the merest remnant of vanity kept me from calling him at once. As things stood, I had nothing to offer him that he could not learn by spending two minutes with a copy of the *Virginian-Dispatch.*

Besides, there was that matter of the Spanish envoy in Washington. To drag him away from that and expect him to do the most elementary sort of groundwork on this Norfolk problem would be a witless trick.

More to hear a voice in that white-tiled stillness than anything else I asked Bowen to show me Adams' clothes. He opened a wall cabinet and brought out an oil-streaked seersucker suit.

I ran the thin, ribbed material through my fingers. There was blood on the coat collar, which was to be expected, and the sleeves. I noted the rusty mark on the breast pocket from a pencil clip. For no special reason, unless it was to try to give an imitation of a competent investigator, I felt along the coat seams, and down to the cuffs of the sleeves.

I held one of the sleeve cuffs closer to my eyes and moved nearer the light. Tom pressed against me, peering over my shoulder. I think I held my breath as I plucked the four black hairs from the cuff. I held them out on my palm. They were about three inches long.

Bowen said: "Adams must have thrown up his arm to shield his face. I found some of his hair on his hands, too."

Tom Larssen cleared his throat, his habit when nervous.

"You're sure these hairs belong to Adams?" I asked Bowen.

Bowen said: "Well, it never occurred to me that they might not." He looked closely at them, made a hissing noise between his teeth. Without a word he reached out with a slender white hand and plucked two or three strands of hair from Adams' head. For some reason I winced violently at his operation, and was not displeased to see Tom's broad shoulders jerk as he shuddered.

"Hmmm," said Bowen, comparing Adams' hair to the black strands on my palm.

It had been a perfectly natural error on Bowen's part. Adams' hair was of a darkness closely akin to black.

Tom and I looked at each other. There was no point in going into the matter of the black dog before Bowen. My feet and legs were urging me again to get under way. I hustled Tom away after the barest exchange of civilities with Bowen, who seemed sorely puzzled at our sudden departure.

"Where to?" said Tom, when we were once more in his car.

"Your office," I said, and deliberately immersed myself as deeply as possible in an uncommunicative silence. The truth was, the inference I had drawn from the back hairs was such a wispy bit of reasoning that I dared not take my mind off it for an instant, for fear it might vanish like smoke.

By dint of concentrating furiously in the car and on the elevator I kept my theory alive and breathing as we passed through the noisy newsroom and into the comparative quiet of the private office.

"O.K., mystery man." Tom tossed his hat on the peg.

"How many of those church notices had Howie copied before he ran out of the office the other night?"

THREE OR four, I think." Tom stuck his head into the newsroom and yelled: "Miss Ramsdell!" A tall, graceful brunette appeared like a conjurer's trick.

"You finished that column of church notes that Howie Sugg was working on the other night?" said Tom.

"Yes?"

"Please get me the originals from the dead hook—just the ones he had copied before you took over."

She was back in less than a minute with four sheets of paper, her brown eyes alight with reportorial curiosity.

"In what order had he copied them down?" I asked.

For answer she disappeared again, returning with a long proof. "Just as they run on this," she said. "I added mine to the four already on his typewriter."

"They haven't appeared in the paper yet?" I asked Tom.

"We run our church notes Saturday—tomorrow—morning," he said; then, "Thank you, Miss Ramsdell."

Miss Ramsdell retired with ill-concealed disappointment. I glanced over the proof, then arranged the originals in the order in which they had been set up. They were the usual type of notice brought in by secretaries of various church and welfare organizations. I noted that Howie had had his contributors well trained, for the originals were all typewritten and phrased in such form that he could have pasted them up if he desired, instead of copying them.

I studied them as I might study the Holy Writ. The first was an announcement of the illness of a local Methodist minister. The notice said that he was confined to his home, and would be unable to conduct services Sunday.

The second told of the forthcoming visit of an Episcopal bishop for a special missionary service the next Wednesday. The notice said that he would be the guest, while in Norfolk, of the rector of St. James's Church.

So far, so good. I was looking for advance dates.

The third notice was less encouraging. It reported a meeting of the board of directors of the "Little Home Ashore" which had been held early on the night of Howie's death, that fatal Wednesday night.

Diligently I plowed through this notice, which informed me that at the meeting, A. Lincoln Knott, executive director of the "Little Home Ashore," had compared the work of the Home favorably to that of similar organizations in the North. Mr. Knott had also reported to the directors on a party given at the Home the previous night, at which a large group of merchant seamen had been entertained by a group of volunteer hostesses with dancing and refreshments.

The last paragraph puzzled me for a minute and I wondered if it was a misprint or a slipped line of type. It said, in quotes: "The wicked flee when no man pursueth: but the righteous are bold as a lion."

Tom chuckled when my descending finger paused and lingered at this line.

"That's Miss Abby Knott," he said.

"Abby Knott?"

"One of Mr. Knott's two sisters." Tom tapped his forehead, "Tetched on religion. Believes that a proverb a day printed in every newspaper will eventually effect a complete reformation of the world. She's a nice little thing, and we compromised by allowing her to add one to each notice we print about the 'Little Home Ashore.' Knott types out the notices himself and lets Abby pick out the proverb. He's very grateful about it; says it keeps her happy—makes her feel she's doing something for people."

"Oh." This was no help. I went on to the final notice—the one Howie had just finished copying when he dashed out of the office.

This was the shortest of all, stating simply that the Rev. Alpheus P. Dorp would return to his home on Hampton Boulevard Tuesday, September 29, after a visit to his mother in Scranton, Pa.

I straightened up and stretched a kink out of my neck. Tom's silence was pregnant. It was a dirty trick, after all he had done for me, to leave him with no more than, "So long, see you tomorrow." But I did. The reason was that I was ashamed to tell him what I was going to do.

I was going to look for a black dog. Or rather, *the* black dog.

Doubts swarmed down upon me from all directions as I left the building and started for Granby Street. The most persistent was this: I was proceeding on the diaphanous theory that Howie's sudden exit from the newsroom Wednesday night had been inspired by something in one of the four notices that now reposed in my pocket.

The critical half of my mind argued that this was an unreasonable assumption. Howie had merely been copying the notices. The chances were that he had been thinking about something entirely unrelated to them. I know that to be possible, for I have done it myself.

"Hell!" I said aloud.

A sailor and his girl turned and stared at me. I tramped on, undecided.

I turned a corner and came upon a taxi stand. That decided me. I would stick by my original theory—if you could dignify it by that name—to the bitter end. And then, and not until then, would I call Kaspir, confess failure, and ask for help.

A driver held a cab door open enticingly. I got in, referred to the first of the notices, and asked to be driven to the home of the sick Methodist minister.

IF BOREDOM can be called a nightmare, then my evening was a nightmare.

I not only loitered in front of that minister's home for a solid hour; I scoured the neighborhood for blocks in every direction. No dog.

My next stop was at the home of the rector of St. James's. Another hour. No dog.

Taking into consideration the area I had covered, I began to tell myself that the law of averages would turn up some black dog any minute. But the law of averages appeared to have suspended operation for the evening.

My plan was to take the "Little Home Ashore" next. But perusal of a city directory in a suburban drugstore near the rector's home showed that the home of the Rev. Alpheus Dorp was only three blocks away. So I went there. There was no black dog at, or near the residence of Mr. Dorp, although I did raise a large white collie who sniffed at my trousers until decoyed away by a black cat that ambled by.

Nor was the "Little Home Ashore" the haunt of a black dog. It was a large, drab brick building just off East Main Street and the red-light district. Aside from an aged Negro who was sweeping out the dim lobby, the place was unoccupied.

The Negro, seeing me lingering before the place, informed me gratis that Mr. Knott—he called him the "Revern' Mistuh Knott"—and his sisters had just left for home, and pointed to a clock that showed quarter past eleven.

He informed me further that there would be a large dance at the Home the following night, which was Saturday—"one o' them exter-specials, suh, wif lots o' rich ladies in them kin' o' sudden dresses." I gathered this meant evening dresses, and mentally congratulated Mr. Knott on his efforts on behalf of the highly deserving merchant seamen.

The aged retainer would have escorted me through the "Little Home Ashore" room by room if I had let him, but I declined. More to check his verbosity than through any particular desire for knowledge I asked him for Mr. Knott's home address. He told me it was in a suburb called Brambleton, and gave me explicit directions. I left him under the impression that I was going to press a midnight call on Mr. Knott.

As I walked back to East Main Street the idea began to appeal to me. Those gray eyes of Mr. Knott's had been shrewd as well as friendly. Too, he came daily into contact with hundreds of merchant seamen; he might prove a valuable ally without knowing it. And if he had just left the Home, I would be able to get to his house before he went to bed.

A taxi was out of the question now, all such conveyances being pre-empted by the ladies of the section and their male friends. I caught a bus. The driver was a talkative soul who knew Mr. Knott well and said that any friend of Mr. Knott was a friend of his. He showed me where to get off, what path to take across the playground, and said to turn right at Vogelsang's Confectionery.

The rest you know. I knocked long and loud on Mr. Knott's door. There was no sign of movement in the house.

It was Mr. Knott's house that I was leaving when the shaggy black dog appeared and followed me to Vogelsang's Confectionery and then across the fields to my Waterloo at the toolshed.

A HAND moved near my face and I ducked. The act of ducking set up a thundering pain behind my left ear. With the pain the will to live and fight returned with a rush. I lashed out blindly.

"There, there, there," said a soothing voice.

I blinked into the moonlight, which turned out to be sunlight, hot and yellow, streaming in through a window.

The nurse was small and swift, with a round, perky face and a cap like a blob of whipped cream. She must have been used to seeing concussion patients returning to consciousness, for she went on adjusting my covers and smiled as she worked. "There, there," she said again, a little sharply now, for I was sitting up. "Relax, Captain Kettle." Then, "What?"

"Black dog," I repeated. "Those two men... Get me my clothes, please, nurse."

My little nurse was shocked. "I'll see the doctor, Captain, but I doubt if..." She faded out. With the opening and closing of the door I heard a familiar voice in the hall; just a word or two, but more than enough to make me shout: "Kaspir! Colonel Kaspir!"

Colonel Stephen Kaspir popped in like a gigantic jack-in-the-box. He saw me sitting up and went "Huh," rather disgustedly. He was wearing his familiar white linen suit, in the folds of which you could hide a watermelon even while he was wearing it, and on the back of his big head rode that frayed Panama he loves like a brother.

In Kaspir's wake hurried Maude, a blond vision in tan sharkskin. Her gasp of "Oh, Mike!" was a shot of adrenalin for my heart, and her cool brown hand virtually completed my cure by patting my cheek.

Behind Maude a young, balding doctor bounced in, followed by the pretty nurse, whose eyes were snapping.

Just as the door closed I caught a fleeting glimpse of another vaguely familiar face in the hall. It belonged to a stoutish man who carried a bunch of flowers and appeared to be looking for somebody. In that muddled moment I could not place those features, and besides, I had something I had to get off my chest before another word was spoken.

"I've found the black dog," I shot at Kaspir.

Kaspir's eyes kindled.

The nurse began, "Doctor—"and the doctor said coldly, "In view of the patient's condition, I must ask you people to…."

By the time I had convinced the doctor that a medically enforced silence would send my blood pressure up into the danger zone, we were all enemies together. Maude was barking at Kaspir, who kept putting his oar in. The nurse was glaring at Maude for adding to the confusion, and the doctor practically washed his hands of my case. We finally achieved a left-handed truce. Maude and Kaspir were to stay for ten minutes, but the nurse was also to remain. The nurse received curt instructions from the doctor what to do when I collapsed. Then the doctor flounced out and the nurse retired to a corner of the room and froze into a statue of disapproval.

Kaspir said: "Now listen, Mike. You gotta—"

"He's going to do exactly what he feels like doing." Maude bit off the words, one by one. "Just that and no more." She patted my wrist. Kaspir made a large, vulgar sound of disgust and turned his back.

"First of all," I said firmly, from under the shelter of Maude's anger at Kaspir, "where am I, what day is this, how did I get here, and why ain't I dead? Those fellows—"

"It's Saturday, the mornin' after the night before." This from Kaspir. "Two cops in a prowl car heard you screechin' for help. They got there just in time to see a pair o' muggs drummin' on your skull."

I was up on my elbow again. "Did they get them?"

"Nope."

I sank back. "How did you two get down here?"

"I—we—Steve got nervous about you last night," said Maude. "He called your friend Larssen this morning about two. Larssen checked the hospitals and found you here—this is St. Paul's, by the way. So Steve and I came right down, by plane." She hesitated, and a nasty glint flickered in her violet eyes. "Steve was airsick. Seven times."

A snicker escaped from the small nurse. Kaspir, stung, whirled.

"Those damn cocktails," he explained loudly. "What about the black dog?"

I MUST admit I enjoyed the next few minutes. It is a rare event when any voice other than his own can hold Colonel Kaspir's attention for more than thirty seconds. I told my tale in fullest detail. I told him of my suspicion that the black dog was somehow connected with the church notices that Howie had been working on.

I noted that the nurse was drawing nearer as I talked. By the time I had made my climax with a fine, dramatic account of the attack on me at the tool-shed, she was leaning on the bed, her pretty lips parted, her eyes like big brown marbles.

"Where's those notices?" demanded Kaspir.

"In my coat." I was annoyed at the absence of praise for my sagacity in finding the black dog.

The nurse handed me my coat. I turned the notices over to Kaspir.

Kaspir shoved out his under lip until his face looked like a bureau with the top drawer sticking out, and studied the notices even as I had studied them the night before in Tom's office.

"Whatinell's this?" he snapped finally. He declaimed: " 'The wicked flee when no man pursueth: but the righteous are bold as a lion.'"

Before I could launch into the story of Miss Abby Knott's plan for curing the world's ills, the small nurse answered out of her trance. "Proverbs," she said. I doubt if she realized she was speaking. "Proverbs, Twenty-eight, One."

"You see—" I began, determined to get my two cents' worth in. To my astonishment, Kaspir bayed: "Shut up." He lowered his eyebrows at the nurse. "Wha'd you say?" he inquired in a bull's bellow.

The nurse cringed, covered with confusion. "That thing you read," she explained feebly. "That was the first verse of Chapter Twenty-eight of the Book of Proverbs. I won a prize once in Sunday School for remembering—"

"How many chapters in Proverbs?" demanded Kaspir. He was not looking at her now. He was looking at the wall. I followed his gaze. There was a wall calendar there. Under the covers my knees began to shake; I wondered why. Excitement of some kind, I thought. But—"

"Thirty-one," answered the nurse faintly.

Suddenly I knew why my knees were shaking. "Before you go any further," I said, "let me tell you that Mr. Knott walked by the door just as you all came in. He was carrying flowers. But I think he was really looking for me."

I was trembling all over now. The image of A. Lincoln Knott, executive director of the "Little Home Ashore" and tireless benefactor of merchant seamen, was large in my mind's eye, and it affected me like the sight of a rattlesnake.

It was as though some trick of my inner eye had stripped Mr. Knott of his camouflage of grave good fellowship and laid bare an evil brain and a scaly soul.

Now I knew why I had trembled outside his home in Brambleton the night before. That was because he had been in the house, although he had refused to answer my ringing and knocking. It was Knott who had set the black dog on me, to follow me, to mark me for others so that the deed might be done a safe distance from the house.

I thought of Howie walking back to his car with the black dog padding at his heels. It was quite plain now. They had slugged Howie, driven him in his own car to the Ocean View road, deliberately aimed the car for the pole and jumped out. And Howie still alive at the time! And Adams! I recalled now that Adams' home was in the Brambleton section. He must have known Knott had a black dog, and decided to take a look around. The dog had followed Adams. But Adams had been able to get hold of the dog. That accounted for the black hairs on him. But the dog's co-workers had arrived and gone to work. And Adams had been removed to Berkley, where his murderers had aimed the police car for the culvert and stepped out just as it was picking up speed.

Strangely enough, I felt no particular rancor toward my attackers, who were most certainly the murderers of my nephew and Adams. That was because I was so sure that it was Knott's ugly, efficient brain we were up against.

"Knott…" I began.

Kaspir said quietly: "He's the bird Naval Intelligence has been keepin' a bright eye on for more'n a year. I looked up his dossier before we jumped down here last night."

"Then why in hell hasn't he been hanged long ago?" I almost yelled it, being understandably unstrung at the time.

"Because," said Kaspir solemnly, "he ain't made one single, solitary false move. Not one. They've tried him out in every conceivable way—planted guys in that Home joint, tapped his wires. Listen, they been checkin' on that Vogelsang at the confectionery, too. Get this: neither Knott, nor his sisters, nor anybody remotely connected with Knott has been in that store or communicated with Vogelsang in any way. In fact, if this Knott was to walk into a Federal Court and make a voluntary confession of some kind, we couldn't dig up enough evidence to make it stick."

Dead silence, during which Kaspir's eye fell on the pretty nurse. "Thirty-one chapters in Proverbs," he said under his breath. He patted her paternally on her starched cap. "Run along, baby," he said. "Captain Kettle's gotta climb into his pants and go places. Maude, you beat it out to a phone and call that Larssen feller and ask him to meet us in his office in half an hour."

Such is the force of Kaspir's personality, when he chooses to sound like an intelligent man instead of an overblown, petulant infant, that I was freed from the hospital with a minimum of argument, and twenty minutes later found myself, groggy but glad to be out, bowling along in a cab toward the offices of the *Virginian-Dispatch*.

COLONEL KASPIR picked up the phone, and I think every heart in the room skipped a beat.

We were a queer-looking crowd, hollow-eyed and weary. It was six o'clock that night, and we were still in Tom's office. We had been there, including Larssen, since ten A.M., digging into files, compiling lists, tearing them up, making new lists, and tearing *them* up.

Now Kaspir held the master list that represented nearly eight hours of labor and thought, and prepared to test it. He was calling Admiral Blank in Washington. He did not look at us, and we dared not look at one another. Larssen leaned against the wall, a dead cigarette in his lips. Maude sat beside me, her hand on my arm, and yawned. But she was not bored.

"Listen, Oscar," said Kaspir into the phone. I made myself glance at him. The hand that held the list was steady enough, but his natural ruddiness had been replaced by a grayer shade.

"These convoy sailin's outa Norfolk," said Kaspir, "they're pretty secret stuff, huh?"

I gathered that Admiral Blank was damning Kaspir for bothering him with insanely obvious questions.

"Supposin' I was to tell you"—here it came—"that I just read in the mornin' paper that a big convoy will pass outa the Capes Monday morning about one o'clock; that it's a helluva big convoy, and takin' the northern route."

All our eyes were upon him as he listened to Blank's reply. We saw his small mouth broaden in a smile of uncontrollable relief. When Blank paused for breath Kaspir said quickly: "Keep your shirt on, Oscar. I was just proddin' you. It didn't get in the paper. But it damn near did."

That had been our one big break of the day, the break which gave us hope at the very start. The paper had been tight the night before, and among the dozen or so columns of type squeezed out and held over for the Sunday edition had been the church notes. When Larssen had told Kaspir this I thought Kaspir was going to kiss him.

Kaspir was explaining to Blank now. It was very simple.

We had compiled a list of, and studied, every notice the *Virginian-Dispatch* had printed for Mr. Knott in nearly a year. As we pored over it, a curious pattern began to make itself apparent. Not the sort of thing you would ever see— unless you were cast in the mold of my nephew, Howie Sugg.

It began to dawn on us about four o'clock. Previously we had wasted considerable time digging for a complex code. It was the very simplicity of the thing which was so disarming.

Each notice contained one of the following words: "large," "medium," "small," or "alone."

Each notice contained one of the following: "north," "south," or "middle." Kaspir informed us, once the light began to shine, that convoys sailing from Norfolk take one of three general routes: the northern route, which usually means Iceland; the middle route, which means straight across, or the southern route, which indicates a trip to the Panama Canal and West Coast.

At four fifteen Kaspir, after a brisk telephone session with Naval Intelligence, had obtained a full list of U-boat attacks and sinkings occurring within a hundred miles of the Capes during the past nine months. When we checked this list against Knott's notices as printed in the *Virginian-Dispatch*, we gave a short cheer and sent out for beer.

I think a concrete example, chosen at random, will make Mr. Knott's system glaringly plain.

On May 3 the *Virginian-Dispatch* had printed a brief notice for Mr. Knott. The notice said that the "Little Home Ashore" was planning a party for a *small* group of merchant seaman who had recently arrived from a port in the *South*.

Appended was the inevitable proverb. This one was: "His own iniquities shall take the wicked himself, and he shall be holden with the cords of his sins." That is Chapter Five, Number Twenty-two.

The *fifth* day of the month. And using the foreign system, 22 o'clock is 10 o'clock at night.

You can understand, then, our excitement when the Naval Intelligence records showed that a small convoy had passed through the Capes on May 5 at approximately 10 P.M., bound for the Canal Zone.

Need I add that the records also showed that the convoy had undergone a savage attack from a U-boat pack—a pack most obviously lying in wait—twenty-odd miles south of Cape Henry, and had been badly banged up?

NEAR THE close of Kaspir's talk with Blank, the Admiral asked the inevitable question. We could tell when it came by the slackening of Kaspir's hands on the phone, and the dogged look that came into his eyes.

How had Knott's information been transmitted to the U-boat wolf packs—the commanders of which were most certainly not on the mailing list of the *Virginian-Dispatch?* Signal lights, shortwave sets—Naval Intelligence had gone thoroughly into these possibilities, and was ready to swear it had not been done in that way.

"We'll get that dope," Kaspir said finally. "You'll hold up that convoy on the twenty-eighth, of course. I'll call you." He hung up and reared back in Larssen's swivel chair.

On the wall there hung a large map of the coastline, and this he looked at a long while.

"You got much circulation down on the North Carolina coast—just below the Virginia line?" he said suddenly.

Larssen said, "Fair." Then he shook his head. "But they only get the mail edition down that way. We don't carry the church notes in that; they're run only in the city edition."

"Got any special mailing list for the city edition down that way?" drawled Kaspir.

Larssen clutched an inter-office phone, dialed two digits. "Jake," he said, "this is Larssen. Jake, do we mail any city editions down Princess Anne County or Elizabeth City way?"

I will not attempt to describe Tom's expression as he listened to the answer, but his voice, as he said "Thanks," was almost lost in his throat. He turned to Kaspir.

"By special request," he said huskily, "we mail one city edition, daily and Sunday, to a man who has a place about six miles back from Albemarle Sound, in Carolina."

He paused. He seemed short of breath.

"Jake Ware, our mailing-room foreman, happens to know the guy," he said. "His name is Vogelsang. He has a brother here who runs a small confectionery in Brambleton."

He paused again, but his eyes told me he was not through. Tom Larssen is not what I would call an emotional man, but the little laugh he gave was brittle with nervous strain.

"Go on," said Kaspir.

"Jake says this fellow Vogelsang has built up quite a business down there," said Tom. "He sells carrier pigeons to the Army Signal Corps."

In the silence that followed, I could see a pigeon winging its way to sea, to where a U-boat waited.

THAT NIGHT shortly after nine o'clock our party, minus Maude, sat in the office of an all-night bakery—a spot chosen because it was less than two blocks from the "Little Home Ashore"—and awaited a telephone call.

There had been two additions to our ranks. The medium-sized man with big hands was Inspector Pitt, of the Norfolk police. The lean, dark, silent one was Detective-Sergeant Dicksen.

The telephone call was to come from Maude. It was already overdue. Kaspir pretended not to be worried. I had stopped pretending.

Faintly along the street came the music from the "Little Home Ashore," where well-scrubbed seamen in their Sunday best were dancing with smartly-gowned girls and women.

Among the girls attending was Maude, in a gown borrowed from Larssen's pretty wife. This was Kaspir's idea.

He had been desperately anxious to make sure that not only Knott, but both his sisters were in the Home Ashore building before we hit it. So Maude had gone there in the guise of a guest, introduced by a committee-woman who was a friend of Larssen's wife, and was to phone us at the bakery as soon as she learned what Kaspir wanted to know. Kaspir was afraid, I believe, that one of the Knott sisters might be staying home so that, at the first sign of anything going wrong, she might telephone a warning to the North Carolina Vogelsang.

When I asked Kaspir why he did not have the pigeon-raising Vogelsang picked up in advance he only snorted.

The bakery office clock said nine eleven. Maude had gone to the "Little Home Ashore" at quarter past eight. I looked hard at Kaspir. He was patting his foot and humming.

I nearly jumped out of my skin when the phone shrilled, but I was the first to reach it. "Maude!" I yelled, almost before I had the receiver to my ear.

"Mike!" Her voice was a scream. "Mike, I'm—"

Kaspir shot to his feet. So did the others. We all heard quite plainly the oath and the blow at the other end of the line; then a crash, then silence.

We did not bother to take the police car that was waiting. Despite my experience of the night before I managed to stay even with Kaspir and the lean, dark sergeant as we sprinted up the street, and that was no mean feat, for Kaspir was running like a man possessed of devils. Behind us pounded Inspector Pitt and Tom.

We wheeled into the brightly-lighted lobby of the Home Ashore. Sergeant Dicksen, who knew the place well, led us across the dance floor between the many astonished couples and into a rear hall.

A. Lincoln Knott was in his office when we burst in. He was in the act of picking the telephone up from the floor. He looked up from his stooping position, and neither Kaspir nor Dicksen nor I missed the quick, instinctive glance toward the door in the far corner of the office.

Kaspir was through that door in an instant, with me on his heels. The narrow hall we entered was dark, but we could hear the scuffling sound at the far end. Kaspir plunged ahead. From the darkness beyond, a man swore and there was a sharp report, deafening in that place, and a spit of yellow flame. Then a blow or two, and the man cried out in pain. I waded in behind Kaspir, groping blindly, and was rewarded, a moment later, by finding myself clutching a limp female form.

At this point somebody in Knott's office turned a flashlight beam down our corridor. It was Maude I was holding, and she was semi-conscious. Beyond us was a heartening tableau. Colonel Kaspir held two persons. His great right hand was closed around the throat of a hard-faced young man I had never seen before. His left was entwined in the faded blond hair of a middle-aged woman who belied her housewifely appearance by clawing at Kaspir like a mad cat and swearing like a barge mate.

We went back into Knott's office with our catch. Kaspir loosed his grip on the man who had shot at him, and the fellow sagged against the wall.

"I take it you're Abby, the Bible expert," said Kaspir calmly to his other prisoner. He turned her over to Sergeant Dicksen.

Knott was sitting behind his desk now, his gray hair ruffled, Inspector Pitt standing over him. "May I ask," he addressed Kaspir, "what is the meaning of this outrage?"

It was Maude who provided the diversion, a horribly indignant Maude whose right cheek was purple from a blow. Wobbling a little, she faced the man whom Kaspir had throttled. "Slap me with a gun, will you?" she demanded, and kicked him not once, but several times, on the shins.

I calmed her and we heard her story. It seemed that Knott had spotted her at once—he had seen her going into my room at the hospital that morning. Dear Miss Abby Knott, with her gentle ways, had lured Maude away from the dance floor and back to the office. There they had jumped her and tied her to a chair.

The mistake they made was leaving her alone for a minute. In that minute Maude had used her head—and her teeth. A pencil was on the desk. Once she got an end of it in her mouth, it was not too difficult to pry the telephone receiver from its cradle and use the pencil point to dial the bakery. It was the sudden return of the hard-faced young man which had occasioned the shriek and other sounds we had heard over the wire. The hard-faced young man had smacked Maude across the face with the barrel of his automatic and then gone for Miss Abby. Together they were wrestling her out the back way when we arrived.

Maude told us that Jessica Knott, the other sister, was not in the building. Inspector Pitt snatched up the phone and got the Brambleton Precinct. "That you, Sergeant?" he said. "Did you get Vogelsang and the other boys at the confectionery? Fine! Now drop over to Mr. Knott's house and grab Jessica Knott. Yes, I said Jessica Knott. And above everything, don't let her use the phone. And Sergeant, if you see that black dog of theirs around, shoot the ———."

"YOU WILL never prove any connection between me and the violence done young Sugg and the detective," stated Mr. Knott quietly.

"You had a good racket, Knott," said Kaspir thoughtfully, "running a clearin' house for seamen like this. What dope on sailin's you couldn't get from your own men on ships, you could piece together by notin' what guys quit comin' here all of a sudden."

"I defy you to prove anything," said Knott. He was the calmest man in the room.

"That was clever, trainin' the dog to put the finger on anybody you wanted bumped off by your Murder, Incorporated, at the confectionery," Kaspir rambled on. "Nope, I know you never spoke to Vogelsang, or his boys. But when they saw that damn dog o' yours followin' anybody at night, they knew what to do…" He was watching Knott's plump face. Knott's eyes were as placid as two quiet pools.

"Young Sugg doped your racket and went to you and accused you," continued Kaspir. "You put the dog on him. And the next night, when Adams came around, you put the dog on him."

He was getting nowhere that I could see.

Kaspir inspected his fingernails. "We ain't pickin' up your pigeon-breedin' pal in Carolina just yet," he drawled. "We're savin' him."

I saw—we all saw—the new expression on Knott's face. He started to speak, but Kaspir held up his hand. "Don't tell me," said Kaspir. "I know. You've never spoken to that

Vogelsang, either. No communication by word or gesture. But bein' as how you're now in custody, and can't issue any more o' those fancy little pieces for the church column, Larssen here is takin' the liberty o' runnin' one for you tomorrow mornin'—as it was dictated by me."

For the space of a breath I was almost sorry for A. Lincoln Knott. His ego must have let him believe to the very last that the carrier-pigeon part of his set-up was still intact for future use by some other agent.

"Read it to him, Larssen," suggested Kaspir, and Knott leaned forward, hands spread wide on the table and something like death in his gray eyes.

Larssen's voice held no hint of irony as he read: " 'The *largest*' "—he stressed the word—" 'dance yet given by the "Little Home Ashore" will be staged in the near future, A. Lincoln Knott announced last night. One of the finest orchestras in this part of the *South* will play for the dance gratis.'"

I gritted my teeth as I watched Knott's face. He was cracking.

"We chose a right nice little Proverb to top it off with," said Kaspir inexorably. "Go on, Larssen."

Tom drew breath. " 'When the righteous are in authority,'" he said " 'the people rejoice: but when the wicked beareth rule, the people mourn.'"

"That's Chapter Twenty-nine, Number Two," explained Kaspir gently. "As you know, Knott, there's a real convoy leavin' Monday the twenty-eighth at one A.M. But your boys won't bother with that. Nope, your gang'll be all steamed up by the news they're gonna receive tomorrow by carrier pigeon from your pal Vogelsang in Carolina, who'll have read it in his copy o' the paper.

"You note," said Kaspir, "that we're puttin' the date at Tuesday the twenty-ninth for this *largest* convoy. That's to give your U-boats an extra day to rally round in force and get all set. You note that we're puttin' the hour for our Tuesday convoy to pass the Capes at two A.M. That'll mean your U-boats'll have to surface in daylight for a crack at it. But they'll take the risk. Because they'll have heard by carrier pigeon that it's the largest convoy of all."

Kaspir's eyes bored into Knott's now, and suddenly his tone took on a sharper edge.

"But there won't be any merchantmen—no lame ducks—in that Tuesday convoy," said Kaspir. "Oh yes, there'll really be a convoy goin' out. But it'll be a kind of extra-special convoy. There's gonna be"—he began ticking off the items on his fingers—"destroyers—and Coast Guard cutters—and mosquito boats—and maybe a cruiser or two—and dive bombers—and two or three blimps— and me. I'm goin' out for the ride, Knott. I wouldn't miss it for a pretty. Not for a pretty. And your name's gonna be mud around the German admiralty, Knott. They ain't gonna like you for steerin' half a dozen U-boats into a trap. Not one little bit."

In view of the situation, I suppose it was some sort of relief for Mr. Knott to leap up and rip the notice from Larssen's hand and then fling himself, raving, upon Kaspir. Besides, what else was there for him to do?

THE SWEET WATERS OF DEATH

THE LOVESICK CAPTAIN
KETTLE AND THE BEAUTEOUS
MAUDE WERE DELIGHTED
WHEN THE HEAD MAN OF
SECTION 5 INVITED THEM
TO COME ALONG ON A
WEEKEND HOLIDAY-BY-
THE-SEA. THAT WAS BEFORE
THEY DISCOVERED: 1) THAT
THEY WERE TO SERVE AS
DECOYS TO BAG A BUNCH
OF BLOODTHIRSTY AXIS
VULTURES WHO HAD SWOOPED
DOWN AND CARRIED OFF A U.S.
ARMY BOMBSIGHT, AND 2) THAT
COLONEL KASPIR'S "BEACH
RESORT" WAS SITUATED ON
TOP OF A POWDER KEG—5,000
MILES AWAY!

CHAPTER ONE
WEEK-END PLANS

THE STRANGEST military trial of all was held recently. It was a hurried affair, largely because the presiding officer was restless from a fresh knife slash along his fifth rib.

The presiding officer was Colonel Stephen Kaspir, my chief in the counterespionage bureau known as Section Five.

Details of the trial are by courtesy of Lieutenant Charlie Wu, formerly head of the Alien Squad of that admirable organization, the New York Police Department, now in charge of Section Five's New York office.

It was embarrassing, my having to ask Charlie Wu what actually occurred on that scented August night at the Locanda of the Sweet Waters of the Marmora—embarrassing because I was virtually present at the trial myself. But I did not know it at the time.

WASHINGTON, SECOND week in August—

Kaspir and Maude and I had just returned from Jacksonville, following the arrest of Kornamann.

You remember Kornamann? He was the vaudeville magician who climaxed his act by making his wife Elise "melt" and disappear inside a glass case, to the eerie accom-

Colonel Noga said, over the threat of the revolver in his
square hand: "Give me the bombsight."

paniment of blue lightning flashes and much sparking and
spitting of electrical gadgets.

Kornamann's act had the peculiar advantage of being
presented on schedule each night. Thus, U-boat commanders knew almost to the minute when to emerge and receive
the vital shipping information that Kornamann was broad-
casting in code even as the audience gaped at Elise "melting" into invisibility before their very eyes.

Upon our return to Washington, after three days and
nights without sleep, Kaspir, with the air of a potentate
bestowing alms on a beggar, gave Maude and me the
evening off.

Kaspir himself purchased a two-pound box of chocolate cherries and five pounds of English walnuts and retired to our headquarters in southwest Washington to stuff himself and—as Maude predicted—think up something to spoil our evening.

"He'll do it, too," said Maude, with conviction. She spoke bitterly, but her violet eyes smiled at me over the rim of her cocktail. We were at the Maison Rouge, jammed cosily close on red leather bar stools, waiting for a table in the diningroom.

Maude's smile and the bare, honey-tan shoulder pressing my black sleeve struck a deep-toned gong somewhere inside me. When it stopped vibrating I was weak but calm. "This is it," I told myself. I drew back as far as the press would allow and looked at her to summon the extra courage I needed.

Maude stared back at me. I saw her violet eyes turn deep and solemn. She knew it, too. Her slender fingers held the martini suspended six inches above the dark mahogany of the bar, and her red lips parted as she drew breath.

I opened my mouth, but no words came out, so I closed it again. I gazed at the cool Grecian upsweep of her blond hair, at the delicately modeled nose and the firm chin.

Her left hand touched my sleeve. A peculiar light gleamed behind the solemnity of her eyes.

"Was that a proposal?" she inquired.

I nodded numbly, cursing my ineffectuality at the one moment when a man should appear at his best. Old night-thoughts began to stalk my brain. Maude has money of her own, lots of it. I have a captain's pay and the prospect, after the war, of returning to an editorial desk on the *Baltimore Sun*. Too, our work with Kaspir in Section Five makes us both the poorest sort of insurance risks. And we live a rack-ety life on planes and trains....

"Quite the nicest proposal," said Maude, softly and thoughtfully, "that I've ever had." Her hand, closing around my wrist, threw my pulses into confusion. "Quite the nicest," she repeated.

I waited, staring at the olive in her glass. In the green liquid surrounding it appeared the reflection of some-thing large and white. My right shoulder telegraphed my brain that someone was tapping it. My brain rejected the message.

Maude looked up. "Mike, dear...."

The tapping on my shoulder was repeated, harder this time. Our table must be ready.

"Oh, for heaven's sake wait a minute," I flung over my shoulder, irritably.

"You got a uniform stowed away somewhere, ain't you?" demanded a neighing voice in my ear.

Maude said something curt and angry under her breath. I turned quickly.

"I said, you got a uniform somewhere, ain't you?" repeated Colonel Kaspir, who had been rapping at my shoulder as a man knocks at a locked door. His yards and yards of white linen suit hung rumpled from his great, tubular figure. In his full moon of a face the Cupid's-bow mouth was pursed thoughtfully, and the small blue eyes were preoccupied.

Maude said, "Oh, dammit, Steve!" in a shaky voice.

"Yes," I replied coldly, "I got a uniform. I think it's in my trunk. Why?" That uniform had been my pride and joy when I entered the Army Intelligence branch early in '40, but I had worn it less than a dozen times. Kaspir had borrowed me from G-2 long, long before Pearl Harbor. In Section Five, uniforms are most emphatically not worn.

"C'mon," grunted Kaspir, and lumbered out.

MAUDE SLID leggily from the bar stool.

"The kid in the three-cornered pants," she muttered, glaring after Kaspir. I had to laugh. The breadth of Kaspir's hips does make his rear elevation triangular from the waist down.

At the curb a taxi, chuffing impatiently, rocked dangerously as Kaspir boarded it like a prize hog squeezing through a gate.

Maude and I climbed in after him and we three became a warm, damp, compact mass sticking to the leather.

The gears clashed and the driver's bullet head turned like a thumbscrew on his thick neck. "Where to, boss?"

To our surprise, Kaspir gave the address of Maude's hotel, three blocks away, then inspected his fingernails with elaborate interest as the cab lurched out into traffic.

We asked no questions—the surest way of annoying Kaspir when he is being the man of mystery. Our apparent lack of interest affected him immediately. He patted the floor with a foot like a mudscow and made sucking noises through his teeth.

The cab, swooping down on the marquee of Maude's hotel, straightened our spines with the violence of its stop. I opened the door and got out, offering a lover's hand to Maude.

"Good-night, Steve," said Maude, poker-faced, preparing to disembark.

That fetched him. "Chuck some frillies into a bag," he said, sour at being forced to give ground. "Get around to the office soon's you can."

That fetched Maude. Dress is a serious matter to her. "Where are we going?" she demanded.

"Li'l beach resort," said Kaspir vaguely. Then, cryptically: "Bring plenty o' that war paint you wear."

"I keep an old inner tube in the hotel safe," suggested Maude hopefully. "Shall I bring that along for you?"

Kaspir, who can't swim, ignored the jibe. Maude marched regally into the hotel.

Back in the cab again, I anticipated him by giving the address of my own hotel. He slumped in the seat and fidgeted.

My hotel wears no marquee, so as not to frighten rural congressmen.

"Well," I said, as we pulled up, "what about the uniform?"

He seemed surprised. "Wear it, o' course," he snapped. "Bring all your papers."

I tingled, but was careful not to show it.

"Step on it," said Kaspir as I hopped out. Whether he meant the driver or me I could not guess. As the door slammed he was neighing to the driver the address of the old brownstone ex-boarding house in which Section Five was born and brought up and still calls home.

Curiosity as to what Kaspir had on his mind kept me from lingering over the delightful experience of donning my uniform. I rationed myself to a single glance in the full-length mirror and hoped Maude would think me half as dashing as I felt.

I debated phoning Maude, but decided against it. When I got her answer, I wanted her lips handy to my own.

A cold pang of apprehension invaded my stomach without warning. Whence this over-confidence about Maude? My hands began to fumble as I chucked identification papers, a change of underwear, and various oddments into a little handbag.

In the cab, streaking through the mellow night into southwest Washington, I sampled over and over the intonation of that "Mike, dear...."

But I could reach no decision.

AS I jogged up the worn stone steps, the fly-specked glass door opened silently. Joe, the Negro houseboy, was there.

Joe indulged in none of his usual minstrel routines.

"General Tancred's upstairs," he announced, without preamble. His coat was unbuttoned and I could see the handle of the .45 in the shoulder holster. Joe holds a law degree from Columbia. It is his misfortune that a prestidigital speed and micrometer-like accuracy with a gun has condemned him to the not unimportant role of inner guard for Section Five.

I used to be sorry for Joe until I learned that his rank and pay are identical with my own.

"Maude here yet?" I managed to make it casual.

Joe nodded. I thought I spotted the tiniest flicker of a smile at the corners of his mouth.

I hurried upstairs into the musty atmosphere bequeathed Section Five by its former tenants and which never leaves it, winter or summer. My shining boots echoed down the third floor hall.

In the anteroom to Kaspir's office waited Maude. Her tan linen suit was a crisp reproach to all the untidy linens in the world.

Kaspir's door was shut. Through it I could hear muffled voices.

Maude cocked her divine head at my uniform. I tried to fathom her reaction. Was it affectionate pride? Or was she wearing her old sardonic armor against sentiment, and laughing at the pristine beauty of my get-up?

She took a hesitant step toward me. I put my handbag down quietly.

"Mike," she began, "I didn't get a chance to tell you at the Maison Rouge, but...."

"Mike Kettle!" Kaspir's bellow nearly shivered the door panel between us. "You there?"

In the midst of a brief, pregnant silence, Maude said, "Oh, hell!" and her underlip trembled.

"Yes," I called back sullenly. "I'm here."

"Whatinell's keeping Maude?" bellowed Kaspir.

Maude's high heels clicked angrily across the grimy floor. She flung open the door.

"Nothing," she answered, acid in her tone. We went in. My face was hot and I saw scarlet spots high on Maude's cheekbones.

Kaspir, sprawled in his swivel chair, chins on chest, treated us to a single scorching glance that saw and comprehended all.

"If you two are through lollygaggin'," he said nastily, "siddown."

Maude's poise had returned. She settled herself as a queen might. Her gracious nod to General Tancred pointedly excluded Kaspir. I forgot to salute Tancred, who was also in uniform, and sat down gingerly.

General Tancred, standing by the desk, overlooked my sin of omission. His large head, with its saucer-like ears, made his small body look frailer than usual. His little black eyes, normally as hard and bright as a pair of diamond drills, were dull with weariness or worry. But most amazing of all was the utter absence of that prickly, wary, belligerent manner which customarily marks his every dealing with Kaspir.

Equally amazing was Kaspir's apologetic: "Sorry to have kept you General. Would you care to stay a little longer?"

I might interpolate here that Section Five is in no way connected with, or subordinate to, G-2. Kaspir's title of colonel derives from the governor of Kentucky. So that when Kaspir defers to General Tancred it is by choice, and under no official compulsion.

General Tancred clapped a shabby cap on the head that contains the best brain in G-2.

"You explain," he said shortly. "I've told you all I know." He bit his lip, gazed at the wall over Kaspir's head. "Arrangements for the plane are being completed now," he said absently. He hesitated. Kaspir rose, looked down at him gravely.

"Good luck to you," said Tancred suddenly and awkwardly. He shoved a stubby hand at Kaspir, who took it with some embarrassment. Then he shook hands with Maude and me as we scrambled to our feet.

Maude gave me a meaning look as Tancred left. This was a love feast. I recalled some of the scenes I had witnessed between Tancred and Kaspir in this office and wondered. Whatever had created a bond of sympathy, however brief, between those two must be a very grave matter indeed.

We sat down again.

"Somebody's pinched a bombsight," blurted Kaspir, then, with a hint of his old bumptiousness, "The Gen's kind of anxious to get it back." He rummaged in a desk drawer and came up with two chocolate cherries, which he popped into his mouth. "The Gen," he mumbled through the juice, "is in a funk." He swallowed noisily and reached into the drawer again. "So'm I," he confessed, not looking at us.

Maude was the first to recover.

"I suppose," she said frostily, to hide a very real concern, "that it would be too much to ask what Mike and I are to do. And when, where, how, and why?"

Kaspir's right paw now held four English walnuts. He tightened his fingers and you could hear the shells splintering against each other. He plucked a sliver of shell from the ball of his thumb, sucked the bead of blood that followed this operation, then hurled shells and nut meats into the wastebasket.

"Mike," he said, nursing the thumb, "you're goin' to this beach resort place in uniform and make open inquiries about Tolliver, Maude—"

"Who's Tolliver?"

SURELY MY question was not an unreasonable one. But from Kaspir's expression you might have thought me guilty of the grossest ignorance and inattention.

"The G-2 feller who had a lead on the bombsight," he explained, with a strained patience that made my scalp prickle. "Maude, you're gonna be a tart that Mike's picked up and taken on a week-end to this hotel. You'll stay in Mike's room, but you'll be dishin' out a glad eye to the other male guests on all occasions. We want attention focused on you and Mike. You got that?"

"Of course," said Maude. "How nice!"

"Ain't it?" said Kaspir, with a leer. He heaved himself to his feet and clumped over to the wall closet where he keeps his spare wardrobe. In a dead silence he shrugged out of his soiled white coat and began to loosen his collar and tie.

"It might interest you to know," said Maude, tapping a cigarette on the dull gold case that cost me a month's pay last year, "that I'm not going anywhere at all, or doing anything…."

Kaspir wheeled and stopped unbuttoning his shirt.

"… until you tell me where the bomb-sight was stolen, who is supposed to have it, and what steps we're taking to get it back." Her pose of chill indifference collapsed without warning. "Really, Steve, this business of making a mystery out of everything!" Her voice was high and a little shrill.

Kaspir frowned, puzzled, and returned to the desk. "Don't you get it?"

I honestly believe he thought he had explained everything in fullest detail.

Maude said, less emotionally: "No, I don't get it."

Kaspir's hand strayed toward the drawer where the chocolate cherries reposed.

"You see," he said gently, as though to a child, "this army bomber made a forced landing near the city. They were gonna destroy the bombsight—matter o' routine. But they cracked up unexpectedly. Four o' the crew were killed, and the fifth feller was knocked stiff as a haddock for eight-ten hours.

"When he came to, he was in a hospital. He scrammed outa there and got hold of some o' the G-2 boys workin' that section. They high-tailed it out to the wreck. No trace o' the bombsight."

He had us on the edge of our chairs now, and made the most of it.

"Naturally, G-2 began sweatin' drops as big as horse chestnuts. The bomber had cracked up near the estate of a wealthy gent named Robin. It was Robin's servants who dug the fellers outa the wreck and took the live guy to the hospital. G-2 was highly interested—account of they'd had an eye on Robin and his household for some little time."

He paused for effect. "Go on," said Maude grimly.

"It seems," said Kaspir, holding a chocolate cherry between his thumb and forefinger and inspecting it for flaws, "that friend Robin left home immediately after the bomber crashed and went to spend a week or two at this beach resort place. G-2 got hold o' the local authorities and told 'em what happened. The local lads got steamed up, too, and arranged to cover all outgoin' trains, planes, boats and kiddie cars."

His lips closed over the chocolate cherry and we heard it squash between his tongue and the roof of his mouth. I wriggled impatiently. Maude's jaw line hardened in exasperation. Kaspir surveyed us benignly.

"Well," he drawled, stringing it out as far as possible, "that left it up to G-2 to smell out the bombsight. Some fellers went one way, some went another, and this bird Tolliver, who's got the longest head of the whole G-2 crowd in those parts, went after Robin.

"Tolliver figured Robin was gonna turn over the bomb-sight—supposin' he had it—to some of his people at the beach resort. Tolliver figured that since Robin had acted on the spur o' the moment—because he couldn't have known in advance that the bomber 'ud fold up right in his own back yard—that his crowd wasn't organized to get it outa the country. He figured Robin was smart enough to know he'd been under surveillance, so he'd never try to take it out himself. In short, Tolliver figured Robin 'ud turn it over to some underling at the beach resort and let the other guy stash it away until things quieted down...."

"Because this was real big stuff. They might never have another chance like this one, and they couldn't afford to miss."

"But where do we come in?" I said. "If it's G-2 work—"

"Keep your shirt on. And quit squirmin', Maude. Tolliver went to this beach resort. He was to report back in twelve hours. He didn't. At the end o' twenty-four, G-2 called the hotel. He'd registered there, all right, but he'd disappeared durin' the night. His bed hadn't been slept in.

"So Robin and his merry men must ha' spotted Tolliver right off. *And* they'd prob'ly spot the next guy G-2 sent in. So Tancred got in touch with me. I said we'd take it on with pleasure if the local lads would keep hands offa the hotel and just continue checkin' planes and trains to make sure some bozo didn't smuggle the bombsight out wrapped up in a dirty shirt."

"So Mike's to show up in uniform and make open inquiries about Tolliver," said Maude coldly. "That's just dandy. How long do you suppose Mike will last?"

"OH, MIKE'S just bait," said Kaspir carelessly, losing interest now. He unbuttoned another shirt button. "So're you. Me and Charlie Wu will be there. We'll be in disguise. Charlie and me will handle it. These fellers are playin' for keeps, you know."

"So I gather from what happened to Tolliver," said Maude. "So Mike and I are the stalking horses, huh?"

"Yep," said Kaspir unfeelingly. A thought struck him. "Before I forget it, Mike"—he picked up a long, official envelope and thrust it at me—"here's your note to General Nassif. You'll have to see him before you head for this beach resort place—get official permission to make inquiries, that sorta thing. But you won't have any trouble with old Whiskers. He's a cagy citizen."

He unbuttoned two more buttons and hauled out an incredible length of shirt-tail. He had his thumbs under his suspenders when Maude, in a voice fairly dripping suspicion, said: "Why was the bomber crew going to destroy the bombsight?"

"Why? Great grief, woman! They'd done their job. They knew they'd be interned soon's they landed."

Interned!

"Don't let me alarm you," I said, "but I'm going to ask a question. What's the name of this beach resort?"

Kaspir's moonface turned smug as a cat's. "It's called...." and here he reeled off some gibberish which—and he knew it—conveyed no meaning at all to us.

Maude jumped up and ground her cigarette under an angry foot. "What does that mean?" she demanded, on a rising note.

"Sweet Waters of the Marmora," said Kaspir sweetly. "The hotel's called the 'Locanda of the Sweet Waters of the Marmora.' Now run along while I change my britches."

Marmora!

"But the Sea of Marmora's in Turkey." Maude clung to the last shred of her temper as a child clings to a toy.

"Yep."

"Are we going to Turkey?" she shrilled.

"Yep. Just outside Istanbul."

Brief interlude, while Maude hit the ceiling.

"Then why in the name of the seventh hell—" this in a half shriek—"didn't you tell us?"

Again Kaspir looked puzzled. "Thought you knew. Besides, what difference does it make?"

Maude sat down, panting helplessly, and glared at him. Kaspir slipped the suspenders from his bulky shoulders and bent laboriously to untie his shoes.

"Then the plane must have been one of those from—" I began.

"Rumania," grunted Kaspir from near the floor. "Been spreadin' joy and light in the oilfields."

"And the Turkish police are helping us?"

"Yep." He straightened up, kicked his shoes into the closet. "An' they're not kiddin', either. They don't want Goering's boys squintin' through one o' those Norden sights when they move in on the Dardanelles—supposin' Goering gets that far—which ain't altogether impossible."

He unbuttoned the top button of his trousers with the air of a man determined to see an ugly proposition through to the end. Maude stepped hastily into the outer office, and I followed. By tacit agreement we abandoned the matter of romance until a more propitious moment. Our nerves were more than slightly jangled.

Ten minutes later Kaspir appeared in the shaggiest of his shaggy tweed suits. He wore a gray homburg hat, a pink shirt, and spats, and he looked for all the world like one of the traveling Britons who once infested Continental resorts and bawled out waiters at every meal.

We left at once for the plane.

CHAPTER TWO
DANGER ZONE

THE FIRST leg of the flight was to Mitchel Field. En route, Kaspir's sole significant action was to open his suitcase, lift the lid of his box of chocolate cherries, and gaze longingly at his favorite fruit. He replaced the lid thoughtfully, without indulging, and wiped his brow.

I noted the green tinge of his mouth. So did Maude. She emerged briefly from her brown study and shouted through the vibration of the plane: "Better cram down three or four, Steve. Settle your stomach."

Colonel Kaspir shot her a glance of pure venom and reeled down the aisle to the washroom.

We touched Mitchel Field for just so long as it took Lieutenant Charlie Wu to get aboard, his squat, cubic figure, solid as a blockhouse, neatly draped in blue summer worsted and topped with a gray felt snapbrim.

I had not seen Charlie Wu since the business of Komagi-chi Yesuda and Den-Kaigi, and it was good to have him with us again.

Charlie Wu's brown millpond of a face and his large, liquid brown eyes showed his pleasure at seeing us. He shook hands with Maude and me and gave Kaspir, who was draped limply over two seats, his brow moist with the dew of airsickness, a purely Occidental grin.

Kaspir rallied feebly. He pointed to Charlie Wu's hand-bag. "You gottee duds, li'l China boy?" he inquired.

"Me blingee," said Charlie Wu courteously. He sat down opposite Kaspir and folded his hands in mock-Oriental fashion on his stomach. "Me pinchee duds from good cousin mine, Wang Lee." His glance strayed to Maude and me and we saw the twinkle deep in his eyes. "Me hunglee, boss man," he said innocently. "You maybe gottee big bowl chop suey in suitcase, huh?"

Kaspir cursed him and turned away.

"Velly solly," said Charlie Wu, with some concern. Then, to me: "Would you mind letting me in on the purpose of this expedition? He"—a jerk of the thumb toward the recumbent Kaspir—"said we were going to look for a needle in a haystack. Then he hung up."

Service planes are not constructed with the soundproof particularity of commercial airliners. I cupped my hands to my mouth and began to explain. When speaker's sore throat forced me to pause, Maude took over.

The twinkle in Charlie Wu's eyes dimmed and died. When Maude was through he thanked us but offered no comment.

I settled myself as comfortably as I could and tried to force a nap, but it was no use. A hard, angular lump of apprehension that was forming just below my breastbone made real repose impossible. Maude enfolded herself in a huge, ulsterlike coat and stared straight ahead. Once she glanced my way and smiled with her lips.

The plane lunged on through the bumpy night air. The co-pilot, a rangy youth in casual khaki, ambled back and dealt out coffee and sandwiches. He was especially atten-tive to Maude, until I became vaguely jealous. Then he returned once more to the dark forward reaches of the machine.

What he told the pilot I don't know, but I can guess, for the pilot, also rangy, and absurdly handsome, strolled among us to make sure we were comfortable. He was especially solicitous about Maude. Later he disappeared, to be replaced by the radio man and others of the crew. They were polite to all of us, but the best of the blankets and flying coats, they brought were lavished on Maude, who finally fell asleep in a deep burrow of wool and fur.

The reaction was setting in all around. Kaspir slept, his great body and long, thick legs suggesting a whale stranded on two small flying seats.

The moment I made up my mind I could not possibly sleep, I dozed gently off. My final waking impression was of Charlie Wu, head thrown back, staring at the ceiling with inscrutable eyes.

We awoke cramped but refreshed, to find ourselves apparently motionless in a sky that was all but blinding with sunlight, five thousand feet over water like deep green marble.

The co-pilot appeared with more coffee and sandwiches. He was most attentive to Maude....

FOR OBVIOUS reasons I cannot lay out our route for you. It was a long trip. Kaspir alternately dozed and was airsick, with intervals of pacing our crowded quarters. When he did this it was like being shut in a telephone booth with an elephant.

The green water yielded to green land. Then more water. Then more land, this stretch a desert yellow.

There were stops, of course, at small landing fields inhabited by various sizes and shapes of brown young men in khaki who invariably formed clusters around Maude when she stepped out for a cigarette and to stare at the bombers, which were everywhere.

Night came again, a superb night like a black velvet curtain. Star colonies raced along beside us, seemingly not a dozen feet from our steady wingtips. Time and space ceased to exist for me. They were factors controlled by the young men in khaki, who materialized in the cabin from time to time to say a word to Maude.

Once more we slept. A heavy hand shook me awake. The plane was no longer in motion. We must have landed again.

"You're sure you know what to do?" said Kaspir. To my amazement, he had his hat on, his suitcase in his hand. Behind him was Charlie Wu, similarly prepared to get off.

"Say…" I sat up, startled.

Across the aisle Maude stirred and regarded Kaspir with sleep-heavy eyes. "Where are we?" she mumbled drowsily.

"Cairo," said Kaspir. "You got it straight, Mike? When you hit Istanbul, let Maude wait in the plane till you've started off to see old Nassif. Maude, sneak away from the airport and wait for Mike at the Hotel Grand Anglais in the Pera section. Mike, once you finish with Nassif, hire a car, pick up Maude at the Grand Anglais, and head straight for the Locanda of the Sweet Waters of the Marmora. It's just below the city, beyond the Seven Towers. Minute you get there, park Maude in the bar and start askin' questions about Tolliver. You got all that?"

I nodded. Kaspir turned to the open port and followed Charlie Wu out.

"Hey, wait!" I sat up, alarmed. "What about you?"

"Gettin' out here," said Kaspir over his shoulder. "Me and Charlie are goin' on by commercial plane."

Maude struggled out from under the blankets and flying coats. "Listen here, Steve Kaspir—" she began warmly.

"Be seein' you," murmured Kaspir. Somebody slammed shut the port through which he had vanished. Our motors sprang to life with the sound of the slam.

Immediately I felt very much alone, more than a little helpless, and, to be frank, frightened. The sense of responsibility which had been growing upon me ever since Washington had now assumed almost overwhelming proportions.

In Maude's eyes were mirrored my own emotions. Her slender hand came across the aisle and I gripped it, hard. She smiled.

That smile helped a lot. Something like determination began to fill the apprehensive void in me. I felt as though I had muscles again, and a mind.

I winked at her. I let go her hand and, with a great show of casual confidence, affected to go to sleep. Minutes later I stole a glance at her. She was asleep. I took it as a compliment to my presence, and shut my own eyes. The next thing I knew, it was day, we were again on the ground and the tall young pilot was saying politely: "This is the end of the line, Captain."

I had a final word with Maude, who was remaining aboard for another quarter hour. Then I stepped out on sunbaked earth, into a warm breeze that whipped sandy, gritty dust around my boots.

The pilot walked across the flying field with me and explained that we were now on the edge of Pera, the northern division of Istanbul, near Kassim Pasha. He saw me into a rickety taxi driven by a villainous-looking Levantine and saluted smartly. The taxi hiccoughed away from the welter of planes, hangars, uniforms, and noises.

I dipped into my blouse for the official letter to General Nassif and read off the address to the driver. He seemed to know at once where I wanted to go, and added a shouted comment in bastard French that I could not understand.

The old cab hurled itself around a group of dirty white airport buildings and stuck its nose down a long hill. Below was stretched the crowded ugliness of Pera which is (geographically) to Istanbul what Brooklyn is to Manhattan.

But beyond Pera—across the narrow gray stretch of boat-littered water that I knew at once for the Golden Horn—rose the mushroom mosques and spidery minarets of that city of cities, Istanbul! I looked again on the seven hills which the Emperor Constantine had chosen to regard as the Seven Hills of the New Rome.

Istanbul! Once known as Constantinople, before that as Byzantium, and before that as the New Rome. Beyond it rose more hills, the hills of Asia Minor, with the snow-capped Bythinian Olympus raising his proud head high.

I caught my breath. Somewhere between Istanbul and those hills of Asia Minor lay a silver spread of water called the Sea of Marmora. In a few hours I would be at the Locanda of the Sweet Waters of the Marmora inquiring about the whereabouts of one Tolliver, who had gone there seeking a bombsight. Would I find Tolliver? And how? And when was I to see Kaspir and Charlie Wu again?

I am glad I did not know then where I would find Tolliver, and how.

The pressing question, however, was whether I should ever reach the office of General Nassif of the Turkish military police.

"*Pas si vite!*" I screamed at the driver, above the hurricane sounds of his motor. "Not so fast!"

He turned his head, displayed white teeth in a friendly grin, and nodded violently. We leapt ahead at even greater speed.

"GOOD MORNING, Captain Kettle," said General Nassif. "Coffee?" He handed back Kaspir's letter and barked something in Turkish at a swarthy orderly. The orderly went out. Some hundred seconds later, while General Nassif was holding a match to my cigarette—a rich Turkish blend I had lifted, awed, from his green jade case—the orderly reappeared with a tray of cups and utensils of gleaming beaten brass.

I had some coffee, thick, sweet, invigorating stuff. I was itching to be off to pick up Maude, but reminded myself that things are not done hastily in this part of the world.

General Nassif said: "May I offer you some advice, Captain?" His English was only lightly accented. He pulled the ends of the thick white mustache that was the only thing about him suggesting age. His dark skin was as taut and brown as an athlete's. The long jaw, the fiercely hooked nose, and the amber eyes were vigorous and ageless.

"If you will be so good," I said diplomatically, setting my coffee cup on the tray.

General Nassif leaned forward, elbows on the darkly shining desk.

"Be very careful," he said.

Since General Nassif knew perfectly well why I was in Istanbul, this sounds like a highly obvious and unnecessary piece of advice. I assure you that it did not strike me so at the time. Perhaps that was due to the general's impressive delivery. Also, he did not look like a man who wastes words in uncalled-for admonitions. My heart beat faster.

"You realize, of course," said General Nassif from under the shelter of his mustache, choosing his words carefully, "why my government does not wish to become identified with your mission?"

I nodded. Turkey's existence today is a hair-trigger affair. I started to mention Maude, then decided against it.

General Nassif stood up. He was lean and tall, with a warrior's head. His shoulders were of a straightness touched with arrogance, but his eyes were friendly enough and a little anxious.

"I trust I may have the pleasure of seeing you again," he said.

"I shall make a point of calling on you before I leave," I promised.

"I repeat," said General Nassif frankly, "that I trust I shall see you again." The meaning of this penetrated slowly. I think I paled.

He did me the honor of escorting me to the door. The room was shaded and cool, but my palms and forehead were sweating.

Near the door General Nassif looked once at the dark orderly. In a breath the orderly was no longer with us, and the side door which closed softly behind him did not show in the paneled wall. General Nassif touched my sleeve.

"I have taken the liberty," he said, in a whisper which somehow did not cost him dignity, "of sending a trusted driver to the Grand Anglais for your young lady. The Locanda of the Sweet Waters is to the south of the city. You will not wish to waste any time getting there."

Then he had known about Maude all the time! My cheeks flamed. General Nassif gave no sign that he noted my embarrassment. I had the uncomfortable sensation that I was a child being looked after by his elders.

This sensation persisted when I hurried into the sunlight outside the massive stone building and saw a wide-eyed and worried Maude sitting bolt upright in the same cab that had brought me from the airport. The same villain-ous-looking driver bounced out and flung open the rusty door with a flourish, baring his ivory teeth in a broad grin of recognition and welcome.

This brigand, then, was Nassif's "trusted driver." It followed that Nassif had taken the precaution of putting us in good hands from the very moment of our arrival.

Maude's tremendous sigh of relief as I climbed in beside her was not burlesque. She slid an arm through mine and drew me against her.

"I thought I was being kidnapped," she said. "But he"— she bobbed her head at our chauffeur—"described you, and said… Oh Mike, I'm so glad you're here!"

She was puzzled. "I don't understand," she yelled—the engine was running now. She was about to say more when the cab, charging suddenly into the traffic, neatly unseated us.

"Aren't you going to tell him where to go?" asked Maude, when I had struggled up and pulled her back on the seat.

I shook my head. "He knows," I said. "He knows."

We zoomed over the Inner Bridge and into the heart of Istanbul proper. The Mosque of Suleiman, with its subsid-iary domes and paired minarets, loomed. I had not been in Istanbul since a summer visit in 1927, and I should have liked to stop and walk once more in Suleiman's vast Garden of the Dead.

But before the thought had fully formed in my mind, the great mass of wedding-cake architecture fled past and dropped from sight around a corner. We passed half a dozen *jamis*—praying places. Overladen *hamals* with dirty feet cursed us as they sprang nimbly aside for safety.

Southward we bore. The driver sang to himself in what sounded like an unknown tongue, and shrugged his shoulders to the beat of his own music.

It was not until we had left the Seven Towers behind, and saw the Sea of Marmora shine out beyond the Wall of Theodosius, that a lull enabled us to hear the syllables of his song: "Mehmemeh-dun tolmay," it ran, over and over. "Mehmemeh-dun tolmay..." Just the single line. Some old Turkish lament, I thought.

Later, somewhere in the midst of the strange night that developed around us at the Locanda, the explanation came to me, and I realized that we had gone to the Locanda to the hoarse strains of "My mama done tol' me...."

CHAPTER THREE
THE LOCANDA

WE WHIRLED through a garden that was a tropical jungle of plane trees and cypresses, roses and lilies and hibiscus. We pulled up before the portico of a long, low, two-story building of white stone that was gradually vanishing from sight under a thousand climbers of blossoming wisteria.

Our driver strangled his engine. In the momentary lull the rich odors of the garden closed over us like a perfumed tent.

I said a momentary lull. Even as our driver dismounted, two ragged, pathetic *hamals,* like jumping jacks, sprang from nowhere and set up a fierce clamor for our baggage.

Our driver cursed them shrilly. A small black boy in brass buttons ran out of the hotel and squeaked at the driver and the gesticulating *hamals.*

Then, in the doorway, appeared a managerial-looking individual in a rusty black coat and faded gray morning trousers, he silenced the contestants with a baritone outburst that figuratively blasted them off their feet. This personage then fixed our driver with a glare of such malignant suspicion that the latter snatched the bill I proffered and was off in a billowing cloud of brown dust, the old cab looking as though it had tucked its tail between its legs.

The *hamals* sidled away, making sullen mouths. The small black boy clutched our bags. I was sorry to see the *hamals* go. They reminded me more than a little of two *hamals* I had seen lounging, like a busted vaudeville team, before the headquarters of General Nassif. Our last link with safety had gone.

The managerial-looking person became mine host of the inn. His *temenahs** were as elaborate and formal in their way as the architecture of the Mosque of Suleiman.

"You arrre most very welcome," he announced, "to the Locanda of the Sweet Waters of the Marmora." A strictly European bow put a period to the speech. "I am Monsieur Gusto," he said, and bowed again.

"I am Captain Kettle, of the United States Army," I said. "That is"—I hesitated carefully and then strung out the pause—"my wife."

Monsieur Gusto's poker face failed to conceal his opinion of my real relationship to Maude. Maude twitched her hips. She was chewing gum.

Gusto led us into a vaulted lobby and squeezed behind the reception desk. He shoved a large, leather-bound register before me, and a quill pen. His skin was only a shade or so lighter than that of the ebony bellboy. At a venture I would have put his ancestry at Greek-Albanian-Turkish, with a little Levantine Jew thrown in. He apparently bathed his longish black hair in olive oil each morning, and his stiff collar was greasily brown where it met his thick neck. He was a nightmare of a French hotel-keeper at one of the better-class hostelries in the Midi section.

---

* Turkish greeting; touching the ground, the heart and the forehead.

I signed the register with a banker's scribble, and, after assuring myself there was no one near the desk, opened fire without delay.

"I have come," I said in a low tone, "to inquire into the disappearance of a M. Tolliver. I believe he was a guest here four days ago?"

MONSIEUR GUSTO became a graven image, all but his expressive brown eyes, which darted glances about the lobby as though peering behind pillars and under chairs.

"I said"—I raised my voice—"that I have come here—"

"I will visit you to your rooms," cut in M. Gusto loudly. "They gives upon the water." He swallowed. "Beautiful rooms. With terrace. It is my pleasure to visit the guests to their rooms."

There was nothing to do but yield to his insistence. Maude clutched my arm as we groaned upward in an ancient elevator that was nothing but a rusty brass cage. Preceded by the inkspot with the bags, we strolled down a carpeted hall to a tall wooden door. This M. Gusto threw open proudly.

"Beautiful rooms!" he announced. He was nervous. He pointed at a small table by the broad bed. "Telephone," he said, with overweening pride.

The inkspot set our bags down, caught the coin I flipped him, and went out like a candle-flame. M. Gusto was throwing open a French window. "Terrace," he said thickly. "Beautiful!"

He was correct in both claims. The rooms (bedroom, with bath attached) were beautiful. And below the terrace reposed another luxuriant garden, this one stretching down to a white stone pier. From the pier the glance traveled over the Sea of Marmora and into the green hills beyond. There were small boats with oddly shaped, many-colored sails on the silver-green water. It was breathtaking. But it could wait.

M. Gusto scuttled back across the room and closed the hall door. Beads of what looked like olive oil oozed from his forehead.

"Now—" I began sharply.

"Yes-yes-yes?"

"About M. Tolliver—a short man with blond hair and blue eyes—" (Kaspir had given me the description).

"I do not know nothing about M. Tolleevaire," said M. Gusto, rapidly and mechanically, as though he had rehearsed the denial many times to himself.

Maude was sitting on the high, four-poster bed. The steady gaze of her violet eyes seemed to disconcert M. Gusto. She had stopped champing her gum.

I brought up my heavy artillery. I touched my shoulder bars. "I am an officer of the Intelligence service of my country," I said. "I have received permission from General Nassif to make inquiries. Tell me about M. Tolliver."

"He came. He engaged a room. He drink in the bar. He walk around. He say not much," said M. Gusto breathlessly, dabbing at his brow with a gruesome handkerchief. He inhaled. "He eat dinner—not ver' much—in my ver' fine dining-room. He walk around some more. Next morning—pouf!—he is not here no longer." M. Gusto spread out his hands, palms upward, to indicate the completeness of Tolliver's disappearance.

"To whom did he talk?" I persisted, transfixing Gusto with a third-degree eye.

Gusto was openly trembling. He stepped to the door, opened it suddenly. A heavy-faced waiter was passing—

very slowly—with a tray. Gusto waited until the waiter's soft tread had died down the hall before he closed the door and once more gave me his attention.

"He did not talk to nobody," insisted M. Gusto, then, averting his eyes from mine, "excep' I see at dinner he talk some little with Manfred...."

"Manfred?"

"Manfred Geist, my *maître d'hôtel*," explained M. Gusto, not without pride. He cocked his head toward the terrace and appeared to listen. "I hear taxi," he said, with ill-concealed relief. "More guest, maybe. I mus' go now." He had the door open before I could stop him. "Come down soon," he urged. "I make you presented to our guests. At the Locanda of the Sweet Waters of the Marmora I make my guests be friends like all one happy family."

"Wait a min—" I began.

"You wish bathe in sea like English people?" inquired Gusto hastily. "Do. Good bathe. Make you ver' clean. You wish small boat?" His short arms moved in gestures suggestive of rowing. "I have boats. Fine! All you want."

"But—"

He was fairly dancing with impatience to be off. "M. Ludwig Robin, my ver' rich good guest, he row boat most days. His wife like ride water." Gusto's English was collapsing slowly in his haste to be free of us and all mention of Tolliver." *"Au'voir."* He performed a cross between *temenah* and a bow and the door closed.

"You wish small boat?" Maude laughed feebly, with a suggestion of hysteria. "You wish for to go dive for bombsight in Sweet Waters of Marmora?"

I DID not answer. I was exhausted. Interrogating M. Gusto had been very much like trying to catch an eel in your bare hands. And about as effective.

I dragged my suddenly weary self to the threshold of our terrace, staring out over the sun-dappled waters.

The beauty of the scene failed to impress me, only its vastness registered. Pessimism came and perched, grinning, on my shoulder. Our whole expedition had been hastily organized, jerky, and disjointed. Turkey was a big country. There was no proof that the bombsight was at the Locanda.

Tolliver had probably gone haring off on a new lead the night he "disappeared." Chances were, the bombsight, or a carefully drawn plan thereof, was already over the border and being studied by eager Germans at some secluded airport near Crete, hundreds of miles away.

I gritted my teeth helplessly. The bombsight—the one well-kept secret of the entire war....

Behind me came quick footsteps. Maude had unlocked her suitcase, was now hanging her meager supply of clothing in a lofty armoire at the far end of the room. There was something heartening for me in this routine. She saw me watching her, smiled, and came over beside me.

Something in her eyes reflected the vagrant thought which had crossed my mind. It was a lovely room. Suitable for a honeymoon.

"I've left room for your things," she said, nodding toward the armoire. She touched my arm and looked along at the garden below, and the sea. "Some day..." she began dreamily, then stopped short.

"I'll have a quick bath," she said briskly. "You wait. I won't be long. Then we'll go down and meet the lads. And have a drink."

With that she left me, to collect a heaping armful of various feminine appurtenances and sail, laden, into the bathroom. I dropped into a curiously made, surprisingly comfortable armchair.

There was a new weakness in my wrists and knees. Another second and I would have had Maude in my arms.

I swore a big, silent oath that I would not, by word or look, try to further my romance until the business of the bombsight was behind us.

From the bathroom came the soft sound of running water. It bothered me. I went out on the terrace, closing the French window to shut out the sound.

Leaning on the ornamental iron railing, I rummaged my mind for some raw material with which to fashion a plan of action. Gusto had mentioned Manfred Geist, the *maître d'hôtel*. Tolliver had talked with Geist. Probably about the wine. Anyhow, Geist sounded German. Worth looking into. And Gusto was going to introduce us to the other guests. Perhaps one of them would betray something at the sight of my uniform.

Slim chance, though. Suppose one did—would I know it? I am a poor physiognomist. One thing: I would meet M. Robin. I decided then and there that I would ask M. Robin some very direct questions.

Not that that would avail me anything. But I might stampede him into some false move that might convey something to Kaspir.

Where in hell *was* Kaspir?

"M'SIEU MOUNTJOY," said Gusto brightly, "I like to present you to Captain and the ver' charming Madame Kettle."

Mr. Mountjoy rose with obvious reluctance from his wicker chair under a palm frond in the lobby. He had a game leg, and leaned on a knobby cane.

"Captain and Madame Kettle," continued Gusto, "I make you present of M'sieu 'Orace Mountjoy, he is of England."

"You keep him," murmured Maude. "I don't want him."

From his great height, M'sieu Mountjoy gazed down sourly at us.

"Americans?" he said.

"Yep," I said shortly.

"Huh!" grunted Mr. Mountjoy. He ignored us and turned his moonface this way and that, looking for someone. "Chang!" he bellowed, so loudly that we all jumped.

I might mention here that Mr. Mountjoy wore a shaggy tweed suit and a pink shirt and spats, and that I was very glad to see him, despite his bad manners.

"That is his servant he calls," explained M. Gusto in a stage whisper. "They are not long ago escape from Singapore."

Maude shifted her gum. "Do you like chocolate cherries?" she inquired, very low, of Mr. Mountjoy. Mr. Mountjoy glared at her.

A shuffle of feet brought Chang. Charlie Wu's cousin must have been a smaller man than Charlie, judging by the skimpy fit of the somber silk servant's costume.

Charlie Wu, alias Chang, bent a look of dog-like devotion upon his master. Not by so much as an eyelid's twitch did he admit awareness of our presence.

"Get me outa here," commanded Mr. Mountjoy. A frigid nod of farewell, and he was stumping across the lobby toward the bar, leaning heavily upon Chang's sturdy shoulder.

M. Gusto was cast down. His "happy family" program had struck a bad snag before it was well under way.

"If you would accompany me?" he said spiritlessly, and led us off toward a secluded corner. Halfway there his shoulders sagged.

"It is Colonel Noga and his wife," he said, glancing from me to Maude. "And Captain Yamura. They are attaches. Ver' charming. They are here to rest."

We froze him with a look.

"You perhaps do not love Japanese people?" he said hopelessly.

"No," I said, clearly and distinctly. "I do not love Japanese people."

Gusto cringed at the carrying quality of my voice. A faint babble of conversation in the secluded corner stopped.

M. Gusto revived for a final effort. "Aha!" he exclaimed, with forced heartiness, "you will like M. Ludwig Robin. And Madame Robin. They are Swiss."

We followed most willingly this time. M. Gusto swept us up to a table near the door leading into the garden on the water side of the Locanda. A man and a woman were playing an intricate form of double solitaire. At our approach the man glanced up, annoyed, but the sight of Maude brought him to his feet and spread a smile of welcome across his fat little face.

Madame Robin's head made a quarter-turn. She was a slender, severe female in black lace, with puritanical eyes. These assimilated and disposed of Maude with a single glance.

Maude had done her job well. A blob of eyeshadow here, a smudge of rouge there, a liberal application of the wrong shade of lipstick—these and a certain provocative swing of the hips endowed her with a raffish air that lay like a social blight over her well-tailored summer suit.

Madame Robin's eyes turned icy. M. Robin's smile shortened. He sensed the drop in temperature. So did Gusto, but he carried on doggedly with the introductions. I felt genuinely sorry for the man.

M. Robin acknowledged us with a small bow and remained standing. His head was wholly innocent of hair, and shiny yellow like a honeydew melon.

Madame Robin's barely perceptible inclination of her pompadoured head was like a slap in the face.

Friend Gusto drew his head down between his shoulders and waited miserably for somebody to say something. Maude tapped her foot and looked away. Robin's smile had set like quick-drying concrete.

Kaspir had told me to make myself conspicuous.

"Please sit down, M. Robin," I said. "I would like to ask you some questions."

Robin sat down. His smile did not waver. Madame Robin continued placing cards on various piles.

"I am trying to trace a M. Tolliver who disappeared from this hotel several days ago," I said. "Did you perhaps talk with him while he was here?"

TO MY amazement, Madame Robin spoke first. "A young man, handsome, yellow hair, fine eyes." She had a thin, flat voice. She did not look up, and her tone did not indicate whether this was a statement of fact or a question.

I took it as a question. "Yes," I said. "Did he confide in either of you as to his plans or his purpose in being here?"

Since I was not expecting any information, I deliberately threw an official rasp into my voice.

"I am a Swiss national," said Robin calmly. "I see you are wearing an American uniform. This is Turkey."

"M. Tolliver was an agent of my government," I said, adding a hint of exasperation to my manner.

"He was not in uniform." M. Robin leaned back. "I do not care to answer your questions, Captain. Please oblige by going away."

"I have received permission from General Nassif of the Turkish police to make inquiries," I said coldly.

"In that case," said M. Robin placidly, "I know nothing about this Tolliver. I saw him, yes. I did not speak with him, except a word or two when M. Gusto introduced us. I am not especially fond of Americans." He returned to his game as though I no longer existed.

I stood a second, furious—not at Robin, but at Kaspir, for setting me up in this senseless role I was playing.

M. Gusto coughed artificially and edged away. Maude put her arm affectionately through mine. "Let's have a drink, dearie," she suggested, in bell-like tones.

I turned on the sad-eyed Gusto. "Anybody else you want us to meet?"

He shook his oily head. "That is all. The season is not yet—" A thought struck him, he dug hastily into his bespotted waistcoat and drew up a thick gold watch. "Ah!" he said, quite happily, "the dining-room is now open. You will meet Manfred. Maybe he will remember something of your friend." He hesitated. "You will like Manfred."

Maude said: "I want a drink."

"But of course. I will send it to your table in the dining-room."

"Double martini," said Maude loudly. "And step on it."

"But of course." M. Gusto shepherded us through the bar and into the restaurant.

In the bar Mr. Horace Mountjoy was explaining to the barman, in a bloated British voice, exactly how to compose gin-and-bitters. The barman, cowed, was nodding violently after each word.

In the dining-room M. Gusto delivered me, with marked relief, into the capable hands of Manfred Geist. He had found our social level at last.

CHAPTER FOUR
THE COVERED BOAT

MAÎTRE D'HÔTEL Manfred Geist was soothing. He listened sympathetically to our plea for martinis and immediately dispatched the lone waiter, one Andreas, the hard-faced, blue-chinned, unprepossessing specimen who had drifted past our room during the conference with Gusto, to the bar for them.

Maude suppled visibly when Manfred told her that there had been few lovely young ladies at the Locanda for many months. I was searching for an opening on the Tolliver matter when, while spreading the handwritten menu before me, he murmured a compliment to my uniform and said that he liked Americans.

"But your name is Geist," I objected. "You are most certainly German."

His bowed shoulders straightened and his watery blue eyes shone briefly.

"I am German," he agreed, his husky voice freighted with pride. He was a bony man in his late sixties, with a long upper lip that cried out for a mustache and the loose, lugubrious jowls of a bloodhound. Then he caught the significance of my remark and the watery eyes hardened. "I am Bavarian," he amended. "You do not think...?"

I have seen that look, that attitude on other Germans when the name of Adolf Hitler is in the air.

Manfred Geist stepped back a pace. His long face became perfectly blank, like a manic-depressive's. His blue-veined right hand snapped up, shoulder-high and palm outward, in as bitter, as cutting a burlesque of the Nazi salute as you could imagine. Then his face darkened and he went through a second's pantomime of spitting on the floor. It was a performance that no Czech, no Pole, no Norwegian could have bettered. Maude brought her hands together in a silent gesture of applause.

I relaxed. Kaspir had said I was simply the bait in this hunt. But I definitely had something there.

"You may be able to help me," I said softly. "I am look-ing for a young man named Tolliver, who was here several days ago. Perhaps you know where he went?"

I cannot describe in detail the change that came over Geist at this point. He moved quickly to my side, but did not answer. I looked up, to see him gazing fearfully into the bar, where the slovenly Andreas watched the barman make our martinis.

"That Andreas," he said, in a voice like a sigh, "I do not trust him. Strange people come here, and he is acquainted with some of them—of that I am sure." His hands, loose at his sides, had begun to shake.

The menu I held up shook a little, too. "You know where Tolliver went when he left here?" I said, staring hard at the list of *pilafs*.

Geist whipped out pencil and pad as though taking my order.

"No," he said, and my heart sank. I could almost smell the fear on him. "But I think...."

There was a rattle in the bar as of glasses being set on a tray. Geist was rigid now, pencil poised above the pad.

"Andreas goes to sleep early," he said, hardly moving his lips. "Come to my room—quietly—about midnight. There we can talk. I will tell you…" He told me where to find his room.

Andreas' slow tread, the tinkle of glasses, came nearer.

"…You have never tasted our *dolmas?*" continued Geist, loudly. "Ah, but you must. I shall bring them myself. After them you shall choose your dinner."

ANDREAS PLACED the martinis on the table and followed Geist out to the kitchen. I tossed off my cocktail at a single gulp. I needed it badly.

The Japanese party was entering the dining-room now. I stared coolly at them. Attachés, Gusto had called them. But Ankara is the seat of government now, and Ankara was some two hundred miles away. There are pleasant summer resorts much nearer Ankara than the Locanda of the Sweet Waters of the Marmora.

The Japanese did not look our way. The older man, who must have been Colonel Noga, was a hard-boiled, crop-haired Jap type. He wore English flannels and a sports coat with a certain air. I wondered at the presence of his wife, a delicate wisp of a woman who looked like a fugitive from a Kesaki print. The Japs do not usually take their women with them.

Captain Yamura was a pale yellow shadow, as inconspicuous as a faint, distant star.

Geist reappeared with a platter of *dolmas*, which turned out to be rice, chopped meat, and spices, wrapped in vine leaves. We burned our mouths pleasantly on these, had another round of martinis, then tackled a noble chicken pilaf with the enthusiasm engenedered by forty-eight hours on coffee and cold sandwiches.

The Robins came in and sat next to us, but they might have been a million miles away.

Finally M'sieu 'Orace Stephen Kaspir Mountjoy showed up, with Chang moving softly at his side, bending under Mountjoy's weight. The sound of Mountjoy's cane on the tiles made him momentarily the cynosure of all eyes.

Mr. Mount joy countered with a sweeping glance of disdain and clumped to an isolated table near the door. When Maude and I, the first to leave, passed him, he was shoveling down pilaf at a tremendous rate and complaining bitterly to Chang, who was doing guard duty behind his chair, of the filthy messes one has to put up with in the Near East.

"Slops!" said Mr. Mountjoy, building up another forkful. He ran a lascivious eye up Maude's fine figure. "Hotels fulla riffraff these days."

The comment was loud enough to be audible to the rest of the dining-room. To stay in character, I looked around angrily as we went out. I thought for a moment that Charlie Wu's impassivity would surrender to a grin, but he controlled it just in time.

Kaspir, however, met my glare blandly. "Riffraff," he repeated, to no one in particular, and bent again to his food.

In the lobby Maude said: "One of these days I'm going to break his fat neck. Why do you suppose he's—"

I shook my head. Kaspir moves in a mysterious way, his wonders to perform. But this time I would be a little ahead of him. I was positive now that Geist's information would prove of real value. And I was not averse to appearing in a good light before Maude, despite my oath renouncing romance.

I glanced at my watch. A long evening ahead. Maude suggested a walk down through the lower garden to the white stone pier.

Evening had imparted a faint chill to the air. I looked around for the tiny black bellboy. But there was only M. Gusto in the lobby, and he was frowning at an account ledger behind the desk. I went upstairs myself for Maude's wrap.

The note had been slipped under our door. It was in a plain white envelope, addressed in a round, featureless hand, to "Capt. Michael Kettle, U.S.A."

I CLOSED the door with my foot and calmed my pounding pulses by inspecting bedroom and bathroom thoroughly. There was, of course, no murderer lurking in wait for me. But I felt easier after the search. The Locanda of the Sweet Waters was beginning to tell on my nerves. I ripped open the envelope.

A single line on a single sheet, in the same round hand. For a second or two the English words conveyed no meaning. Then my hands tightened on the cheap paper.

"Do not neglect the covered boat." That was all it said.

I had made one thing glaringly plain since my arrival at the Locanda. That was my interest in Tolliver of G-2. Somebody, then, must have answered my question. This was undoubtedly a lead. Perhaps Geist had sneaked up the back way during dinner. Perhaps the fluttery M. Gusto had put it there. Perhaps—I held my breath—Tolliver himself was still in the vicinity.

"Covered boat," it said.

I jumped to the French window, went out on the terrace. Below, the garden was shadowy in the gathering dusk. Beyond shone the white stone pier. I strained my eyes. On one side of the pier, half a dozen rowboats rocked gently in the ripples. On the other side near the land, was a larger craft, the size of a small cabin cruiser. It was covered with what looked like tarpaulin!

The writer of the note must have known that I should easily be able to find the boat referred to. Otherwise he would have given me more details.

I snatched Maude's white woolen wrap from the armoire and ran down the hall. On the elevator I managed to compose my face and iron out some of the tension that was cramping my limbs.

We strolled lazily, aimlessly into the smothering odors of the garden. We paused to light cigarettes, and I showed Maude the note.

There was no one on the pier. Maude sat on a stone bench and gazed out over the lapping waters—smoking, enjoying the breeze.

I slid over the edge of the pier and into the open cockpit of the covered boat. The tarpaulin covering was drawn tight over the little cabin and tied with tap ends of rope just at the entrance.

I put my mouth near the knots. "Tolliver!" I called softly. "Tolliver!"

No answer. Above me, Maude stood up, humming softly to herself.

My hands fumbled at the simple knots—the palsy of overdrawn nerves. Somehow I undid them. The small wooden door swung open easily. I stepped down.

The match that flamed in my hand showed nothing but the usual litter of odds and ends one finds in a boat laid up for the winter: a spare anchor, a hand-pump or two, a tin horn, a sail rolled up like a blanket on one of the seats.

Rolled up! Sails are usually folded away. Besides, this craft, although built like a felucca, was a motor launch. It did not even have a mast.

I began to unroll the stiff canvas. The instant I touched it I knew, by that queer instinct aroused by the presence of death, what I should find.

Half a minute later I succeeded in striking a second match and beginning my feverish examination of Tolliver, late of G-2. A minute later, under the feeble glow of a third match, I was examining the grisly wound which....

Maude's ready whistle pricked me like a knife point.

There was no time in which to restore Tolliver's canvas shroud. The main thing was to get clear of the boat. I rapped my head smartly against the overhead hatchway as I bounded hurriedly out into the cockpit.

An instant's frantic scrambling put me on the cool stones of the pier. Maude was already sauntering back toward the garden. I caught up with her, and had just broken my quick stride to fall into the easy swing of her long legs when, around the corner of a giant flowering bush, we met the waiter Andreas.

Andreas had replaced his black jacket and greasy dickey with a sweater which, along with the pair of oars on his shoulder, gave him a semi-nautical appearance.

"You desire boat, sir?" he inquired. "It is fine night," he added, but without conviction.

I said no, that we had just come down for a look at the water.

"M'sieu andMadame Robin make the little excursion each night," persisted Andreas, indicating the oars. "It assists in eating the dinner."

I took it he meant "digesting." Again I declined. But Andreas interested me. His salesmanship was so negative.

He didn't want us to go. And his eyes, in the dusk, were oddly hard and bright, and he was breathing more quickly than his exertions seemed to warrant.

HE WENT on. Maude and I speeded up. She asked no questions. At the door of the Locanda we stood aside to let the Robins pass. Madame Robin wore a shawl. They did not speak.

The Japs were not in the lobby. Nor were Mr. Mountjoy and Chang. Gusto, behind the desk, still wrestled with his accounts.

One thing was quite clear in my mind. My lone-hand stunt was over. I had to see Kaspir.

I said to Gusto: "Where is M. Mountjoy? I would like to play a game of cards with him."

A pathetically transparent effort, I admit. Gusto's eyes widened. "He is in his room," he mumbled. "The number twenty-two. But—" His manner hinted that he would as soon visit a cobra as the explosive M. Mountjoy, and his air, as I turned away, said: "Well, it's your own funeral."

We used the stairs. Outside Kaspir's door we stood stock still a full twenty seconds. Then I opened the door and we went in quickly.

Kaspir and Charlie Wu were playing cribbage at a small table under an ornate lamp. Somehow the sight, after what I had just been through, infuriated me. It was so typical of Kaspir to have, thought to bring a cribbage board along on a presumably desperate expedition of this kind. And they had Kaspir's box of chocolate cherries between them, and Kaspir's mouth was full.

Charlie Wu pitched his hand on the table and stood up. Kaspir laid his cards down slowly, reluctantly. Maude helped herself to a chocolate cherry. Kaspir put the lid on the box.

"I've found Tolliver," I said.

"Where?" Kaspir spoke as though I had found a penny.

"In the cabin of a boat down at the pier. Dead. Stabbed." I ran the words into him like needles.

He rose, mammoth in the half light. "Stabbed!" His surprise was genuine.

"Yes, stabbed," I said hotly. Then a thought struck me. "Not exactly stabbed," I faltered.

His eyebrows shot up. "Whaddaya mean, not exactly?"

Charlie Wu had moved in. We were a compact group now, clustered around Kaspir like small vessels around a mother ship.

I described Tolliver's wound. It had begun under his left armpit, so far back as to touch the shoulder muscles. The knife had traveled shallowly around his side, but as it neared the heart region, guided between two ribs, it had suddenly become very deep. Then, emerging, it had turned shallow again and died away in the center of the body just under the breastbone.

A single slash, it must have been incredibly expert or just plain lucky.

"It must have sliced his heart almost in two," I concluded. Against my arm I felt Maude's slight shudder. Kaspir pushed out his under lip and threw back his big head. That denoted thought.

I thrust the mysterious note at him, but he evinced only a mild interest in it. I told him about my date with Geist at midnight and he acknowledged the information vaguely. I mentioned the Robins going for a row and he jumped like a stuck pig.

"Get back down there right away," he snapped. "See what happens when they come in. And from now on, for the luvva Christmas, keep away from me—unless you get yourself in a hell of a jam."

"How about Geist?" I flared back. "You still want me to see him?"

"Sure, sure." He snatched his coat from the back of a chair and put it on. Irritably: "For Pete's sake get movin'. Me and Charlie can't get outa here till you two leave."

MAUDE AND I stalked out with the dignity of two bums being hustled from a saloon. As I closed the door Kaspir was picking up the phone. I heard him jiggling the cradle and yelling "Hey!" We took the elevator down. M. Gusto was no longer at the reception desk. He was seated at the old-fashioned switchboard further back, saying nervously into the mouthpiece: "Yes-yes-yes, M'sieu Mountjoy. I will struggle to achieve General Nassif at once. But I do not think…."

Kaspir must have let go at this point. M. Gusto flinched and put his hands to his ears. "Yes-yes-yes," he said hastily, and began manipulating cords and plugs.

Maude said: "I hope Steve realizes that he's about to blow the works." It was quite obvious that Gusto would listen in.

Again we set out through the garden. It was nearly full dark now, and the black foliage and heavy odors were somehow sinister. Andreas had gone. I was about to speak when—

"You have change your mind, sir?"

Maude went "Oh!" and her hand shot to her throat. I was badly startled myself.

Andreas had spoken from the cockpit of the covered launch. He was lounging there, smoking a cigarette.

My heart was thumping furiously. "No," I said curtly. "I haven't."

"I think the Robins are coming in." Maude was peering out over the dark waters, and she was right. A boat was nearing the far end of the pier, the oars dipping in even, unhurried strokes.

Andreas flipped his cigarette seaward and clambered up. We followed him toward the pier's end. When we arrived he was holding the painter with one hand and assisting Madame Robin up the short flight of steps cut in the stone. M. Robin followed.

M. Robin spoke in French. "We had the misfortune to lose the anchor, Andreas," he said, without expression. "Please inform M. Gusto, so that he may put it on our bill."

"Bien, m'sieu." You might have thought that every guest who took a fifteen-minute row lost his anchor.

M. Robin handed Andreas a coin and took his wife's arm. They passed within three feet of us, eyes straight ahead.

Andreas, whistling softly to himself, made the boat fast. He removed the oars, shouldered them.

"Bon soir, m'sieu—madame," he said. I could have sworn to a certain grim humor in his tone.

Silent, we watched him swallowed up by the black garden.

"Mike," said Maude, "that anchor—you don't suppose—"

"Yes," I said, a tight feeling in my throat. How could a man taking his wife for a sedate row in the cool of the evening lose an anchor? There was no doubt about…. And yet, that fat little man, that severe little wife in her black shawl—

Once more I went over the edge of the pier and into the cockpit lately vacated by Andreas. The tarpaulin covering of the cabin was still untied at the entrance.

A single match sufficed this time.

"Gone?" said Maude, when I rejoined her.

"Gone," I said huskily. "Buried at sea, by M. and Mme. Robin, with Andreas assisting."

We turned our backs upon the sweet waters of the Marmora.

"He was young, wasn't he?" said Maude.

"Yes." I took her arm, much as Robin had taken his wife's arm.

Tolliver had been young. That round face, that corn-colored hair must have been attractive to women. No doubt Tolliver had a sweetheart somewhere, or a youthful wife who was proud of his picture, and kept it in a silver frame by her bed.

We went up through the garden for the last time that night. My shakiness had left me. Anger—the cold variety—had come to me at last, and it was welcome. The stimulant I needed for this night was already at work within me.

Also, I experienced a sort of shame that I, who could see forty ahead, should be alive and healthy, with Maude at my side and work before me, while Tolliver, with his greater claim on life, lay deep in a cold and alien sea, his open eyes staring back, unseeing, at the curious fish.

CHAPTER FIVE
MISSION AT MIDNIGHT

MAUDE STIRRED on the bed and thrust her tan arm under the shaded bedlamp. I held my own wrist watch to the light.

"Ten to twelve, Mike."

I rose from my chair in the deep shadows of the room. Maude swung her shapely legs over the edge of the bed and slipped her feet into her shoes. She took the coat of her suit from the foot of the bed and put it on. She patted her blond locks into place. Then she took up her handbag.

"You'll stay here," I said, noting these preparations with some alarm.

She smiled. That was all. She hefted the handbag significantly.

"Look at your gun," I advised. I had earlier in the evening sneaked into the bathroom to examine my own.

She fished out her little gunmetal .25 automatic and pressed the clip release. The clip popped into her hand. It was empty.

"Somebody must have dropped in while we were out on the pier," I said. "It's no use looking in your suitcase. Our cartridges are gone."

"I'm going with you anyhow," she said defiantly. "If you think...."

"Then come on," I said.

The hall was deserted. We opened the service door at the far end, as Geist had instructed me in his final hurried whisper in the dining-room, and tiptoed along a narrow passage lined with linen closets. Another door, and we were in the wider hall of the servants' quarters.

Geist's door was the second on the right, and he had explicitly warned me about knocking.

I stepped into a room so opaquely black that for a moment I stood paralyzed. By the time I recovered my nerve, the faintest rustle of garments, the lightest whiff of perfume, told me that Maude was beside me.

I took a step forward. My foot touched something that moved with a delicate tinkle.

The sharp click of Maude's handbag followed immediately. A thin beam of light from her tiny pocket flash angled down beside my feet and searched slowly along the bare boards.

It was a knife I had kicked. I remembered at the last moment to use my handkerchief in picking it up. It had a long, thin blade, razor-sharp. The handle was barely thicker than the blade. A sleeve knife, made to lie flat against the arm.

The beam of Maude's light lingered on the blade. Clean as a whistle. Suspiciously clean and shiny. Very recently cleaned.

The flashlight beam abandoned the knife, to poke here and there about the room. It shone along the foot of an iron bedstead, then on a blanket. There were feet under that blanket, stiff and motionless feet.

The beam crept along the ridges that were legs under the blanket. Even now I can remember the look of that blanket's coarse weave.

On went the light, to the pillow and what lay on the pillow.

Then the beam jumped away from the bed and danced briefly about the room, stopping on a wall switch. I reached out and flipped the switch. There was no longer any reason to fumble in the dark. We blinked painfully in the sudden illumination.

Geist looked very peaceful there, head on the pillow, blanket drawn up around his chin. His eyes were shut, and the pendulous jowls that went so oddly with his long, thin face were loose and still. His long arms lay outside the blanket, and the skinny hands were white as a flounder's belly.

A stride took me to the head of the bed. To my warm palm Geist's bulging forehead was quite cool.

I think I must have gone slightly off my nut at this point. You see, I had been counting on Geist more than I would have admitted to anyone but Maude.

The blanket came away with a whoosh as I yanked it. Geist's limp arms flopped down on the sheet underneath.

The old man was dressed in shirt, trousers, and bedroom slippers, just such a costume as he might have worn to receive us at that hour of the night.

I ripped open the flimsy shirt. The thin-bladed knife was in my mind.

There was no wound—absolutely no mark or wound on the head, neck, or upper part of the body. There were several small round scars on his chest, but these were plainly from ancient wounds.

I snarled something at Maude. I had a flash of her set mouth and flaring nostrils as she bent to help me.

We stripped Manfred Geist's stringy-muscled boniness naked on that creaking bed. We turned him over. Not a wound, not a drop of blood.

In a faraway voice Maude said: "His shoulders, Mike...."

I EXAMINED the shoulders again before I shook my head. The two barely visible red streaks on the shoulders were nothing. Tight suspenders, perhaps, or an ill-fitting stiff shirt probably caused them. The skin was hardly abraded at all.

I thumbed back the eyelids. The washed-out, protruding eyes were no longer watery, but set, like jelly.

Maude leaned over, stared into the eyes. She drew back and seemed to be looking at his cheeks. I noticed for the first time that the cheeks were unnaturally flushed.

"Apoplexy," suggested Maude.

I laughed weakly as I threw the blanket over the naked body and twitched a corner of it to cover the dead face.

The feverish fit was still upon me. We began a search of the room. It was inconceivable that Geist had been so foolhardy as to leave anything in writing, but what else was there to do? Maude went into bureau drawers. I patted the threadbare suits in the narrow closet, peered into the dust under the bed and pulled out a bulky, imitation-leather suitcase. I undid the straps and raised the lid.

The suitcase contained a pair of dirty socks and a brown canvas week-end bag. Probably Geist's private supply of liquor, I thought, as I took the thing on my lap and pulled at the zipper tag.

Maude was watching me from the bureau. Now she joined me on the edge of the bed.

The zipper opened easily. For a full thirty seconds neither of us breathed or spoke.

Then Maude said uncertainly, "Do you mind if I snivel a little, Mike?" and put an absurd white handkerchief to her nose, as women do.

I don't know what I should have done in another minute. Sobbed like Maude, perhaps. Or danced. Or sung. Or all three.

I clutched the canvas bag convulsively. The hard contours of the bombsight were indescribably grateful to my hands.

The blood was in riot in my veins now, so that I did not even hear the door open, was not aware of the third person in the room until a floorboard creaked.

Colonel Noga said, over the threat of the revolver in his square hand: "Give me."

Behind him Captain Yamura slipped into the room like a breath of foul air and moved to the foot of the bed, near Maude.

Maude's eyes were momentarily insane. She said savagely: "Listen, Mr. Moto—"

There was no hesitation whatever in Captain Yamura's actions. He laid the flat barrel of his automatic along Maude's temple as unconcernedly as he might have swatted a fly. Maude's shoulder struck me as she toppled backward on the bed.

The single glance from Colonel Noga to Yamura warned me, but by then it was too late.

I would like to be able to report that I sprang up and pulverized the pair of them in a tigerish battle, with dialogue. The bald truth is that Yamura's automatic swung again as I was rising, and after that the events became vague and unreal. I remember attempting, from the floor, to reach Noga's slippered feet, but Yamura must have swung again, for colored lights exploded in my head and I dropped a million feet into the abyss of unconsciousness.

NOR CAN I recall Maude's ministrations which, many minutes later, helped me back to the surface.

Suspended above me was a great gray face. The faint glow of the shaded lamp burned my eyes like a photo-flood. I shut them quickly, then forced them open again. My surroundings swam into some sort of focus.

It was Kaspir's room, all right. Beside me on the bed sat Maude, regarding me with an expression that penetrated even the thunderous ache of my battered head. One of her hands held the little handkerchief, now red, to her temple. The other held a cigarette.

The great gray face belonged to Colonel Kaspir. Kaspir was a very different man from the beefy, belligerent Brit-isher of the dining-room. His Cupid's-bow mouth was drawn thin now, his nostrils were pinched, and above his sunken eyes the sweat hung in his bushy brows. I did not know where Kaspir had been that night, but wherever it was, it must have been undiluted hell for him.

I turned my head uneasily on the pillow. The dark figure crouching at the hall door must be Charlie Wu. I struggled up on an elbow and opened my mouth.

"Not too loud, Mike." Maude spoke quickly. She told me later that my eyes were frantic, and that I was about to shout.

"We found the bombsight," I told Kaspir, barely controlling the impulse to yell. This was a nightmare. Why weren't people running around, fighting and shooting, to get that bombsight back? I sat up straighter. "Noga and Yamura came in...."

"I told him," said Maude gently. "All about it."

"But they took it," I insisted to Kaspir. "Noga and Yamura." I couldn't believe Maude had made the situation plain, else what was Kaspir doing standing calmly there while Charlie Wu peeked through a crack in the door. I clenched my fists. "Don't you understand? We found the bombsight in a suitcase, and—"

"Keep your shirt on," said Kaspir, for the second time that night. "Me and Charlie put it there."

"For God's sake, Steve!" Maude shot to her feet, the violet eyes furious. So this was news to her, too. "You mean you—"

"Bait," said Kaspir cryptically. Then, softly: "Anybody come along yet, Charlie?"

Charlie Wu, still kneeling, shook his head slowly.

It was Kaspir's tone that stopped Maude and shook me to the core. The bluff, the forced confidence behind his easy words were as ghastly apparent as the sweat on his face.

One fact alone stood clear in my mind. Kaspir had had the bombsight in his possession and had had the unbelievable gall to gamble with it. And he had overplayed his hand.

I was too weak to curse. Had I been alone, I think I should have shed tears of an unbearable disappointment. I sagged back on the pillow and tried to stiffen my jaw. There was silence for perhaps a dozen seconds. Then, outside in the hall, swift, furtive footsteps that died away almost the instant they passed our door.

Charlie Wu stood up and walked over to Kaspir before he spoke. Don't tell me the Chinese are incapable of showing emotion. Yet his voice was phelgmatic enough.

"That was Yamura and the woman," he said. "They had suitcases."

"Then you'd better get going," said Kaspir tightly. His eyes had caught fire.

"Wait," he said, "you better take a gun—just in case."

For answer Charlie slid from his sleeve something that gleamed in the half light. The long, thin blade was very familiar. I learned later that Charlie had possessed himself of it when he helped Maude bring me away from Geist's chamber of death.

"This'll do fine," said Charlie Wu, and was gone.

Kaspir began to pace the room with careful steps. I noticed that his left shoulder was drawn in against his side, as though by a stitch of indigestion.

A period of waiting seemed to have set in. I wanted to talk, but was unable to trust myself to address Kaspir. Maude had withdrawn the handkerchief from the bloody bruise on her temple and was leaning against the foot of the bed, eyes shut, her quick, irregular breathing showing that her nerves were not yet dependable. For my part, I explored my skull with wincing fingers. Two large, juicy bumps I found.

"You told him about Tolliver?" I said to Maude, at a venture. She nodded without opening her eyes.

Kaspir started for the door, changed his mind, resumed his pacing. It seemed impossible for his huge frame to move as quietly as it did. Once he stopped, grimaced as though in pain, and sat down. But he was up immediately.

In spite of my anger I felt sorry for him. His brassy armor of bluster and indifference is such a well-turned imitation that I am prone to forget he is equipped, underneath, with the nervous system of an overbred horse.

Whatever his gamble, he had paid, and was still paying, full price for it. I watched him more closely. It came to me that unless our game took a turn for the better within a very few minutes, Maude might have another, and more difficult, invalid on her hands. I sat up again and put my feet on the floor, determined to remove myself from her list of troubles. With the faint creak of the bedsprings Kaspir gave a start, then swore foully.

THE HALL door opened and closed. Charlie Wu was in the room. I saw the fierce elation in his eyes even before I noted the brown canvas zipper bag in his hand. He was breathing hard, and across the front of his silk jumper some dark liquid had spattered.

In that moment Kaspir came alive, filling out exactly as a dry sponge swells in warm water.

Charlie Wu zipped open the bag. Maude was on her feet, I was out of bed, in nothing flat.

Awed, we looked into the bag. Crammed in on top of the bombsight was a large crumpled sheet of paper. Charlie Wu pulled this out and handed the bag to Kaspir to hold. He spread out the paper.

"Not bad, considering the short time he had," he said.

My knowledge of draftsmanship is nil, but Noga's hurried sketch of the bomb-sight did look like a fairly competent job.

There were several dark blotches on one corner of the sketch. Charlie Wu ran his thumb meditatively over one of these and gazed at the fresh red smear. Then he wiped his thumb on the side of his pants.

Kaspir said, with a catch in his voice: "You're double-damned sure he's…?"

Charlie Wu chuckled.

"Yamura and the woman must be wonderin' what's keepin' him," said Kaspir. "I guess we can start movin' on schedule now."

Relief nearly overwhelmed me. Of the Locanda of the Sweet Waters of the Marmora I had had enough and more than enough.

"Whereinell d'you think you're goin'?" snarled Kaspir, as I beckoned to Maude and started for the door.

"To pack," I said. "It won't take us more than—"

"Siddown," said Kaspir. I sat, and began to tremble. Every moment I stayed in that accursed place would, I felt, mean a day off my life.

Charlie Wu stuffed Noga's drawing back into the bag. Kaspir sat down to the long-necked telephone and began to jiggle the cradle. It was quite a while before someone answered.

"Give me, please, the room of M. Robin," said Kaspir, in the excellent French he produces on occasion. His voice was hard and husky and completely unlike his ordinary tone.

He drummed on the table with impatient fingers. He did not have to wait long. M. Robin must have been sleeping lightly.

"This is Andreas," said Kaspir hurriedly, still in French. "Come quickly to my room. Geist is dead."

"Robin's startled voice crackled from the receiver in a question.

"Noga," said Kaspir at length, and hung up.

Charlie Wu looked doubtful. "When Robins gets to Andreas' room and finds out it wasn't Andreas who called him…" he objected.

"Listen," said Kaspir, "when they find Geist—and sneak a peek into that cubbyhole where the bombsight was, d'you think they're gonna worry about details? Take the door, Charlie." His long arm went out toward the bedlamp and the room was snapped into darkness.

The faintest crack of light appeared in the doorway as Charlie knelt once more to his vigil. I couldn't stand the pressure. I groped my way to the door and peered out over Charlie's shoulder, into the passage beyond.

I give M. Robin, tubby little man that he was, credit for being able to move quickly in an emergency. It seemed that I had hardly settled myself at the door when Robin and the dour Andreas went by, walking very quickly, in the direction of Colonel Noga's room. Andreas had a gun in his hand. Soon afterward we heard a door open and shut.

Charlie Wu must have heard my intake of breath. He went "Shhh!"

It was just as well that he did. There was a flicker of movement across my limited range of vision into the hall. I caught the merest snapshot glimpse of Captain Yamura, also hastening to Colonel Noga's room. He must have run up the stairs, for there had been no sound from the elevator.

Charlie Wu's whisper drifted back into the darkness. "Yamura."

We heard Kaspir pick up the phone again. Whoever was on the switchboard must have been alert this time.

"Gimme Gusto, quick," said Kaspir. "Oh, that you Gusto? This is Mountjoy. Listen, Gusto, you better get a couple o' your pals and hop right up to the Jap's room—yes, Noga's. There's gonna be—"

I jumped as the shot, presumably from Noga's room, cracked out along the hall. A cry followed, but whether of fear or anger or pain I could not tell.

"… a hell of a row," concluded Kaspir in the darkness. We heard him hang up.

Two more shots confirmed this diagnosis.

The light went on.

"Get along to your room," said Kaspir to Maude and me, with an urgency that was like a physical shove. "Get in your pajamas. You've been asleep. Got that? And for the luvva Pete don't make a move until you're called."

Maude said: "But Steve—"

"Hurry," said Charlie Wu, and opened the door a dozen inches.

We fled along the carpeted hall on shaking legs, past the stairway leading to the lobby below. And just in time, too. Purposeful feet were pounding up that stairway. I shoved Maude into our room, turned for a final look.

M. Gusto and two more men were racing down the hall toward Noga's room. I looked again. Yes, Gusto's companions were the *hamals* who had lounged before Nassif's headquarters and who had appeared so quickly and mysteriously at the Locanda.

INSIDE OUR room, Maude, without a word, vanished into the bathroom with a pair of white linen pajamas. I had barely time to climb into my own before she reappeared, garbed as Kaspir had ordered. She had washed the blood from her temple, and the abrasion was now hidden under a white scarf, wound around her head and tied in a coquettish knot.

Without a word she flung herself in the bed, face down, head pillowed on her arms. There was a sob or two—the final release of overwrought nerves. Then her breathing became slow and regular.

She did not stir as I passed the bed on my way to the bathroom to make my own repairs.

I suppose I should state that when I returned I gallantly chose the armchair for my couch of the night. I did not. Too much had taken place for me to abide by any sticky and senseless little moralities. I stretched myself quietly beside her, and the surest gauge of my physical and mental condition is the fact that I went to sleep without giving her another thought.

M. Gusto and the first rays of the sun must have arrived simultaneously. His knock brought me up with a start. I staggered to the door.

Many things had changed in the Locanda during the night, among them M. Gusto. He had lost his fawning manner. Now he was formal. He held his head high, and there was an authoritative glint in his eye.

"General Nassif has the desire to see you at once immediately," he said. "Be pleased to come below to my office when you have dressed yourselves."

CHAPTER SIX
MILITARY COURT

"**MY ADVICE** to you all is to depart from here—and from Turkey—at once," said General Nassif, a little while later, downstairs.

Kaspir nodded gravely. General Nassif's voice was not unfriendly, but it was very official, and a flat command lay behind his polite phrasing.

We were seated around a low, copperfaced table in Gusto's office. The inevitable coffee apparatus was being tended at intervals by Gusto himself.

We were all dressed for traveling, even Charlie Wu, who had resumed his blue summer worsted.

"You do not, I suppose," said General Nassif evenly to Kaspir, "know anything of the tragic events of the night?"

Kaspir shook his head. I was relieved to see him regarding Nassif with the large respect that I happened to know the general deserved.

"Not a thing," said Kaspir. "We recovered the—er—item we were after early in the evening, from Geist. It was hidden behind a panel of the wainscoting in his closet. We—er—persuaded him that it was to his advantage to turn it over to us. Of what happened afterward we have, of course, no knowledge." Never had I heard Kaspir pick his words so deliberately.

General Nassif received this without blinking.

"Captain Kettle," continued Kaspir, "has reason to believe that either Geist, or Andreas, or Robin murdered our agent Tolliver with a knife. He believes you may be able to locate Tolliver's body if you will drag the waters a short distance beyond the pier. We would appreciate it if you would turn the body over to our people in Istanbul."

General Nassif nodded thoughtfully. I was restless. This absurd conversation was nothing but a thin coating of ice over a deep and turbulent stream of events.

"Perhaps you might be interested in hearing what occurred during your slumbers last night," said General Nassif, leaning back and gazing at the figured ceiling. For some reason I glanced at Gusto. A sardonic little smile vanished from the corners of his expressive mouth as he caught my eye.

This time it was Colonel Kaspir who nodded.

"It would appear that M. Gusto, without knowing it, has been host to two units of Axis agents," said General Nassif, without batting an eye. Nobody moved.

"Of the Gestapo branch," he went on unsmiling, "were Manfred Geist, whose real name was Von Gessler. He did some very able work for Germany in the Balkans in 1917 and 1918. He was very efficient with a knife. He had a brain also."

A train of thought set out in my mind. I remembered that Kaspir had done some Intelligence work for us in the Balkans around 1917.

"Also," went on General Nassif smoothly, "there were Andreas and M. Robin. M. Robin has lived in my country many years, posing as a wealthy Swiss. On the other side were Colonel Noga and Captain Yamura and Noga's Japanese woman, who was not his wife."

I dared not look at Maude. I had a feeling she was blushing.

"For some reason—I do not know what—trouble came about between these two units last night," said General Nassif. "I might say in passing that we in Turkey have observed that there is no real collaboration between the Secret Services of Germany and Japan.

"Be that as it may. Whatever the cause, the trouble assumed serious proportions. From the admirable report that my Major Gusto has made to me"—here Gusto bowed low—"I gather that, for reasons of their own, Colonel Noga and Captain Yamura found it advisable to—er—liquidate Geist, using an ancient but little-known Japanese method."

I thought of Geist's unmarked body, and a thrill crawled up my spine. Maude was leaning forward now, openly hanging on the general's words.

"Andreas and Robin," continued the general, "retaliated. They killed Noga with a knife when Yamura was not present. Yamura returned to find them in Noga's room—and Noga dead, with a knife on the floor. He fired. They fired. Andreas is dead. Yamura and Robin are both badly wounded. They are in our custody. Already I have received inquiries from their respective embassies. The embassies are highly excited."

A seraphic smile had come into being under the general's white mustache, but his voice did not hint of it.

"I fear," he said, "that the ill-feeling already existing between the German and Japanese agencies in Turkey has been immeasurably increased. But you gentlemen, and you, Mrs. Kettle, will not weep over that."

"Nary a tear," said Kaspir. He stood up. We all stood. General Nassif bowed gallantly to Maude, held out his hand to Kaspir.

"I have engaged a suite for you at the Hotel Grand Anglais," he said, "where you may rest until your plane departs this afternoon. A taxi is now waiting for you. I am happy your mission was successful. But please"—General Nassif's tone sharpened—"do not come back again."

Kaspir bowed a crooked bow. He had the grace to blush. We left.

IN OUR gaudy suite at the Grand Anglais we inaugurated the new day with much Scotch and some soda. There was little talk among us until two young attaches of the American staff arrived with an honor guard of four swarthy Turkish soldiers and relieved Charlie Wu of the brown canvas bag which had never left his hand since the early hours of the morning.

As the door closed on their politely withheld curiosity, Kaspir draped himself over a quilted sofa and exhaled a sigh of relief that rustled the silken curtains. He drank deeply of his Scotch-and-very-little-soda and squinted sideways at Maude and me.

"What's eatin' you two birds?" he demanded rudely. He winked at Charlie Wu.

We didn't say a word.

"You wonderin' who slipped you that note tellin' you where to look for Tolliver?" he persisted.

We maintained our stubborn silence. It was not easy.

"And who killed Tolliver?" he tempted.

Maude said resignedly: "Yes. You know damn well we are."

Kaspir looked happy. The weight was off him now, and his self-rising spirits asserted themselves. Also, false modesty is not one of his failings.

"Robin's servants got hold o' that bombsight by pure luck," he began. "Robin took it and scrammed to the Locanda to see Geist. Geist was the head man of Robin's crowd around these parts."

Geist! Geist the helpful, the sympathetic, who had given us such a beautiful burlesque of the Nazi salute. Kaspir's shrewd eyes searched our faces, and in our surprise he found his reward. He swelled.

"Robin turned the bombsight over to Geist," he said, now launched and away. "Nacher'ly, they wanted to rustle it outa the country. But the Japs showed up, and the Turkish police were lurkin' in the bushes, so they didn't dare. So they stowed it in Geist's cache until things eased off a little.

"Then Tolliver showed up, askin' questions. They didn't waste time on Tolliver, this bein' a serious matter. Geist put on the act he later used on you, Mike—"

I thought of how anxious I had been to get to Geist's room the night before. I shivered. Who could blame Tolliver for falling for Geist's gem of acting? Maude drew breath sharply.

"My guess is," said Kaspir, "that Tolliver hardly got inside the room before Geist knifed him—usin' that peculiar slash you found on Tolliver's body, Mike. The point kind of feels its way along the ribs till it hits the soft spot. Then it cuts the heart in two and comes glidin' out again. And whoever gets it is dead. No fancy heart surgery's gonna save him.

"They bundle Tolliver down to the pier. What keeps 'em from dumpin' him in the drink right then I don't know. My guess is, the Japs showed up. So Geist and Andreas and

Robin did the next best thing and tucked Tolliver away in the boat for future disposal.

"A waitin' game now begins. The Japs know the bomb-sight's on the premises but can't find it. Geist's crowd is afraid to move for fear of exposin' their hand to the Japs.

"Then Mike shows up and goes around puttin' his foot in things—just like they'd expect an American to do.

"So Noga figures he can use you, Mike, to blunder in and start somethin'. He knows where Tolliver's body is. So he slides that note under your door and sits back to see what you'll do."

KASPIR WENT into the Scotch again, then set the sweating glass down on the floor—or rather, on an expensive Turkish rug, for we had the best suite.

"Then Andreas catches you messin' around the boat, Mike. They figure it's time to get rid o' Tolliver, regardless o' the risk. It's brazen, the way they have to do it, but they ain't worried. Because Geist knows you'll be along to visit him later, and he's gonna take care of you then."

I shuddered again. Somehow Kaspir's offhand words made the picture horridly clear—Geist waiting for me, that terrible knife up his sleeve, his ugly face tense.

"So you report to me and Charlie," continued Kaspir. "When you describe Tolliver's wound it starts me wonderin'. I'd misfigured Robin for the head man. But that wound—I was in the Balkans in '17. There were a couple o' British agents turned up dead about then—in Albania, it was—with wounds like that. And there was a strong suspicion that a gent named Von Gessler had guzzled 'em.

"So strong, in fact, that a Britisher by the name o' Apple-shaw went around one day and pumped three-four slugs into Von Gessler and left him for dead. He was sure he'd fixed Von Gessler, although he had to grab the next boat out and couldn't wait to see. So sure, in fact, that after the war, when a rumor started that Von Gessler had survived, everybody in London, led by Appleshaw, tagged it as a damn lie. Which goes to show....

"Anyhow, that wound made me wonder. I'd seen Von Gessler once or twice in '17, but not close, and he was younger then, around forty. That wound was too much like the ones we found on the Limeys to be a coincidence. To strengthen my case, I called old Nassif—who knows as much about this end o' the world as any livin' man—and he said he'd heard from good sources back in '20 or '21 that Von Gessler had recovered and made it home to Germany.

"*Also*, this feller here called himself 'Geist.' Which, in German, means 'Ghost.' So it looked more'n just possible that he'd got leave of absence from hell for a few more years....

"So Charlie and me we called on friend Geist about 10 last night and"—here Kaspir glanced at Charlie Wu—"argued with him. And the upshot was, damned if he didn't tell us where he was keepin' the bombsight!"

I snorted disgustedly. The rest hung together. But that last was a flat lie.

"We were gonna take it along," said Kaspir, unheeding, "when it occurred to me that Noga and Yamura must be keepin' a leery eye on all proceeding that night. So we stuck it in the suitcase where they could find it easy. Remember, they were watchin' Mike, and it was ten to one they'd follow him down to Geist's room to see what he and you, Maude, turned up."

"I suppose some sixth sense told you they wouldn't blow our brains out to get the bombsight." Maude's hand went to her bruised temple. There was a curious light in her eyes.

"I told you before," said Kaspir shortly, "that we were playin' this round for keeps. D'you think I *liked* lettin' you two walk into what was comin'?"

Maude looked long and searchingly at him. "No," she said slowly, "I don't."

Kaspir was actually relieved.

"Anyhow," he said quickly, "they took the sight offa you. They were all for leavin' in a hurry. Noga sent Yamura and the woman downstairs to get the car ready, while he made that sketch as insurance against losin' the sight itself in some fracas.

"So I sent Charlie along to get it back. Noga was gonna put up a fight anyhow. That much was certain. What harm, then, in lettin' Charlie fix him with that knife—Geist's knife—so's it would look to Yamura like one o' the Germans had done him in? And Charlie didn't object, did you, Charlie?"

Charlie Wu smiled his long smile. "Not in the least," he said amiably.

"After Charlie got the sight back," said Kaspir, "it was just fun, settin' Andreas and Robin onto findin' their old buddy Geist murdered according to the old Jap method. You notice they didn't waste any time goin' for Noga and Yamura once they'd seen Geist.

"And then Yamura comin' back and findin' them with Noga's body—and Noga killed the same way Tolliver had been. Charlie was careful to do it Geist's way.

"After that it was simply a matter o' gettin' Gusto and his merry men up to stop the fuss before everybody got killed. You see, I wanted one or two of 'em alive so's they could run straight to their chiefs and bear strong witness to the treachery o' their dear Axis partners."

MAUDE BIT her lip. "But Steve—leaving that bombsight for Noga—that was a godawful risk to take. Suppose he'd got away with it?"

"Yep." Kaspir thrust out his under lip belligerently. "But looka the results. In less'n twenty-four hours every Nazi right up to Hitler is gonna believe, beyond the shadow of a doubt, that the Japs not only killed a German agent to get hold o' that bombsight, but also that the Jap government's holdin' out and lyin' when they assure the German State Department that they ain't got it.

"*And,* not a Jap in the world but won't believe that the Germans have still got it, after first slaughterin' Noga to take it from him. Now ain't that worth a chance?"

Maude said abruptly: "When did Noga and Yamura kill Geist, Steve? And how?"

I looked up, amazed at her tone.

Kaspir refused to meet her eye. He stood up suddenly and unbuttoned his shirt. On his face, without warning, had appeared that green, pinched look he gets when he is airsick.

The shirt stuck to his left side and he pulled it loose with a grunt of pain. We goggled at the thin brown line of dried blood that extended from his left armpit across his heart and lost itself in the hair on his bulging chest.

"I asked a question," Maude reminded him angrily.

"Gotta step into the bathroom and cobble up this scratch," mumbled Kaspir, ignoring her. He lumbered across the room, through the bedroom beyond, and into the bathroom beyond that. The door slammed.

Charlie Wu's broad face was serious. "I'm not sure," he said, "that you'd care to hear what happened to Geist."

Maude stamped her foot.

Charlie Wu said: "All right. Steve and I went to see Geist, as Steve told you. Geist knew, the moment we stepped into his room, what we were there for. He pulled that knife. I barely caught his arm in time. You saw"—he jerked his thumb toward the bathroom—"how close he came.

"Steve said, 'Hold him, Charlie,'" went on Charlie Wu. "It wasn't easy, Geist was pretty good for his age, and evil as a cobra.

"Steve sat on the bed, and I hope nobody ever looks at me the way he looked at Geist. He said: 'I'm constitutin' myself a military court, Von Gessler. You killed Tolliver in cold blood. You killed Benson and Throckmortin in Tondek in '17. You got anything you wanta say?'"

CHARLIE WU was reproducing Kaspir's staccato speech perfectly, but there was no humor in his performance.

"Geist cursed him—in three or four languages. Oh, that old man was bad clear through. Then Steve said, with his eyes all hollow and his nostrils spread out: 'O.K. I'm puttin' you under sentence o' death. *And* you'll be executed immediately.' You notice he didn't mention the bombsight even though he still didn't know where it was. My flesh began to creep a little," said Charlie Wu, low, "because I knew from the way he talked that he was going to do it.

"With that, Steve went over to the big wicker chair in the corner of Geist's room and turned it upside down. Then he began tearing up a sheet."

Charlie Wu paused. "I think," he said, "that he went through that rigmarole about the trial to salve his conscience over what he knew he was going to do. Because he'd made up his mind.

"Geist looked puzzled until we tied him along the back of the tipped-over chair—at about a forty-five degree angle, with his head down. Then he caught on—before I did. He began to squawk for mercy. He tried to buy Steve off by tellin' him where the bombsight was.

"I don't mind telling you," said Charlie Wu, a little huskily now, "that I was puzzled, too. Geist squawked some more and Steve gagged him.

"Then Steve said: 'In a little while you're gonna die of apoplexy, Von Gessler. It won't hurt much. No more than shootin'. Not near so much as a knife. And you're an old man.'"

"Then what?" said Maude tensely.

"He died," said Charlie Wu. "He was old. Lying at a steep angle that way, the blood ran into his head until something burst. He struggled some just before the end. Then we put him in bed, and cleaned up, and put the bombsight out in the suitcase, and came away, after...."

"After what?" I put in faintly.

"After Steve was sick," answered Charlie Wu, "out of the window. I knew how he felt. I was pretty rocky myself. He told me when we got back to the room that the Japs use the apoplexy method pretty often to finish off elder statesmen who start bucking the Tokyo military clique. It looks good, and it's sure-fire. The best doctors in the world would say he died of apoplexy.

"And Steve says that the Gestapo is thoroughly aware of that peculiarly Japanese method of finishing a fellow off. He says that's what'll prove to the Gestapo that it was Noga and Yamura who knocked Geist off. Say," concluded Charlie Wu, "you won't let on to Steve that I told you about him getting sick, will you? He's afraid you'll think he's soft."

We said, in faint voices, that we most certainly would not.

Across two rooms a door opened.

"Hey!" bellowed Kaspir, "whaddaya say we go downstairs and tie into some grub?"

Colonel Kaspir was himself again.